HellBo
Antholo

curated and edited by

Jaime Powell

A HellBound Books® LLC Publication

Printed in the United States of America

CONTENTS

OTHER HELLBOUND BOOKS

HellBound Books' Anthology of Horror

The Gates

Cory Andrews

I think anyone who has repented in their life, and I mean seriously repented, not for the venial sins but for the mortal, has thought to themselves, *was it enough?* Enough to not be cast into the fires of Hell when their physical body ceases to breathe. Enough to ascend to God's palace in Heaven

Is it the destination the repentant man fears? Or is it the fear that he will not meet his beloved family, friends, and pets in the afterlife? That he'll be banished from the utopia of Heaven, letting the just and righteous down one final time.

No Rainbow Bridge.

No Pearly Gates.

No Eternal Life.

Only pain and suffering. For eternity.

These worries came often to Dave DiBruno in the small hours of the night despite ending his wicked ways well over twenty years prior.

In the spring of 1998, in the small rural Pennsylvania town of Bennet, there wasn't much to do for the misfit teenagers. The ones not focused on finding their fame under the Friday Night Lights. The ones without the smarts or encouragement to pursue education past the twelfth grade - if they could pass that. The ones destined to work a monotonous job at the mill for forty-five years, get their sweetheart knocked up three times before twenty-five years of age, and have a beer gut before forty.

These social outcasts were the ones who usually found themselves rebelling against their institutions and their churches. Though one could hardly blame their anger at the church—the Catholic Church more specifically—if you consider the scandalous headlines dominating the news at the time. As too often is the case, the young, ignorant, and unguided confuse their disdain of the wicked infiltrators of the church with God himself.

While the jocks practiced for the big game, and the smart kids diligently hit the books preparing to get out of Bennet, you could find these stoners, sluts, punks, and drunks wasting their youth in the woods of Bennet at a secluded spot dubbed 'The Gates'.

To get to The Gates you had to wedge between a hole in the fence behind the Daily Fresh Bakery, slide down a hill full of vines, poison ivy, jagged rocks, and fallen trees. Then cross the train tracks and bushwhack for a good mile before coming to an unmarked country road.

Crossing the road and walking north past a giant boulder that looked like the face of a witch brought one to a clearing in the woods where the trees split wide, and a hill of tall grass gradually inclined to the foundation of the old Bennet County Insane Asylum which burnt to the ground in the late 1930's. The death toll from the fire remains the single largest loss of life in Bennet County to this day.

Right before the land begins to climb toward the site of

the old hospital is a set of old rusty gates. The local legend says crossing The Gates is akin to setting foot into a realm of Hell. Those who have stepped in the tall grass beyond The Gates report hearing the screams of the mentally ill as they burned alive, fire trucks being unable to access the remote location where the patients were kept hidden away like a dirty secret.

Bad luck has been known to follow those who pass The Gates.

But it was the sins that happened near the ash and melted-beer-can-filled fire pit in front of the rusty portal that would have Dave DiBruno wondering if the repentance and forgiveness he had begged for in the years since would *be enough.*

Dave couldn't remember how many times he and his friends had hung out at The Gates before the blasphemy and sacrilege started. In the beginning it was typical rebellious teenager stuff; hanging in the woods smoking pot, drinking cheap beers, starting fires, getting the girls to flash, and blasting loud music through battery powered stereos.

Then his friend, Chris, complete with spiked leather wristbands, a mohawk, and the worst attitude of the bunch, met them one day at The Gates with a bookbag full of Bibles stolen from the school they attended, St. John's Catholic.

"You guys hear about the perv, Father Louie?"

"Oh, no. Don't tell me we got one of them sick-o priests in our town," Cheryl said as she took a drag off a cheap cigarette and adjusted her low-cut Anarchy T-shirt.

"Bastard got caught touching Will Donnegan's little brother in the confessional booth."

A collective sound of "ugh's," and other utterances of disgust came from the group of stoners and punk rockers.

"I swear the church is the real enemy in this world. The ones we should really be throwing our middle fingers at.

Not school, our parents, or even the cops for the most part. But the church. All they want is to tell us how to live our lives and make us feel guilt. Then what? They molest kids and beg for handouts when they are tax exempt. Well, if that's the way of God, I'll side with the Devil." Chris ended his tirade by dumping the bag of Bibles in the middle of the unlit fire pit they sat around.

He doused the pile of holy scripture with lighter fluid, struck a match, lit a joint, and yelled "Hail Satan!" before tossing the match on the pile and lighting God's word ablaze.

Led by Chris, the misspent afternoons in the woods quickly began to change after that. He acquired books detailing black magic rituals that he passed around to Dave, Cheryl, Cheryl's younger sister Tina, Will Donnegan, and others who would come and go.

The punk rock about youthful outcast's rebelling against government and society was replaced with Norwegian black metal. The songs were hymns for Satan worshipers and blasphemers. Members of these bands had even been dubbed "satanic terrorists" by media outlets after burning down churches and committing sacrificial murders in Norway.

They carved pentagrams into trees, spray-painted rocks with blasphemous declarations and upside-down crosses. And the Bible burnings continued. Worst of all, Chris had taken to stealing chickens and even baby goats from a local farmer and using the top of a flat boulder as an altar, sacrificing them.

Cheap beer was swapped for cheap hard liquor. They willingly laced their pot with angel dust or whatever illicit street drugs they could find a few towns over. And unbeknownst to the rest of the group, Chris acted the part of cult leader when he scored LSD and took less than everyone else before leading their first black mass at The Gates.

Despite how hard Dave tripped that night, it was the first time he had the thought that he would need to eventually distance himself from this group for the sake of his soul.

When night fell, the fire pit roared, and the drugs kicked in. Chris, adorned in a black hooded-robe and the rest of his coven nude, commanded Tina to lay on the ground in front of the fire pit. He had Will place rocks on her outstretched palms and ankles. Sniffing the air, he looked at Cheryl and asked, "Cheryl, are you menstruating at the moment?"

Her dry mouth opened but not a sound came out. Her glazed eyes went with the nod of her head.

"Remove what keeps your blood from flowing and squat above your virgin sister," Chris said to Cheryl.

She did as told and the blood and clots dripped like big drops of rain falling from a leaf on a warm spring day into the shallow well of her sister's stomach. Sparks from the fire cracked and hissed and fell on Cheryl's back, but in her numb state she did not feel them sting her skin.

Satisfied with the pool of blood on Tina's stomach, Chris cast Cheryl aside and told Will and Dave to kneel on each side of Tina and masturbate until they filled the fleshy goblet of her stomach with their ejaculate.

When the boys' semen mixed with Cheryl's menstrual blood, Chris led his acolytes in drinking the filthy mixture. He then knelt as if he were kneeling in church between Tina's legs intending to defile the girl.

That's when Dave had had enough.

"Chris, this is going too far!" he shouted, pushing him away from Tina before he could enter her sex.

Chris's eyes seemed to glow red in the light from the fire as he stared back at Dave. He stood, reached inside his cloak, and produced a double-edged dagger with a gleaming, sharp point.

"How dare you interfere with the ritual!"

"You're not any better than those evil priests in the church!"

That set Chris off. He charged Dave with every intention of sinking the dagger into his gut. Dave, still naked as the day God made him, grabbed a thick branch meant to keep the fire going and swatted the steel out of Chris's hand just in time. The two threw punches back and forth before finally being separated.

Tina and Cheryl, despite being key parts of the attempted black mass, just calmly sat on a log, dazed and smoking cigarettes.

Dave dressed and left the woods for the night, making the miles long trek back to town alone.

In a move that Dave would later regret, he and Chris reconciled, each chalking up the whole night to their drug intake. Over the next few weeks, the group had their usual gathering at The Gates without any incidents. Chris even stopped the animal sacrifice.

The final night of communing for the flock came in late September when the air turned chilly, leaves fell, and summer turned to fall. They assembled as the sun began to fall below the horizon. The devil music blared as the group gathered kindling for the fire. Chris supplied a bottle of Evan Williams whiskey stolen from the liquor store. Dave brought the marijuana; he sat on a tree stump rolling joints. The sisters stole painkillers from their mother's medicine cabinet.

An initiate Chris invited to join them that night was named Dillon Jacobs. He was their age, but had been held back twice, still a freshman. Not because of behavior but because he was mentally challenged. Dave wondered what the hell Chris was thinking inviting him out here.

They got into a circle around the fire, Dave lit a joint, inhaled, and passed first to Chris. Chris took three hits—

one more than the standard puff, puff, pass—before handing it to Dillon.

"Uh, nah, sorry. Can't smoke, I'll get in trouble."

Chris looked annoyed. "If you wanna hang out with us, Dill   on, you'll smoke."

Dillon gave into peer pressure, clumsily took a hit and had the biggest coughing fit the group had ever seen, making them howl in laughter.

Dave looked at Dillon and said, "Hey, Dillon. You know what everyone has to do on their first night out here with us?"

"Uh, smoke pot?"

"Well, yes. But you already did that. If you wanna be part of the group, you have to cross The Gates and stay there for five minutes."

Chris put his hands on his hips and smirked. He was happy that Dave, who had seemed to go soft on him a few weeks beforehand, was seeing what Dillon was made of. And the whole thing had been made up. None of them had crossed The Gates. They had known the local legends since they were little kids, and it was one of those things they were all still superstitious about.

"Wha…over there? No way, Dave!"

Dave and Will Donnegan grabbed Dillon by his arms and dragged him toward The Gates. "Come on, little baby. What're ya scared of? Tall grass?"

The rest of the group laughed, jeering Dillon.

"Quit acting like a little girl!" Cheryl said, making her sister giggle.

The sound of The Gates opening was like the screech of a forest animal at night as the fangs of a predator sunk into its soft belly. Dave pushed the sobbing Dillon through and quickly slammed The Gates shut. When he did this, the fire which had been roaring, quickly died down to charred embers giving off barely any light.

"What the…" was uttered by a few in the group.

Then the screams began.

"Dave, open The Gates!" Will shouted.

The clank of metal jarring as Dave tried to open The Gates could barely be heard over the screams of what sounded like more than just Dillon Jacobs. It was the desperate screams and groans of a multitude of men, women, and children in agony.

Will grabbed a quarter piece of split wood, wrapped a piece of his shirt around it, doused it in the cheap whiskey, struck a match and created a torch. He approached The Gates where Dave was still struggling to open the rusted metal. When Will stood next to Dave and they looked toward the grassy hill, they almost screamed themselves.

Dillon Jacobs stood naked in the cool autumn night. He worked a pocketknife into the flesh of his stomach, carving a pentagram. He stared at Will and Dave, his eyes turned as black as a raven's feathers.

"Come. Join us," Dillon said in a hollow voice not his own.

Dillon approached The Gates, so close he could reach across and touch Dave and Will. He looked down and then back up at the boys on the other side. "Guys, I don't like it over here. It's really… hot. I think I gotta get home soon or I'm gonna be in trouble."

He then smiled so wide the skin of his lips peeled back to his ears revealing a set of yellowed teeth as sharp and jagged as broken glass.

Dave took the torch from Will and shoved it into Dillon's mouth causing the possessed boy to roar. In a moment, Dillon's whole head caught fire. The screams from the invisible ghosts behind him grew louder.

The whole group now stood against The Gates watching the ball of flame run up the hill to where the old foundation of the mental hospital was. When Dillon, or whatever it was that possessed him, reached the top, he disappeared from sight. Seconds later they heard a crash in the distance. It could be assumed that Dillon Jacob's body crashed through the charred, rotted floorboards of the Bennet County Insane Asylum.

"Good job, Davey. You just performed our first human sacrifice," Chris said, slapping Dave on the back. Dave turned and slugged Chris so hard he was knocked unconscious for a good twenty minutes.

The group disbanded after that night, never to gather in the woods again, and barely speaking with one another as well.

Missing child posters and news reports went up over the next twenty-four to forty-eight hours. None of the teenagers dabbling in the dark arts that night said anything, though. They all played a role. Plus no one would ever believe the truth.

Dillon Jacobs's body was never found and eventually the search parties had to go to try and find new missing people or in the case of the volunteers back to their lives. Seven years later, Dillon Jacobs was officially declared deceased.

After that night, Dave committed himself to turning his life around, turning back to Christianity. He still had his problems with the hierarchy and customs of the Catholic C hurch but found contentment when he switched to a Protestant congregation.

He liked the idea of the pope being denied, and the confession of his sins could be between him through Jesus to God. He spent time everyday reading the King James Version of the Bible, the first time he felt truly connected with the holy scripture. He attended mass, participated in charity, and tried to be a good man every day. But still he wondered if it would *be enough.*

Then in October of 2005, the day after Dillon Jacobs

was declared dead, Will Donnegan was declared dead, too. A search and a declaration of death without a body wouldn't be necessary for Will, though. He was found burned alive in a basement apartment he rented in Bennet. Will nodded off several minutes after injecting heroin and a lit cigarette ignited the couch he lay on.

Dave left condolences on an online memorial but didn't attend the viewing or the funeral. Of the five there that night, Dave was the only to turn back to Jesus, making him an outcast to the outcasts. He only briefly spoke with Tina at a gas station, and even that was four years back.

In October of 2010, Dave, now a manager at the local supermarket and aspiring to become a pastor at his local church, got quite the shock when he opened the *Bennet Daily* newspaper one Sunday morning. Cheryl's picture looked back at him from the obituaries.

Passed away at home. At twenty-eight years of age, that usually meant drugs or something worse. Sure enough, at the end of the obituary donations could be made in her name to an addiction and recovery center.

Five years later, Dave was happily married to a nice church girl he met during his first year as a pastor. She was pregnant with their first child, a baby girl. One day in early fall as Dave raked leaves and his wife lay on a hammock nearby reading on her smartphone, she said, "Oh dear Lord. How terrible."

"What is it, hunny?" Dave asked, taking a break from raking the leaves and sipping on sweet tea.

"Last night a nurse at the psychiatric hospital near Philadelphia was killed by a patient who escaped his restraints. He bludgeoned her with a bedpan before stabbing her repeatedly with broken glass. Says here the poor girl was from Bennet."

A lump formed in Dave's throat. He had heard Tina became a nurse. Didn't know where. Didn't know if she was taking little kid's temperatures, wrapping sprained ankles, or dealing with the mentally ill. But he felt he knew the answer to the question he was about to ask his wife.

"What's her name?"

"Christina Wilson."

Damnit.

For the first time, Dave thought about the timeline and the connection. He laughed to himself and thought *well, at least I have either five or ten years left. Only Chris and I are left from that night.* He'd seen Chris's name in the paper a few times. DUI. Domestic Violence. Possession. He worked for a shady back-alley mechanic that likely doubled as a chop-shop.

Five years can feel like a short time or a long time depending on the situation. Dave's paranoid thoughts eventually left him. A child, a church, a job, a wife - all plenty to occupy his mind.

By October of 2020 the old, unmarked dirt road that led to The Gates had been turned into a heavily traveled road that led to new homes, a few warehouses, and a strip mall full of franchised fast food restaurants.

Development and city folk relocating to the suburbs had reached Bennet. But small patches of woods remained. The Gates still stood. The foundation of the insane asylum still among the tall grass.

Dave had become a volunteer EMT after befriending several paramedics who attended the church where he still acted as a pastor. The time spent volunteering had left him feeling fulfilled. He was truly happy with his life. The misspent days of his youth never crossed his mind anymore.

A call came in for a car crash with an already confirmed fatality one fall night. Guy in a truck flying around a bend smashed head-on into one of the trucks leaving a warehouse. Dave didn't drive the ambulance and didn't realize where he was until he stepped outside on the scene. The bend in the road was right where they crossed all those years ago to head to The Gates.

Dave approached the officer on scene.

"How bad?"

"Bad. The passenger wasn't wearing her seat belt, she flew through the windshield, smacked the pavement, and slid thirty feet. Took most of her skin off. Corpse looks like a damn pepperoni pizza. We know the driver. Real piece of trash named Chris Snyder. Gotta rap sheet longer than the Delaware River."

Dave could barely get the words out to ask the officer about Chris's condition.

"He's over there by the trec line. When I arrived, he was dragging himself across the ground toward the woods. He made it all the way off the road and died as I approached him. I smelled the booze before I even saw his face. Shame he had to take the girl with him."

If the last five years went by fast, the next five years went by excruciatingly slow. Dave read scripture for hours every day even at the expense of sleep. Had every conversation with God he could in the hope that his soul would be spared from the infernos of Hell.

Then when October of 2025 came, things happened almost too perfectly. His wife had taken to chaperoning their daughters cheer squad and they had been invited to participate in a national competition in California. They would be gone for the first week of the month. If Dave came to believe in anything the last five to ten years, it was that there are no such things as coincidences.

He hugged his wife and daughter tighter than ever before. "I love you both so much. Be careful and have fun."

"Dave, is everything alright?"

"Yea, I'm fine. I'll just miss you two this week."

"I love you, Dave."

"I love you, Daddy."

When they were gone long enough for Dave to be sure they wouldn't be coming back for anything forgotten, Dave placed life insurance policies, his will, a password book, and other documents neatly on the kitchen table.

He was going to face this head-on. What was the alternative? Wait in his room all week. Maybe the house would burn like the insane asylum did. Maybe some nut would break in and shoot him. He was going to face the devil head on.

Armed with a cross around his neck and his faith, he headed for the woods. Instead of driving, he took the long way on foot. Just like when he was a teenager. Despite the bakery being shuttered for ten years, the hole in the fence remained.

Sliding down the hill, old voices began to fill his head. *I'll side with the devil. Hail Satan! Drink her blood! Come. Join us. You just sacrificed a human.* But the worst voice in Dave's head was his own, asking the same questions over and over. *Was my repentance enough? Is my faith strong enough?*

He came to the new busy stretch of road where five years prior he had seen the corpse of the man who got him into this whole devilish mess in the first place. Dave was halfway into the southbound lane when a sports car whizzed around the corner, almost striking him.

The gust of wind from the speeding automobile blew his hat off. On instinct he turned around to retrieve the cap and a big-rig came whizzing around the corner. He dove back into the woods at the last moment, narrowly avoiding the eighteen-wheeler.

After catching his breath, he made a dash across the road. It'd been twenty-seven years since he last stood here. He could smell the marijuana, hear the black metal, and see the flickering of a bonfire in his mind.

Dave made his way through the undergrowth of the forest, past the rock that looked like a witch's face, and now stood in the clearing. The fire pit remained. Trees vandalized with satanic symbols remained. The blasphemous spray paint remained. And The Gates remained. Twilight drew near.

Dave approached The Gates and placed his hands on the rusty bars.

"Whatever entity lies in wait, be gone! You are no match for the Power and Spirit of God Almighty!"

Dave felt the heat as he opened The Gates, hearing the screech of the rusted metal. Sweat broke out across his brow. The cool fall air now felt like the desert in the middle of July.

Hunchbacked figures with charred, melted flesh, eyeless faces, and lipless mouths stared back at him. The only one not burnt was the boy standing in front staring at Dave. Dillon Jacobs.

The Gates closed behind Dave.

It had not been enough.

Conscience

Kathrin Classen

It wasn't as hard as I thought it would be to kill someone; I knew more intimately than any other person in the world. I idolized him and did everything he asked me to do for him. When we were in the same room, his mere presence defined me. I was his and his alone.

But in the end, I wasn't enough for him. He was going to leave me. Just like that. After everything we've been through together. He said he needed a change, that his life had grown tiresome. In other words, he had grown tired of me.

In the beginning of our time together, I used to stare at his face, committing every detail to memory. I knew it better than my own. His words were gospel, wise and profound. We were grafted together, inseparable… or so I thought.

The night he told me he was leaving, it was like the ground had given way to a deep, dark chasm and I was falling into it. I was in denial. This was some sick joke. He would never leave me. Never! But as the weight of his words soaked in, a fierce, intoxicating rage took root.

I used sodium cyanide crystals in the mashed potatoes I made for our last dinner. I added plenty of garlic and salt to hide the taste. I couldn't believe I could use something so ordinary, so benign for such a terrible purpose.

As I stood by the kitchen counter idly peeling the potatoes, I tried to imagine what it would be like when he took that first bite. Would he know immediately what I had done to him? Or would it take the greater part of dinner before the cyanide rendered the oxygen in his body as totally useless?

Would his body spasm like in the movies or would his death be peaceful? He would lean forward for the next bite and just… stop? His head falling limp right into the mashed potatoes and peas? I imagined getting up from my chair, quietly walking toward him and as gently as I could, lifting his face up and wiping it clean. He was a beautiful man, after all. It wouldn't be right to bury him in such filth, even if that's what he deserved.

I reflected on our life together as I loaded the plates with potatoes, freshly steamed vegetables, and a chicken I roasted for this special occasion. He was all I knew. From when I was very young, I was his lump of clay. He molded and pressed me to become just like him. To think like him, feel like him. Who would I be when he was gone?

I couldn't imagine him being with someone else. Teaching someone who wasn't me. Touching them in the way he did me. It couldn't happen. If I couldn't have him, no one could. Or so the old cliche goes…

When we both finally sat down to dinner, it was already pitch-black outside, the winter bringing with it long, cold nights. He smiled at me and congratulated me on a marvelous feast. I think he thought me a mouse as I nodded in the light of his approval.

Little did he know, he was dealing with a cat carved out

in his own image. He took the first bite and I waited. Nothing happened. He took another and then another. I took little bites of the chicken, waiting as if for Christmas day, the anticipation tingling throughout my whole being, but still nothing happened.

Finally he looked up and asked why I wasn't enjoying the food I worked so hard to prepare. I mumbled something about not being hungry and started to think I had done something wrong. But I didn't worry for too long.

He looked up at me suddenly, fork suspended in the air halfway between the plate and his mouth. A frown creased his brow and for a moment, he looked like a confused little boy. I wanted to laugh, to clap my hands with joy.

But I just sat there, completely still as I watched him moan and grab his chest. He fell to the floor and retched, putting his finger down his throat in one last effort to rid his body of the poison. But it was no use… He was too late.

It almost took until dawn to dig a hole deep enough to bury him. I was grateful the mild winter had damped the earth. Pure adrenaline coursed through my veins as the shovel cut through dirt and loose rock. I was exhausted to tears by the time it was done, afraid I wouldn't finish before the sun rose and gave away my terrible secret to the waking world.

It would be a lie to say I didn't cry for losing him. I knew I had done a terrible thing. His blood was on my hands.

I took his legs and pinned them under my arms to pull him into the backyard. I was sweating, stumbling over my own feet. His head made a sickening thud on the ground when I finally got him outside. For a moment I had to retch myself, my empty stomach offering nothing for the effort.

I was grateful for the all-consuming darkness of the winter night as I finally rolled his body into the waiting earth. It landed quietly, the ground swallowing him up for all eternity.

***

Now, I am driving to our little cabin deep in the woods. Our little piece of paradise in the chaotic world. He built it for me as a gift when I first came to him. The road on which I am driving is narrow with many hairpin turns. The cabin is close to a well-traveled hiking trail, and it's a wonder our hideaway hasn't been discovered.

It's raining and the road up the mountain is slick and shiny, reflecting the glare of the headlights back at me. And even though I cannot see it, the terrifying pull of the sheer drop on the right side of the road raises my anxiety.

I can hear my heart pounding in my head, relentless in its assault. I am sweating, the fine hairs on my upper lip catching the moisture as it forms little beads until they are large enough to join the others that are rolling down my face. My fingers have gone numb from gripping the steering wheel, whether from terror or excitement, I don't know.

What have I done? *What have I done? Stop it!* I tell myself. I scream to let out the pain, the rage, the confusion. In the confined space of the car, the sound echoes back at me in loud, monstrous tones. I am ashamed to be crying again. And when I finally gain control over my unbridled wailing, the silence is deafening, so thick and heavy its weight crushes me.

For the briefest of seconds, I am back in our dining room and I see his cold, dead eyes staring up at me, accusing glint shining from the light in the overhead lamp. That annoying twinge of remorse invades the edges of the memory. I lash out and imagine him leaving me behind. Being with someone else. I imagine myself slapping that condescending grin off his face and I feel satisfied.

I lose focus on the road and underestimate how slowly I should take the next sharp turn, the back tires skidding toward the cliff edge. I swear loudly and manage to force them back on track. I take a deep, calming breath and try to imagine I am out for a normal drive in the mountains.

The rain is coming down harder now, pelting the wind-shield with such ferocity that my view outside the little sphere of light beyond the headlights is all but impossible.

I wipe sweat from my eyes but turning the heater off is not an option, the fog on the glass hanging around the edges, ready for the slightest chance to crowd in and take what is left of my vision. I am almost there. Almost free of him and from what I have done.

A large formless shadow looms out of the darkness right in front of me. I slam hard on the brakes to avoid hitting it. The tires swerve to the left, then the right; the rear of the car hanging for one terrifying second over the edge of the cliff until momentum carries it back into the trees. I don't even register the obscene smashing sound of the car as it careens into old-growth cedars: the splintering wood, bending metal, and cracking glass.

For one blissful moment, my brain doesn't connect with my body. The reality of what has just happened stays tucked in a little bubble outside of space and time. Until that bubble bursts and horrifying realization comes crashing into me.

I can't breathe, a sharp, angry pain in my side. My head feels a hundred times its size resting on the rough fabric of the airbag, the powder expelled during activation turning to a white sludge in the relentless rain. Along with this cold, hard hellfire spitting from heaven, I feel something warm slowly making its way down my forehead and onto my neck and shoulder.

I can't see, the skin around my eyes bruised and puffy. The primitive part of my brain is in charge, telling me to get up, get out, and move to safety. I listen, struggling against the stubborn seat belt until it finally gives way and I tumble out of the open front door. I lay there for a moment, aware that I'm not alone.

Four large, heavy hooves come toward me, the heat of its foul breath ruffling my hair with every exhale. The devil, I think deliriously. The devil is here to claim me for what I did to him.

At that moment, I know I am not ready to die. I want to state my case. I want to scream that it's not my fault. But even as I plead with death, I know I am grasping at straws. I want to shift the blame away from me, but there is no hiding the truth in the end. *I killed him.*

The creature comes closer and I lay as if in death, not willing to admit to myself how hard the terror is gripping my gut, twisting it around like a grotesque balloon animal. With one final sniff, the black giant grows disinterested, sparing my life as it lumbers away, antlers held high against the torrent from above. It was just an elk that had stood in the middle of the abandoned road, no longer curious to what had disturbed his evening walk. I scold myself for being so childish and afraid.

Blood and rain mix with sweat as I heave myself upright to sit, shivering beside the tangled mess of   what man made and nature claimed; a canopy of branches shielding me from the worst of Mother Nature's harsh temper. I can't help but think she has a right to be angry with me. I upset the natural order of things with what I have done.

Slowly and with great effort, I pull myself up on the driver's side seatbelt, leaning heavily on the upholstery until my feet are firmly under me. I need to assess the damage to the car. But I know even before I stumble back to get a better look that it is hopeless. The front of the car is buried deep in the trunk of a tree and the frame is bent at an unnatural angle. I will have to walk from here.

I make my way unsteadily back to the pavement, surprised to see how far the car traveled before being stopped by the gatekeepers of the forest. Here, there is no cover from the rain and no reassuring light from the ruined head-lights. I squint into the darkness to get my bearings, acutely aware of the pain radiating through my whole being. I can't remember the last time I was in such agony.

I shuffle forward on the road, grateful there are no roots to trip me and no rocks to block my slow progress. I live through an eternity in the few minutes it takes me to limp around the last tight curve I took coming up the mountain.

Finally, I have a full view of the road I traveled so many times in the past. I am about three miles away from the turnoff that will take me to the cabin. Three miles doesn't seem that far but I know better. I will be in anguish, suffering through the torture I surely deserve.

I am turning toward the direction of the cabin when something catches my attention out of the corner of my eye. The hairs on the back of my neck stand on end. I am not alone. Slowly, so slowly, I turn to face in the direction of the movement.

There is nothing. I am alone on the road. Just me and an elk hiding somewhere in the shadows. *Get a grip.* It is now a game of survival until I reach the cabin, and I will lose it if I don't get a hold of myself. But as I turn back, a tall, brooding figure stands directly in front of me. I inhale sharply and stumble backward to remain standing.

My breath is coming hard and fast. The pain in my ribs is intense as it radiates through the whole of my being. *It is the elk. It has to be the elk.* But elk do not look like men.

They do not wear his brand of cologne.

I can't feel the rain anymore. The gusts of wind against my back are nothing. My fingertips tingle and my mouth is dry. I can smell him here with me. It is like he is right in front of me, but I know that it is impossible.

Lightning fractures the world around me and for a second it is as bright as day before I am plunged into a darkness deeper and heavier than should have been possible. The figure in front of me has disappeared but it is not gone. I can feel his breath tickling the fine hairs on my skin. I am blind, and when the thunder cracks and breaks the sky around us, deaf as well. I blink helplessly, desperately, to no avail.

Another furious flash lights up the sky. My blood freezes in my veins, the beating of my heart stilled to silence when my sight is restored, and I see what is in front of me. The amorphous creature–for it is not a man, not anymore–looms over me, dark and brooding.

I scream, my terror bubbling up from the deepest part of my soul, clawing and scratching its way out of my throat and into the world. I fall back on the hard cement of the road, my head bouncing off of it; sight exploding into a million shimmering stars.

The creature lets out a howl of rage; its foul, rotting scent flowing toward me on the wind, clinging to me, seeping into every pore. It lingers above me, breathing in the sight of my helpless fear. I am ashamed to be so terrified, and try to gather what little reserve of strength I have left to stand. I need to face it… No, that's idiotic. I can't face this thing. I need to run away from it. And I know if I don't move now, this creature, this hound from hell, will be the last thing I ever see.

Another bellow brings me out of my stupor and I roll onto my stomach. The shaking in my arms and legs betrays my efforts to get up, to run, to get away from the creature. I curse myself for the weakness that seizes me. I am better than this. I am stronger than this.

The creature lowers itself on all fours, unnaturally twisting its head from side to side, studying its prey as it surges forward in a grotesque mockery of movement. Its joints are unhinged, its bones broken, snapping and reshaping, bone grinding against bone as it draws closer… and closer… and closer…

The rotting breath forces itself into my nostrils and deep into my lungs where it sits, burning, decaying, breaking me down from the inside out. I try to scream, but the creature has stolen my voice. My body, paralyzed in fear, betrays me, leaving me to be consumed by this beast of vengeance.

Slowly, it draws itself up and over me, mere inches from my face. Jowls slick with sickly green saliva rest above me. Where eyes should have been, only two endless holes, an eternity lost in them. Fear grips me harder, like razor wire pulling apart my skin, shredding the muscle, tearing tendons from the bone.

The endless terrible faceless creature tilts its head as it inspects me and then *he* is there looking at me. For a brief second, he is there in all his confident beauty. I want to run to him, to hold him, to tell him I'm sorry. So, so sorry and I want him back with me.

His face contorts as his lips curl at the edges, then stretch and strain until his face is a contorted, inhuman mass of lips and teeth. He opens them, letting saliva drip to my skin, the flesh bubbling up where it touches, separating from the muscles underneath as acid hungrily consumes me.

I shouldn't have done what I did… *I shouldn't have done what I did!*

Horrified, I watch on as he eats bite after bite. With every little piece of me that is devoured, I grow more and more numb, despondent to his revenge. He is an animal, a ravenous beast. The pain comes in sharp, overwhelming waves.

I shouldn't have done what I did…

Visions of Hell

William Presley

The dead man stood facing away from the camera, hands tied to his ankles so that his back was flat enough to eat off of. His entire posterior was now an open cavity that allowed a mass of entrails to seep down the backs of his legs, and little army men had been positioned along the intestines as if climbing a ladder. In the upper lefthand corner of the frame, the photographer held a knife between the victim's severed ears in the shape of an erect phallus.

In the upper right, one of the corpse's lungs was balanced neatly on a plate at the top of his scalp. The more precarious bits of the piece were supported by the willow branches that ran throughout.

I turned my head with a grunt, counting the raindrops that pattered against the plated windows of the police loft in an attempt to forget what I'd just seen. "The self-portrait in Hell. Hieronymus Bosch. It's from *The Garden of Earthly Delights*."

"Well, our perp is calling it *Without Breath to Complain*, and there's a lot more where that came from." The detective drew my attention back to the computer screen, where a series of snuff photos were for sale as non-fungible tokens. "I have to tell you, I've seen bad… but not worse. The artist calls himself Switch. That's all we know. This NFT shit's on a blockchain – can't trace it."

"All of his pieces look like Bosch recreations."

"That's what we figured."

"Then why did I have to see that? What, exactly, were you hoping to get from an art historian?"

"We were hoping for some insight. Obviously the two artists share a similar source of inspiration."

"Religion. During the time Bosch was active–late Fifteenth, early Sixteenth Century–there was a heavy focus on sin and punishment. Those themes factor quite heavily into his work… and perhaps explain the name 'Switch.' Other than that, I… I don't know what to tell you. Is there any connection between the victims?"

"No idea. So far, this is the first victim we've ID'd, and only because someone here recognized him. The guy had two or three domestics under his belt just from neighbor complaints. Probably why the wife never reported a missing person. I can't for the life of me figure out why she had ten kids with him."

A gruff voice interrupted our conversation. "Another one of the victims had twelve." I turned around to see an older man standing behind us. "Glen," he nodded. "Dr. Randolph."

Glen leaned over to introduce us. "Grace, this is Detective Marston. He's working with me on this case. Sounds like we have another ID."

Marston grabbed the mouse and scrolled down to the picture of a severed head fastened to a pair of feet, a scarf tied beneath its chin. "Mark Forsythe. His co-worker called him in this morning. A couple of deputies just went out to the house with the chaplain, so the widow should be about ripe for questioning if you want to head over. They're in Silica."

"I'll go, too," I interjected. Both men shot me an apprehensive glance, and I quickly added, "Not to talk! Only observe."

"Grace, I—"

"Glen, if you want me to help you understand the killer, then I need to understand who he's targeting. There's got to be a pattern."

"Your call," Marston shrugged as he walked away.

The remaining detective pushed a few strands of brown hair from his prematurely wrinkled forehead and sighed. "Fly. On the wall."

Without another word, I was ushered into a black SUV and soon found myself winding through the bowels of Toledo. The art lover in me couldn't help but appreciate the gilded age facades of the decaying shotgun houses lining the streets, each emblematic of a city whose outskirts combined every worst feature of a small town and industrial wasteland.

Dive bars and smokestacks, steel bridges and rusty train tracks – all drawn together under the gray Midwestern sky. And yet, the mellow ambience it created quickly melded into one of foreboding as we approached some of the more isolated pockets of the county.

Indeed, by the time we pulled up to a lonely white ranch house, there was a pressure in my chest I couldn't quite place. It was only made worse by the little girl on the porch swing. She was wrapped up in a fairly one-sided conversation with her doll, nodding in quiet agreement as her inanimate companion seemed to whisper in her ear.

"It's always fun when the whole family's crazy," the detective muttered before ringing the doorbell.

Both girl and doll appeared annoyed at the sudden noise, and I was struck by a pair of piercing blue eyes that drooped into a look no five-year-old should be capable of.

One that said she'd seen inside my soul and was thoroughly unimpressed with its contents. Thankfully, her glare was broken when a dowdy woman in a denim jumper greeted us.

"Mrs. Forsythe, I'm Detective Glen Harwood, and this Dr. Grace Randolph. She's visiting us from Ohio State. May we... come in?"

"Please, yes. Of course." Her tone was so artificially sweet that it was almost grating, and I noted her attempt at a vocal fry when she apologized for some non-existent mess on the way to the living room.

Glen immediately jumped into his textbook condolence speech, but I was too busy gawking to listen. Somehow, this house was even eerier on the inside. Twelve kids, but no toys. No pictures.

And, come to think of it, several missing doors. One might actually assume this family had just moved in were it not for all of the Bible verses painted across the walls. Then it hit me – I knew what this was. I knew that blank stare on the widow's face. My own mother used to stare at me like that when she'd lock me in the kitchen pantry with my father.

My thoughts were seized by memories I'd spent the second half of my life trying to repress. I was eight years old again, cowering in Father's shadow as he loomed over me with a PVC pipe for sneaking leftovers without permission.

My first instinct was to get away, but... I had nowhere to go. There was barely enough room to breathe in that pantry, let alone run. Besides, that would only make him madder. Make his swings wider.

I had no choice but to bend over and accept my punishment. "Foolishness is bound in the heart of a child!" *Thwack.* "But the rod of correction shall drive it far from him!" *Thwack*. "Happy shall he be, that taketh and dasheth thy little ones against the stones!" *Thwack*. *Thwack*.

It took everything I had to ground myself back in the present.

"Where do you go to church?" I blurted out, the smallest hint of a Southern twang creeping through my voice.

My question seemed to catch Mrs. Forsythe off guard. "Well, we're… we're Christian."

"Yes, but *where* do you worship?"

"We… do home services."

Detective Harwood shot me a side eye, and I quickly bit my tongue. In fact, I didn't say another word until the car door had slammed behind me.

"Glen, they're Fundies!"

"Huh?"

"Fundamentalists. They're Christian Fundamentalists. That's your connection between the victims. It looks like they were both part of the Quiverfull movement."

"I'm still not really following."

"They believe every kid they have is another arrow in God's quiver, so they have as many as possible. Think Duggar. And there's this book they all read—*To Train Up a Child*. It's… basically a manual for abuse. I didn't pick up on it at first, but the title of the NFT you showed me is a quote from that book. 'A proper spanking leaves children without breath to complain.'"

"So, the killer is targeting Fundamentalists. Why?"

"Because he *is* one… or, at least, was *raised* by one. This is an extreme version of a common problem. Trust me, I grew up with this shit down in Arkansas.

These people isolate their kids, beat the Devil into them, and then teach them to repress basic human instincts like sexuality until they're so emotionally stunted they can't function in the real world.

"That's why they produce so many little creeps and per-verts. And when one gets caught doing something really disgusting, you know what they do? Cover it up. Handle it 'internally.' No need for the rest of the world to hear their dirty laundry. That wouldn't be bringing glory to God's name."

"You think they know who it is and that's why they're not reporting each other missing? They don't want the state involved?"

"I'm not sure if they *know* who it is, but I bet they have an idea."

"Hang on." Glen pulled into a parking lot and started typing something into his phone. "It looks like there's a so-cial hall they use for homeschooling meetups over by the old power plant. I say we take a little detour and see if any-thing there can help us identify some of the other victims. Maybe someone will actually talk to us."

"I doubt that."

"Even if all they do is stare, you'd be surprised how much information you can get out of silence when you ask the right questions," he chuckled, putting the car back in drive. "Now this… uh… this might be a little too personal, but how did you escape that lifestyle? I mean, if you don't mind me asking. Sounds like the parents keep their kids on a pretty tight leash."

"There was a youth group I drove my younger siblings to a few times a week. I was supposed to sit in the car and wait for them, but… I used to sneak off to the local library. A pretty tame rebellion if you think about it. I was just so transfixed by this idea of a room full of information   my parents couldn't censor. It almost seemed… dirty. I loved it.

"Anyway, long story short, I discovered a passion for art and struck up a friendship with the librarian. I think she felt bad for me. Help me apply to college. It took a lot of sneaking around to get the documents I needed, and what I couldn't get, I forged, but eventually I got offered a full ride to a state school in Indiana."

"How'd your parents take it?"

"They never knew. One day, I grabbed everything I could carry, bought a bus ticket, and never looked back. We've been no-contact since."

"You ever miss anything about that lifestyle? I know that sounds like a stupid question – guess I'm just wondering why it appeals to anybody."

"The appeal is in petty tyranny. Commanding a brood of fifteen children is the closest a lot of these men will ever get to feeling powerful. There was definitely nothing in that lifestyle for someone like *me* to miss. It was awful, plain and simple. I actually laughed to myself the other day when I heard a student complain about growing up Catholic. Like, kid, you have no idea."

"I definitely don't," the detective shrugged. "I come from a long line of detectives, and we tend to be a pretty skeptical bunch. Wasn't much religion in my house growing up. My father used to say we were probably all going to Hell anyway, so why worry about it?"

"You would have liked the seminar we had last week! I swear the art history department attracts the weirdest people. This speaker was working on a series of paintings about how we *do* all go to Hell… at least in a manner of speaking.

"Apparently, he'd read somewhere that the brain is hyperactive in the first few seconds after death, so he portrays the entire afterlife as one of those three-second dreams that feels like it lasts forever. And, in that dream, we relive weird mashups of all the moments that left the deepest scars on our psyches. Our worst memories. Over and over again."

"Sounds like he needs a handful of Prozac and a stiff drink."

"Something like that," I laughed as we pulled up beside a drab brown building.

"Hmm… lights are on. That's a good sign."

We walked in to find a lone janitor waxing the floor of the reception area.

"Have a minute to chat?" the detective asked. "We're with the county sheriff. Trying to get some info on the people who own this place."

The janitor shrugged, rubbing a hand along the back of his bald head. "Couldn't tell you much – never met any of 'em. Don't even know their names. They deal with my company, not me. Heard they're kinda weird, though."

"Mind if we look around?"

"Knock yourself out. I think there're some pictures in the backrooms, but I don't really remember. They only pay us to clean the other half of the building every couple weeks."

Glen thanked him and led me through a few sets of double doors. We stopped when we reached a dining hall, where several ten-by-twelves of previous meetups were hanging on the wall. "Christ," he muttered. "That's a lot of denim."

"See anyone you recognize?"

"Mmhmm." He took out his phone and snapped a few shots. "Over here. Top row, far right – one of our victims. That might even be another one in the middle row. Come on, let's see if there're any more photos in the next room."

We headed into the gymnasium at the very rear of the building, and even before the detective flicked on the lights, the smell of raw sewage and overripe fruit tipped me off to a nasty surprise. Indeed, there, in the center of the basketball court, was a decapitated corpse high up on a homemade throne.

It had been left to decay for so long its sagging skin had

turned an off shade of blue, and on its neck rested the sculp-
ture of what could only be described as a demonic bird
head. There was another body, too – this one suspended
from the rafters with its front end stuck in the bird's mouth,
a paper mâché pigeon protruding from its anus.

I backed up, sweat collecting on my trembling palms,
my heart lodged so firmly in my throat it kept me from
vomiting on myself.

"Dear God!"

The detective only sighed. "Guess I better call this one
in. Creative little bastard, I'll give him that."

The hours following our discovery saw me floating
around a deluge of investigators and technicians like a lost
puppy. I was interviewed, interviewed again, and then left
to stand in a corner, still fixated on the macabre creation
before me. I was about ready to sneak out when I saw Glen
making his way over to me. He looked pale, frantic even, a
strange tone in his voice.

"Grace, we have a problem."

The detective handed me his phone, where the latest
Bosch recreation was already up for sale as an NFT. This
one even featured a special cameo – a detective and an art
historian staring in horror from the bottom corner of the
frame.

"Eck!" A shudder ran up my spine as I realized the
killer must have been watching us from one of the windows. "That's just... eck!"

"Is that an academic term?"

"I don't even know what else to say. I almost feel vio-
lated."

"Yeah, I... yeah. This is definitely next-level creepy.
But, uh... what do you make of the title? *If No Contest
Arises Naturally.*"

"It's another quote from that book. I'm paraphrasing
here, but it's something like, 'If no contest arises naturally,

arrange one.'"

"So, he wants to play cat and mouse."

I handed Glen his phone back, brows furrowed. "No… I don't think that's it. This sounds like an invitation, not a challenge. He *wants* us to find him. I mean, think about it. Whoever did this isn't trying to be a tv cliché. There's something deeper going on here."

"I don't need to think about it – we're off the case. Turns out we have a couple of these Fundies in the department. They've been asked to take over. Some happy horseshit about cultural sensitivity."

"Wait, what? No! This is what I was talking about! This is what they do! You let them handle their own case and we'll never hear about it again."

"Grace—and I'm gonna be real direct with you here— I don't give a damn anymore. This guy knows what I look like. A quick search on the department website would give him everything he needed to track me down. I'm not about to play that game. I've got young kids. I don't want him skulking around our house. *They* created this monster, so let *them* wrangle it. If a few wife beaters and child abusers get eaten in the process, well… it's hard to feel bad."

"You think the problem is going to stay contained? Because I'll tell you right now, it never does. Sure, they start with the people they know. Josh Duggar started by groping his little sisters. And his parents? They made sure to get the 'right' cop involved by going to a family friend—a friend who, by the way, *also* ended up being a pedo.

"Josh goes free to be healed by the power of God, and twenty years later, gets busted with infant torture porn."

"This is a different situation. People are dying here."

"Exactly."

But my argument fell on deaf ears, and I was eventually escorted to my hotel room. With nothing else to do, I sat in front of the mirror to remove my makeup, cringing at the face that stared back at me. My mother's face. We'd always looked alike with the same wide-set gray eyes and blonde waves.

Yet now, I could also see her distinct worry lines starting to snake across my forehead. And I hated them. Hated that the older I got, the harder it was to forget my past.

In some ways, I'd always be that scared little girl in the kitchen pantry, praying that Jesus would just take her to Heaven. I knew that; I'd accepted it. But I refused to be the woman who locked the door behind her. I had been scarred by an evil no longer isolated to the households that perpetuated it. An evil that had taken on a new form – one that would soon venture out into the general population. And, in my own irrational mind, I convinced myself I was complicit if I did nothing to stop it.

"If no contest arises naturally," I repeated. That *had* been an invitation, yes, I was sure of it. In fact, not only did our killer want to be found, he seemed annoyed it hadn't already happened.

It's not like he was making it hard. All the NFTs were publicly available, and each of them—save the one from the gymnasium—were taken in the exact same location. A location nobody had been able to identify. Perhaps standing right over us while he took our picture was the artist's way of saying we were missing something right in front of our faces. But what was as obvious to an artist as it was inconspicuous to a team of cops?

And then it hit me: the pipe joints.

Though the concrete walls and arched windows of the backdrop had been generic enough, the cast iron lion heads that held together the ancient plumbing were absolutely beautiful. I'd seen them before, too, on an architectural tour through the city. I even had a picture, with the location marked in my phone as an abandoned papermill.

So, I did what any psychotic moron would do –

armed myself with my personal handgun and called a ride to a serial killer's workshop.

Unfortunately, the trip proved to be lengthier than I realized, with the sun having long set by the time I arrived. This left the red bricks of the three-story building to glitter like rusty scrap metal in the dim glow of the streetlights. I looked from the boarded-up front door to the open window on the second-floor fire escape and sighed. Was I really about to climb up there? Could a PhD really be this dumb? I had my answer when I felt the first rung of the ladder clasped against my palm. "Better dumb than a coward," I mumbled. Indeed, I'd been given a chance to stop a serial killer and expose the people who'd made my childhood a living Hell in one fell swoop. I would not let that go to waste.

That's not to say, of course, I had any confidence in my decision. With every inch I climbed, so too climbed my heart rate until I was a sweaty, shaky mess. I couldn't even find the strength to pull myself onto the exit platform; I had to flop. I did finally manage to slip inside, though, and was shocked at how abjectly dark a room with such large windows could be. I was actually reaching for my phone when I felt the floor start to shudder. Then a sound like splintering wood. Next thing I knew, I was in a freefall that lasted only seconds before I landed in what felt like a ball pit.

Flash. A sudden light ripped through the space, lingering just long enough for me to see I was in some sort of vat surrounded by plastic green orbs. *Flash.* To my right, I noticed the fileted remnants of a man's face stretched out on a mounting board. The empty sockets where his eyes should have been were accentuated with black paint, and clay mucus dripped from his nose to his sagging lips. *Flash, flash, flash.* I finally realized the bursts were coming from a camera, the photographer's silhouette looming on what was left of the second-floor balcony. I watched as he ran down a flight of stairs and into another part of the building.

I hopped out of the vat and began to chase him. "Wait!" I called. "You wanted me here, damnit! I'm here!"

A blinding orange glow struck me as soon as I crossed the threshold of the next room. Photography lamps— an enormous set. The killer had switched them on to reveal none other than Glen himself, whose body was splayed out on the strings of an oversized harpsichord. In his left hand, he held his severed tongue, in his right, his teeth. The resulting cavern at the bottom of the detective's face drooped in horror at his organs—still connected to his open abdominal cavity by strands of vasculature—as they hung down from the different notes of the instrument.

"Why?" I gagged, falling back on the wall for support.

An attractive young man stepped out from behind the display and pushed a shock of dark hair out of his puppy-dog blue eyes. "Because I heard the detectives talking outside while I was taking your picture. They were gonna assign the case to one of my father's friends, and then what? I get swept under the rug? They track me down and drag me to another stupid camp? I had to give them something they couldn't cover up."

"What, you mean shaving your head and forcing you to dig random holes won't cure your inner psycho?"

"You… you know about the camps?"

"Of course. I grew up Quiverfull. And now I'm an art historian. You and I actually have a lot in common. Let me guess, you got into Hieronymus Bosch by sneaking into the library?"

"It was the only place I could use the internet."

"And now you're doing this because you want to hurt the people who hurt you? Kill who you can and expose the rest?"

"That's part of it. But honestly… I just like killing. It's true what they say, you know. Some people are born evil."

"You weren't *born* evil, they *made you* evil. And if you trust me, I can help you. There *is* real help out there… in the real world. You don't have to keep doing this. We can still expose this awful cult for what it is – still tell your story."

He pulled a gun from the pocket of his hoodie. "How 'bout we start now. Call the police and tell them where you are. Let them know there's a present waiting!"

"If that's what yo—"

"Call the fucking police!" The gun trembled in his hand. I began fumbling with my phone, breathlessly explaining the situation to a 911 operator. He nodded with approval. "Good, now say my name. Dylan Forsythe. I want them to know!"

I did as I was told, my voice becoming more frantic. "Listen to me, don't send someone random. I need you to get in touch with Detective Marston. Jim Marston. Please. I'm going to hang up now – he'll know what to do."

As soon as I ended the call, Dylan turned to walk away, but I pulled out my own gun. "You know I can't let you leave."

The young man sighed, still facing away. "I really didn't wanna do this. You were one of the good ones;   I was gonna let you go."

He whipped back around, and both of us fired a shot. We ended up falling away from each other in agony – Dylan with a wound through the head, me with a hole in my chest. I closed my eyes to the sweet lullaby of approaching sirens. "*Yes!*" I thought. "*Wait… no. Where are they going? Here! In here!*" The noise had faded away.

I forced my eyes back open, only to find Dylan standing over me. "No! How are you still alive?"

The killer let out a laugh that quickly became something deep and guttural, his face morphing into that of my father. A PVC pipe materialized in his hand. "Welcome to Hell,

Grace."

Bone Broth

John Schlimm

"Okay then, you look good and secure, not going anywhere. Gorilla Tape is the best, isn't it? It never let me down yet. And your La-Z-Boy looks nice and comfy. Just settle in now and relax.

"Do you know how special you are? I couldn't just pick anybody for this, not like the other ones where I had more leeway. Believe you me, I took a lot of time scouting through many towns and cities looking for someone just like you—photogenic, cute in that lovable girl-next-door way, not too young but not too old, someone who I can trust to communicate effectively, single with no distracting strings attached to a boyfriend or husband or kids.

"Someone with total Rom-Com star allure.

"That first day I saw you a few weeks ago, I just knew you were the one. You know what caught my attention first about you? Your blue eyes. I spotted them from a mile away. Those are some real bankable puppy-dog eyes you've got. I bet you can convince people of anything with those eyes, and get away with anything, and pull some serious heartstrings. I'm counting on that.

"So first things first: I'm going to give you the back-story, and I need you to listen very carefully. It's important you remember as much as possible. It'll actually be to your advantage later on.

"No one has ever heard this story before. Not the real version, anyway.

"When I was a kid, my father told me I had spectacular eyes, too. I bet you've even seen these green eyes before. He once proudly described them to *Time* magazine as a 'rare shade between polished emerald and lizard skin,' and he told me they would ensure I'd be famous forever.

"But he was wrong.

"About the 'famous forever' part.

"My father and mother were often wrong, including with their decision to buy me when I was three years old. That may just have been their biggest mistake.

"Do you know they actually sent talent scouts out across the country looking for me? Can you imagine your parents doing that?

"The instructions to the scouts were very specific: healthy, thin, white, baby boy, three-years-old, clear skin, light brown or blonde hair, symmetrical nose and lips, small ears, and with a sparkle in his eyes.

"My parents could do this, and quietly, because my father was still one of the biggest directors in Hollywood at the time—this was around forty years ago in the mid-eighties. And my mother was a former actress, tapping out her career in a popular soap opera during the sixties and seventies before hitching a ride on my dad's coattails. Boy did she ever get screwed over. She's a cautionary tale for all the gold-diggers out there: be careful what you wish for!

"By this point, they were in their early fifties. Mother was reduced to a trophy wife who stayed mostly at home—the way my father preferred it, managing our estate in Beverly Hills. Meanwhile, Father was flailing in shark-infested waters, watching his once esteemed, Academy Award-winning career as a film director fade away because no one wanted his style of police and cowboy movies anymore.

"Mother desperately wanted a baby since that had been put on hold to protect her size-zero figure during her TV years, and Father desperately needed a new project to keep his name up on the big screen to stay relevant. That's where I came in.

"Oh, I'm sorry about the tape across your mouth, I can tell it's uncomfortable, but I have no choice. Surely you understand, I can't have you screaming. Hopefully the tape around your wrists and ankles is a little comfier. I certainly don't want to cut off your circulation! If you just stay still, that'll help.

"So where was I?

"Oh yeah, so my father gets a once-in-a-lifetime, kill-two-birds-with-one-stone opportunity dropped in his lap. His agent called one day in the early eighties and said   the king of suspense and terror, author Horas Clyde, whose latest masterpiece at the time *Devil Eyes* was topping every best-seller list, was now looking for the perfect director to adapt it into a movie.

"Turned out, Horas was a huge fan of my father's cop and cowboy movies, and thought he could bring something fresh to the horror genre this time. *Devil Eyes* was the story of a young, Bible-thumping couple desperate to get a new kid after theirs tragically dies, then one day a beautiful, angelic little five-year-old boy with light-colored hair and twinkling eyes just shows up at their farm in Maine.

"After trying to find out where he came from with no luck, they decide to keep him for themselves—they believed his arrival was a real honest-to-God miracle!

"You're probably too young to have seen the movie and its sequels when they came out; you likely weren't born yet, but maybe you saw them later on or read the book—it's still popular, a cult classic really all these years later.

"Anyway, shocker   -shocker   , that little miracle kid turns out to be the son of Satan. Kind of a predictable storyline these days, but it was groundbreaking back then. Some libraries even banned the book, and some theaters refused to show it, which just made people want to read and see it even more.

"Oh, I can tell from your wide eyes you're enjoying this. Believe you me, this is all leading up to something real big for you! A role of a lifetime just for you.

"When this project was dropped in Father's lap, he saw it as his one-way ticket back to the top of the almighty Hollywood pyramid. When my mother learned about it and read the script, she wanted to play the wife in the story, but Father told her she was out of her mind—that no one would believe someone as old as her, let alone a washed-up soap actress, was a fresh, naïve, dewy-eyed young farm wife from Maine. But he had an idea that would make her happy, too.

"A baby!

"The success of the movie adaptation of *Devil Eyes* fell squarely on casting the perfect child for the role.

"Father figured he had about two years of development work to complete before the film went into production, which meant he had one-to-two years to find the perfect kid for when the cameras started rolling. And he wanted an unknown child he could groom and control from the start.

"With the production company and studio on board, a team of the industry's best talent scouts were dispatched across the U.S. to every nook and cranny to find that perfect child—who my parents would adopt so my mother could have a new pastime and so my father could turn him into a star in order to revive his own career. The scouts were authorized to offer up to $200,000 for the kid.

"I know, right! That was a fortune back then! Have you

ever thought about what your parents would have paid if they had to buy you? You're pretty special, so a bargain at any price!

"The scouts visited tons of orphanages, foster homes, homeless shelters, certain convents that were well-known as dumping grounds for unwanted kids, and other places, and they sent dozens of photos back to my parents in Beverly Hills for consideration.

"But Father and Mother rejected every child in every photo. They told me the kids in the photos were 'too fat, wrong color, dull eyes, crooked mouth, weird nose, the ears were too big, the hair was too dark or too curly.'

"But after six months, a scout hit paydirt in Flank Hollow, Kentucky—a small coal-mining town stuck between two hill ranges. Only one road runs through the middle of it. It's not a place you plan on stopping in unless you live there and have no choice.

"That's where they found me, living with my Mamaw in the same small house she grew up in and her momma before her. I was three years old, and fit the casting call requirements to the letter, and then some.

"Both my birth parents were dead—overdosed, six months apart when I was one. Mamaw had lots of health issues and could barely get around, and couldn't take care of a toddler, and no other family members wanted me, they all had enough problems of their own.

"Back out in Beverly Hills, as soon as my parents saw the photo of me that the talent scout sent them, they were sold! Or, rather, I was sold. My green eyes are what sealed the deal. I checked off all the required boxes, but my eyes are what got my father on the phone to that scout to tell him to offer my Mamaw whatever she wanted, just get me back to Hollywood with no strings whatsoever attached.

"And boy did my parents get a bargain, believe you me. The scout offered my Mamaw and an uncle who had come sniffing around $75,000 to start the negotiation. They'd never seen that much money in their lives, nor had they ever negotiated for anything. One handshake, a few illegible signatures on a contract that secured their silence and stated my Mamaw and uncle never knew me to begin with, and a suitcase stuffed with cash was handed over—SOLD!

"The flight back was my first time on a private jet, though I don't remember it.

"I can tell from your confused eyes, you're wondering how a three-year-old could remember all that all these years later. I don't, exactly. Several years back, let's just say I *persuaded* my father and mother to tell me all this, the real truth, not the one they and their publicity team created at the time.

"For the next two years, my new mother basked in pretending to be June Cleaver while my new father was cultivating a star. I rarely ever left our estate during that time. Our place out there is called Casa Dahlia. It was built in the 1940's, and has twenty-five rooms, a pool, tennis court, and the outside gardens have only dahlias growing in them.

"Do you know there's like seventy-thousand named varieties of dahlias? My favorite is the Black Jack—it's big and pointy, with deep-red petals that surround its black heart in the middle.

"I had everything a normal kid could ever wish for—one whole room was nothing but video and arcade games, there was a music room, a candy store room, a sports room, a stuffed-animal room, a full-size home theater, even a bouncy room inside just like the ones you see at other children's birthday parties in backyards.

"The bed in my bedroom was a giant spaceship I could crawl into every night and emerge from every morning, and the room was outfitted by a topnotch interior designer to look just like you were in outer space.

"An army of nannies, doctors, teachers, acting coaches,

dance instructors, and stylists were brought in to tend to me and train me. Mother and Father called them my Care Team. No kids were ever brought for me to play with or be friends with. My mother would always say to me, 'I'm the only friend you need, and you're the only friend I need.'

"Then, when I was five, we finally began filming *Devil Eyes*. We were on location in Maine, way out in the country where location scouts had found the perfect farm to use, just like they'd found me years earlier. Mother, and my Care Team, were there with me the whole time. We stayed nearby the set in an old Victorian mansion that looked like something from a scary movie itself. My Care Team was housed in some outbuildings on the property.

"Filming took several months, then about a year for my father's team to edit and finalize the movie in post-production. Each day, I'd go over my lines with Mother at the house and I'd have my hair and makeup done there. Then she and I would be driven to the set where I'd film my scenes and do any retakes before we were promptly driven straight back to our rental house.

"No one on set was allowed to talk to me, unless directly involved with a scene I was in. Father insisted there be a mystique around me at all times.

"When I was seven, the first movie was released and I made my official debut as the five-year-old Amon Peters in *Devil Eyes*. The name Amon means Marquis of Hell, commander of lesser demons. Charming, especially for a kid, right?

"Ha ! I bet your childhood wasn't quite as colorful as mine, huh? Have you seen *Devil Eyes*? . . . Come on, blink or nod, or do something. . . . Hey, what's with those heavy eyelids? Now don't go falling asleep on me in that La-Z-Boy, or I'll have to set you on that wooden desk chair over there.

"I promise, we're getting to the part you probably want

to hear most about. But it's important you have this back-story. Besides, it's not every day you get to sit and visit with a bona-fide Hollywood legend, is it? You best soak it all in! Besides, you're not going to be anonymous yourself for much longer.

"So the movie hits theaters and, no surprise, with Horas Clyde's and my father's names attached to it, *Devil Eyes* was the biggest film of the year, and the highest grossing horror film to that date. My father knew this would be the case, so by then, while I had been six like Amon would be, we had filmed *Devil Eyes 2*, which was in post-production, and we were midway through filming *Devil Eyes 3* that called for a seven-year-old Amon, which I was at the time.

"The premiere and everything that came after the first movie was crazy. I was old enough to remember it all. To my father's credit, he proved once more he had a keen eye for undiscovered talent, because I became the breakout star. My photo was on magazine covers and posters, I made appearances on talk shows, there was even an Amon doll and Amon Fan Club.

"I did public appearances where I'd be surrounded by hundreds, sometimes thousands of people. They were never allowed to touch me, or talk to me, or even get too close, but they'd all yell, 'AMON! AMON! AMON!.'

"I'm telling you, my father was determined at all costs to maintain the aura of Amon, the devil's spawn, everywhere I went.

"For a few public events to promote *Devil Eyes*, I literally sat inside a red glass case—a cage, really—that my father had specially constructed, like I was a creepy doll or zoo animal, or truly the son of Satan. The case, with me in it, would be carried into malls by big burly, uniformed men to the accolades of screaming fans, then once on Halloween on stage at the Hollywood Bowl, and inside Mann's Chinese Theatre for a special screening.

"By the time the sequels rolled around over the next two years, I was eight and then nine, and too big to fit in the glass case. Because I was older and, according to Father, not as cute anymore, my public appearances on behalf of *Devil Eyes 2* and *Devil Eyes 3* were reduced to nothing more than a few choreographed print interviews where a publicist wrote and submitted my answers, along with air-brushed photos that made me look cuter than I was.

"It's not like anyone was going to see me out in public, and realize I wasn't that cute anymore, because I never left Casa Dahlia. Father did all the TV interviews for the sequels.

"Can you imagine what it's like playing a devil child when you're only a child yourself? Your parents bringing in real-life satanists, occult leaders, demon experts, ghost-hunters, psychics, and others to coach you about how a real son of Satan would act. It sure worked though; I was very convincing. But, believe you me, it can mess with you real bad.

"One scene in *Devil Eyes 3* called for me to attack a cow as it laid in a field, and they used a real cow unbeknownst to me until it was too late. My father told me it was a dead cow from a farm nearby, and that it had died of natural causes.

"But it wasn't dead at all, only tranquilized by the production team. You, in fact, are the first person to ever hear this behind-the-scenes story. As soon as I hit the cow with the ax, it spasmed and made a sound I'll never forget.

"I was stunned at first, then I heard my father scream at me, 'Keep going!' So I did, until it was dead for real. By the end of filming the scene, I was drenched in blood.

"I was so convincing as Amon that some fans out there even believed I was actually the son of Satan. Can you imagine having wackos screaming outside your house when you were a kid? They'd be out there at all hours, waving crucifixes and throwing Holy Water on our front gate. A few priests even volunteered to perform an exorcism on me, all for a fictional role I played. For my parents, all of that hype just meant *Cha-Ching, Cha-Ching*!

"Oh, the tape on your mouth looks like it's peeling in the corner. Can't have that now, can we? Here, let's put this new piece over it.

"Come on now, I'm not making you uncomfortable getting this close to you, am I? No reason for that, we're just like two old friends, and I'm pouring my heart out to you here. You can trust me, I promise. Besides, you should feel honored to see these famous green eyes up so close!

"Okay, there, that's better. That piece of tape will hold that sneaky little corner down and stick for as long as we need it to.

"Anyway, after three years of back-to-back blockbusters, it all stopped.

"For me, anyway.

"I was typecast as Amon, so no other roles came my way, and the franchise had run its course so a *Devil Eyes 4* was out of the question—Horas Clyde saw to that. On the rare occasion when I was considered for a role, my parents always turned it down, even the one-time John Hughes came knocking, wanting me to play the mischievous kid in *Home Alone*. Did you know, I was his first choice for that role?

"But, nope! I had been bought and paid for, for a specific purpose, and that deal had more than paid off for my parents and fans. My parents had always intended for me to be a one-hit-wonder cash cow. Forever, and only, Amon! Father and Mother still get royalties from those *Devil Eyes* movies to this day. Meanwhile, no one ever wonders what Amon grew up to be. But, believe you me, they're about to find out, big time.

"My father landed a few more directing gigs after that,

thanks to my performances, before he was then labeled by studios with the Hollywood death knell of being over-the-hill and out-of-touch, especially among the hot young directors in the mid-to-late nineties—dudes like Quentin Tarantino, the Cohen brothers, Spike Lee, Kevin Smith, James Cameron, Wes Anderson, Chris Columbus, and Tim Burton—all rock stars.

"But I wasn't done. I had been . . . I *was* famous, and I wanted to stay that way. Three whole rooms at Casa Dahlia are filled with *Devil Eyes* memorabilia, especially Amon stuff—movie posters, scripts, my costumes on miniature Amon mannequins, the kill weapons I used in the movies, the Holy Water bottles, crosses, rosaries, and Bibles that the various actors portraying priests had used on me before I made sure they met their Maker, and one room is an exact replica of my bedroom from the Maine farmhouse.

"Growing up, after the movies were done, I'd often sneak in there late at night and crawl into Amon's bed to sleep. I still think about that farmhouse today, and dream about the amazing life I could have had there with a normal family.

"For the next several years, I was kept under house arrest by my parents, with most days at Casa Dahlia just being me and my mother, and our shared Care Team that had since been reduced to a homeschool tutor for me, a chef, housekeeper, and gardener, and a combo therapist-slash-meditation guru for my mother. I honestly think she was banging that guy the whole time, because they'd spend hours in her bedroom, and he'd often spend the night.

"Then something really awesome happened when I turned fifteen! Horas Clyde, who had written the novel and script for *Devil Eyes* and the scripts for the two film sequels, got hit by a semi-truck while out walking one afternoon. *Splat   !*

"When his widow was going through his things afterward, she found an unpublished sequel manuscript to *Devil Eyes* that was simply titled *Amon.* The book publisher scooped it right up, as did the original production company and studio that had done the first three movies. And my father was called back again to direct.

"The new storyline was about Amon as a—*wait. for it.*—fifteen-year-old teenager.

"*Amaaaazzzing,* I know, right? I can tell you're amazed, and you probably know where this story is headed, but, believe you me, you'd be so wrong!

"I assumed the role was mine. I mean, why wouldn't it be? I was fifteen at the time, and I *was* Amon!

"But you know what they say about people who *assume*, don't you? It just makes an ass out of you and me. Father was the biggest ass of them all. I sure hope your father isn't like this.

"When I asked him about returning to the role that I, and my green eyes, had made famous, my father laughed. 'Are you out of your mind?' he scowled. 'Have you looked in the mirror lately? That pimply pizza face and stringy hair. You're a scrawny, gangly kid with a squeaky voice who we keep hidden so no one will see you. You're an embarrassment. And maybe think about taking a shower sometime soon, sonny-boy. You should just be grateful to your good ole father for what he did for you the first time around.'

"As he spoke, I remember eyeing the shelf of Oscars behind him, thinking what it would be like—that it would be the most spectacular thing—to grab one and bash his skull in.

"'Besides, we've already cast this unknown kid from Oklahoma to play the teenage Amon,' Father told me. 'He's a fifteen-year-old athlete with the build we need; we can easily lighten his hair, and he can pop in colored contacts to match Amon's eyes.'

"'My eyes!' I yelled back at him.

"He laughed again, and said, 'Yeah, right.'

"Remember me telling you about all the gardens at Casa Dahlia being filled with only dahlias? Thousands of them. I spent that whole night cutting the heads off of every dahlia in every one of those gardens. All except my favorite, the Black Jacks. I used a big pair of garden clippers, and by morning I could barely move my arms.

"Seriously, was your father a jerk like mine? Just nod your head or blink your eyes. . . . *Come on, nothing?* Guess you're not in the mood to play along at the moment. We're going to have to snap you out of that. You don't want me to think it was a mistake coming here, do you?

"Oh, and my mother also got screwed over again, too, when development on *Amon* got underway. There was a role for an actress to play Amon's grandmother in this new movie and she pleaded with my father to let her at least audition for it. But, nope. 'You just don't have the look we need, sweetheart,' he told her. 'You're a little too pretty, even for your age.' Mother was still in her fifties at this point.

"I hope no bastards ever treated you or your mother that way, have they? . . . *Still nothing?* I'm going to have to give you some media training here. There's an art to doing an effective Q and A. But we'll get to that soon enough.

"So two years later, *Amon* debuted to a very disappointing box office and the reviews sucked, which was so awesome! My father's career was officially in the toilet. However, the teen who played my part went on to star in some successful vampire movies right afterward and his career is still going strong today. Those roles belonged to me!

"*Okay, there we go.* I can tell by your eyes you know who I'm talking about. I never mention him by name. Bet you even had a crush on him, maybe still do. He's a hunk for sure. *People's* Sexiest Man Alive twice now. Those should have been my magazine covers. I've fantasized about bashing his head in, too, with the Golden Globe he won a few years ago.

"So now to the part you've been waiting for. How I ended up here in your lovely little house! This place really is like a cottage out of *Better Homes and Gardens*. You have a fantastic eye for quaint and cute, but not in a cheesy-make-me-want-to-puke way.

"By the time my father's career ended and he resigned himself to humiliation and seclusion at Casa Dahlia, my mother had also become a recluse addicted to daily cocktails of pills her therapist-slash-meditation guru and other doctors happily doled out. By then she'd also butchered her face with numerous procedures, surgeries, injections, lasers, you name it.

"A lot of *Devil Eyes* profits went to pharmacists and plastic surgeons!

"On the rare occasion she left the house and on the rare occasion a paparazzo recognized her, Mother's photo would end up in those 'Where Are They Now?' columns and once in one titled 'Believe It or Not, They're Still Alive.'

"They took to calling her the Lion Lady because of how her once-beautiful face now looked. Sadly, it's just nasty.

"Meanwhile, I was seventeen and determined to become famous again. Their lives and careers were over, but I refused to believe mine was. I was no longer going to be held prisoner; I was determined to do something so spectacular that no one would ever forget me—the real me, the star, not some five-year-old from decades ago. I wanted my real name to go down in history books.

"That's when it hit me: I would become the most famous serial killer of all time. It was the role of a lifetime! And it would capture a huge audience, if done correctly.

"Ha! I bet you didn't see that twist coming, did you? I don't know though, you look pretty smart. I bet you got all straight A's in school, didn't you? Maybe you knew where this was heading the whole time. But don't assume what *your* role is here, believe you me. Don't want to make an ass out of yourself, do you?

"I spent the next three years researching, planning, and strategizing every single detail. I wasn't going to just give the world—my audience—blood and gore; I was going to give them the full package, a complete production unlike anything anyone had ever seen before.

"An epic, multimedia masterpiece!

"I read everything I could get my hands on about Bundy, Gacy, Dahmer, Gein, Ridgway, The Zodiac, Ramirez, and others—learning what they had done right and where they had screwed up. They were all artists, but each one had flaws that tripped them up. I wasn't going to let that happen to me. I was determined to be in control from beginning to end.

"Not only was I going to be the lead actor again, I was also going to now be the producer, director, and script-writer.

"As much as I hated my parents, they had taught me a lot. My father taught me about setting a scene and telling a story, and my mother taught me about acting. She was really a great actress in her day before my father erased her star from the world. In many ways, I suppose, she was a prisoner, too. But she chose that path with him out of her own need and greed, so we can't feel too bad for her, can we?

"Over the past twenty years since then, my production has played out flawlessly.

"To date, I have now killed one person in each of the other forty-nine states, as planned. Each in a different style, each person different from the ones before—no connection between race, gender, age, or anything else like that, so no obvious trail. In cities, small towns, backwoods, beaches, along stretches of remote highways. Each kill was made to simply look like a one-and-done tragedy.

"I bet right now you're thinking to yourself, *But, wait, I never heard of you? You're telling me you butchered forty-nine people across the country and no one knows about it?*

"Am I right? Is that what you're thinking?

"Oh, great, there's a nod! Welcome back to the conversation! Fun fact: did you know at any given time in the U.S. there are twenty-five to fifty active serial killers on the loose?

"Now you're probably wondering, *But what about me? How do I play into this brilliant production of his?*

"Just hold on to your panties, my friend—and we are friends now, bonded for life. I'm getting to that. And, oh boy, you are going to love it!

"I only did a few kills a year, and far apart from each other. A librarian in Elkton, a rancher down in Roswell one year, then the next year an accountant near Seattle, a grandma in Salisbury, and a kid in Miami. Zero pattern to any of it. All random, except for one thing.

"I'm sure you've heard how a lot of serial killers will leave a calling card behind. To taunt police and victims' families. I didn't want to be too obvious, but I knew I had to leave something that would later be a great topic for debate and discussion among the media and my fans. Something that would inject a bit of humor and down-home charm into the narrative.

"So after each killing, I mailed a handwritten recipe for Bone Broth to the local police department.

"Smooth move, right? The perfect mix of quirky, mysterious, and touchy-feely. I can tell you're impressed! And naturally you're probably wondering why bone broth, right on cue. Especially since, funny thing is, I'm a vegetarian.

"When I was around thirteen and trapped at Casa Dahlia, I roamed around the property a lot. We have this one building, a storage building, toward   the back end of the property.

"It's huge, more like a warehouse. It has mostly stuff like scripts and costumes from my mother's time on her soap opera and from other projects she'd done before my father ended her career. There are also things from Father's career stored in there as well. As a child and teenager, heck even now, I would often think about lighting it on fire, just so I could see the horrified looks on their faces.

"So anyway, this one day I was rooting around in there and I came across a small brown suitcase. A child's suitcase buried under a pile of old newspapers. It was old looking, and dirty. It had 'TRASH' scrawled in all caps across the front, in what I recognized as my mother's handwriting.

"When I opened it, I found neatly folded kids clothes, a bag of petrified cookies, and a handwritten recipe for 'Bone Broth.' On the back of the scrap of paper, there was a brief note: 'This was your momma's favorite recipe of mine. Love, Mamaw.'

"My parents never made a secret of the fact I was adopted, but the story they and their publicist at the time spun around it was a complete fabrication. And I was clearly never meant to see that suitcase, but someone, perhaps a nanny from way back, had pulled it from the garbage and hid it in that building, maybe hoping someday I would find it.

"Later that night, believe you me, I confronted my parents with the suitcase. My father was drunk and nursing a bourbon, and my mother was in la-la land with her own cocktail of pills. At first they denied it, but then I grabbed an ice pick and threatened them. They just sort of gave up, and spilled the beans, the whole rotten can of beans. Father even showed me the contract my Mamaw and uncle had signed. It was all kind of anti-climactic.

"However, years later when I was in Kentucky—that time it was a bus driver who I got a few miles after his last drop off, and I made it look like his bus lost control and went over an embankment—I decided to go to Flank Hollow.

"I saw Mamaw's house, though she was long dead by then. I've only been back to that state—my home state—one more time, but not to Flank Hollow. I went back for the dedication of the memorial bench for the bus driver out in front of the one school. Before I left, I carved my initials on the bottom of it.

"Good, I can see you're really into my story now, which is awesome since I have a very special starring role for you to play a little later. By the way, a hilarious side note: a few years ago, my mother stuck that same ice pick in my father's left leg during an argument. I laughed my ass off when I heard about it. He was fine, the cry baby, and the story never got out. But, then again, no one cares about those two anymore.

"By the time I was out on the road, doing my thing, Father and Mother were essentially burnouts back home in Beverly Hills with zero clue. All the invitations—to parties, premieres, openings, new projects—stopped for them, soon relegating them to the Land of Has-Beens.

"They still have no clue what I'm doing out here, but that's going to change very soon. I just hope they can hang on long enough to see it all play out. They're in their nineties now, and living, breathing proof that only the good die young.

"All this time, they've thought I was just out on the road trying to *find* myself, against their better judgment of course but they soon lost the will to put up a fight and keep me imprisoned at Casa Dahlia. The best part: they've been bankrolling everything I've done the whole time.

"Killing only two or three a year also gave me the time to put together the larger multimedia package to ensure my star will never burn out once the time comes. And, again, this was thanks to the world I experienced because of my parents. No one can ever say I don't give credit where credit is due.

"From the beginning, I wanted my unique calling card of the Bone Broth recipe to be something that would likely not even ring a bell until the very end when I, myself, revealed it as a prop within my larger epic production—even though I was sending it directly to police departments, so it was literally right in front of their faces this whole time, for twenty years.

"After every kill, I'd handwrite the recipe, being sure to disguise my real handwriting on different stationery and other pieces of paper, then send it off to the local police department. No return address, and it was always post-marked from that town or city. I'm sure the majority of those were tossed in the garbage, but maybe a few made it home to wives to try out.

"Did you know Bone Broth is really healthy for you? I bet you didn't know that. Ever try it? . . . Aw, come on, you're not playing along with me again? The least you can do is nod or blink a few times. I'm trying to have a conversation with you here. You don't want to be remembered as a rude hostess, do you?

"Well anyway, while it makes me want to puke, Bone Broth is rich in collagen, gelatin, glycine, proline, chondroitin, and a bunch of minerals like calcium, magnesium, phosphorus, and other stuff. See, I told you I did my research.

"For each kill, I'd scope out a location and potential victims for weeks, sometimes even months. Then I'd stick around for a while after, enjoying the news coverage and even attending wakes and funerals. All forty-nine have remained unsolved to this day, and zero mention ever of a Bone Broth recipe. I'm very proud of that, believe you me!

"Also, at each scene, I took photos, including of the Bone Broth recipe, all of which I carefully catalogued and stored in a rented space in LA. Eventually, I want it to be very easy for police, lawyers, judges, juries, and especially the media to connect each victim with their related ephemera—that'll make the process go much quicker so we can get to the really fun parts.

"Whatever weapons I used, like the fork, barbed wire, plastic bags, a pencil, once a broken Mason Jar, I also have those carefully packaged and labeled in that storage space. I even archived every outfit I wore during the kills. I bet those, especially, along with the weapons, will be popular with crime museums. Maybe even the Smithsonian! Oh, and for charity auctions!

"Once I was in full swing, and had my modus operandi, as they call it in the biz, down to a foolproof system, I wanted to have control of my story when it came time to tell it. I want to tell it myself in my own words. After all, these past twenty years are my Magnum Opus!

"For this part of my plan, I wrote a memoir manuscript, telling all, from Father and Mother buying me from my Mamaw in Kentucky to my role as Amon in the *Devil Eyes* franchise to details about my successful, unprecedented run as a serial killer.

"The manuscript is already over eight-hundred pages, so it may have to be published in volumes. Each victim gets his or her own chapter, detailing everything, including how I never got caught, which is pretty impressive now with so much technology, cameras everywhere, and iPhones pinging, and DNA.

"It would sound like bragging to call myself a genius, but come on, right? The book may even become a blueprint for other aspiring serial killers!

"But don't you worry, there's still one last chapter to be written, all about you, which I promise I will get to, believe you me.

"Here, let me put this small pillow behind your head. You look like you're getting a stiff neck. We can't have that now, can we? We need you to be fresh and ready for your close-up.

"While I was writing the memoir manuscript during the past two decades out on the road, I was bitten by the writing bug. So I also wrote a novel manuscript—a *roman à clef* it's technically called, based on my true-life story. Plus, my real life is certainly as good if not better than *Devil Eyes*, so I wrote a movie script for it, and also another script for a limited series about me that I'm sure Netflix will gobble right up!

"Finally, and you're going to love this, I just know you are, I can tell, especially since I saw all those cookbooks in your kitchen and even more on the shelves in your living room.

"I wrote a cookbook manuscript in which all the recipes use—*Wait. For. It.*—bone broth!

"The cookbook might be a bit much for some folks, but just the existence of it will make reporters pee themselves with excitement. I can see the photo shoots now in prison of me doing cooking demos.

"Come to think of it, I don't think there's ever been a cooking show done inside a prison. Has there? Whoever my new agent ends up being, *and it won't be Father*, I'll have to have them pitch that to the Food Network.

"As for the other projects—the books, the movies—I don't plan to make a cent off them. That would be twisted, and just plain wrong. Besides, I don't need money.

"I plan on donating all profits I make from those projects, and anything else, such as licensing my name and image for T-shirts and sweatshirts, household items, action figures, you name it, to all the victims' families via a charitable foundation I plan to set up. After all, believe you me, I couldn't have done any of this without them!

"And think of how much publicity forty-nine murder trials in forty-nine different states will generate, plus whatever they charge me with for you here! It'll be years of non-stop traveling and press junkets.

"I've also been carefully studying different young defense attorneys who I think would be a good fit for me, for the long haul. I have my eye on a particularly sharp one in New York.

"She hasn't lost a murder trial yet, though I plan on confessing everything, because why would I want to hide my masterpieces from the world any longer? I'm about to turn her into a big star, too, just like I'm doing with you. Spread the wealth, is what I say.

"*Okay, okay,* I can tell you're about to conk out on me here. It can't be because I'm boring you. We've come a long way—you and me—today, and it would be a shame if you fell asleep and missed the rest, so here it goes, *drumroll please* . . . here is what your starring role in my production is going to be:

"First-off, congratulations, you get to live! Yay!

"From the start, I planned for Number Fifty to be very special, *yes indeedy*.

"Even with all the memorabilia I've archived from my forty-nine-state tour, and all the manuscripts and scripts I've written, I always knew I would still need one last thing: a witness. Someone who survived, who I let live to share her perspective on what it was really like to come face-to-face with a dashing real-life superstar-turned-monster. I'm sure that's what the press will call me, a 'monster.' Ha! Like they're not monsters.

"Therefore, you get to be my final girl. My very own Laurie Strode, who, by the way, I got to meet when she came to the premiere of *Devil Eyes*. I had such a crush on her when I was Amon's age.

"Oh, don't cry! I know you're happy about how amazing this all is, but no need to go all weepy-weepy on me. I need you to stay focused here. Do you know   I never once saw either of my parents cry, not even happy tears like yours when great things were happening?

"I don't cry either, unless it's for a role.

"But I get it, I really do—this is an incredible moment for you, for sure the biggest thing to ever happen to you in your life. I promise I won't let you down. I'm about to make you famous, *world famous*!

The other forty-nine will become famous, too, but more like home-state heroes. You, though, are going to be next level! Folks will want selfies with you and your autograph, and I bet you'll get paid lots of money to do interviews, write your own books, probably even to consult on the scripts I've written.

"That's all fantastic! You'll bring such a raw, honest, been-there-done-that energy to everything, and all with your bankable girl-next-door charm. And I'll always be just a phone call away, and more than willing to mentor you. Navigating fame can be a real bitch, believe you me.

"Hey, *you know what?* I could even see us doing a joint interview at some point down the road. I bet Oprah and others would pay millions for that! But now I'm getting way ahead of myself.

"Okay, back to the plan: Tomorrow morning, I'm going to call the police and turn myself in. In addition, I'll give them the address of the storage space in LA where everything is boxed, labeled, and in alphabetical order according to state. They'll surely know where Casa Dahlia is, and that's where they'll find my book manuscripts and movie scripts.

"As for you—Number Fifty—we are literally sitting in your file box, right here on Squirrel Lane. In fact, I bet after tonight and tomorrow, this house becomes a popular tourist stop. You'll probably even be able to charge for tours!

"So I will call the local police in the morning and confess just enough to get them here. Once here, and of course later on, I'll tell them everything they need to know. I have no secrets to hide, and why would I want to? I've even decided I'll grant my first big exclusive live interview in prison to Anderson Cooper. I like his empathetic nature, and he's got great eyes, too, just like you and me.

"*Ohhhhhh*, I bet you're wondering about the Bone Broth recipe for my stop here. Fear not, here it is. This is Mamaw's original copy she put in my suitcase. I saved it just for you, Number Fifty.

"Seriously, please stop crying. I know you're happy and excited about all of this, but we still have business to take care of here. There will be plenty of time for celebrating later.

"Now here's the best part, the exclamation point for my fiftieth, and final, stop on my national tour: when the cops arrive here, around lunchtime, they'll find your front door unlocked. They're going to smell something delicious simmering in the kitchen on the stove.

"When they finally reach your kitchen, their mouths watering, they'll see you and me at the kitchen table. I already have it set with your red-checkered bowls next to spoons carefully centered on your pretty embroidered-linen napkins.

"We'll pick out something real cute for you to wear, something that will show up nicely in photos for the police photographer and when the reporters arrive. I even brought a special outfit to change into tomorrow morning. Because those photos are going to be seen around the world.

"On the stove, the police will find a huge pot of Mamaw's Bone Broth—enough to feed their whole precinct station.

"If anything, and despite my parents, I've learned to be hospitable!

"I'd love to have the cops over sooner, but making Bone Broth takes time, and I'm already pushing it with it being this late at night now and planning on having them here by noon tomorrow. So you and I need to get moving on the final prep work.

"I have just about everything I need already in the big pot on the stove—five quarts of filtered water, three tablespoons of apple cider vinegar, two large, chopped carrots, four celery stalks all chopped, two small bunches of parsley, a large onion chopped up, a parsnip, a leek, and two crushed cloves of garlic.

"Now for the best part, the part that will turn you from unknown into all-out *icon*: your left leg bones—your femur, tibia, and fibula—and foot. I'll skin the bones, but probably toss the whole foot in the pot, along with some tendons and slices of muscle for good measure. I don't want to skimp, this is for the cops after all and we owe them all the gratitude we can give them.

"I promise this won't hurt too badly. I've studied a lot of YouTube videos about anatomy and surgeries, and I also learned how to care for amputated limbs, create tourniquets, bandage them—and that'll just be until they get you to a hospital where you'll have clear sailing.

"I even practiced on a deer, and he was able to walk away on three legs a day later. I bet he's still out there, happy as can be. So you'll be just fine, believe you me.

"And, don't worry, this small saw here won't make much noise. We don't want to be *those* kinds of neighbors. Plus, I decided not to put plastic underneath you to protect the La-Z-Boy. This way, your chair will be a shoo-in to be included right next to Archie Bunker's at the Smithsonian!

"Come on now, enough with the crying! Don't make me second-guess choosing you for this starring role. A great actress can control her emotions, no matter what they are. I totally get this debut is about to become the greatest day of your life—been there, done that, but save those happy tears for later.

"And please, I beg of you, stay still, I don't want to screw this up.

"Okay, here we go!"

Blood in the Cut

K.L. Lord

From the 2019 Diary of Lila Durn

Thursday, October 1

The pearl handled straight razor was a rusted mess when I found it in an antique shop in Old Towne. Despite the condition, it called to me. Being the connoisseur of blades you know I am, I brought it home and cleaned it up.

Today it is sharp and clean.

I keep setting my pen down to admire my handiwork. Light from the overhead glints off the metal as I twist it back and forth. The pillows on my bed have slipped down and the iron of my bed frame bites into my back.

As I write this, I relish the pain and push my shoulder blades in harder. I want it to be enough. I know you don't believe me because I've said it a million times. But I always mean it when I say it.

Especially to you.

Unfortunately, the small pain is nothing but a temporary distraction. My beautiful new straight razor is splayed open, resting on my thigh. We both know I like to pretend there is some ambiguity in my impending actions. There is not, but the ruse gives me some measure of control, which I desperately need.

At least you never judge me, even as I fill your blank pages with ink and smudges of my own blood.

Tonight the catalyst is a dark, hollowed out nothingness in my chest. Empty as a bottle of cheap tequila on girls night. Days have passed with this weight bearing down on me. Life is dull, as if run through a filter that removes all semblance of pleasure or pain.

I am an empty chasm, and if I do not act soon, it will only get worse. We both know this is true. The pearl handle of the razor is cold in my left hand as I press the sharpened side into the bare flesh of my left thigh, still writing to you with the other hand. I rested it there for several seconds to build anticipation.

Sigh.

I've done it, and managed to get another smudge on the clean white of your corner. The pain was sharp but faded quickly. Blood beaded, then drips down the inside of my thigh. The moment I've been craving.

I closed my eyes for a few minutes and rested my head on the wall behind me, like a heroin addict settling into the high. There is no "high" here. Not in that sense. Instead, I feel level for the first time all day.

The pain and blood bring me back to the surface again. I *feel* again, and that is a small bliss I cannot find any other way. The weight has lifted.

If you've never known the dredges of depression, my actions are likely shocking and distasteful. It's not something to be talked about outside of therapy and forced group share.

But being dead inside, that void of emptiness, is its own unique kind of pain. You can be having the best day of your life—getting a promotion, being loved by family, getting engaged—and none of it matters. In this instance, you are incapable of feeling or enjoying anything.

Not that any of those things are happening to me. I've driven away anyone who ever loved me with my inability to stay stable and healthy. You, dear journal, are all I have left.

And my blades.

It's hard to explain to your partner that they just took you to dinner, bought you flowers, and told you they loved you and yet you're still inexplicably depressed. Neurotypical brains cannot comprehend this notion.

They see me as selfish and hard to please. I stared hard at the sharpened edge and wished I knew another way to be, all while pressing the blade back into my flesh.

Sweet release.

The second cut compounded the sting of the first, centering me and bringing me back to some semblance of myself. A thin trickle of blood seeped out of both cuts I have made, giving me a twisted air of satisfaction. If it weren't for the relief, for the momentary grounding, I wouldn't do this ruinous thing. And it is fully ruinous.

My last two partners left because I couldn't stop, and they couldn't cope. Yet, here I am, sliding blades into my delicate skin once more. Because it works.

Sometimes.

This is one of those times. I'm grounded again, watching the blood seep out a drop at a time until it streams down my thigh in a thin ribbon.

One more time and I will have to start my day. I press the blade to my flesh, millimeters above the last cut, and slice in slowly.

I wish I didn't have to work today.

The new rush of pain washes over me. Time to start my day.

October 1, part 2

I know I'm back sooner than usual, but moments before I was about to walk out the door, my supervisor messaged me to tell me a water main broke. It's not safe for us to go to work today. We have a paid day off. I sat on the sofa with tears cascading down my face for a full ten minutes before I came to fetch you.

Sick days are in short supply, having used them for days like this earlier in the year, and mental health days are not embraced by most businesses. I stripped down and crawled back into our favorite place, pulling the blankets up and turning on the television.

The cuts from an hour ago are still red and angry. I run my fingers over them, remembering my wish. No work. A coincidence to be sure.

Sunday, October 4

Sunday funday, my ass. All of the cleaning and laundry needs to get done so I can function during the week. But I am exhausted despite twelve hours of sleep. The extra day off seems to have done no good. Instead, I've spent the rest of the weekend sleeping in excess.

The numbness from earlier in the week has given way to a twitchy anxiety. I am restless and want to peel my skin from my body.

This is the opposite of the non-feeling emptiness. The constant swing between the two states is arduous, to say the least. My darling journal, is "normal" even a real thing? I'm starting to believe it, like so much else, is nothing but a social construct designed to make me feel bad about myself.

I lay in bed for hours trying to reconcile my feelings—working up the energy to break you out and write it all down. A tightness grips my chest while my heart hammers away, leaving me breathless and shaking.

I've been crying off and on for a long time, and I am nothing but an exposed nerve. Do not judge me, dear journal, for being weak. Despite my shaky hands, I know what I need. I need my beautiful pearl handled blade…she will make me feel better. This time there is no pretext. I want to cut myself.

I *need* to.

I need clarity and relief, even if it won't last. Even if you don't understand. As low as I feel, I do not care. Those few precious moments will be worth it.

When I pressed the sharp edge into the skin of my right thigh, letting the pressure cause its own kind of pain to amplify the experience, I found solace. The pressure is a more solid pain, less sharp, than the actual cut, but soothing in its consistency. I slid the blade across the skin, leaving an indentation in the wake of the blade. For a moment nothing happened. After a few scant seconds, blood beaded, welled, and dripped over. Not enough. It took three more times, until relief finally came.

I don't want to be alone tonight.

Blood smears my freshly laundered sheets, adding to the stains. Once again, I've cut myself for feeling too much, for feeling so lonely I want to die. And I'm not done. There's now a deep fifth cut in line with the rest, deeper and oozing more blood.

I squeeze my thigh to encourage the flow of red, wishing I could just get laid. For someone to touch me, hold me, if only for one night, to take the edge off the crippling sadness in my soul.

October 4, Part 2

He is pulling his jeans over his perfect hips and dressing to go home. Perhaps I should wait until he leaves to start writing, but I really don't care. Pretty sure he doesn't either, since he pulled on his shirt as he walked out of the room without a word. On another night, that might have bothered me.

But tonight I'm relieved to have this stranger leave with no fanfare or discussion. I only went out because I was lonely and Mel insisted I meet her and the girls at the bar. At the club I could drown myself in music and hopefully find someone to fuck.

I was in luck.

The cacophonous sound of the live band filled the bar, making it impossible to hear. But I wasn't there for the music. I wanted something more physical to soothe my jagged nerves. I could barely hear what the hipster, long hair pulled back into a man bun, was saying to me. We were two drinks into the exchange, and he still seemed interested. This man was attentive, flirty, and couldn't seem to take his eyes off me. Not a feeling I'm used to.

We danced a few times, and after that he wouldn't leave my side. I paid for nothing the rest of the night. His eyes were all for me, and he seemed kind and gentle.

At the end of the night, I invited him to come home with me. He agrees. This man knows his way around a woman's body. For the first time in ages, my orgasms were genuine. He worshiped my clitoris with his tongue for a considerable amount of time before driving his magnificent cock into me. I cannot recall the last time I felt so good.

The skin-to-skin contact is just what I was craving.. Every stroke of his skin against my own was a lightning bolt.

Before he dressed, he put his number into my phone and showed me the contact. DICK. And his phone number. I giggled and went back to writing this. He's gone now, and I'm feeling better than I have in ages.

Unrelated, the cuts on my thigh seem to be more irritated than usual. I keep everything sanitary to avoid infection. But I'm wondering now if I forgot to put antibiotic cream on them today. Note to self, be more diligent about keeping things clean.

Wednesday, October 7

The coincidences of the last week don't feel like coincidences. They feel like... magic. Work was sucking the life from me, and yet I got an extra day off. I've been so lonely, and I finally found someone to hook up with who wasn't repelled by my weirdness.

These things don't normally happen to me, as you know. Instead it was like something made it happen. Ridiculous.

But I've been so out of sorts. Dorothy Parker's "Resumè" now resides in a spiral around my arm. The experience is somehow a blur. Tattoos are a way for me to cope. They bring me the pain I need to cope in a way that is socially acceptable. A new tattoo should have been more than enough to help me cope and get me through my itchy period, but this time it was not even close. I barely remember the pain well enough to revel in it.

I smacked the raw words with my bare hand, trying to draw forth some sensation that will satisfy me. Too dull. I am forced to slap the fresh ink several times in quick succession, until it stings, and I can't focus on anything else. The pain grounds me, as it usually does, but relief was fleeting.

Friday, October 9

Thank Fuck It's Friday. That's not the normal saying, but I don't fucking care. I'm tired. Work was trash this week, and I am tired. All I can think about is DICK and our night together. What if his name is actually Dick? All he entered into my phone is MR. DICK in the contacts.

I can't stop laughing every time I think about it. Who would voluntarily call themselves that in the twenty-first century?? No matter. He's texted me dirty messages and dick pics all day, and I'm here for it. Besides, he's down to meet me at the club again tonight.

I still feel touch-starved, despite our recent rendezvous. My neediness has been an issue in most of my relationships. Right now I don't want a relationship. I just want someone to fuck me senseless, to wrap their body around mine, and go home when we're done. A guy who logs himself as DICK in my phone is the perfect candidate. I'm off to meet him at the bar, appropriately slutted up. I'll let you know how it goes.

There's only one concern I have: the cuts on my thigh are very finicky. They aren't healing as well as they should. I don't want to say they are infected, but they are a bit angry. I've slathered them in antibiotic cream, bandaged them, and squeezed the flesh in the guise of rubbing in the cream. No one needs to know that's a lie.

MR. DICK need never know any of it. Certainly not about the two fresh cuts on my left forearm, the ones I made while wishing he'd come home with me again; they were meant to reduce my stress for tonight's date. I just desperately want tonight to go as well as our last time together. I need the validation more than I'd like to admit.

Saturday, October 10th
Mr. Dick came home with me again, no questions asked. We drank and danced and made out relentlessly. I brought him home again, and he did not disappoint.

I wanted the darling MR. DICK to leave once all was said and done, but he cleaned himself up and came back to bed. The sex was amazing, don't get me wrong. But I don't know what to do after. It's not something I've had to do.

As much as I crave attention and skin-on-skin contact, cuddling after sex feels foreign and awkward. I know that's a testament to the men I've been with and how they've treated me. Post-coital, with nothing to distract us, he noticed the bandages on my thigh and my arm.

Honest answers sprung to my lips before I could stop them. I told him the truth. I never tell anyone but you the truth. The look on his face as I admitted I cut myself because of my depression and anxiety lingers when I close my eyes.

Wonder turned to horror to disgust in a matter of seconds. I could see the wheels turning in his brain. If I'd wanted him gone before, he was ready to go after that. Hearing his two-time hookup had some serious emotional baggage was apparently a major turnoff. That's one way to get a man out of your bed, I suppose. He stammered some excuse about needing to get up early and left.

After he left, I unbandaged my arm and leg. The wounds were raw and weeping, as if they were only hours old instead of days. I sprawled out on top of the covers and put on *Law and Order SVU*, my mother's words about letting your wounds "breathe" at night echoing in my mind. The banter of Benson and Stabler played in the background, but I couldn't focus.

My mind wandered to a million places.

None of them helpful.

Time ticked by and I couldn't sleep. A priest was accused of abusing children. Sweat slicked by brown and dampened my sheets. The high of MR. DICK was long gone. The itchy, twitchy feeling is back. Which is why I'm writing at this unholy hour.

All I can think about is the razor biting into my skin. I want it. I need it. But I've already cut myself three times this week. Three. That's a lot, even for me. I don't know if things have ever been this bad. I can't remember. Normally, as you know, I cut myself once in a while when the urge becomes too much to bear and I can't ignore it anymore.

I resisted for another whole episode. The SVU team

caught the bad guy, as they usually do. A more satisfactory ending than real life often has.

In real life, the pedophile priest gets reassigned by the church. The date-raping college boy gets off with a slap on the wrist.

My mind slides over all of this as the episodes progress. Eventually, I slide out of bed, cool air puckering my damp flesh and stinging the myriad of wounds.. The straight razor is in the drawer in the bathroom.

A valiant attempt to keep it away, at a distance.

I barely noticed the cold bathroom tiles on my bare feet as I dug through the drawer to pull out my darling friend. I took the blade back to bed and looked at the old cuts. My left arm and right leg were inflamed. So I got up and got the antiseptic and antibacterial ointment. I cleaned the wounds meticulously and coated them in ointment. This hasn't been an issue before, but maybe I hadn't cleaned the new blade well enough before using. I rubbed it furiously with alcohol, determined to kill any lingering germs.

With every moment that passed, the urge deepened. I needed this, whether I wanted to or not. Blade in my left hand, I dug into the underside of my right forearm.

Sting.

Gasp.

Blood.

Relief.

Wish upon a star for a better life. Whatever that means.

Monday, October 12

The promotion was mine. They didn't even interview anyone else. My supervisor called me to her office after lunch and gave me the news. I nearly sobbed in relief. Everything had been so difficult for so long. I needed the raise, the confidence boost, all of it. She smiled at me throughout and told me how happy they were to have me on the team and moving up. I left feeling better than I had in so long.

When I got home, I had to change all of the bandages on my body. The number is growing and none of them seem to be healing properly.

Maybe now that I've been promoted, I will relax enough to heal like a normal person. My thigh and both arms are still weepy like fresh wounds. In all my years of cutting, I've never seen anything like it. I have to keep them all covered when I'm out or they will bleed through my clothing. I showered and slathered them in antibiotic cream, hoping they would dry out and scab over while I slept.

I put on old episodes of *Drag Race* to distract myself, but just like *SVU*, it doesn't really work. My mind hones in on the shining pearl handle of that straight razor. I've pulled you out to keep myself distracted, but I just keep circling back to that blade.

I can write about anything and turn it into an allegory for the cut I crave so deeply. As Ru announced new challenges, I poked at my existing cuts, trying to satisfy the need for pain and release. But ultimately, it didn't work.

I feel so weak, but there is no substitute for cutting. Especially with this blade. There's something magical about this blade. My unspoken wishes keep coming true with each cut, but I know the connection is all in my head.

Only lunacy would let me believe this pearl handled straight razor from an antique shop has some mystical wish fulfillment. Even I know, in my desperate and half delirious state, understand this.

Yet...

I dug into the other thigh, four, five, six times. Each stroke brought beads of blood that I relished. The pain centered me. I knew exactly what I wanted. My loneliness is front and center. Sure. I can call on MR. DICK and he'll show up. I can go to the club and find some other dick to fuck, but none of it means a thing. They don't want me for me. They don't want to keep me as their own. I'm nothing more than entertainment. So I cut. Again and again.

What else am I supposed to do?

Friday, October 23

For the last month, I've gotten everything I wanted. The promotion at work, all the dick I could handle. And then some. But I'm not happy.

The cuts line my arms and legs like exclamation points no one asked for.

Nothing is healing.

Even MR. DICK doesn't want me anymore. The festering wounds are a turn off, even to that fuckboii. I've tried everything. Peroxide. Alcohol. Antibiotic creams. Instead of getting better, they are worse. Puss oozes from each cut and I don't know what to do. I know I should go to the doctor, but they'll want to know what happened, and I'll end up on a 72-hour hold. I've been there and not willing to go back.

So I keep dressing the cuts. Hoping it will be enough. Yet they weep.

Saturday, October 24
I can't stop.

October 25

I called out from work. Everything hurts. The cuts on my arms and thighs ache constantly, and they look infected. Blood pounds in my head, making my brains hurt. I can't focus on anything anymore. The only thing that brings relief is the next cut. But I'm not healing like I should be. It doesn't make sense. I keep the wounds clean. I change the bandages twice a day and use antibiotic cream. More than I've ever done before. Yet, every cut I've made lately is open and weeping a rank puss. That's the other reason I can't go to work. The smell. I can't escape it.

Rotting flesh.

Disease.

I took another shower and scrubbed myself raw with antibacterial soap to no avail. The hot water and soap stung my skin to the point of tears.

When I got out, I patted everything dry, slathered the wounds with ointment and covered them. Within the hour, yellow and green puss soaked my bandages, and the stench was back in full force. What the fuck is happening? I took a handful of painkillers and crawled into bed to write to you. My only true confidant.

The television blares in the background. Another episode of *Call the Midwife* to distract me. It doesn't work. I'm trapped in some kind of loop, worse than usual. I don't recognize this pattern. In the past, the cycle of depression, cutting, bouncing back, was something I could count on. It was a short span. A week or two at most. But I feel like there is no escape now. I'm in this, and it will never end. Not until I finally die.

Despite my reservations, the small voice in the back of my brain   whispers "this is wrong." I reach that gleaming handle. Blade sharp and beaconing. I stroke the length of the blade, bringing it to my lips for a kiss. Deep inside, I know I shouldn't.

This is wrong.

But that doesn't matter.

I *need* this.

My forearms are wrecked. Thighs were not much better. The blade called for something fresh and untainted, so I traced a line on the inside of my left calf. This is uncharted territory, and the flesh was not prepared for the pain I brought to it.

I gasped, barely able to apply the proper pressure. In the end, the line was more jagged than most, but the pain soothed my soul. I leaned back into the pillows, not paying any attention as to where the blood flowed. Instead, I clicked "next" on *Call the Midwife* and let other people's pain wash over me.

I woke up with my bloodied leg stuck to the sheet. Peeling the skin away from the fabric was an endeavor, and tears streamed down my face. Blood and puss crusted the sheets.

I hadn't bothered to bandage my leg after the latest cuts. A big mistake. I looked down at the mess that had become my left leg. A real human leg could not possibly look like this. Each cut was swollen and red. Yellow and green viscous fluid seeped from the older wounds. Veins of dark purple and black spread out from the cuts like toxic spider webs. A slow, but steady oozing of plasma leaked from the newest cuts.

I know I can't keep this up, but I don't know what else to do. The darkness bounces around in my head like a ping-pong ball, tainting everything it touches.

Happiness.

Stability.

Normalcy.

They seem like such foreign concepts right now. This depression has removed me from reality. It's as though I'm Alice in the looking glass, seeing her real world with no way to connect to it. Feeling dead inside is no joke. Or maybe it's the cruelest joke of all. I can see the life I could have, but I'll never reach it. Instead, I'm trapped in a fog that never fully lifts.

You are my lifeline, but I don't think you are enough anymore, my dear diary. Things are too hard. I'm too fucking tired. If I'm being honest, tonight's stains are not the first upon these sheets. I've been living in squalor for some time now, and I cannot remedy the state of things.

Sunday, October 31
Days have passed, and I haven't even been able to write in you. I haven't left my bedroom much, either. Food has been off limits since last we spoke. I choke down some water each day, and that is a struggle. My disconnect is deeper than it's ever been.

Work means nothing. My leave is about to run out, but it's fine. I don't care anymore. Work is nothing but another thing holding me hostage in this mortal coil.

The only thing that matters is this beautiful pearl handled blade.

It's sharp and clean.

Never lets me down.

Tremors wrack my hands, probably because food no longer means anything to me. Even still, I manage to open the lovely blade and bring it to an untouched portion of my right inner thigh. The sharp metallic sting against my leg is heaven. Nothing else makes me happy these days. Just the sting. The slow beading of the blood. Red and hot. Life.

One more time.

One.

More.

Time.

Summer Of '74

Jane Nightshade

It had to be Barkley, the eager-beaver beagle, who found the lady at Taylor Mountain, Washington State. Charlie, fourteen, knew his family's other two dogs were neither as curious nor as energetic, which was why he preferred Barkley as a walking companion. Halfway through their noon outing on a deserted trail deep in the forest, Barkley ran ahead while Charlie relieved himself against a tree.

Just as Charlie was zipping up his pants, the beagle began barking in a wild and urgent manner.

"Here! Here!" cried Charlie, hustling in the direction of the furious noises. "What's all the fuss about, Barks?"

He followed the sound up a small incline through a ton of brush and saplings. At the summit of the incline were much larger pines and firs, shadowing a tiny clearing of tall grass. Barkley was in the grass, running to and fro with manic energy, in time with his high-pitched yelping.

What could be the matter with the crazy old boy?

He'd never seen the beagle so frantic.

Then he saw the lady's foot. It was poking out of the grass, still wearing a red, platform-heeled shoe. It looked very still and white, almost like it was made of marble.

Charlie stomped through the remaining grass until he saw Barkley, who lowered his barking tone and ran to his master, jumping up and batting at the boy's pant legs.

He saw the rest of the lady, then. She was lying on her back, wearing a pair of floppy blue jeans and a plaid shirt that was open down the front. There was no bra and the open shirt revealed bruised, mottled breasts to the sky. She had a mass of long, light brown hair that partially covered her face and neck.

Charlie cried out and then froze, uncertain of what to do. Barkley quieted down to wary growling and sat, waiting for his master to do something. Charlie supposed he needed to check if she was really dead. He believed she was, but a decent person would make sure. He knelt beside her and pushed the hair away from her face.

Her face was not a pretty sight. Maybe she'd been pretty once, but that was a day or so ago. Her eyes were bulging and sightless, her face blotched with black and purple contusions.

There was a deep, angry red-and-black furrow around her neck. She was definitely dead. Charlie decided she'd been strangled by a rope or other ligament because of the marks encircling her neck.

The thing he had to do, then, was to go back to his family's summer cabin and call the police as soon as possible. Then he would have to answer questions for hours, at least going by the cop shows he watched on television. His life would be disrupted and he would become a minor celebrity temporarily, a nine days wonder, a sound bite on TV. He disliked attention in general and wasn't thrilled with the prospect.

Still trying to process his macabre discovery, he stood up on wobbly legs and called "let's go," to the beagle.

They set off at a quick pace until some yards away, in a

stand of especially lofty grass, Charlie stepped into a steep, rocky hole. He heard a sickening snapping sound and felt a sharp, stabby pain in his right ankle. He fell to the ground amidst the grass, shouting in agony.

"Oh fuck, oh fuck, I think I broke my ankle! Oh fuck, it really hurts."

Barkley began to bark again, loud and fearful. Charlie realized he was in something of a pickle. No one knew where he was. He'd told his mom he was taking the beagle out for a walk in the woods and that was it.

Their cabin near Taylor Mountain was in a fairly isolated area and his parents were so trusting of their few neighbors they left their front door and trucks unlocked. They didn't expect Charlie to keep them updated about his whereabouts, as long as he did his chores and arrived home in time for supper.

Eventually, someone would come looking for him, but that would be hours later—maybe they wouldn't even find him until tomorrow morning. Which meant spending a night out in the open. It was June in Washington State and he probably wouldn't freeze, but it would be a very, very uncomfortable night.

Not to mention the corpse some yards away, which would draw wildlife. Charlie shuddered at the thought of a bear or a cougar wandering onto the scene, with him barely able to move.

Barkley was his only hope. He had to make the beagle understand. He retrieved his Boy Scout pocketknife from his jeans pocket and cut off a piece of his green Led Zeppelin T-shirt. It was his favorite, but this was no time to be sentimental. He placed the piece of cloth at the beagle's feet and commanded:

"Home, Barkley, home! Get help! Now!" He raised his arm and pointed in the vague direction of the cabin. "Home!"

Barkley understood. He nudged Charlie's face briefly with a wet nose, and then took the piece of cloth in his mouth and ran off into the brush in a golden-brown blur of fur and churning little legs.

Through his pain, Charlie was relieved and elated.

Barkley will fix this. He's a very smart dog. He was glad he'd taken Barkley out that morning instead of Spider, his mother's elderly Yorkshire terrier, who was half-blind.

Charlie waited, bored and miserable, lying on his stomach, his head and shoulders propped up by his elbows. His ankle throbbed and the grass was itchy and uncomfortable. Insects crawled on him and some of them made minuscule prickly bites or stings on his exposed skin. He heard something snapping twigs up the incline and shrank into the ground as best he could. He hoped it wasn't a bear or even an angry elk with huge threatening horns. Gingerly, he lifted his head and peeked through the grass.

It wasn't a bear or an elk. It was a man.

Charlie felt a heart-leap of joy and relief. What luck! Someone who could help. He started to call out to the man but something stopped him at the last minute, his jaw dropping from trepidation. The way the man was moving, going in a straight, sure line toward the lady's body.

Why, he's been here before!   He knows exactly where that body is and why it's there.

Charlie shut his mouth. The implications were obvious. This was the man who had placed the body in the grass in the first place. This was the killer who had cruelly strangled her and dumped her remains in the woods like a dead feral cat run over by a car.

He watched the man through the grass, praying silently he would not be discovered.

The man was lanky and pale skinned. Charlie estimated him to be in his late twenties. He was wearing a beige turtleneck shirt and brown corduroy flares with a wide leather belt and what looked like Adidas tennis shoes.

Charlie saw now that he was carrying something that looked like a woman's cosmetics bag. He watched as the man sat next to the dead lady and, incredibly, began to talk to her.

He couldn't hear exactly what the man said, but it was punctuated by strange gestures of tenderness—stroking the lady's hair, straightening her clothes, crooning to her like a lover.

Then he opened the bag and took out something. Charlie raised his head a bit higher and craned his neck. The man applied the mystery object to the lady's hair. Charlie soon realized it was a woman's hairbrush. *He was brushing the dead woman's hair!*

Later, the man took other objects out of the bag and applied them to the lady's face. They were too small to recognize from Charlie's place yards away in the grass, but from the gestures the man was making, it looked like he was using lipstick and other cosmetics.

Charlie watched the macabre grooming rituals with a sick fascination. He had completely forgotten about his accident and Barkley's quest for help. He was so intent on watching the bizarre scene, he had only a vague sense of the pain in his ankle.

The man finished his grooming and then did something even more extraordinary. He took off the corpse's jeans, spread the legs apart and began doing unspeakable things to it.

Charlie was confused at first, but when he realized what was happening, he recoiled and felt an overwhelming wave of nausea. He fought the urge to retch and eventually lost it. He turned his head and puked into the grass. He tried to do it silently, but it was impossible and he made loud vomiting noises. He hoped he was too far away for the man to hear him.

But the man, apparently, had the heightened hearing capabilities of a predatory animal. For he jerked his head up and scanned his surroundings. He lit upon the big stand of grass where Charlie was lying and stared directly at it, sniffing like a wolf or coyote.

Charlie tried to make himself as small as possible. He felt ice growing in his veins and his ankle began to throb ominously again.

The strange man got up, adjusted his pants and strode quickly toward Charlie. Charlie was seized with terror. He tried to think of a way to escape but there was nothing. Wriggling away on his belly toward another stand of high grass to hide in?

There wasn't time.

And the man could find him in a new place just as easily as in his current place. He prayed for Barkley to show up with help before anything bad happened. But the way it looked at the moment, his life was hanging by a thread. This killer—for that's what he was, Charlie was sure—wouldn't let him live long enough to tell anyone what he saw.

Soon Charlie was staring up into an ominous face looming over him. It would have been a handsome face, but for the frightening look of detachment on it. Dark, wavy hair framed an angular visage with opaque blue eyes that looked almost black. Above the eyes were swooping charcoal brows, and below was a slim straight nose over thin, spreading lips and a strong, slightly cleft chin.

"Grass isn't a good place to hide," said a mechanical voice. The weird detachment vibes could be heard in the way the man spoke as much as in the way he moved. How he stood, his voice, the light in his eyes, all told of a man who lived in his own world, according to his own rules.

Charlie struggled to sit up. "I didn't have much choice. I'm hurt, and I can't walk or run." If he was gonna die, he didn't want to go out on his belly like a worm. Sitting up with his injured leg splayed out in front of him, Charlie noticed the man's pants' fly was open.

Gross. He shuddered inwardly.

The man followed Charlie's gaze and quickly zipped up the open fly. "You saw it all?"

"Yes."

The man bent to the ground and picked up a large, ugly stone. Charlie's heart fluttered wildly.

"You have to understand," the man said, still in the mechanical voice. "There's nothing like the feeling of total power over another human being. *You are God.* A boy your age may not understand it now, but you could when you are my age. *Wouldn't you like to feel like God sometimes?"*

Charlie eyed the stone nervously. "I've never really thought about it. I have a hard enough time just keeping up with my homework and after-school sports." He felt now that his only chance was to keep the man talking, talking, and talking until help arrived—if it even arrived at all. "When was the first time you felt like God, yourself?"

"Oh, what a good question. You're a smart boy, aren't you? I was about your age, fourteen, fifteen." The man bent over, so his face was closer to Charlie's. His breath smelled like a faint odor of death.

"There was this little girl on the street my family lived on, in Tacoma. Anne M. She was eight. Dark-haired little pixie. There was something about her, some sparkling life force, that I wanted to obliterate. It was offensive to me somehow. They never found her. I laughed about it to myself, afterward, for a long time. How I'd tricked them all. Yes, I felt omnipotent and all-powerful. It was a wonderful feeling. After that—" the man shrugged. "I just always wanted to recapture that wonderful feeling."

The man straightened up, shifting the heavy rock from hand to hand. Charlie gulped and tried not to think of what the rock and the gesture represented.

"I don't really want to kill you. You're not my type. I don't feel any sparkly life force coming from you that I want to dominate and subdue. This is not personal. It's just self-preservation. I'm the coldest son-of-bitch you will ever know, when I'm looking after myself."

"Wait!" said Charlie desperately. "If you want self-preservation, you should leave as soon as possible. I didn't come here alone. I came with... a friend. Then I fell and broke my ankle. He went back to get help. They could arrive at any time and catch you here with that... lady."

The man shook his shaggy head. "I can't take the risk... if you're telling the truth about your friend, I'd better kill you quickly then and leave. But I'll try to make it as fast and painless as possible."

Painless? screamed Charlie in his mind. *He means to bash my head in like a rotten pumpkin on Halloween.*

"I won't tell," Charlie cried. "I won't, I swear. I don't even know your name. I want to stay alive, like you. I want to feel the power, the omnipotence someday, too."

"You... do? You want to be like me?" Charlie saw with amazement a glint of surprised pleasure in the otherwise dead eyes. *He is human after all. He can be flattered and manipulated.* The realization gave Charlie some hope.

"Yes," Charlie lied. "Yes, I want to be like you. I'm already taking notes in my mind about how you dress, how you walk, how you talk. I want to grow up to be just like you."

"Really? You really feel that way?" The man pushed a stray strand of bushy hair away from his face. He sounded uncertain, as if assessing what to do, and finding himself uncharacteristically undecided. "You want to understand the power, the control. You want to be God."

Charlie nodded vigorously. "Of course. I'm special, almost as much as you are. I've got the vision."

The man hesitated. As if the information was new to

him, and he was struggling with how to process it.

Charlie pressed his rhetorical advantage.

"You'll have to move… her," he stated authoritatively. "You'll have to do it quick, too, before help comes from my friend. And move her far enough so that dogs can't smell her. My friend has a dog with a keen sense of smell."

A distant, almost dreamy look flashed in the man's eyes.

"Yes, I suppose I should," he said finally. He put down the heavy rock. "Don't go anywhere, young man. I'll be right back."

Charlie let out a huge, relieved burst of lung volume. "Yeah, sure, dude."

Charlie watched while the lanky, thin man redressed the dead lady, and then grabbed her by the ankles and dragged her into a glade of thick, dark trees.

At least I've bought myself a bit of time. I'm really surprising myself with my ability to manipulate this man.

But Charlie's mother had always said he could sell popsicles in a snowstorm if he wanted to, so perhaps it wasn't so surprising, after all. "You've got the gift, Charlie," she would say. "You can go very far with the ability to convince people to do what you want them to do, if only you would try."

The words comforted him as he waited for the dangerous stranger to come back. He felt like he was almost a match for the obvious psychopath now, with his newly recognized confidence.

The stranger was taking his time finding a new hiding place for his prize. Charlie imagined him taking a while because he was doing… things… to the body and quickly put it out of his mind. Then he heard a familiar bark and he knew Barkley had gotten help and returned at last.

He heard the beagle and a couple of other sets of footsteps come up the incline, and then he saw the dog, followed by his father and brother.

"Over here," cried Charlie, waving above the tall grass he sat in. "Thank god you found me!"

"Charlie!" exclaimed his dad. "Are you all right?"

"Aside from what I think is a broken ankle, yes." Barkley ran for Charlie then, and Charlie mauled him with pets and rubs. "Good boy, good boy, Barks!"

"Looks like you'll be out of commission for a while," smirked his older brother, Todd. "More babes for me at the public pool in Issaquah, then."

Suddenly Barkley broke away from Charlie's embrace and ran to the center of the little clearing, and sprinted around in circles, barking and yelping.

"What's gotten into Barks?" cried Todd. "There's nothing there."

Charlie hesitated. It was now or never. And he never quite could understand, years later, why he opted to go the way he did, at such a young age. "Probably smells a rabbit," he said smoothly.

"How are we going to get you out of here?" asked his dad.

"I know!" said Todd. "We can use that old army cot you keep in the truck to make a stretcher. The legs fold under." Charlie's dad agreed it was a good idea and Todd left and shortly returned with the cot. The two of them helped Charlie onto the makeshift stretcher and hoisted it, his dad in front and Todd in the back.

"Come along, Barks—we're leaving!" Charlie shouted at the still-barking beagle.

Todd and his dad carried him away, back to the service road below, where Charlie knew his dad's Ford pick-up truck would be waiting. He'd have to ride in the truck bed and get bumped around a lot, but it wasn't that far back to the cabin so the agony wasn't going to be long. Overall, he felt great to be alive.

However, before they set off down the incline, Charlie sensed a malevolent presence and looked back, toward the thick trees where the stranger had disappeared, a little more than an hour before. He squinted and scanned the shadows and then his eyes were rewarded. A flash of brown and beige, a blob of a pale white face. The stranger was watching them leave.

Charlie wasn't sure it was the exact same place. That was, until he climbed the scraggly incline and stood in a grassy clearing. Then, and only then, could he feel the evil energy that was still somehow clinging to it.

The place where he had almost died twenty years before. He was standing on the spot where the girl's body had been, and over there, approximately, was where he'd broken his ankle and lain in the tall grass, waiting for Barkley to bring help.

He had kept the promise he made that summer day in 1974. He never told anyone about what he'd seen at Taylor Mountain. Not because he felt any fealty or sense of honor toward the vile man he encountered. No, not even a year or so later, when he and the rest of the world knew the identity of the man who had almost killed him.

No, he kept the secret because, over the years, it became his talisman, his special power.

*I bested a cruel and evil kille*r, he would think, and he suddenly was transformed from a shy nerd to a confident and assertive extrovert with a rare gift for gab. It stood him well through high school, then college, then work, and—when he felt like it—with girls.

He enjoyed the power, the omnipotence, when he was able to bend most people to his will. He became extraordinarily successful as a stockbroker. Unlike his inadvertent mentor, though, he knew when to quit. He never got care-less or complacent with his manipulations, his dogged pur-suit of that special feeling over the fates of others.

He turned and hiked down the incline and back to the rough trail that led to the service road where he'd parked. At his Land Rover, he noticed a sort of amateur memorial some yards away, near a clump of ferns along the shoulder of the road. It was similar to the little shrines that people leave all over the place for victims of traffic accidents.

Charlie trudged over to the shrine. It was a weather-beaten wooden cross with a plaque nailed to the center. At the foot of the cross was an arrangement of plastic flowers, faded pathetically from rain and snow.

Painted on the central plaque were block letters that read: IN MEMORIAM. Below that, in smaller letters, was the legend: "Remembering those who were found here as victims of serial killer THEODORE ROBERT BUNDY in 1975."

The sign ended with the names and vitals of four tragic, unfortunate young women.

Charlie shook his head and fought the urge to chuckle. Ted had been so reckless and slapdash, especially toward the end. Plus, he had those disgusting perversions that con-sumed him and made him heedless. Charlie was more dis-ciplined; he would never allow himself to go out the way Ted did, frying in a Florida execution chamber while mobs outside clapped and cheered.

He had a body of his own to dump, a short walk away in the back of the Rover, but he damn sure wasn't going to leave it in some random, easily disturbed spot on Taylor Mountain.

###

All The Sweet Things

K. John O'Leary

The wind bit into my exposed legs, furtive snowflakes caught in the hair covering my shins. I was wearing a hoodie and track shorts and damned myself for not throwing on jeans before leaving the gym. I'd assumed the heat I'd generated during my workout would see me all the way home—a pretty dumb thought in the midst of a Michigan winter.

It was only 5 PM but the sun had already retired for the night, draping the world in shadow. I had left the streetlights behind, turning onto an old, cracked road that ran through the industrial part of town.

It was a Saturday evening, so the warehouses and factories stood silent vigil over the delivery trucks lining their parking lots, the vehicles nestled up against their walls like overgrown, suckling piglets. Only the light from those massive, brutalist structures lit the way—sickly light, all of them that same burnt shade of orange.

I'd taken my AirPods out. I felt fine walking through downtown with them in, where getting mugged was a distinct possibility—a normal occurrence you'd joke about over beers the next day, yet this place put me on edge, had me looking over my shoulder, jumping at any sound which broke the silence—a bird taking flight, a rat scurrying under some garbage. The only other person around was a lone custodian sweeping the steps of one of the buildings. He stopped and watched me as I passed, raising a hand before returning to his work.

I wondered what had compelled me to take this route. It added a good ten minutes to the walk home, after all, and wasn't particularly scenic. My question was answered when I saw the rotting factory up ahead—its spires blackened, its windows mosaics of shattered glass like glaucomatous eyes, the fence surrounding it promising swift punishment should anyone trespass.

To locals it was known as "The Candy Factory," its status as a proper noun somehow audible when spoken aloud.

It was noticeably older than the other buildings in the area, composed mainly of brick rather than the smooth concrete the other structures favored, and with at least some thought put into its general design. It was larger, too, and a massive sign on its front announced it as *Thompson Treats, Candy Co., Home of the Thompson Guarantee!*

I sniffed the air and swore I could smell something sweet—cinnamon and toffee and caramel. But behind each scent was something else, something burnt, with a carcinogenic and strangely meaty edge.

It had drawn me here, the factory. Or, more accurately, the memories associated with the place had. Five years prior I'd been sitting with my older brother Jacob on the hood of his car. We'd parked across the street from the building and were drinking cheap beer.

I gave no thought to the fact Jacob was going to drive us both home. He was my older brother, and at fifteen I looked upon him with an admiration I'd never admit to. I never questioned his immortality. Jacob would live forever, and by extension so would I.

We'd stared at the warehouse and drank, talking mostly about nonsense, and occasionally about Jacob's plan to join the military. We danced around the subject of his leaving, only grazing it, mistaking, as young men often do, vulnerability for weakness.

Finally, I'd asked why we were here—why we were staring at a dilapidated old factory.

"You like horror stories, yeah, Rye?"

"I guess," I said. In fact, were one to open my backpack, they'd find a dog-eared copy of Carrie, my first foray into King.

"You know the story behind the Thompson place?"

"They say there was a fire."

He took a swig of beer. "Yup. Anything else?"

"Not really. People say it's haunted. What a load of shit." I looked at Jacob for confirmation that I was correct—that it was, in fact, a load of shit, but his face remained impassive.

"Maybe not haunted. Can't say I believe in ghosts. But what happened there will leave a mark on a place. Some buildings get, I dunno—I guess 'scarred' is the right word for it. And if it's bad enough the land itself goes bad, turns rotten, and nothing decent can grow there again. That's how you get tracts of land like this, left untouched for decades. People can sense it isn't right, that the soil's wrong. Know what I mean?"

"Yeah," I said, lying.

He pointed at the building with the bottle. "So yeah, there was a fire. It was 1975, I think. Nobody knows how it started or how it spread so fast. Some say it was arson but far as I can tell, Thompson was pretty well-respected around here.

"Good wages, good benefits, no scandals. It was some chemical reaction, I'd guess, or a mechanical fuck-up. Just a stroke of profoundly shitty luck. At least it happened at night when most of the workers were home. The building was almost empty. Almost."

He moved his bottle upward, staring down its length as though aiming down a sniper's sight. "Up... there. Those windows at the very top. See 'em?"

"I think so."

"Apartments, built special. That's where Thompson lived with his family—a wife and two kids. I don't remember their names. The man was serious about his job, I'll give him that. Imagine living where you work. Christ."

I didn't bother mentioning that, as a soldier, he would be doing just that.

"So, they were in the building when the fire started?" I asked.

"Yep. Sleeping. They say there was a big grinding sound, like something was breaking apart, and Franklin must've run downstairs toward   the vats to see what was up. See, inside the factory are—or I guess were—these huge vats of sugary goop: toffee, caramel, bubble gum, whatever, just tons of vats of pink and orange and brown ooze, you know? So, he runs down onto the main floor where all these massive metal vats are and he's scrambling around trying to find the source of the sound, then—bam!"

Jacob slapped the hood of the car; I jumped, the beer bottle smacking against my front teeth.

"Fuck," I said.

He smirked. "That hurt? Think how Thompson felt. One of the vats explodes, then another, then another, and before you know it the poor bastard is buried under thousands of pounds of boiling goo. Christ, can you imagine? Man dedicates his entire life to candy and is boiled alive in the stuff.

"Can only hope the explosion killed him or knocked him out before he was, you know, encased. Authorities never could find exactly where his body ended up, since his skin melted and then the candy hardened."

He finished off his beer and flung it toward the warehouse, the glass smashing on the street. "Apparently his bones are still there somewhere, in the hard candy. Nobody in their right mind wants to buy the land and deal with that sort of cursed shit, scraping a man out of his candy tomb."

"You're fucking with me. His bones are still there? Come on."

He gave me a look that told me nothing.

"And his family?" I asked.

"Ah," he said, lighting a cigarette. "The fire had spread, and the floor was basically covered in sugary lava. There was nowhere for them to run." He inhaled, deep. "They burned."

The memory faded. I looked at the section of street where the car had been; I could picture it clearly, a shitty silver 2004 Honda Civic. It was gone now, and so was its driver. A few weeks after our conversation he'd packed a bag and vanished without warning, leaving no trace or note—all he left was a gaping absence where he once had been—a black hole which tore the family apart in its event horizon.

I turned back to the factory, at those small windows at the very top where the Thompsons had lived, trying not to imagine them burning. A gust of wind blew from the north, from the direction of that monolith, carrying with it that damn smell.

I squinted out into the black and noticed… something. Movement.

In one of the windows there seemed to be a figure, a silhouette, and it was gesturing, but surely not, surely—

"Hell of a thing," said a voice.

I turned fast, my ankle twisting, the pain almost knocking me on my ass. The custodian I'd seen earlier stood a few feet away, hands in his coverall pockets. "Woah, steady on."

"Christ, you scared the shit out of me."

"Yeah, I can tell. Apologies. Thought you heard me coming, but guess your mind was somewhere else. Your leg okay?"

I exhaled, chilled breath dancing nervously in front of my eyes. I tested my ankle, which burned fiercely. "It's fine. No worries, man. Everything alright?"

"Was going to ask you just that question," he said. He wore a ball cap advertising some team I'd never heard of, and his coveralls were a light blue, stained in places by oil and dirt. His shadowed face was smooth, making his age a mystery. "It's almost 10 PM and you're out here staring at the old Thompson place. In shorts. In the middle of winter. Not exactly the picture of normalcy."

"Just curious," I said.

"That so? Ya know, I happen to recall a certain feline that was curious, as well. Not planning on doing some silly? Say, sneaking in?"

"The thought hadn't crossed my mind."

"Well, wouldn't blame you if it had, kid. Hell of a thing, as I said, the Thompson story."

"My brother told me all about it. 'Hell of a thing' is putting it mildly."

"I suppose it is, I suppose it is." He looked out at the building for a moment before shrugging. "Honestly, I often wonder why they haven't demolished the damn thing. The land must be worth something. It's like they've decided to keep it as a memorial. But to what?"

He sucked in his breath and seemed to come to a decision. "So, wanna see inside?"

"Seriously?"

"Hell, why not? I manage the lot, keep it clean. Well, relatively clean. Only so much you can do for a place like this, one that's seen…" He trailed off. "Well, anyway, if you'd like I can let you sneak a peek. Can't let you wander or anything, or take any pictures, but it will at least satiate that curiosity of yours."

"I mean, I appreciate the offer, but why? Isn't that against the rules?"

"Well, because I know you wanna see it, and, more importantly, because I know you *will*. If I don't let you in to see it properly now, you'll let yourself in one night and get yourself hurt.

This ain't the place for urban exploration, and I'd rather not find your corpse in one of the apartments the next time I make the rounds. That place has seen enough death, I'd say, and not just of the Thompson variety. So the deal is, you step in, have yourself a gander, and then you never come back. Sound good?"

"Yeah, man. You've got a deal. Thanks."

"Alrighty then." He walked to the front gate, fiddling with a large keyring. The lock took a few tries before it decided to comply.

"Damn thing needs replaced. Well then, come on in." He pushed the gate open with his shoulder, which screeched at the indignity of it. I walked onto a field of grass, tendrils of cool air dancing from their frosted blades and up my legs. There was no visible path leading to the entrance, though I didn't doubt there had been one once.

I heard the gate close behind me. The factory loomed like a living thing, like a sleeping beast. I couldn't take my eyes off of it, at once revolted and entranced.

"The Overlook," I said.

"Hm?"

"It reminds me of The Overlook Hotel."

"Never been," he said, continuing on ahead, hands in his pockets. He whistled as he went, a repetitive, familiar melody I couldn't place, the tune broken up only by the crunch of frost underfoot. I had begun to shiver, though from the cold or something else I couldn't say.

Finally I asked, "Is what happened to Thompson true?"

"Suppose that depends on what you think happened."

"That they, well, burned alive. Him and his family."

I couldn't see his face, but knew he was smiling by the lilt of his speech. "They burned, yeah. Some say they're burning still."

"What?"

"Never mind. It's just an old ghost story. You'll see how it really is, kid—a place like any other."

The smell of candy grew stronger the closer we got to the building, became cloying, aggressive. Even the air itself felt more viscous. I stopped and began to cough, my eyes drawn to the apartment windows.

And there it was again, the silhouette. It was moving now—waving frantically.

"There's someone up there, man," I said.

"Where?"

"The apartment. Someone's waving, or..."

"Ah, for fuck's sake. Sometimes kids break in and get stuck in one of the rooms. The doors are so rusted, they basically lock themselves in. Found a junkie up there once. He'd been there three days and seemed a few hours from death. Ironically, I think the drugs kept him alive. We should probably lend the poor bastard a hand, yeah?"

He turned to me. In the oily shadows of the street I hadn't seen the custodian's face, not really, the streetlights having served only to amplify the shadows underneath his cap. But I could see him clearly now, in the honest and unflattering light of the winter moon.

My first thought was that his flesh wasn't right. It was too smooth, beyond what any plastic surgery could possibly achieve, and he had no lips, the flesh curving into a mouth filled with uneven teeth. And his flesh was pink. Not ruddy or chapped but *bright* pink, glimmering wetly like bubble gum left out in the sun.

That's when I knew the person in the window wasn't waving to me—they were warning me off.

"You okay, kid? You look like you've seen a ghost. Then again, given where we are, maybe you have. A place can only drink so much blood before it starts to get a taste for it, I guess. Someone once told me places get *scarred*."

His voice had changed when he said that last bit, the tone with a mocking edge. I took a tentative step back. The man in the window had his hands pressed firmly against the glass, pushing at the pane, as though the act could physically move me away from the factory. A warning, yes, that's what it was, but it may already have been too late.

"Look, man, I'd love to help, but I'm actually gonna head home. It's late, and I, uh—yeah, you have a good night." I walked backward   , not wanting to turn my back on the custodian. My ankle roared with every step on the uneven grass. He followed my progress, walking slowly, hands still in pockets, his posture hunched, red-rimmed eyes searching.

"Jesus, something's spooked you. Is it that asshole in the window? Look, if someone's stuck up there, I may need your help getting him out. We may have to drag him, and I ain't as spry as I once was. As a bonus you get to see the room where Thompson's family... *slept*."

"I can call someone. The cops. They'll help you out. That guy's trespassing, anyway, right?"

"Ah, no use, no use, I'm afraid. The cops don't come here, kid. They're smarter than all that. Truth be told, nobody steps foot in this place, not even the damn graffiti artists, and they'd vandalize their own mothers' graves. Yup, there aren't many who'd willingly go through that gate. Something about the air of this place has people running, its memories carried on the wind. But there's the occasional oddball drawn to it, if that's even the right word to call them. Kids like you—and like your brother."

"What did you just say?"

The custodian's smile widened, causing his skin to stretch like putty. "I think you heard me just fine, Rye. Isn't that why you came here in the first place? To see Big Bro? Well, why stop now? Come say hello. He's been waiting an awful long time. It's funny—he didn't hesitate at the threshold like you. He waltzed right in. But then, you always were less sure of yourself than little Jakey."

"You're full of shit. You don't know my brother."

"Yes, I do. Better than you, by now. Ah, we talk all the time, him and I. I made his life sweeter. I think he sees that now. I can make your life sweeter, too. After all, there's no curfew in the Thompson family, and you don't even have to eat your vegetables before dessert. You and Jakey can share a caramel crunch, or maybe even a toffee delight. Such sweet things you'll eat, and each treat backed by the Thompson guarantee—that after just one lick, you'll be part of the family."

His hands reached out from the pockets of his coveralls, in each palm a pile of sweets wrapped in silver packaging. They glimmered in the moonlight, and each bore a small Thompson logo—a red, cursive T with a full-stop in the shape of a wrapped piece of candy.

"Come on in, son," he said, his voice different now, *wetter*, like something was hot and bubbling inside of him. "I give my family all the candy they could ever want. They're eager to meet you."

A pink light was visible underneath the entrance doors, spilling out into the night, and in my mind I saw what lay behind that threshold: caverns of writhing gelatinous toffee slithering up the walls, tunnels of the stuff like the intestines of a great beast, containing countless hidden things in their bubbling recesses. I saw men and women and children boiling in the slime forever, as a creature walked the pink halls replacing pieces of himself with the oozing sweetness all around him.

I saw Jacob begging me to run.

So I did.

I sprinted toward the entrance. The man said nothing, or maybe I just couldn't hear him over my heart pounding in my ears. My ankle burned and threatened to give, but still I ran, praying my legs carried me just a little bit farther.

The gate had been relocked. Of course it had. I would have to climb. I risked a look back and there he was, hands in pockets, walking calmly my way, whistling that tune. He gave a wave.

I began my ascent. The cold links bit into my flesh and my foot kept slipping on the wet metal. Then there was a pressure on my exposed right leg as he grabbed at me, somehow closing the distance in an instant. His skin was soft but his grip cold and vice-like; I was sent sprawling onto the grass. He was on me immediately, his left arm pinning me down as the right tried to force something into my mouth—a piece of candy, small and red.

"Open wide," he said. "Here comes the choo-choo train. Such sweet treats we'll all share. There's no end to it, no end, no end at all. The Thompson *fucking* guarantee!"

I lashed out before the thing could touch my lips, knowing it couldn't, that if that candy grazed any part of me it would be over, I would be at his mercy. I was shouting *get off get off get off* in a high-pitched voice I was sure belonged to someone else, someone much younger.

I accessed reserves of strength I didn't even know I had; I scratched at his face like an animal and was horrified as a segment of his flesh sloughed off with ease, revealing rotting muscle and sinew beneath, the meat seeming to glow from within as if a fire burned in his guts.

He was in hysterics, either laughing or crying, my lips now closed tight against the reddish drool and chunks of pink skin which fell from his mouth and onto my face. Still some got into my mouth and I could taste the sweetness of him.

I shoved him off, God knows how, and he lost his balance, his candies sent flying. He stumbled and one of the candies was crushed under his heel. Something inside of the candy, something red and thick but with a yellowy-white center, burst onto the grass like a lanced cyst. His expression became one of great pain. "No!" he screamed. "*No!*"

I jumped onto the fence, still high on adrenaline, no longer feeling my skin tear against rusty metal, ignoring the blood running down my sleeves. I was up and over, collapsing as my legs made contact with the concrete.

He was at the gate when I looked back, his 'candies' retrieved or forgotten, fumbling with his keyring, hands trembling; he looked angry, his staring eyes lit from behind by that churning inner fire.

"I'll have you," he said. "We'll be a family yet. Thompson Treats is a family company. Above all else, it's a family company."

Again, I ran.

After some time, I found myself sitting on my bed, fully clothed, still wearing my backpack. I had a vague recollection of my trip back to the house but felt much like a drunk does after a night of binge drinking—the trip home was blurred and unreal, a collage of fuzzy polaroids.

I sat there for a long time; I could almost feel my brain trying to repair itself, rationalizations covering up the mental wounds like bandages—bandages upon which were hastily-scrawled messages like "*I was dreaming.*"

But their material was weak and fell away in the face of the memory's clarity, at the reality of my pulsating ankle and the pink gunk still trapped under my nails—bits of the man's face. I sniffed at my fingers and flinched at the scent of artificial strawberry.

I showered, cut my nails down so low they bled, threw my clothes into the trash and fell into a shallow sleep. I dreamt I was crawling through gelatinous, pulsing caverns, surrounded by the moans and screams of those trapped inside. I was following someone, and though I could never quite get a good glimpse of him, I knew him by his old New Balance shoes, by his ratty jeans. And something was following me, too, something with a bubbling voice, which spoke of family and eternity. Whenever I slowed I would feel its fingers grazing my exposed legs.

I woke up the next day feverish, covered in cold sweat, my body trembling. I slipped in and out of consciousness for two weeks, reality melding with dreams, the room's walls melting, becoming soft, hands pushing at them from without, some begging me to help them, others telling me to join their family.

I saw figures flit in and out of existence, blurred shapes standing in the dark corners of my room, facing the wall like chastised children, whispering, moaning. My mother cared for me, but would not spend too long in my room, for (as she would tell me later), I kept muttering Jacob's name again and again, each syllable hitting her like a physical blow.

Then, as happens with such ferocious illnesses, it passed. One day I woke up and felt better. The shakes were gone and I was able to eat and drink, even stand.

I let another week go by before revisiting the factory. It was 11 AM on a Tuesday, the sky clear and the sun bright. The factories were alive with activity and the air was filled with sounds both human and mechanical. The custodian was gone, and so, too, was the malevolent air of the place.

When I reached the Thompson Treats factory, I was shocked to see it surrounded by construction workers, with most of the structure covered in tarp and the topmost floors of the place completely gone.

A worker stood outside the gate smoking a cigarette. I nodded at him and he nodded back.

"The old factory's coming down?" I asked.

"Uh-huh," he said. "A long time coming."

"Tough gig."

"Yeah? Why's that?"

"You know, all that hardened candy on the first floor. And the bones."

He furrowed his brow, giving a look normally reserved for people who take a seat beside you on the bus and proceed to have an animated conversation with the voices in their head. "How's that?"

"From the explosion. The vats. Thompson's body."

He shrugged. "You too, huh? I've had a few people ask me about this place. No offense, but I have no idea what you're talking about. I know there are plenty of legends about old buildings like this, but I don't know shit about any hardened candy or an explosion or bones. The vats are empty. Rusted, sure, and a pain in the ass to disassemble, but empty. And there's some fire damage on the top floor, and a terrible fucking smell, but that's about it."

"I don't get it. I heard the vats exploded and killed Leonard Thompson."

"Well, I don't know what you've heard, but I know what I've seen. This ain't no haunted house. It's just a place like any other. It gets spooky at night, sure, and the smell gets to you, but that ain't a surprise. I guess some say they hear sounds, voices, but I'm thinking they—and you—should probably cool it on the horror stories." The man dropped his cigarette and stamped it out. "Anyway, break's over. Have a good one."

He turned and opened the gate—it gave a familiar screech.

When I got home, I did as much research as I could about the history of the place; there was surprisingly little about the closure of the factory, which happened in the mid-1970s, as Jacob said. There was a fire, and the Thompson family did die, and there were some hints at foul play, Thompson having some loose connection to the mob back then, something about smuggling—but beyond that, I was at a loss.

A man being entombed by candy would surely be head-line news, wouldn't it? I saw no reason for that to be sup-pressed. There'd have been countless books written about it. Clearly, Jacob had taken a grain of truth and expanded on it, turning it into a ghost story rather than the simple, horrible tragedy that it was.

This explanation satisfied me, for a time. I figured that while walking home that night I must have already been sick, the fever growing, only the cold keeping me from feel-ing my brain heat up.

Like a shitty horror movie I had hallucinated, maybe dreamt, the entire escapade. A man with candy flesh—how ridiculous it seemed to me in the light of day, as I watched bored, swearing men tear apart an old brick factory that had seemed so large, so ominous, after the sun had gone down. It was no Overlook—it was just a place filled with sad memories, better left forgotten.

This might have been enough, had it ended there. Per-haps I would have forgotten the entire thing and moved on. Only I can't, for the dreams continue. Every night I chase Jacob, farther away from him than I was the night before, and every night I am chased, the bubbling exertions of the creature behind me closer still.

And sometimes as I lay awake at night, keeping the dream at bay with coffee and Red Bull, I hear someone whistling a discordant tune outside. I know now that it is the Thompson Treats jingle they used to play on the radio:

Try one now and you will see, Thompson's amazing guarantee! Have a lick, you'll say 'Golly!' and you'll be part of our family!

The tune starts down the street and grows louder, until it seems someone is standing right below my window. Then it stops. I do not look outside, and I pull my blankets up over my nose to block out the smell of burnt candy and rotting meat. Hell, with noise-canceling headphones on, I can even convince myself there is no tap at the window.

And when I step outside in the morning to find a single piece of candy on my doorstep, wrapped in silver and emblazoned with a red T, I kick it away—kick it onto the street where it will be crushed by the tire of a passing car, at which point it will burst like a living thing, its jelly center looking so much like blood.

Nevertheless, I will close the door and remind myself all is well.

Because it was only a dream. Only a story. And stories have no power.

Jukai

Dante Bilec

I ignore the sign at the entrance of the forest pleading to have me reconsider killing myself. It is written entirely in Japanese, but I know it says: *Life is a precious gift from your parents. Try to think calmly once more about them, your siblings, your kids. Don't keep it to yourself, please talk to someone.* I walk by it without a second look.

None of it pertains to me. No parents, no siblings, no kids. *Ojiisan*, Japanese for grandfather, isn't mentioned, but I add, *no Grandpa*.

As if I need any more validation for my choice.

I walk into the forest equipped with my backpack containing a coil of rope, my phone, a bottle of water and a lighter. I bring no ribbon to tie to a tree. If you need ribbon in the Jukai to help retrace steps, you should reconsider your reason for visiting.

The *Tamagotchi* Grandpa gave me when I was ten is in my pocket. It stopped working two years later, around the time he went missing on holiday in Japan, but I still carry it with me to remind me of him.

The first steps are effortless with all the man-made trails for hikers. Once I pass the cordoned-off section of the forest with the *No Entry* sign, the path forward becomes unclear and progressively more dangerous.

I drown in green with each step. My pace slows to a slug's and I use the trees for support to withstand breaking any ankles walking on uneven ground. For a moment, I find it funny and ironic that I am trying to prevent harm to myself, but it's necessary until I find the right place—the place that speaks to me.

I thought about this for a long time. Preparing even. Most recently, I searched for a tutorial on YouTube on how to tie a noose. Yes, those types of videos exist, and all of them start with a disclaimer that you should avoid watching if you are having suicidal thoughts.

I laughed every time I saw that. Who else would be watching a how-to video about noose tying? Boy Scouts, who have learned how to tie every other knot?

Learning was easy, and I became so skilled I could tie a noose blindfolded. That was when I knew how I wanted to do it. It was the only thing I was ever good at.

You're probably thinking I'm sick or depressed and that I need help. If I were to post this plan online, people would reach out and say, "Don't do it. There is always a reason to go on; we're here for you." But why does it have to come to a person wanting to kill themselves before anyone cares?

Most times, by then, it's too late. If anything, those same people trying to talk you away from the ledge lead you to it in the first place.

They are all full of shit. They just want to look like decent people when they don't even know your name. I could remedy that by offering my name, but why would I tell anyone now? I am no better than any other dried-out leaf on the forest floor to be stepped on.

I've tried to elevate my station in life.

I started with my body as my dad always told me to toughen up. I spent five days a week at the gym. My muscles grew the first few months, but the newbie gains wore off faster than I could pound back protein shakes.

I was far from those fitness guys on Instagram—or Dwayne Johnson or Thor. Just mediocre. Like everything else in my life. I injected myself with steroids after that, but I ended up with back acne so severe I bled like I was flogged with a whip covered in thorns every time I lay down.

I had taken advice from the wrong person. How tough was my dad really when he died from liver cirrhosis at fifty-five? Fucker couldn't even hold his alcohol.

My outlook was distorted. Weak and hideous doctors at the hospital, where I worked as a housekeeper, received attention from some of the hottest women.

The difference between myself and them? Money. Too late for me to go to medical school (as if I could get in), so I dabbled in other ways to improve my financial means. I did it all—crypto, drop-shipping, affiliate marketing. All I managed to do was feed the pockets of online get-rich-quick schemers.

At least I had my housekeeping job throughout my pursuit of financial betterment. That is until the hospital decided to cut my hours. Now I can't even afford rent for my shitty apartment, for which most decent people would be ashamed.

The only out for me would've come through the sole talent I have—or think I have. Drawing. I always loved manga, so I decided to make my own to hopefully get published by a magazine in Japan or the US. I thought my idea was original.

It was called *Watashi no Saiba Tomodachi,* meaning *My Cyber Friend* in Japanese. Eventually, I changed the title to *Tomodachi Cyber* because I thought it sounded better.

It told the story of a lonely, thirteen-year-old computer genius who created a friend in his computer with artificial intelligence so complex it ultimately became sentient.

The cyber friend helps the boy gain prominence, wealth, and status and stops global crisis by infiltrating the most top-secret areas of the internet.

Rejected.

There are mangas about everything from superheroes to soccer, volleyball, and even cooking. Still, I guess my idea was just too moronic.

So here I am in the Jukai. Aokighara Forest, Suicide Forest, where hundreds of people go to end their lives each year, beckoned by the vengeful spirits of those left to die in the forest back when it was acceptable to abandon the elderly once they became too much of a burden. The Japanese call them the Yurei.

Here I am with nothing but wasted effort, worse off than ever. In this life, I'll only ever be the nobody with a teaching degree who ended up cleaning old people's shit off the floor of the hospital because he couldn't get hired in what he was educated to do. Sure, I like old people, but have you ever smelled C-diff shit? It is the worst smell in all existence, and I'm done with it.

I remember reading somewhere that no matter how rich or poor we are, how beautiful or ugly, how influential or ineffectual, in death, we are all equal. I'm ready to feel equality. I will die prepared and willing, and everyone indulging in their lives now will someday be decrepit, soiling themselves and fearing their final resting place in a bed with detritivorous worms.

I'm coming, Grandpa.

The next time I turn around, I can no longer see the *No Entry* sign. Everything looks the same in all directions. Minutes passing feel like hours. Or maybe hours are actually minutes. My digital watch gives me no indication.

When did it stop working? My phone is a failure, too. I walked in with a three-quarter charge, and now it's dead. At least it's light out. For now.

The sunlight doesn't seem as strong.

Most would panic, but I feel more at ease than ever. I pull my water bottle out of my backpack, take a long drink, and continue forward.

Morbid peace sparks within me and grows stronger with each step deeper into the Jukai. It makes me want to sit against a tree and rest my eyes. I am tired from the thirteen-hour flight to Narita Airport in Tokyo and the two-hour train ride from Tokyo to Kawaguchiko, but I fail to resist the eerie beauty of the forest beckoning me within. I'll have plenty of time to sleep soon enough.

As I move deeper into the forest, I pass artifacts left behind by those who came before me. I stop at an abandoned camp with evidence of a prolonged stay. The tent collapsed on a torn sleeping bag, pill containers, and empty bottles of One Cup Sake.

I find a can of Zippo fluid near the fire pit next to a pack of cigarettes and legal documents underneath. It had rained on the papers, but I could still make out some of the text. I know enough Japanese to make out the word *rikon—divorce* on the page. I see no ribbon anywhere.

"Hello?" I call out.

No response, but I'm used to that. Hopefully, whoever was here found peace. I move on to keep pursuing mine.

Past the camp, I trek by trees for miles. The sunlight continues to fade, and I still don't have a spot. I take another swig of water and then hear my stomach growl.

I last ate during the meal service on the plane, and now I feel it. I regret passing by the *Konbini* without buying food, but I reassure myself with a reminder that my bowels will be clean when I finally do it.

I've heard when people commit suicide, they often piss

and shit themselves involuntarily. I won't have control over that, but I want to reduce the chances.

I see red in my periphery.

I discern red ribbon tied to a tree, unraveled beyond my line of sight. Upon closer inspection, I see it is still intact and vibrant, indicating it was connected to the tree not long ago. I follow it, wondering what I will find at the end.

The Jukai guides me.

When I arrive at the end of the ribbon trail, I discover an abandoned reel on the forest floor covered by leaves. It is the spot where someone made their final decision and where I will make mine.

It isn't the ribbon reel that captivates me, but what I find just a few paces away. A manga magazine. I was never religious, but nonetheless I feel something unseen helping me. I bow my head in silence, thanking the Jukai, some Yurei, and even Grandpa for leading me here.

I drop my backpack, unzip it and retrieve my coil of rope.

Time to set myself free.

I stop with the rope in my hands. My visibility is reduced with the sun long set. Sure, I could tie a noose blindfolded, but I choose to avoid any risks. The only thing worse than a suicide is a failed suicide. I gather enough twigs and branches in the surrounding area to build a fire. When I set them for optimal burning, I realize I don't have any kindling or a knife to make some.

It pains me, but the manga magazine is the only thing I could realistically use to start the fire. I grab the magazine, sit near my twigs and branches, and rip pages out. I only take what I need to start the fire and leave the rest intact.

With as little as four pages, the twigs and branches successfully catch fire. The sight of flames evoke a strange feeling in me. I can't really explain it. I am renewed and oddly satisfied. I start gathering more branches for burning to enjoy the fire through the night.

The firelight then illuminates the images in what is left of the manga magazine. I fail to resist picking up the damaged magazine and flipping through it.

The pages contain the usual manga fair, like samurai, ninjas, pirates, etc., until I stumble upon a full-page image that stupefies me: one of a happy-looking humanoid sharing a laugh with a boy. I bring the magazine closer to the fire to see the image more clearly. The additional light verifies I am not hallucinating.

Tomodachi Cyber.

My manga story. The one supposedly rejected. I leaf through the entire first chapter. Was my story stolen?

No.

I could practice reading Kanji more, but I know all my Hiragana and Katakana characters. Right underneath the title of my story appears my name written in Katakana. I'm somewhere in between elated my story was printed in a manga magazine with credit given to me, and indignant the publisher hadn't paid me.

In all my excitement, I forget the Jukai and my final camping trip. I place the manga magazine in my backpack and add a few more sticks to the fire. The forest is shrouded in darkness, but the fire provides enough light to illuminate my surroundings.

Everything is different.

The longer I look at the trees, the more intimidated I become. They are gnarled. They veer off in every direction, and I am left unbalanced. Jagged moss-covered roots dig into an uneven ground—rapacious claws clutching deep into their prey. They are ready to impale me with their branches.

No longer do I feel I'm in a peaceful forest but digested in the belly of a vile beast.

I consider my coil of rope for a moment. Fingers crawl

down my spine and send me to shivers.

I can't do it.

I have so many chapters of *Tomodachi Cyber* to publish, not to mention ideas for other manga series. Tomorrow, I'll make my way back to Tokyo and visit the offices of the manga magazine. I'm convinced the publisher has a logical explanation for my missing payment. I am confident for a solution—if I can make it through the night.

I have no food and little water, and I am so deep into the forest that navigating a path out will be onerous at best, especially in the dark. Leaving the forest is a task best left for the morning.

I lie near the fire and blanket myself in as many leaves as possible. Before resting my head on my backpack, I add more branches to it and watch the flames dance more wildly. Inside myself, something dances along.

\#

Morning. I'm woken by an ominous chill. I can only just see a smattering of the gray and somber   day through the tiny holes in the forest canopy above me. First, I take the manga magazine out of my backpack and find *Tomodachi Cyber*. Still there. Guess I am of sound mind… for a guy who considered suicide hours earlier.

The inside of my mouth tastes rancid so I take a tiny sip of water from my bottle. Only a quarter of the one-liter bottle remains. My back and neck are sore, and my stomach continues to rumble. I put everything into my backpack and waste no time getting to my feet.

If I delay any longer, dehydration and starvation will complete the task I had initially set out for myself. How would I start my new life? Life as *a mangaka*—a manga artist and writer.

I'll rent a place outside Tokyo and live off whatever money my manga stories earn. The pay likely will be on par with my rate as a housekeeper, but at least I'll like what I'm doing. Who knows? Some of my work may become as popular as *Dragonball* or *One Piece*.

I snap myself out of my reverie. *Need to get out of this forest first.* I follow the reel of ribbon I found on the ground the night before back to where it was originally tied. I was so sure I didn't need ribbon. I never thought I would be following someone else's trail to get out—someone who is probably dead. I wince at the thought.

I take my first steps and it finally happens. Focused on forming an escape plan, I neglect to mind my foot placement on the uneven ground and I stumble, colliding into the ground. I launch the reel of ribbon in the process. As I pull my face out of the leaves and spit bits of dirt and moss from my mouth, I hear a sound that has been absent from my mind for the better part of twenty-five years—my Tamagotchi *beeping*. My ears must be ringing from the fall.

The need to get out of the forest is now acute.

Back on my feet, I search for the reel of red ribbon and notice it had been sent flying at least ten meters and landed near a tree with a thick trunk. Slightly visible from behind the tree, I see...something. My stomach jumps into my throat. I'm unable to settle on what I'm seeing at my distance. The only logical explanation materializes in my mind—it was the original owner of the ribbon reel.

"Hello?" I call out, not expecting to receive a response.

I need to confirm if a body is hanging behind the tree, if only so I can inform the authorities. Taking the utmost care to maintain my footing, I approach the tree.

Then I hear it again.

This time, there is no debate. My Tamagotchi *is* beeping.

I pull my old friend out of my pocket. It still calls out for me when I place it in my palm. What startles me is the screen functioning like it did over two decades ago.

How is this possible? I tried everything to repair it, and

now, of all times, it decides to come back to life? I inspect the screen and find no egg and no little Tamagotchi happily bouncing around. What I see instead freezes my blood. A little ghost next to a tombstone—it's the death screen.

I check the dead Tamagotchi's stats and it shows this one died at fifty-nine years old. Fifty-nine is a number that always stood out to me only because it is the age at which Grandpa went missing on his holiday in Japan.

This is absurd. My Tamagotchi must be reacting to the increased magnetism of this forest. Electronics were known to behave erratically in the Jukai. I don't know; I'm not a scientist. I put the Tamagotchi back into my pocket and continue moving toward the tree.

I take five steps before the Tamagotchi beeps again. It greets me with the same death screen. When I check the stats this time, the device tells me the Tamagotchi died at thirty-five years old.

My age.

In terror and panic, I throw the Tamagotchi. Just as swiftly do thoughts of Grandpa force me to regret it. The Tamagotchi is the only thing I have left of him. I decide to look for it later and that inspecting what is behind the tree is more important.

I move closer with awkward steps forward. Before I reach the tree, a stench forces itself into my nostrils and causes me to keel over and nearly vomit. The noxious, sickly, sweet stink smells worse than C-diff shit a thousand times over. I raise my shirt over my nose to dull the smell. It does little good, but I manage to stop gagging.

Only when I find myself standing over the ribbon reel do I realize what is behind the tree. I believe I am prepared for it.

This time, I actually vomit.

I hear my Tamagotchi going off again somewhere in the background. With the taste of bile at the back of my throat,

I stand up straight to reaffirm what I see. I forget about the smell, my Tamagotchi, my manga story, the Jukai, and my life.

The person hanging from the tree is decaying, with maggots crawling on him in select places. The rope around his neck digs into putrefied flesh to the extent that he struggles to remain suspended. Soon, he'll be hanging by his cervical spine. He'll eventually be free of the rope when the bone wears away, but it will be at the cost of being detached from the head.

At the bottom of his right pant leg, fecal matter worms through. The thought of shitting at the moment of death always disturbed me. I look up into his eyes, as far away from there as possible. One is gone, long rotted away or eaten by carrion birds, and the other is slightly open. Even in this state, I recognize him.

He is me.

Be Back at Three

By D. H. Parish

Emily opened her eyes and looked into the darkness. She was breathing rapidly and could feel her pulse racing. But it was okay, she told herself. It had all been a dream. What that dream was she could not remember, its foggy substance dissipating, although it must have been rather bad.

Most of her recent dreams had been bad. She reached over to her nightstand and looked at her phone to check the time. It was only 12:45. She had gone to sleep after her date had ended and had been out for less than two hours, yet the night already seemed long.

The room still dark, Emily sat up in bed. She was more awake than she wanted to be. She reached over on her covers and grabbed the remote, turning on the television bolted to the wall just past the foot of her bed. John had been the one who had fixed it there early in their relationship, although watching television in bed had been more his thing.

The guide screen came on, welcoming her to a world she didn't often enter. She scrolled past late night talk shows she had no interest in, television reruns she never wanted to see, news stations she never watched, and finally came to a movie title she wasn't familiar with: "The Stairway." Three stars.

It had just begun. She selected it. "With a title that pedestrian," she muttered to herself, "maybe it will put me back to sleep."

The television initially remained dark as what sounded like a Bach fugue played on a harpsichord. The screen slowly lit to reveal a set of gray concrete basement stairs, descending left to right. An arm reached out from the lower right-hand corner of the screen, its wrists striated with red, raw cuts, its hand grasping the lowest stair and slowly pulling into the picture a body behind it.

A second hand reached out to the second step, with great effort dragging the body upward. She watched the man's sure and deliberate progress up the steps, one by one, gaining elevation by force of his arms only, as if he had no use of his legs.

The music kept its somber pace but grew louder and louder. She felt unnerved watching this scene. It took her a minute to recognize what was wrong: the body had no head.

"That's disgusting," Emily cried out, gasping at the realization. She turned off the television. The screen went black. And then four words, visible for perhaps less than a second, appeared on the blank screen in scrawled red lettering: "Be back at 3.'

"Jesus!" she muttered to herself, her pulse bounding once again. What the hell was that?"

This was not going to help her sleep. She took some deep steady breaths, just as the therapist had told her to do in situations like this. It was just a movie, and given the time it was airing, a bad one at that. She did not want to turn on the television again, so she looked at her phone to check out the title.

Knowing what it was about might be calming; truly understanding something reduces anxiety about the unknown, or something like that. But there was nothing online. It was a film so minor even IMDb couldn't be bothered to mention it. That knowledge alone, however, was itself reassuring.

She just needed to try and drift off again, remember how her day had been good, how well her date had gone. "Emily, all is well," she comforted herself, "you just need some sleep." She shut her eyes and counted backward by sevens: 100, 93, 86, 78, no, 79, 72 . . . oblivion.

She woke abruptly a second time, again anxious about something unknown, again the room pitch black. She reached out for her phone and checked the time: 1:53. "Dammit." she whispered. She was wide awake, again disturbed by some quickly forgotten, nebulous dream. What to do? Maybe read?

She picked up the Kindle next to her bed. She scrolled through the various books in her library. She was always reading something, be they novels, romances, or biographies, but rarely finished anything. If it wasn't for the electronic reader, she would probably have a mountain of books towering precipitously over her bed, ready to crash down.

She looked through her collection and, somewhat surprised, found a copy of the Bible. She hadn't remembered adding it, as it wasn't something she would typically choose to read. But maybe this was fortuitous. Didn't people used to open their Bibles to a random page to seek guidance?

"The Bible should be sufficiently calming and boring; it always put me to sleep in church." Emily chuckled to herself. She chose a random chapter from a random book ("Judges it is.") and started reading:

"And her master rose up in the morning and when he opened the doors of the house and went out to go on his way, behold, there was his concubine, lying at the door of

the house, with her hands on the threshold. He said to her, 'Get up, let us be going.' But there was no answer. Then he put her upon the ass and rose up and went away to his home. And when he entered his house, he took a knife, and laying hold of his concubine, he divided her, limb by limb, into twelve pieces, and sent her throughout all the territory . . . "

"Holy shit!" she uttered, surprising herself with the sound of her own voice. "Of all the boring Bible passages I could have chosen, I found the one with graphic depictions of dismemberment?" She powered off the device. As she did, a message flashed on the screen, white scrawled lettering on a black background, identical in style to what she had seen before on her television: "Be back at 3."

Emily was breathing heavily now, almost panting, as if she had just run a mile. What did that message mean? She didn't believe in ghosts, did she? This wasn't some message from beyond, threatening her? No, it was just her anxiety. That said, she reasoned, the occasion called for some pharmaceutical help.

She needed it, even if she had had a few drinks during the date (although not as many as he had had). The room still bathed in darkness, she threw off her sheets and quilt, rose from the bed, and strode the familiar path to the bathroom. She turned on the lights and caught her image in the mirror.

She looked awful: hair disheveled, eyes sunken, and visage pale as the proverbial ghost. Emily turned on the faucet and splashed cold water on her face. She had probably lost weight too, she reckoned, and not in a good way. She needed to move on. Oh how she hoped this new guy would be the one.

She opened the medicine cabinet behind the mirror and stared at the shelves of toothpaste, compacts, eyeliner, lipstick, and dental floss, locating several amber pill bottles standing on the bottom row. She was always nervous about potential addiction given her brother's history and her own tendency toward obsession, but if she ever needed a sleep aid, now was the time.

She grabbed the one labeled Xanax, twisted open the child safety lid, fished out a tablet, and swallowed it with a gulp of water from a cupped hand.

She shut the cabinet door, turned off the lights, and walked back to bed. As she waited for the drug to do its thing, she tried to calm herself down—self-soothe. This was all just her anxiety, wasn't it? There was no specific reason she should be this anxious right now, although generalized anxiety doesn't need something specific to be anxious about, does it Emily?

What had her therapist said? She should not blame herself for the breakup; those happened, and some people just aren't meant for others. It didn't mean failure. It was a part of life, of growth. It was okay to mourn the passing of a relationship, but that was just it: it would pass.

For now, she needed to take care of herself. Something new would come. Indeed, she had already maybe found someone new. It was still early, and maybe Zach was not everything John had been, at least not yet, but such things took time.

You can't know someone after one or two dates, can you? Still, she missed that easy intimacy she had had with John. As the Xanax kicked in, she drifted off, pondering the mysteries of human connection and romance, a smile creeping its way onto the corners of her lips as she did.

Emily jolted awake, feeling as if something had smacked her in the head. "The movie stairs! Those were my basement stairs!" She reached over and looked at her phone: 2:51 AM   .

"Almost 3! What should I do? Should I call the police? No, they would think I was crazy, drugged up." She turned on the lights and sat up, throwing her legs over the side of the bed.

"No, it's just my anxiety," Emily reassured herself. She would check out the stairs and prove to herself there was nothing there, that everything was fine. The messages were just her imagination.

Clutching her phone, she slowly made her way down to her kitchen, to the door leading to the basement. She hesitated before opening it and descending. Should she take a weapon? There wouldn't be anything dangerous for her down there, would there? Still, she would feel better with some protection.

She drew the large chef's knife out of its butcher block holder and gripped its black handle tight in her right hand, the mere weight of it giving her an increased sense of safety.

Emily paused at the door and inhaled deeply. There was nothing to be worried about, she told herself. She turned the handle and pulled the door open, all without a sound. She reached out and gently tugged the light cord hanging from the naked bulb at the top of the stairs.

Click.

Nothing.

No light.

Her heart beat a little faster. "It's just a burned-out bulb, Emily. Normal problem. Just a bad coincidence. Doesn't mean anything." She transferred the knife to her left hand, grabbed her phone, and turned on its flashlight. She aimed its light at the gray stairs and slowly climbed down each of the thirteen steps, one at a time, her slippers making only the slightest thud with each footfall.

She could see nothing unusual at the base of the stairs, thank God. But what was that noise she was hearing? It seemed like music; was it that fugue music? No, her mind, and maybe the Xanax, were playing tricks on her. That was all.

She reached the second to last step and turned on the switch at the bottom of the stairs. The full basement came into view, fluorescent lights now humming. It looked as when she had last seen it.

The washer and dryer, the couch, the big television, the keepsake cabinet. All were in order, all were undisturbed. There was nothing unusual. No harpsichord music. No headless man crawling on the floor. It had all just been a dream. Thank goodness she hadn't called the police.

Then she heard a noise, a rustling, quiet but persistent. She froze, trying to listen. This was not normal. But where was it coming from? She gently put her phone down on top of the nearby washing machine and switched the knife back to her right hand.

She concentrated intensely. There was one additional room in the basement, an extra bedroom she had built for guests. The noise seemed to be coming from there. She walked, stalked toward the door, and put her ear to it. The noise was definitely coming from behind it. But what was it? A mouse? A rat? She grabbed the doorknob and twisted it slowly, and pushed. It swung open quietly.

"Oh God!" she yelled.

Zach was exactly where she had left him after their date, bound to a chair and gagged tightly. But he was awake now, wide awake. He had somehow overcome the alcohol as well as the loads of Xanax she had surreptitiously added to his drinks earlier that evening. He was trying, despite her own expert work, to saw his way through the ropes on his wrists, using a small penknife on a keychain he had likely been carrying, his chair scraping on the wooden floor with each back and forth movement.

That was the noise! Had she forgotten to empty his pockets? How could she have been so foolish, so careless?

Zach looked at her with wide, frightened eyes as she

glared back at him. He grunted but could not scream.

"Oh Zach," she chided, "you need to stop this right now!" She rushed at him with the chef's knife and stabbed repeatedly at his hands, dealing him multiple oozing lacerations until he finally dropped the penknife, relinquishing it with an anguished gasp.

She kicked it away from his reach, walked over to it, and picked it up between her thumb and index finger. She then walked back and held the knife in front of Zach, shaking it at him, scalding him with it like a child.

"You scared the hell out of me! You need to stay away from such things! They are dangerous! What did you think you were doing? If you had succeeded, you would have ruined everything!"

She closed the penknife and put it in her robe pocket. "Things were going so promisingly, Zach! Well, I guess every relationship has its stumbling blocks. Now you behave!" She paused before continuing in a more moderate tone. "My therapist says I need to be more forgiving, to myself and others. Well, Zach, I forgive you. But please don't do this again. If you do, it won't end well."

Her voice then became softer, almost coquettish. "And get some rest, dear Zach. We have the whole day ahead of us." She winked at him and shut the door.

She considered those wide eyes that had been staring at her. They were so blue. Not unattractive, but not the rich brown of John's eyes. Could she live with them or would she have to change to them, pluck them out with her knife and put in new ones? That was probably a discussion best saved for a third or fourth date, when they knew each other better.

Her therapist had told her she should move more slowly in her relationships; they would approve of her restraint, her growth. Yes, this would be healthy for her.

She picked up her phone and plunked herself down on

the couch where she and John had, not so long ago, spent so much time together. It was 3:01 AM. The message she had received hadn't been a bad omen after all. It had been her subconscious warning her, protecting her. Or maybe, she wondered, someone else was looking out for her. Or maybe, it was an invitation?

That last thought, however fanciful she knew it was, brought her some real joy. She picked herself up off the couch and walked over to the cabinet that stood just next to the large-screen television. It contained assorted ceramics and knickknacks she had collected over time, memories of trips and special occasions.

On the top shelf was the biggest, most important item in the collection, a large glass jar. She considered it and its precious contents for a moment, putting her hand out to touch its cold exterior. She wrinkled her brow before addressing it. "Were you trying to warn me? To protect me?" She carefully picked the jar up with both hands and placed it down with a squish on the couch cushion next to her.

She turned on the television, looking for something soothing and romantic. She found a movie that seemed to fit the bill, "Love Eternal," and turned it on. She tilted the jar so she could look directly at the formaldehyde-preserved head within, its brown eyes still wide open, its mouth even wider.

Eternally so.

"I know you don't love these movies, John, but indulge me tonight. Boy, do I need it." She pulled John's severed head out of the jar by its wet, wavy hair, yellowed liquid splashing on the couch as she did so, and placed it on her lap so its eyes faced the screen. The head's dampness felt deliciously cool on her thighs.

On screen, a couple embraced and kissed passionately under a lamppost in a drenching night-time rain. She lovingly caressed John's wet hair, breathing in the pungent smell, imaging John and her as the lovers on screen.

John may have wanted to end things, but he was still here, at least tonight, and no doubt glad he was, or why else was she warned. Maybe she did believe in ghosts after all.

The Nameless Girl

Whitney McShan

When I reflect and examine my life up until the events which I will detail here, I have great difficulty relating to the girl I once was. I feel as though I am straining to make whole a shattered image, all refracted light, and distorted angles I cannot piece together.

The only tie that binds me to that girl now is unending death. I bore witness to so much death it has in its own way become prosaic. This story begins with death, and I hope now that it ends in death as well.

My father owned a funeral home, and it is where we lived all of my life. He worked as both the embalmer and the funeral director. Throughout my teen years I assisted where it was appropriate, primarily with small, administrative tasks.

I fear through thoughtless errors I often caused more work for him, but he was rather progressive and believed it important I learn the business. When I was nineteen, I was given the role of mortuary assistant and became more involved with the preparation of those who in decorum we referred to as "clients."

Our town was not large, nor did it have anything of note beyond a mental asylum that sat twelve miles to the East of our home. It had only been in operation for three years at the time of these events, but it was not infrequent for us to be called upon to direct the funerals of those who had died on their premises. To my admittedly limited knowledge, the primary causes of death were age and disease.

Though, occasionally we would receive murders, suicides, and even once a guard who died under circumstances that remained mysterious to me.

It was the summer after I began my role as mortuary assistant when we received my first and only client from the asylum, and while I do not now recall any particularities like the day of the week or the time of day, I vividly remember how hot it was. When my father informed me   a new client would be dropped off shortly, I could not shake the dread that immediately settled upon me like a thick, enveloping fog.

I attributed it to the heat, as working with the dead in temperatures over 80 degrees was immensely challenging. But, at that point I had gained enough experience to learn there was little to do but get on with it, so albeit begrudgingly, that is what I did.

That afternoon Father had been occupied with creating funeral arrangements for a well-respected local family, so I took it upon myself to receive the body. I sat on the porch so as to stay in the shade while I waited for the delivery. There was a pleasant smell of wildflowers on the breeze, and a persistent, low buzz as is common for the time of year.

However, my attention continued to be stolen away by the sharper sound of horse flies circling in their nagging way around me. I had little skin exposed, yet somehow still was continuously assaulted with their painful bites. Just as

I was certain my entire body would be overtaken by a rash as a result, I heard the rhythmic sounds of approaching horse hooves.

As the modest funeral coach rounded our dirt path past a dense bunch of oak trees, I caught a glimpse of the driver. I recognized him as Frederick Davies, a ghastly fellow with slender, gaunt features and an almost gray pallor.

I once made the observation to Father that Mr. Davies looked quite a bit more like one of our clients than some of those which he had delivered, but he scolded me, reminding me of the importance of Mr. Davies work and the toll it likely took on him.

Still, though I cannot name the cause or truly the nature of the feeling itself, I did not enjoy his company. As the coach slowed in front of the porch where I sat, I felt a growing sense of unease.

"Good afternoon, ma'am," he said.

I stood and returned a courteous nod.

"Good afternoon, sir." Motioning to the back of the carriage, I asked, "Who do we have here?"

"Strange one, she was," he said as he hopped off the driver's box. He walked slowly as he rounded the coach to the back door, "Though I suppose they all are."

Inside the coach was an unadorned wooden box which I knew from previous experience the asylum used to transport all of their deceased. To the left of the box sat a distressed brown leather case. Mr. Davies opened the case, and provided me with a folder from inside. I glanced at the first page, to confirm all the necessary details were included.

"No family?" I asked.

He shrugged. "I do not prepare the paperwork, ma'am. All I know of this one is that she was odder than many I have seen, and that says something."

"I imagine it does."

With surprising grace given his sinewy frame, Mr. Davies unloaded the box from the coach onto an unfolded wheeled contraption. He looked at me expectantly.

"Right then, let's bring her inside."

I led them through the back halls of the funeral home to our small embalming parlor. It was a solemn room designed for functionality above all else.

Despite the years, I had never gotten used to the smell. No matter how clean it was, or maybe because of it, the air always smelled of rubber and something slightly toxic. It was both too dull and too sharp and made my head ache. I think in convincing myself that was the reason I avoided the room, I felt more courageous than I was.

There were no windows, and I had only lit one lamp prior to Mr. Davies's arrival. The dim, flickering light cast shadows I am sure less practical minds would find quite frightening. In the center of the parlor sat a worn, utilitarian table where Father prepared the clients for their final rest. There were three metal cabinets placed against the walls that stored the tools of our trade. Atop the counters, were large glass jars of the necessary chemicals for embalming.

I removed myself from the room to allow Mr. Davies to transfer the client onto the table. It was silly, I knew, and I felt like a little child, but still. There was something I found so undignified in the act of moving the dead, and Mr. Davies did unsettle me so.

After only a few moments, the door creaked open, and Mr. Davies pushed the now empty box ahead of him. On its top sat a single piece of paper. He motioned toward it, "Will you sign, please, ma'am to confirm you have received her?"

I obliged, and with that, our business was concluded. I led him back outside and stood in the shade as he loaded his coach. Once settled into the driver's box, he gave a curt nod goodbye and gently whipped the reins to spur its horses into motion. I sat and watched until the coach was beyond the oak trees and out of view.

It was strange then, the sense of dread I still felt. I had attributed it to both the heat and the visit from Mr. Davies, but it seemed to be a heavy presence stuck upon me. I was still holding the document he provided on our new client, and in what I suppose was procrastination I decided to review it before starting my work.

While it was uncommon, it was not entirely unheard of for us to receive clients who had no known familial relations. I could not recall any client so young as this one, though, who had no family. According to the document, her age was unknown, but the physicians estimated   she must have been in her early twenties.

Her name was also unknown. The institution appeared to call her Mary, but I assumed that was simply out of necessity. There were a few notes scrawled about the page that indicated the physicians believed her to be schizophrenic and delusional.

While no witnesses were named, it stated that she died of suicide. She somehow secreted herself away in the medication room over the dinner hour and took large quantities of a variety of anti-psychotic drugs. She was not found by the orderlies until this morning.

Suicide meant she might be denied a Christian burial. How sad it was to lose all so young, and to be divorced from even God's grace. But perhaps he would see fit to show the poor girl mercy given her mental failings. I would have to remember to say a prayer for her.

I certainly felt no better after reading the document, but I knew I should not delay starting my work any longer. Father would handle the embalming, but I needed to prepare the poor girl first.

I deposited her file in a desk drawer where we stored our other client documents from the month, and then went next to the washing room where I changed into my planer working clothes and apron. Upon my return to the embalming parlor, I found Mr. Davies had covered the client with a grimy off-white sheet with faded, horizontal red stripes. It was not one of ours, so it must have come from the asylum with her.

I tied my hair back out of my face and lit a few more lamps, making the room feel a bit less eerie. My role as an assistant was to prepare her for embalming, which consisted primarily of washing her, combing and styling her hair, and sometimes I helped with the application of makeup. I gathered the wash bucket, cloths, and soaps from our supply cabinets and set everything up on a small metal stand next to the embalming table.

I pulled back the sheet, exposing her face and gasped. She was strikingly beautiful, and while I had no conscious expectations of her appearance, I suppose I did think of asylum patients as more unfortunate looking—flawed as though that prejudice may have been.

Her skin was smooth and without blemishes, and I would swear it seemed almost translucent in the lamp light. She had deeply dark brunette hair which laid atop her slim shoulders. Her lips were so full and crimson that I thought to myself how odd that she would have applied makeup before her suicide.

I noticed then her lips were slightly parted, revealing sparkling white teeth. Something in her expression deepened my sense of unease. I was not so learned as my father, but I had seen a great many corpses throughout my life. I could not name why, but she appeared differently to me than any of them.

I dipped my cloth into the wash bucket, and gently ran it across her lips to remove her makeup, but none came away. In disbelief, I repeated the motion several more times, adding more soap or warmer water. She was not wearing any makeup. I could not understand how a woman who died the evening prior would still have such vital colors about her. Truly I felt I must have looked more like the dead than she.

I felt such paranoia then and I was embarrassed by it, but I watched her. With such intensity I stared at her chest, straining to see even a hint of shallow movement. I felt her neck searching for a pulse, however faint. I cannot say for how long I did this, but it was a considerable period.

Of course, there was nothing. The young woman was dead, and selfishly I was grateful because that meant no one had witnessed me behaving so foolishly.

I took a steadying breath and finished washing her. After combing and braiding her hair, I covered her once again with one of our clean sheets, disposing of the filthy one she arrived in. I emptied and sanitized the wash bucket, and with forced meticulousness put away all of my supplies.

My work was done, and that was a mercy. While I have never been particularly squeamish, I can admit that even in the best of times I did not enjoy my profession. It was my father who handled the more gruesome aspects, but I unfortunately had to bear witness to most of them.

This time, however, I felt so deeply and inexplicably unsettled that I decided I would insist upon a break. Perhaps I was ill, coming down with something that the heat was exacerbating. I would clean myself, go to bed early, and awaken with a clearer mind.

I do not know what drove me to it, because it is not something I had ever done before, but before leaving the parlor, I placed my hand on her covered chest and said aloud,

"I am sorry whoever you are that your short life was so troubled." And then I prayed, "Eternal rest grant unto them, O Lord, and let perpetual light shine upon them. May the souls of the faithful departed, through the mercy of God, rest in peace. Amen." With that, I left.

I checked in on Father and it seemed as though all of the family excluding the deceased's brother had left. It appeared he and Father were making payment arrangements for our services. Not wanting to disturb them, I left a quick note on his desk to inform him our new client was cleaned and prepared for embalming. I added I was not feeling well, and would be taking an early rest.

Given my strange mood, I anticipated a fitful night, but I slept more deeply than I had in years. When I woke in the morning, I felt as if I had been drugged. It was as though I had to push against an invisible resistance, like molasses in my veins, slowing both my thinking and movement. Once out of bed and dressed, I began to gain a bit of foothold and felt alert enough to make my way downstairs for breakfast.

On most mornings, Father played operetta as he dined, but as I descended the stairs it was unusually quiet. Upon entering the dining room, there was no sign of either father or our normal breakfasts. We were far from overly lavish meals, but by this time in the day there was usually tea, bread, preserves, eggs, or porridge all set across the table. Perhaps he was feeling ill as well and slept in.

I began back up the stairs to check for him in his room and felt once more a heavy dread settle upon me. With each step a gnawing pit in my stomach grew, until the time I finally opened his door and felt as though it might burst.

His room was empty, and his bed, made. He was up and about then, and there were only so many places within our small home he could be. I presumed something went wrong last night with the financial arrangements, and he was delayed in beginning his work on our new client. The process was in many ways a race against time, so he must have skipped breakfast to get to it.

Looking back now, I am not sure I believed that even then. If I had, I would not have felt so incredibly afraid.

I went straight away then to the embalming parlor

where I was met with a closed door. The silence was profound. It was more than the absence of our usual operetta that troubled me. The funeral home was often quiet, but there was something tangible and oppressive in its quality now.

As I reached for the doorknob, it seemed as though any sound would shatter this fragile moment and send me spiraling over an unknown precipice.

I steeled my nerves and opened the door, straining to see inside the parlor. The lamps were unlit and the only illumination came from the small bit of natural light pouring in from the hallway. I took a few cautious steps inside and noticed immediately the smell.

It was a pungent and obscene combination of rot and iron and earth that threatened to curdle my stomach. Before I had the opportunity to make sense of it, I took a misstep and my world tilted upon its axis. With a sickening thud, my head collided with the hard floor.

I think I lost consciousness, but for how long, I cannot say. When I came to, I attempted to push myself up, but my hands slid against the slick floor. I was horrified at the possibilities of what the substance I was soaked with could be. Slowly, I managed to stand, and I walked carefully to the counter to light a lamp.

What I beheld then will haunt my nightmares for eternity. My father laid sprawled upon the floor in a grotesque display. His pallid face was frozen in an expression of agony, with his eyes wide in terror, as if he witnessed death itself coming for him.

A pool of crimson blood spread like a rug beneath his contorted form. His neck appeared torn open, all that remained was mangled flesh scarcely able to connect his head to his body. I recoiled in horror, screaming as I tried to run from the room. I slipped again, and in my terrified desperation crawled out on my hands and knees as I wept.

Once past the doorway, I collapsed prone onto the floor and sobbed so heavily I could hardly breathe. After some time, I stood and turned back to the parlor.

A realization dawned on me with bone chilling clarity. Mary was gone. I considered in a desperate grab for my sanity that my father's murderer had stolen her body for some foul purpose. But I knew. I knew she had killed him. I heard folk tales of what could become of those who took their own lives, cast out from both Heaven and Hell.

I had to run. I could take a horse into town and get help.

It was as I stood up from the floor that I heard a soft humming behind me.

I was paralyzed, unable to turn and face the monstrous entity moving toward me. I screamed in hopeless terror.

Then came a gentle shushing, like that of a mother to an inconsolable child. I felt her breath on my neck and feared I might faint.

"Will you not look upon me, kind girl?"

Her voice was musical and commanding. I felt my resolve flickering like candlelight against an encroaching darkness. I turned, unable to stop myself and my breath hitched in my throat as I faced her.

She stood in front of me, so uncomfortably close, looking just as she had on the table. Her pale skin shimmered in the dim light, and her eyes like pools of midnight stared intensely at me with something resemblant to curiosity. Her beauty was spoiled however, by my father's blood upon her face.

"You," I whispered. "You murdered him."

She tilted her head at that, and stood silently for a moment before asking, "What is your name?"

I did not want to tell her. I did not want to be known by a monster.

I took one step back as I said, "You are dead, and I would like for you to leave."

"I am dead," she seemed to contemplate the idea as she spoke it. "Where shall I go if not a funeral home?"

I continued moving backward and in an imperceptible instant she closed the distance between us and inhaled deeply, breathing in my scent.

"A nameless girl like me. Shall I call you Mary as well? Come with me, nameless girl."

She was predatory, but more than that, there was something animalistic in her countenance. I knew   if I were to run, she would kill me. It would be reflexive, like a cat swatting curiously at a mouse.

"And where am I to follow you to?" I asked.

She smiled at that, a beautiful, bloody smile.

"Oh, my nameless girl, what fun we shall have together!"

She led me back up the stairs, where in a perverse reversal of our roles, she insisted on helping me bathe. Oddly, the sense of unease I had been assailed with since her arrival had all but faded.

The worst had come to pass, and now I would wait for death to claim me. I sat silently and statuesque in the tub, the water turned a sickly brown from father's blood as she cleaned my hair. She talked the whole while of the places we would go, the experiences we would share. How insane she was.

After dressing me, she laid me in my bed and instructed me to rest while she prepared a meal for me.

Days passed that way, as if I were trapped in a ceaseless nightmare. She doted upon me in an inexplicable show of twisted devotion. She forced food upon me all while I grew weaker by the hour, withering in unending, numbing terror. It was as if despite her monstrous nature, she felt some pull to care for me now that Father was gone, rotting away on the floor of the embalming room. If our circumstances were less gruesome, I might have thought it something akin to being honor bound.

On the third day of my imprisonment, she left the home for the first time since Mr. Davies had brought her to me. We were nearly out of food and a trip to the well was necessary. I think she had genuinely come to fear for my well being. I was too weak to escape; she must have been confident in that. Though we did not speak of it, we each knew she had been feeding upon me. How else was it she could retain such vitality as I slipped closer and closer to death?

I was lying on my bed, exhausted and without hope. She sat gently next to me and placed her hand atop mine. Her flesh was soft and warm.

"You are not well, my nameless girl," she said. "You eat too little and lose your strength. What foods would you like for me to prepare you?"

"You steal my strength as you steal my life."

She seemed pained by that, her expression turning sorrowful. "I do regret we did not meet before my transformation. I would have liked us to be friends. This is not a world built for those like myself, so I was locked away to wither and perish without kindness or witness.

But in my death, you witnessed me. You were the first to show me any humanity since my childhood. Now I am to exist in this unlife. We are bound, nameless girl, by forces beyond my comprehension. I am sorry to you for that, but nevertheless it is true."

She kissed my temple, and her lips lingered for a moment as I shuddered.

"I will return shortly, and you will be strong again."

I drifted into unconsciousness then, something deeper than sleep, and when I awoke it was to screaming. I heard footsteps, pounding up the staircase and saw the man F ather had been in meetings with the day he died. He must have come for a final viewing of his brother and found F ather in his horrific state. He looked pale, as if he had just been sick as he ran to my bed.

"Oh, poor child, poor child," he cried, shaking as he scooped me into his arms.

The next several hours are fragmented in my mind. He carried me down the stairs and placed me in his carriage. I slipped in and out of consciousness on the frantic, bumpy ride into town. I think I was taken to a doctor, but everything happened rather quickly.

Other men came in, asking me questions about my father, and what had happened to the both of us. A kindly old man, who I believe was the physician shooed them away.

Once I had regained sufficient strength and the physician was confident I was no longer at death's door, investigators returned. I told them my story in its entirety, knowing of course how it sounded. But what else could I say? The looks in their eyes were so alien to me, an infuriating mix of disgust and pity that in time I came to know all too well. They thought me insane, and there were instances when I half agreed.

In lieu of any sensical explanation, I was accused of Father's murder. The prevailing theory I believe was that my fragile female constitution was warped by a lifelong exposure to death.

I never had the opportunity to stand trial but was instead carted to the asylum where even old Mr. Davies keeps his distance from me. To be a pariah in a place such as this is as isolating an experience as I can imagine. I grieve for my father all while bearing the weight of a crime I did not commit.

Despite the hatred I feel for Mary, or whoever she is, I find myself longing for her. I think I understand now how suicide had freed her of the life I am now imprisoned within. I have considered it often for myself, but at times I swear I hear her humming in the night. Without words, she calls for me.

I know somehow she is coming for me, perhaps through the bond she insisted we share. Whether she comes to free me, kill me, or an unholy amalgamation of the two, she is coming.

Echo Cove

Keiran Meeks

His shoulder was warm against mine as I sat beside him. Even through the damp layers of clothes that separated our bare skin, I could feel the heat of his body seeping into mine. He smelled like body odor, cigarette smoke, and the crusty sea salt that coated everything on Echo Cove. Sitting so close I could almost taste the dark cloud hanging over him.

An island town is always one storm away from being swallowed whole. Back down to the seabed from where life began.

His head tilted toward me; a thick clump of wet hair falling into his eyes before he shoved in a big hand and pushed it away. Our eyes met across the small space between us. Unshed tears made the blue of his eyes glitter under the dim bar lights. He was beautiful, even in his misery or maybe because of it. He was cracked open; the softness of his insides was spilling out. Exposed. What stared back at me was broken, alone, and so beautiful it hurt to look.

Echo Cove was often struck with the dreaded fear that this might be *the one*.

"People call me Fin," he said as we made our hellos and

introductions.

I remember him saying it just like that. *People call me Fin.* Not *my friends call me Fin*, not *you can call me Fin*, or any of the usual ways people introduce a nickname to a stranger. That is just what people call him, like it was out of his control.

He knocked on the bar top without breaking eye contact. I looked away first, down at his hand, and watched the wedding ring glow against his pale skin. I didn't mention it, nor did he, though I know he knew I saw.

The bartender slid a glass of amber and a beer in front of us without a word. The beer was lukewarm and tasted sour and metallic, the same as always. Fin drank his glass with single-minded focus as someone swallowed a spoonful of cough medicine. He sniffed loudly and fisted his eyes. I wondered then what was going through his mind that finally made those pooling tears fall.

When the silence between us became unbearable I mentioned the turn of the weather, how the ocean had been angry today, and wondered how long the storm would last. He softly hummed in response. I glanced at him in the corner of my eye to watch his face. He stared blankly at the bar top, new tears pooling in those glittery blue eyes.

There was something comforting in the closeness.

"I'm divorced," I told him on a sleepy Wednesday afternoon. I can't remember if he asked or if my words were pulled from a desperate need to form a connection. "He took our kids and moved back to the mainland about three years ago."

"That must be lonely," he said through a whiskey grimace.

I think we all get lonely in our own way. I've never needed others to make me feel like a person, but having no one to tell when something funny happened or when I got a promotion at work, that is hard. That's where loneliness grows—the good times, not the bad.

I no longer remember if I told him this.

I saw him once outside the bar, shuffling down the sidewalk like anyone else. From inside the bookshop, I saw his form across the street. Stunned to see him outside the four walls I grew so accustomed to comparing him with, I sat my finds down on a table and hurried out of the store before I lost sight of him. He walked with his head down, staring at his own feet like he was afraid of tripping. He did not notice me running across the trickling traffic.

I called out to him; it took three times to make him pause, and another try to make him turn. His brow wrinkled when his eyes found mine. I slowed to a walk and then stopped at his side.

"Hey," I said. I was suddenly very embarrassed at having chased him down with nothing to say.

"Hey," he repeated slowly. In the full light of the sun, he was pale and gaunt, dark shadows hung under his eyes. He seemed on the verge of sickness.

"I saw you," I told him, "across the street," I pointed over my shoulder. He followed the movement all the way to the bookstore. When his eyes pulled back to settle on me again, his brows rose slowly into his hairline.

"I wasn't sure you existed outside the Lighthouse Tavern." His words stung, but I wanted to believe the slight tug at the corner of his mouth meant he was joking.

I smiled and bumped my shoulder into his. "Where are you headed?"

Together we walked side by side like real people who know each other in real life. Fin was headed to the post office; he had some parts for his plow delivered from the mainland. The sun was shining, the air smelled like spring, and we were walking together. It would've been easy to grab his hands, to lace our fingers together and hold on tight. His fingers brushed mine, our pinkies nearly tangling.

As we slowed, ready to cross the intersection to the post office, a woman shoved a sheet of paper into Fin's hand without so much as a glance before moving on to speak to someone in the small group forming around her. I noticed the noise of the crowd only as Fin froze in step to examine what he'd been given. People moved in close, pushing against me, their combined voices humming like insects.

It was a missing person's flier for a woman named June Digger. Thirty-seven years old, last seen leaving her office one week ago. She was pretty. Dark hair and blue eyes. I recognized her as the face that stood dry and cracked on a bench in the downtown square. The real estate agent promised everyone a fair deal on their dream home.

Now, she was missing.

"Did you know her?" I asked when Fin still hadn't moved.

He startled like he'd forgotten I was there, then shook his head. "I'm sorry," he said, "I'm sorry. I need to go home." He shoved the paper at me, then turned on his heels and began briskly walking back the way we had come. The flier was wrinkled and damp.

"My wife—" outside under the bar's back awning, it was near midnight and raining. My stomach was sour, and my lower back hurt. I just wanted to go home and sleep. I leaned back against the damp brick and inhaled a small breath of the cigarette that was giving me a headache.

"Her name was Emily," his voice was dry and hoarse. "She disappeared ten months ago." His eyes glittered under the dim street light. He exhaled smoke through his nose like fog. "They never found her body, but they closed the case. Declared it a suicide."

"That must be lonely," I said.

He turned to me, and with the light at his back, he glowed beautiful and cracked like a stained glass window. Smoke danced between us, and I could see the scope of our future laid out before me.

I could see him lean in, I would meet him halfway, and we would kiss. I could see his hand slide under my shirt and feel the warmth of his calloused palm scrap against my skin.

His fingers stretched so wide they would close around my heart. I could hear him invite me back to his home, where we would sink into one another and become something new, connected, and whole.

The vision began to fizzle and blur as I tried to conjure the image of him without his grief, without his ache. Who would Phineas Oda be without his misery? Could he even survive?

Just as quickly as it came, that view pinched closed, and I was left standing in the rain, looking up at him as he looked down at me. He nodded gently, then bid me goodnight. As I watched him disappear down the alley, I could still feel the ghost of his touch on my skin.

They say Echo Cover got its name from the unique shape it formed. Something about the bend of the rock and land reverberates sounds from the ocean all the way up to the land high above. It was a neat little trick islanders showed tourists, like putting your ear to a conch shell to hear the ocean.

But the stories say that when they first discovered the island, the settlers would attribute the call of the waves to lost soles wailing from the sea. Some accounts say it was more than just the sounds that echoed back. Some say everything echoes here.

The night a phone call with my sister kept me from the bar, I arrived two hours later than our usual unspoken time. Fin was paying up his tab and readying to leave.

Standing beside him, arms crossed tightly over her chest, was a woman named Tilly I knew worked at the post office.

She was not smiling, and neither was Fin, but it was clear from how close they were standing they were leaving together.

Betrayal and disappointment overtook me. Part of me knew I should not care. The other part of me wanted to scream. I slid up next to Fin at the bar and asked if he was leaving; his gaze shifted to the woman beside him before his eyes dropped, and he confirmed he was.

Tilly was pretty. Her brown hair was professionally streaked with blond, and her nose was splashed with tiny freckles. She smiled meanly at me. Her front tooth was gray.

I waited to the count of one hundred before I followed them out.

The sun was only a sliver over the horizon, but the lights in the parking lot were already lit. I could see Fin and Tilly's forms clearly as they ambled down the sidewalk.

Fin walked with a curve of his shoulders, hunched into himself as though trying to become invisible, his arms curled around his middle. He was a kicked dog, avoiding anyone and everyone's eyes. Tilly walked with her arms crossed, shoulders brushing against Fin's. She spoke a little, though I couldn't hear what she said. Fin never responded, and she eventually stopped trying.

I was lucky that Echo Cove was small enough that most residents walked through town. I followed along a few yards behind. I don't know what I was hoping to see. I had yet to plan what would happen when we reached their destination.

They didn't head toward any neighborhoods. They walked past shops and streets across town, where roads became cracked and sandy. They held hands as they climbed over dunes to a deserted beach of jagged rocks and crashing waves. When they reached the edge, where the high tide splashed around their ankles, they embraced, and Tilly's shorter frame curled into Fin's.

The beach was loud enough for me to follow undetected, with plenty of rocks to hide behind. I settled into the wet sand a couple yards away from the couple and watched as they kissed. Tilly's green acrylic nails clawed sensually at Fin's shoulders and back. The beach smelled like rotting fish.

I only noticed the debris washing ashore farther done the beach once the sheer amount became impossible to ignore. Broken bits of fish, tails of seals, fins of dolphins, octopus and squid tentacles, legs and wings of birds. Two human arms, a man's hand, three human legs, and a naked woman's torso, bloated and discolored. Wave after wave of rotting flesh.

And then, slowly, like the death flutters of an injured bird or beached fish, it began to move. Flopping and undulating a disorganized tempo, the decomposing debris began to crawl together, seeking other broken bits. My body was frozen as the flesh started to fuse, taking the shape of something that wanted to live again. As the pieces crawled atop one another and the mound began to rise, I realized with dawning horror this flesh wanted to be human.

The head that rolled atop the now-standing form could have once been female. The skin was bloated and bruised gray, and the hair was long and black and tangled with sand and seaweed. The eyes were bulging and blue with sickly yellow sclera.

The creature began to move toward the distracted couple with an awkward hunching shuffle of human legs, thin bird talons, and a hobbling slide of a mangled seal tail.

Neither noticed as the creature moved close, shuffling forward on uneven legs. Fin's arms enclosed around Tilly's small frame as the creature reached out toward the pair with two human arms and a rotting gray tentacle.

My body was moving, exposing myself from the safety

of my hiding place before I could even think.

I screamed, I called out. *Please notice, please, god see.*

The warning was lost in the noise of crashing sea and cutting wind. My legs were moving, the sand shifted dangerously underneath, and the brief image flashed in my mind of stumbling, breaking my ankle, crashing into the ground where I would fall and sink and be lost to the world forever. But my body stayed upright, and the creature was upon the couple.

Tilly's scream was loud enough to cut through the air. It was pure basic-level fear, a primal sound forgotten with our rise to the top of the food chain. Fin held tight to one arm as the creature grabbed the other with far more arms.

All the strength hidden behind those curled shoulders meant nothing in the face of a monster. It got its prey, hands, tentacles, and fins wrapped tight around her, pulling her, dragging her back toward the sea as she thrashed, flopping around like a worm on the end of a hook. Fin was jerked with her, stumbling in the sand, falling to one knee, and pushing back upright without losing his grip.

Close enough to see the whites of Tilly's eyes and the tears in Fin's, he finally saw me. I was still running, moving toward   the fight, but when our eyes met, I saw something there that made me freeze, like a deer under car headlights.

His grip on Tilly faltered. She jerked her arm back and used it to hit the creature, jabbing at the gaping fish heads adorning its body. The beast flinched, and Tilly was free. She tried to run, but after only a couple steps, she crumpled violently. The crack was nearly as loud as her scream.

Then, the creature was on her. It didn't try to return to the sea this time. It only opened its mouths, dozens of them, all filled with teeth, and closed around Tilly's face. With a loud, wet crunch, the screams stopped. Blood spurted, and Tilly's body convulsed in the thing's clutches.

The creature pressed Tilly close to its chest when her body fell limp. As I watched, frozen in place, the bloated body opened up, and Tilly's remains were absorbed. She sank into the thing's body, accumulating into the collection. The creature's body pulsed, vibrating. Parts writh. Others squirmed as though trying to escape themselves.

A hand closed around my forearm, and I flinched, so consumed by the sight before me I didn't even notice Fin's approach. When I peered up at my expected savior, his face was grim, mouth pulled down in a wrinkled frown, eyes watery and distant.

I said his name and tasted it on my lips, but he shook his head hard like an angry bull.

"You shouldn't be here," is all he said as he began to walk, pulling me with him.

Once again, a glimpse of our future flashed before my eyes. He would lead me to safety, dragging me through the sand. *Don't look,* he would say; *don't look at what that monster does to poor Tilly.*

I would squeeze my eyes tight because he was warm and strong, and even in his sorrow, he would keep his eyes open all the way back to solid land. We would embrace and be grateful to be alive. We would walk back through the town hand in hand, closer now after what we survived.

The future closed once again as he pulled me into the creature's waiting jaws.

It moves quicker this time. It doesn't bite. There was no time for me to scream. Even the human hands were cold and sticky. It smelled like the sea and rot and lightning. It snatched me from Fin's waiting hand and enclosed me against it like a hug.

There was no pain as I was consumed.

Fish mouths gaped against my skin. The creature cooed in my ear. I turned my head as my skin began to fuse with the creatures. Fin was there, watching. Tears spilled over, droplets danced down his cheek. I watched with aching eyes as he reached out and brushed a strand of dirty black hair behind one of the creature's rotting ears. Then my world went black.

The light came back slowly.

One eye at a time.

She and I and all the others lost at sea.

Nothing more than echoes.

Gaki

Josh Darling

The bedroom Marilyn pulled me into didn't fit the house. The bed was cheap. The walls, bare. There was no mid-century Rococo Revival furniture that decorated the rest of the house. The transported palace had way too much dark wood for a guy who made the bulk of his billions in tech. Old-school New York money was about the dark wood.

They were also about shipping European mansions and castles via ocean freight to Long Island for their homes. Marilyn's husband was a self-made billionaire. He started out like most billionaires. He got millions in interest-free loans from his dad to start his company.

"Look at me," she said.

Her eyes were a faded blue from girlhood summers in East Texas and years on yachts in her teens. Her twang trained out of her in California. Even if she couldn't act, she'd still be nabbed off the street and ushered in the modeling/movie industry.

Film isn't my thing.

Being around her made my breath quicken and heart race. There wasn't much I could do about it. Thinking of my fiance downstairs enjoying the party, I swallowed.

Without breaking eye contact, she locked the door. She pushed me against the wall. She kissed me, forcing her tongue into my mouth.

I couldn't say anything.

No matter her motives, a woman like this kissing you is an insane ego boost.

I kissed her back, betraying Emma a staircase and a few rooms away drinking champagne with her friends and my business colleagues including Marilyn's husband.

She broke the kiss, panting.

"Am I named on the bonds as the recipient if anything happens to Rasmus?"

She bit my jaw and kissed my neck.

She'd been in a string of B-movies. She'd had a bunch of seductive scenes, a few nude scenes. There were sites dedicated to her head Photoshopped onto porn scenes. This isn't unusual for celebrities, even ones whose movies aren't direct to streaming.

"Yes, but only if he dies of natural causes…"

She pushed my shirt up.

She bit where my ribs and stomach met.

"How much would I get?" She was on her knees, those huge blue eyes looking up at me.

She'd probably never heard a man say *No* to her.

I wasn't just betraying Emma, but my father's investment firm.

As much as I'd love to have my cock in her mouth, I didn't love this woman.

Her hand over the front of my pants was fire. There's always that feeling that guys like me, no matter what kind of car we drive—even if it is a Porsche, and we're total Wall St Alphas, don't land women like her. Yeah, banging a headlining stripper at a high-end gentleman's club is crossed off my bucket list as is dating a model—Emma used to be one. This is different. This is something that would be actual news…

Having her there on her knees, had my mind swirled with pornographic delights. I wouldn't be able to cum on her face, she'd have to swallow. Then we'd go down-stairs and I'd buddy up to Emma. Would she smell my cum on Marilyn's breath when they fake hugged as Marilyn pretended she cared what the little people think of her?

Emma, with the engagement ring I put on her finger.

She almost drank the damn thing last week. I had a waiter at 21 hide it in a champagne flute.

I couldn't think…

Marilyn yanked the waist of my pants, getting me back to reality… which didn't feel real. "How much?"

"It's hard to say…"

She ran her hand over the front of my fly. The heel of her palm pressed my shaft.

"It feels very hard, but I think you can say."

She stroked my cock through my pants.

I was almost hyperventilating.

"Stop for a second, I can't think…"

She paused, then bit at the air in front of my cock, a reminder to make with the info. This was client-privileged information. SEC rules aside, it could be bad publicity if it got out…

I could fuck her doggy style on the floor…

I focused on the ceiling.

I closed my eyes trying to remember.

"Gross assets you'd receive would be about a hundred million. There's no income tax, but there is an estate tax that applies to assets over thirteen million, which'll be close to forty percent. New York State will want their cut. That'll be sixteen percent, after taxes, you're looking at forty-six million-ish, but that's a ballpark figure."

I lowered my head.

"That's it?"

"With my firm… yes."

Anger flashed on her face for a second, as if to say *that cheap ass billionaire*. She switched modes back to sex kitten.

"Is there any way to funnel that to an offshore account so I wouldn't have to pay any taxes on it?"

"It'd be hard…"

She caressed the front of my pants, "Mmm, very hard?"

My body pulsed with want.

"I'm not going to jail for you," I exhaled.

She tugged my belt against the buckle "Rasmus is a greedy creepy piece of shit, I want more for what I've had to put up with from him for the last three years."

There were memes about them. Jokes about how a frail, balding, billionaire, who reminded most people of the evil boss on the Simpsons with more hair, could marry her. Their fifty-five-year age difference was a footnote in every article about them.

"This is all hypothetical?" I huffed.

"Not at all," she smiled.

I grabbed her hands. "Let's take a break for a minute. "

She got up and walked to the window.

With actors and women this beautiful, it's hard to tell what's real.

She turned as I stuffed my shirt into my pants, the fabric pressing against my erection.

"He's had me followed, tapped my phone—"

"People still tap phones?" I said.

"He *cloned* my phone, he has goons who hack into everything I do. I had to get a burner phone at a convenience store and even then I was followed. I stopped sleeping with him about a year ago, but he put cameras in the bedroom. He's not blackmailing me, he knows he can't do that, he's just stealing any privacy I have. He does this to everyone. He's made a separate fortune blackmailing people by hacking them."

"Divorce him."

"I signed a prenup, I'd get nothing, he has to die. Even then, I'm not getting a whole lot."

"Forty-six million is nothing to sneeze at. The annual interest is about two and a half million, rounded up."

"Forbes has him valued at thirty-two billion, that's fuck you money."

Most men try not to stare at women's breasts, with Marilyn you stare at all of her.

"Oh yes, I made mistakes, big ones. He is charming, well, was. I was attracted to his intellect, but I made the mistake of not being attracted to him. The more and more I thought about him, the more and more it occurred to me, the intellect wasn't real. He knows how to make money through cruelty and connections."

"That's all and good, but I'm not going to be part of a plot to assassinate my firm's biggest client."

"There's nothing you can do about it. The plan is in motion, don't worry, no one will know, and don't freak out when the lights go out. He'll die of natural causes… soon."

"Why are you telling me this?"

"Because it doesn't matter, maybe because I want to confess something to someone. I grew up Catholic…"

Five years ago she would have been graduating from Catholic school. I pictured her in a white shirt, plaid skirt, knee-high socks…

She continued, "I found out he started bugging me when I went to confession. I didn't believe in God anymore when I was confessing, I needed someone to talk to. He figured out ways to cut me off from friends and family. A therapist you can pay off. He would withhold my allowance and what could I do?"

"That's beyond me."

"While everyone was prepping for this party, I was clearing everything out of this room—not the servants, me. That's what I had to do so I could talk to you. I'll totally suck your cock if you're into it.

That man is so repulsive. He smells old, his skin is saggy, and he can only get a hard-on if I cry for him, that's why he says he married me, because I can cry on cue. Sex with him is gross. Getting him hard was easy, he could only cum if he saw the company gaining on the stock market. You're not bad-looking, and the idea of sex with someone young is hot after two years of that old man grunting on top of me."

"I'm probably an idiot here because you're one of the most beautiful women I've ever seen in my life, but I love Emma," I ached to be inside Marilyn. "You telling me about this plan makes me an accomplice after the fact. I'm legally obligated to tell the authorities."

"It doesn't matter, he's already been dealt with. No matter what you tell anyone, the greedy bastard will be declared dead of natural causes."

I'd already seen Rasmus walking around the party in his tux. He held a champagne flute in his left hand. His right hand was free to shake and greet guests as they approached him.

Turning to leave, she muttered behind me, "Rasmus is a greedy fucking bastard…"

I headed outside to cool down.

There were about seven hundred-plus guests. Half of them were inside. The rest were around the pool. From an outsider's perspective, you'd expect more celebrities, actors, rock stars, and influencers.

The reality is this crowd didn't care about them. The artistic types only had a few million dollars. The people here were financial celebrities. Their great performances here were in profits. These rock stars didn't sell out, they bought in using generational wealth. These influencers shifted global financial markets.

Stylish gas heaters surrounded the pool as an October mist twisted over the surface. The chilled evening air made wearing a jacket easier. This was Rasmus' autumn/winter house on Long Island. It was closer to the city, reducing his commute time by a half hour. His summer home in the Hamptons took forty-five minutes to get there.

Beyond the pool were three acres of lawn and four helicopters waiting in the darkness. One belonged to Rasmus, and the other three I don't know. An illuminated dock stretched into the Long Island Sound.

His yacht was not in.

The sprawl of the estate would have put Gatsby to shame—his story set a few towns over.

Emma was not with the outside crowd.

She had done runway modeling, not something one gets famous for. It was a thing her mom had her do to keep her bulimic for family photos. It also guaranteed she didn't put on weight while in college. They were California people and image was everything.

When she chose poly-sci over majoring in theater, her entertainment lawyer father sent her an Academy Award statue crying black magic marker tears.

That's how she tells the story of choosing to s*plit the difference and become a communications major*. I met her when the PR firm she worked at was hired for the online trading division of my father's firm.

I headed inside the house.

Rasmus said, "Oh, the poor child workers."

People around him giggled and laughed.

He was holding court in the middle of one of his many living rooms.

Emma was next to him texting on her phone.

He smiled at her.

I had the unfortunate image of him fucking a crying Marilyn while watching a stock ticker on a tablet.

"You know, you might want some better spin on that, not that I work at a PR firm," Emma grinned back.

Touching her elbow, he laughed, "But, but," he swallowed a gulp of champagne, "I don't care. You talk about PR, but I've got stock in BHP, Gen Corp, China Molybdenum, and Cobalt Blue Holdings, and those are the ones I can remember off the top of my head. I've got so many holdings in East Asia I'd have to double-check what I own.

I don't care if children die, as long as the money comes in. I'm not some twisted pervert who went to Epstein Island, all I care about is profit, not how I look. Nike and Disney do the same thing and they're hip."

"Yeah, but Nike and Disney have awesome PR so they are way out in front of that stuff. To the average American, those companies are woke."

She was trying to land a whale of a client for her firm. If she could get him to sign off on a PR campaign, even a small one, she'd make partner.

Fixating on him touching her elbow, I thought of the tabloid press he'd gotten for his alleged affairs. Letting go of her elbow, he fanned himself with his open hand, "Hot in here."

I couldn't tell if he was making an awkward pass at Emma. His face flushed maroon.

"Whoa, I may have had a little bit too much," he said, shaking his head.

It was the first time I'd seen Rasmus admitted to fault.

One of his bodyguards approached.

"I'm fine, I'm fine," Rasmus looked at me, "Junior, your wife is trying to pull a fast one on me."

I was a IVth, not a junior, but I didn't care. My firm wanted the old bastard's investments.

"The thing about PR is, it's a lot of money, for a whole little of opinion, and I didn't get to where I am by caring an iota what anyone thinks."

"Not even the people who love you," Marilyn drained a champagne flute.

The lights went out.

Some women made a surprised *oh* sound. Party guests used their cell phones for lights. Parties like this are not for fun. More business gets done at gatherings like these than during the weekdays in offices. Things are agreed on here. The lawyers figure out the details and the language during billable hours.

Emma's cell phone cast light upward, "At least it's interesting." she winked at me.

The bodyguard mumbled into his cufflink about watching the perimeter.

"Aren't you going to fix it?" Rasmus said.

"I'm going nowhere, this is how I'd kick off a kidnapping," the bodyguard shot back.

"Shit, I think I'm having another heart attack." Still holding the champagne flute, Rasmus clutched the left side of his chest. "Can someone call an ambulance, like now, I'm having a heart attack. Get the defibrillator from the hallway closet."

After dialing, a wave of phones illuminated faces.

Rasmus sat on the floor.

Emma pressed the screen to make a call on hers.

I reached for mine.

After d   ialing, I put my phone to my ear.

"You assholes drink my champagne, enjoy my home, ogle my wife's tits and ass, and use my fucking money for your causes, but none of you can get a fucking ambulance here? You people are useless leeches. I'm going to take back everything I gave each of you. It's all mine and I'll have more and you'll have nothing, anyway."

He lowered himself to the floor.

In seconds, Marilyn supported his head. She helped him to recline on the Persian carpeted floor.

"Is there a doctor in the house?" she shouted.

How couldn't there be?

Easily, if she planned this…

She put her ear on her husband's chest.

"Somebody help," she screamed.

Tears glistened on her cheeks. They glowed orange reflecting the flame of the outdoor heaters.

The bodyguard knelt beside his client. He spoke into his cufflink. Counting, he started pushing on Rasmus's ribs doing chest compressions.

"We need a doctor, now!" Marilyn shrieked.

Another security guard grabbed her by the back of her arms. He lifted her to her feet, and shouted "Please, call an ambulance."

"Can you call?" Emma asked.

I looked at my silent phone.

The screen said *Dialing*, but in the upper right corner *Searching for Signal*.

I have no idea what the other people in the house thought was going on. Somehow, Marilyn was jamming the signal. She probably found a tech geek or some crazed fan to do it for her.

An overweight balding man huffed his way to the bodyguards beside their client on the floor.

"I'm a doctor," he said.

The bodyguard, with a cell phone to his ear, said, "Save him."

"Oh, I don't…"

"What's the matter? This man is having a heart attack. We're giving him CPR, can you help?"

"I'm a researcher, I do gene splicing experiments with mice."

Another bodyguard came up from behind the doctor, "Get his shirt off." He carried a red box with a stamped heart with a yellow lightning bolt in the middle. It was a defibrillator.

They ripped open Rasmus's shirt.

The bodyguard with the defibrillator squeezed gel onto the paddles. He rubbed them together, then pressed them on Rasmus's gray-haired chest.

"Clear."

Rasmus convulsed.

Marilyn's jaw trembled.

She did an amazing job playing her part, or maybe she didn't anticipate her billionaire husband having a defibrillator handy.

The bodyguard on the phone screamed "Fuck!"

Someone from the back of the room called, "No one's getting a signal."

The bodyguard giving Rasmus chest compressions talked into his cuff link, "Bring the van around front."

The guard on the phone felt for a pulse, "I've got nothing."

"Clear!"

Rasmus convulsed.

Marilyn shouted for a doctor again.

The room filled with mumbles.

Both of the bodyguards sweated thick beads of worry.

"I'm still not feeling anything."

"Clear!"

Into the cufflink, "We're going to need the immobilizer. We'll keep defibrillating him until we get to the hospital, he has to be DOA at the hospital."

"I think you've lost him," the research scientist said.

"I still don't have a pulse, and shut the fuck up, fat boy," a bodyguard shouted.

"Clear!"

Rasmus seized on the floor.

Emma and I pressed our phones to our ears. We redialed *911* every few minutes but were stonewalled by digital silence.

The snippets of conversation moved in a panorama behind me:

If he's dead, the market is going to dip tomorrow.

At least the children slaving away for him in China will still have jobs.

Too bad I can't live stream this, I'd make bank.

I wondered if any of that would make it to his eulogy.

The bodyguard with the defibrillator called "Clear!"

A faint white shape darted out of Rasmus.

It dissipated.

The bodyguard talking to his cufflink made an awful noise. A mewing mixed with pain.

He stuck his tongue out. In the air, an invisible force pinched it.

The end of his tongue disappeared.

Blood shot forward. He held his hands before his face. Keeping his mouth open, a waterfall of crimson fell over his chin.

A faint trace of Rasmus's ribcage flashed in the air, his hands on the guard's face.

It went invisible.

"Holy fuck," I said.

Emma didn't move.

She smacked at her chest as translucent blue teeth bit the exposed top of her breast.

Subcutaneous layers of skin broke, forming a concave circle.

It broke off her.

The chunk of flesh vanished into the air. Blood slipped

through her fingers pulling down the front of her beaded Elie Saab dress.

Marilyn ran down a hallway.

I'd never seen anyone sprint in heels.

Emma fell onto the Persian-carpeted marble floor.

Rasmus's jellyfish-like body glowed overhead then turned into nothingness as another woman in a black Vera Wang dress slapped at her face. Within seconds, he took a piece out of her cheek. The great hole exposed teeth.

I got on my knees, "Are you okay?"

I cradled Emma.

The bodyguards drew their guns. They pointed their weapons at the Rasmus thing floating in the air.

She winced, clasping her hands to her wounded chest.

"Let me know you're okay?" I said.

"I'm not fucking okay, this fucking hurts."

The bodyguard with a goatee of blood fired his gun. Half the people in the room ducked. The rest stampeded for the doors.

Rasmus grabbed onto a running man and drifted with him for a second. Rasmus bit the back of the man's head. This bite sunk into the flesh and cracked his skull. The man fell to the ground. He seized, his pink brains leaking out on the hand-knotted Persian rug.

One of the bodyguards kept his gun up as the other examined their coworker's gaping mouth.

"Let's move."

The men abandoned Rasmus's body.

The ghost—let's be honest and call it what it is *a ghost*—chased party guests out of the front of the house. As it went, it ripped pieces out of Rasmus's various underlings and their spouses.

Emma growled in my arms.

She touched the crater in her flesh where her breast and ribs met.

"Fuck that's going to leave a scar," she said, "I want to throw up, it hurts so bad…"

Hot and cool leaked from her onto my hands.

The guests screamed running for the front gate. Some hid in the topiary in the acreage between the main Estate building made from the European transplanted castle, the garages, servants' homes, and the horse stable. The wives hiked up their gowns, ditched their heels, and outran their fat ass husbands.

Car alarms blared in the driveway as European sports cars started and crashed into luxury sedans in the chaos.

"I can't fucking believe this," I said, "he's a ghost."

"He's a wraith," Emma said.

"A what?"

"Call me an ambulance…"

Using my thumb, I dialed 911 again…

Searching for Signal…

I redialed and redialed.

"What's a wraith?" I held the phone to my ear hearing nothing.

"A vengeful spirit. Didn't you go to summer camp and tell scary stories? Anything?"

"Yeah, still no signal. Do you think you can walk?"

"This hurts so much, but yeah…"

"Let me get you vertical, this way you're not using your upper body for anything."

A lean man in his early sixties with white hair trotted into the room, "Don't move her. She's more likely to bleed out. You're not going to get a cellphone signal, I have a feeling they're being jammed. This feels strategic."

"What should I do? Wait around for that thing to come back and kill us? I need to get her to a hospital."

"You're not going to get out of here. Some asshole who got his face bit off got behind the wheel of one of those Ferraris from the sixties –he floored it into the front gate. It didn't explode, but it's on fire. The gates in one piece, and that says a lot for craftsmanship."

The front gate was made out of stacked stone and heavy wrought iron spiked bars.

"It's a shame, really," the white haired man continued, "about the car that is."

"I don't know what to do," I shook my head.

Between Emma's fingers, the wound revealed itself. It was an inch or two deep.

Dropping my phone to the floor, I pulled off my Burberry silk tie "Use this." Balling up the tie, I put it over her wound.

I'd dropped acid in college, this didn't feel like that. Those hallucinations I could tell weren't real, no matter how solid they seemed.

This was different.

This was a reckoning of the laws of the universe. A man had died. His translucent ghost exited his body and flew around his house and front yard biting people.

That was real.

It was a thing that happened.

If ghosts were real, did that mean all spiritual beings of the world were real? Did good and evil exist? Was all that bullshit in the Bible and/or Quran real in some way? Would I have to answer for the things I'd done?

Emma wailed in my arms.

"Marilyn did this," I said.

"What?"

"Fifteen minutes ago she told me she was going to kill him. She was asking me all these questions about finance and stuff."

Given Emma's condition, I figured it wasn't the best time to mention Marilyn offered to suck my cock.

"Find her and offer her to the ghost," Emma returned to making agony sounds.

Yeah, sure, it's not a crime to kill someone by offering them to a ghost. *Rasmus had already killed a number of his party guests, what would one more be? Would anyone even believe what happened?*

The asshole was biting chunks out of people. There was no way I could get pinned for it.

Yes, I love Emma—even with a hole in her chest a plastic surgeon might not be able to correct.

That blue eyed, blonde haired, fake titty bitch was going to die.

On the front lawn, people scattered in tiny schools like minnows evading a predator.

"Can I leave you here? I'll find her, I'll bring her to him, but I need to know it's okay. You're the love of my life, you know that?"

"I'll die if you don't do it fast enough, I feel light-headed…"

I lowered her head to the floor.

I pulled off my tuxedo jacket and placed it between Emma's head and the floor.

I smiled at her. Maybe it was to reassure her or myself, but in that moment, my love for her was more real than ever before.

I started down the West Wing of the transplanted castle.

The interior walls were Tudor stucco, not the stone surfaces seen from the outside. This kept the interior from looking like a giant dungeon.

I assumed Marilyn had headed this way. Everything happened so fast. Minutes ago, I'd seen a man die, become a ghost, bite chunks out of millionaires, which caused a minor existential crisis, and endanger the life of my fianceé. She could be some place else in the giant house.

I crab-walked down the hallway.

It felt the right way to hunt a movie starlet.

Heading down the corridor, I heard a conversation…

Mixed words.

The language was Asian but I couldn't place the country.

Rounding the corner, a man talked a million miles a second.

Takashi Ito, he'd made billions with an online fashion platform. Last year, he'd been to the International Space Station. He was nice enough, but once he started talking, that was all he talked about.

"Gaki, gaki, gaki," he said.

He paced the room, redialing his phone, speaking to no one.

"Hey," I said.

"I'll pay you a million dollars if you can get me past the gaki." He redialed his phone.

"I don't know what that is. You see Marilyn? Someone needs to tell her about Rasmus."

"It's a hungry ghost." I'd say his English was perfect if he didn't speak with a British accent.

"I get that, but I think it's a ghost that needs the right kind of food."

"Get me past it."

"My fianceé is bleeding out."

"Five million…"

I restarted crab-walking in the hallway.

I tread with the same feeling in my gut as when I'd been on Safari.

Marilyn was a lioness needing to be cut down.

Crying echoed down the hall.

When Rasmus couldn't be revived, the bodyguards fled.

They didn't care about Marilyn.

Their assignment a failure, they escaped with their lives.

She wasn't paying them.

The sobs were feminine.

Previously, I'd heard those sobs at the premiere of the indie drama *The Travels of Lafcadio Hearn* –a super boring art film about an Irish translator who travels the US in the 1800s and marries a former slave.

I'd stalked the right path.

She was close.

She'd found a room with a few embroidered couches, the kind stuffed with horsehair and had an old-American puritanical stiffness. She knelt behind one of the couches. I got on my haunches and did my best not to look down her dress at her semi-famous breasts.

"I did this, this is my fault…" sobbing interrupted the rest of her words.

"This isn't your fault. Hey, who knows what's going on? This is some wild stuff."

Did it sound natural? Or did I sound like a pervert offering a child candy to get them into the back of a van?

She didn't stop with the boo-wooing…

"Marilyn, I need to tell you something, and I hope it's not weird, but I wanted you. Earlier, when I said no to you, it wasn't because I don't desire you. It's because I want you that bad. I wanted to start things right with you. Thinking there was a chance I could be with you, I wanted to break things off with Emma. I wanted to start clean and right with you."

She raised her lyrical blue eyes.

Makeup streaking down her face didn't look bad on her. Her natural atheistic was the kind that no matter what she did—makeup, no makeup, a psychotic crumbling mess— she'd still be just as sexy.

She pushed her tears off high cheekbones.

"I'm sorry, I should have taken that into consideration…" she sniffed the air.

Her crying stopped.

She'd been waiting for someone, she needed emotional support to pull this off. I guess the guy with access to her husband's funds made as good a shoulder as any.

We were both hunting…

"I don't want you to think I was with Rasmus for the money. I really loved him. As he got more and more controlling, I started to think of you, you became my dream of escape."

"I know how to get out of here. Rasmus, the ghost, whatever that thing is, it's on the front lawn. I can't believe I'm saying this, but he's haunting closer to this side of the property. I was thinking we head straight across to the other side. We have to move fast, he's taking bites out of people left and right. He's going to run out of people soon."

She snorted, her acting outperformed her work in pictures, "What about Emma?"

"She's dead. Honestly, it's a relief. I realized everything I want was in that room about fifteen minutes ago."

I'd like to thank the Academy of Motion Pictures for this award…

"Let's get out of here, and then we'll figure out what's next for us."

She slipped her heels off and followed me.

We headed back. Passing the open door with Takashi still trying to get a signal on his phone. He fixated on the window watching the front lawn.

Taking Marilyn's hand, I led her down the hall. Both of us jogged until we reached Rasum's corpse and Emma on the floor. Tears in her eyes, she pressed my tie to the wound in her chest.

"You said she was dead?"

Grabbing Marilyn's arms above the elbow, I pinned them behind her back.

"What the fuck!" she screamed.

"Rasmus, I've got her, take your revenge, you son of

bitch."

Marilyn thrashed her head back, almost catching me in the mouth. Her hair whipped my face with a rush of air. The back of her head pounded my chest. Kicking in the air, I had to support the weight of her body.

"Rasmus, you piece of shit," my voice echoed off the vaulted ceilings.

Marilyn started slipping through my grasp.

I clutched her wrists, I didn't know how much longer I could hold her.

My thumbs ached fighting to hold on to her.

I pictured carrying Emma out of the transplanted castle. I'd hold her crossing the threshold of the massive lawn and get her to a waiting ambulance—a meaningless fantasy if Marilyn escaped.

Whipping and jerking her body, her movements a grand-mal seizure of resistance.

Getting a hand free, Marilyn spun. She dragged her nails down the front of my face.

Focusing on the pain, I let go of her, clutching my wounds.

Red dots speckled my palms.

She broke the skin.

Marilyn was fast.

She was almost to the other end of the room when Rasmus passed through the wall cutting her off. She sprinted toward me.

Rasmus barreled down on her.

As the distance between us diminished, I knew I needed to catch her.

I darted for her, she tried to cut around me.

Ungentlemanly as it is, extending my arm, I clotheslined her, catching her neck. She hit the floor and I turned, pinning her. Choking, she coughed.

Rasmus floated over us.

Wheezing in, she cocked her arm and punched me in the nose. She'd worked on a few action movies and I guess they taught her how to hit because before I could get my hands to my nose, blood and snot spurted on her cleavage in a snorted money shot.

"Ew, gross," she said.

Marilyn kneed me in the balls.

I doubled over.

The pain was instant and shooting.

Pushing me to the side, she hopped to her feet. The translucent specter grabbed her, pushing her across the floor. She flailed at it. Her hands passed through the thing clutching her. Its mouth opened like a snake unhinging its jaw.

I didn't care what happened to her.

I got to my feet as best as I could.

Clutching my balls, I headed for Emma.

Marilyn screamed behind me.

Looking back, Rasmus wasn't following. His teeth were sawing through her gown to get a huge chunk of her stomach and ribs. My ears twitched at her screaming.

He didn't seem to be stopping or losing power.

I made it to Emma.

Her eyes were closed.

Not knowing if she was dead, I slid an arm under her.

"Be gentle, it hurts so fucking bad."

"Good, you're alive." Smiling, I tasted the blood trickling   from my nose.

I lifted her. Carrying her wedding threshold style, I was out the front door fast. I headed for the front gates of the mansion.

In the distance, the bonfire of an antique sports car smoldered.

The blaze, a beacon for the front gates.

Men in tuxedos and women in designer gowns hid behind trees and massive sculptures. In the escapes of grass, some darted for the gates.

Why were there no cops?

This has all happened in a few minutes…

Had no one escaped?

I began jogging, trying my best to not bounce Emma around. I worried the turbulence would make her bleed out. She had one arm behind my neck. The other hand pinned my blood soaked to tie over the hole in her chest. Panting, red drops of my blood mixed with hers on her stomach.

Pain seeped into my arms and back from carrying her.

I didn't know how much farther I could go.

There was so much driveway left.

"You have to go faster honey, the Rasmus is out of the house," Emma said, looking over my shoulder.

Racing down the gravel driveway, my Italian loafers felt like slippers made of brick.

I focused on the distant car fire. While others criss-crossed the lawn in a panic or hid, my plan was to make a straight line for it.

"He just got Whitney Van Den Ende, I hated that bitch. *Faster honey…*"

The flames from the car flared for a second.

My shirt clung to my sweat-soaked body.

Would the car explode?

How would we fit through the gate?

The gate was sixteen feet high, iron, and spiked, like an exaggerated gate from an old cemetery.

I'd crossed more than half of the front lawn when the screams rose around us.

"He's getting close again, *faster…*"

My lungs burned.

Smoke wafted in my face, my eyes teared…

Red and blue lights flickered in the distance.

The calvary.

"It just got Max Bornstein *faster*…"

Running plus the weight of her in my arms made me question if I could do this. We might have crossed a half mile or so of his front yard but that didn't mean I had anything left in me. A hundred feet from the bonfire of late-sixties Italian automotive perfection, the heat reached my face.

The car had rammed the gates. One of the gates rested on top of the car. The other was set on the diagonal hanging onto the stone frame by its upper hinge. Given our luck, it would fall on us passing under it.

Police cruisers stopped in front of the gates. Cops got out and watched.

The bastards wouldn't enter the gates.

A man in a black tuxedo approached them shouting…

Emma slipped in my arms.

With a bounce in my step, I raised her back into the bridal hold.

She slipped again. Stopping, I did the same move, getting her back into position.

"He's right behind us, *faster*…"

I sprinted.

I gave it everything.

As the flames from the car began scorching like desert heat, Emma shrieked.

A cold jolt pressed against me, as my arms felt buoyant.

Emma kicked as incorporeal hands passed through me, grabbing her, stealing her from me. Rasmus lifted her into the air.

His ghostly mouth closed around her throat.

She beat at the air connecting with nothing.

Rasmus flickered opacity. For a second, his jellyfish body seemed tangible. Then he was gone.

The side of her neck burst out.

Air-cooled blood rained down on me.

He released her.

Her body hit the gravel.

Dead, she clumped over herself.

No, I didn't check, I bolted for the gate.

I ran around the flaming car.

Passing under the gate, I raised my hand. It was a tight fit.

I screamed.

Hot iron burned the inside of my hand.

Maybe I'm a coward.

Maybe I'm an asshole.

I am alive, and that's real.

The cops looked at me like cows in a pasture gazing at a passing car.

"What the fuck are you assholes doing? People are dying in there, go save them," the words exiting my throat burned.

No one moved with urgency.

"What the fuck is wrong with you? Do something,"

I said.

"Sir," an officer gestured at the gate behind me.

Rasmus floated parallel to the gate eyeing the cops. Seeing him, I jolted.

"It's okay, they can't cross iron," he said.

"What?"

"Every few years something like this happens. You know, people think ghosts happen over years, but they can happen at the moment of death. Every now and then, one of these rich and greedy types dies and they're still shit heads after death."

I couldn't process this new reality.

"Why isn't my fiancée   a ghost, busy eating people?"

"I don't have all the answers, I can just tell you what happens."

"Why not tell people about this? What is wrong with you assholes?"

"Would you believe anyone if they told you about this? Follow me," the officer said, leading me to his car. He opened the passenger side door. Getting in, I kept my feet on the pavement.

Shocks of pain radiated from the balls of my feet to my heels.

More people headed for the gate, the cop cars giving them hope.

Rasmus picked them off as they attempted the run for safety.

The officer said, "Daylight weakens spirits," I couldn't hear the rest of what he said. There was too much to process. There were the big existential questions, and the little questions, like what was my life now without Emma?

Ambulances pulled in along the iron fence to help those who made it through.

I stayed in the car, waiting for sunrise.

Dead Mall

Paul Lonardo

Up until the moment they spotted the old theater, everything had gone as expected; not much different than any of the other 'dead malls' that they investigated and documented for the two-million-plus subscribers over the past three years.

Prior to that, they'd made a pass on all three floors. With her iPhone, Anneke had captured all the haunted imagery the team would need for their next episode.

Aiyden would edit the content, Channing would add extra commentary, and she would upload the final product onto their social media sites.

She had recorded the vestiges of humanity; left-behind scarves, gloves, and coffee cups. She had documented the conquest of nature; empty bird nests, intricate spiderwebs, and an active wasp hive. Latex gloves and discarded syringes were strewn all over the place, and they even came across a .38 shell casing.

But then Channing pointed toward the other end of the third-floor promenade. "Hey, we haven't been down there yet," he remarked.

"You sure?" Anneke asked. "I think we have."

The truth was Anneke had seen more than enough already. In the high-intensity brightness of their handheld LED flashlights, it looked to her that Channing and Aiyden were becoming less human the longer they remained inside the three-story wasteland of empty retail stores that had been vandalized and picked clean by scrappers.

She didn't know why, but she felt like they were all becoming part of the desolate environment they had invaded.

Once they caught sight of the ticket booth below a marquee that still held the title of the last movie that played in the theater, *SCREAM 3*, Anneke knew there was nothing she could say that would convince them to leave.

"Holy shit," Channing howled. "Check out the old movie that was playing when this place closed. What was that, like forty years ago, dude?"

"More like twenty, I think," Aiyden told him.

"Come on," Channing said. "Let's go in."

Anneke slowly panned down to the theater doors and walked in behind Channing and Aiyden. The screen at the front was empty, but some of the seats were not. Aiyden noticed them first and screamed, startling Channing. "What the hell's your problem?" he began, then he saw them. "What the fuck?" he mouthed quietly, questioning what he was seeing.

Anneke, still looking through her phone at what she was filming, did not see the heads until she looked up from the screen. She sucked in a mouthful of air and   froze. For a moment, no one spoke, as if anticipating the people sitting in the total darkness of a theater in a dead mall would suddenly turn around to see where the intrusive light was coming from. But these midnight matinee filmgoers remained perfectly still.

"H-Hello." Aiyden's voice cracked with fear, and he began taking small, apprehensive steps backward toward the door.

There were about six people seated in front of the theater, and when Channing directed his flashlight toward the back, he revealed at least a half dozen more. The light illuminated their faces, which were shocking and frightful. Their mouths were hinged open in a frozen rictus of laughter, the jaws separated far wider than humanly possible.

"They're mannequins," Channing said with a sense of relief.

"What?" Aiyden said, stopping his progress at once.

Channing walked up the aisle toward the closest mannequin. It was just a torso that included the head and arms. "Anneke, make sure you get this," he said. "Come closer."

Anneke struggled to keep her hands steady as Channing spoke to their followers.

"This is exactly the way we found them," he began. "We were about to leave when we found the theater, and these creepy mannequins spread all around, none of them seated together, their mouths open wide."

Anneke was hardly listening to him as she followed him around from one mannequin to another. They were all wearing various-colored wigs and faded shirts or tank tops. Some of them had no arms.

"It's hard to tell if they're laughing or screaming," Channing continued. "They've just been sitting here in the dark like this for decades, as if waiting for the projector to turn on and the movie to start. Finally, the show has started, only they're the ones on camera.

So creepy.

Who would even make mannequins with expressions like this?" He stepped out of the way and whispered to Anneke, "Get a close up of this one."

She zoomed in on the mannequin's gaping maw, but closed her eyes and held them tight.

"All right, you guys ready to go?" she asked when

Channing concluded his cryptic discourse to their followers.

Before anyone could voice a response, a shuffling noise out in the promenade drew their attention. They turned their heads toward the door and listened in rapt silence until whatever it was stopped.

"There's someone in here with us." Aiyden whispered.

"Fuck that," Channing said extra loud. "It's probably a squirrel or a racoon or something. This place must be infested with rodents."

"We got everything we need for the episode," Anneke said. "Let's just get out of here."

"I'm with Anneke," Aiyden asserted. "That sounds like a good idea to me."

"Hold on," Channing began. "You think there are some others in here, maybe there are. So why not get it on film. All we really got right now is just another empty mall."

"And the mannequins," Aiyden added.

"And the mannequins," Channing conceded. "But even if you're wrong and I'm right, at least we'll get a family of cute little skunks or something to include in the episode. People love that shit."

"Only if there *is* someone in here, they could be dangerous," Anneke said. "A crazed homeless guy or drug dealers or the cops or…" She stopped there.

"Or what?" Channing goaded, an impish smile giving himself away to her. "What are you afraid of, anyway? Leave the camera on so the subscribers can see you cry. Because that's about the only thing that will make this episode worth watching. Cry. Go ahead. You know you want to. That's all you're good for, anyway. You're a useless little bitch, and you know it."

"All right, Channing, that's enough," Aiyden intervened.

Anneke glared at Channing, trying to play it cool, but

she found herself being seduced by him, anyway. He knew exactly how to push her buttons. But being domineering with her in this situation made her feel even more vulnerable, which only added to her sexual excitement.

Aiyden didn't want to be in the theater with the two of them or the mannequins any longer, and he walked out by himself, willing to take his chances with whatever was out there.

The thing that caused him the most anxiety was when Anneke mentioned the potential of police involvement. He was the only one who was over eighteen, and with his past infractions for breaking and entering, criminal trespassing, and conspiracy, he knew he could go to jail if he ran afoul of the law again.

Swiveling his flashlight around, he searched the darkness for any trace of animal presence. Everywhere he aimed, there was nothing to see. The upper floor of the massive pedestrian promenade was completely empty. Even the light fixtures had been pilfered.

There wasn't even a shopping cart in sight. The windows of all the stores were broken, and glass shards covered the floor. The security gates had been ripped apart. There were no handrails on the upper floors. Portions of the ceiling had collapsed and there were pools of standing water, brown and frothy, with clots of rodent hair floating on the surface.

The stench of mold and rot was overwhelming. It was so dystopian. The place reminded Aiyden of that abandoned amusement park in the Ukrainian town that had to be evacuated after the Chernobyl nuclear accident.

He turned around to see what was keeping Channing and Anneke and instantly drew back with a sharp yelp when he noticed someone standing directly behind him. As soon as he saw the uniform and hat, he started to explain what he and his friends were doing there.

"We were just leaving, officer," he began. "My friends and I post social media content for…" He stopped when he realized he was talking to a mannequin dressed as a police officer.

He tapped the mannequin's cheek with an index finger to be sure it was fake. It made an empty, hollow sound and he laughed lightly.

Channing and Anneke emerged from the theater. "That movie really sucked," he joked. When he saw Aiyden he said, "I see you made a new friend."

"This wasn't here when we came in," Aiyden said with panic in his voice.

"Sure, it was," Channing told him.

"I didn't see it, either," Anneke said.

"All right, you didn't see it, but it was there. Just like all the animals living in this place that you don't see but are here."

"I'm done with his place," Aiyden announced, and headed off.

"Me too," Anneke said, and followed.

"Pussies." Channing punched the mannequin in the face. The fiberglass cop fell to the floor with a thump. "You're both pathetic. Afraid of these things." He kicked the dummy, sending it scuttling across the floor and then walked away, in no hurry to catch up with the other two.

Anneke shut off her phone and stuffed it into her pocket, trading it for her flashlight.

As Channing lagged behind, he started to get a strange feeling that he was being watched. He stopped to shine his flashlight around, but he didn't see anything. Before he started moving again, his flashlight suddenly went out and he was engulfed in total darkness.

Anneke and Aiyden had already started walking down the fixed escalator to the second floor.

Channing heard a shuffling sound behind him, and he

frantically struck the flashlight repeatedly to get it to work. It blinked several times before remaining on. Turning quickly, he shined the beam behind him but there was nothing there.

He didn't want to act like he had been alarmed in any way, walking slowly down the escalator to join his friends. They were on the first floor as he was still descending to the second when he heard something moving on the floor above him.

He turned in that direction without using the light and saw a shadowy figure at the top of the escalator. He couldn't be sure it was there, and he was even less sure   it was a mannequin with the face of a demon, maybe even the devil himself, so he told himself it was only his imagination, and continued on.

When he caught up with the others, he didn't tell them what he had heard or seen.

While walking through the shadowy promenade, from the vacant shops behind them and in front of them came a series of shuffling sounds of the kind   someone might make when they dragged their feet—heavy feet—feet that were not flesh and bone.

"Do you hear that?" Anneke asked, looking directly at Channing.

"Still think it's animals?" Aiyden chimed in.

"Let's just get out of here," Anneke said. "Hurry."

As the shuffling continued, she got no argument, not even from Channing. When they reached the corner of the mall where they had entered through a jagged hole in the masonry no more than an hour earlier, there was a vacant store instead.

"What's going on here?" Aiyden said. "This isn't where we came in."

"We must have gone the wrong way," Channing announced.

"No, this is where we came in," Anneke countered. "I remember. The escalator was in front of us."

"We went the wrong way!" Channing shouted. According to his way of thinking, speaking the loudest made you right. By that measure, he was right a lot. "We got to double back." The noise suddenly stopped. "Let's go." He led the way, Aiyden and Anneke hesitantly following.

Anneke gasped and they all froze as the edges of their beams caught unexpected images of mannequins occupying the otherwise empty shops all around them. They were just regular department store mannequins in a variety of sizes and poses, displaying clothing lines that had long since gone out of style.

"Those definitely weren't here before, Channing." Aiyden's voice was weak. He was trembling.

"Someone's fucking with us!" Channing yelled. "I'm going to kill whoever's doing this." He reached into his pocket and withdrew a double action knife. He slid the switch, releasing the blade.

Hearing a sound above, Channing raised his flashlight, directing it up to the third floor. Something moved away from the light near the top of the escalator.

"All right, you fuck, you want to play games. I can play, too." Channing charged toward the escalator and started up, flashlight in one hand, knife in the other.

Aiyden and Anneke turned to one another, their expressions fraught with concern and terror.

Channing disappeared somewhere on the top floor. They could see the glow of his flashlight and hear the anger in his voice. "Where the hell are you? Come on out."

A moment later, the faint light above was extinguished and Channing screamed.

"Channing!" Anneke called out. "Are you all right?"

Even as she spoke these words, something came tumbling down from the third-floor promenade. Anneke looked up and screamed seeing the human form falling from above and landing just a few feet in front of her and Aiyden.

They jumped back in horror as a sharp splintering sound echoed around the empty hall and the mannequin exploded, sending limbs and chunks of plaster out in every direction. The decapitated plastic head spun around several times before coming to a rest, faceup, looking eerily like Channing.

Anneke was too stunned and sickened by the sight to say anything.

"Stay here," Aiyden told her.

"Where are you going?"

"Channing's still up there." His eyes were wide. "I'll be right back." He did not sound convincing.

She tried to grab his arm, but he pulled away before she could secure a grasp. "No, wait. Aiyden don't leave me here." She could only watch as he mounted the frozen escalator and slowly walked up to the third floor. His light got fainter and fainter, then it disappeared completely, and it became preternaturally quiet.

She called out to Aiyden several times, but no reply came. Left alone, there was no stopping the dread from squelching any hope she had of escape.

She started to feel her throat tighten and her arms and legs stiffen. She knew she had only two choices, and she didn't like either of them. She could go look for Channing and Aiyden, who might still be alive, or she could head for the other end of the mall in search of the exit and run the gauntlet between the mannequins that had appeared.

She chose the former and mounted the escalator, nearly tripping over the first riser.

She strained to force her tight muscles to pull her body up the steps. On the second-floor landing, she considered stopping and remaining between floors, avoiding the danger from both above and below until dawn, when the natural light would illuminate this condemned mall of horrors and free her from its clutches.

However, she noticed her battery-powered LED flashlight was already growing weaker. Fully charged, the device should have provided eight to twelve hours of battery life, but Channing's and Aiyden's had already shit the bed, and this forced her to move faster.

Although it was a struggle, she ascended the escalator steps as fast as she could, calling the names of her friends before reaching the top. She prayed to hear the comfort of a familiar voice, but she wasn't expecting it. The silence was still better than the scuttling sounds.

Looking around at the empty shops, they all looked the same, except one. The mesh-like metal gate was intact and pulled down. Someone wearing an orange jumpsuit was standing just a few feet inside.

The person was the exact size and body type as Aiyden. She didn't say anything as she crept closer. It soon became clear that it was a mannequin in the exact likeness as Aiyden, even the synthetic hair was the same length and style. She noticed   his hands were handcuffed behind his back.

Anneke shook her head, rejecting what her eyes were telling her.

"This can't be," she mumbled softly as she stepped backward toward the escalator, intent on going down and executing Plan B. As she turned toward the stairs, however, she caught sight of two oddly positioned mannequins in one of the ransacked shops.

A naked woman with long, dark hair was laying across the lap of a seated man who was wearing a leather hood over his face and nothing else. The man's right hand was raised, holding a black braided leather flogger with a wood handle. The woman's alabaster butt cheeks were fire engine red. Anneke shined her flashlight directly on the woman's face, which was cocked in her direction. The expression on

the mannequin was one of complete submission and ec-
stasy. It was her own face.

Anneke felt every muscle fiber in her body grow taut,
beginning in her extremities. Her fingers locked and she
could not manipulate them. Her limbs began to harden and
there was nothing she could do about it. With her head and
neck fixed, she watched her arm transform into firm,
smooth plaster, and then she could no longer move at all. In
the next instant, her flashlight went out and she became part
of the dead mall forever.

The Dollhouse

Martyn Lawrence

Why is it that when your dog breaks free of its leash, it always makes a beeline for the creepiest place in sight? That was the thought running through Jilly's head as she watched her little brown dachshund dart through the gate into the dark, unkempt garden surrounding the house at the end of the cul-de-sac. Surrounded by trees from the neighboring forest, the old Victorian home sat in almost permanent darkness. Rumors had long swirled about the strange reclusive old man living within its walls, though no one knew anything for certain.

"An old pervert," the kids would whisper. "Just a lonely old man," the adults would mutter dismissively.

"I heard he murdered his whole family in there," Jilly's older brother would tell her when they were younger, relishing going into gory detail about the supposed massacre. "I heard he got kicked out the circus for being too creepy." The never-ending rumors varied wildly, but rumor was all they ever were.

Shoulders slumped in defeat, Jilly sighed and slowly shuffled alongside the overgrown hedge that sat behind a small brick wall surrounding the front garden.

"Rudy…" she whispered as loud as she dared, voice

quivering. It was nearly midnight on the quiet street, neither the time nor the place for shouting after your wayward best-friend. She stopped in front of the gate that looked like it was held together by rust and held her breath awaiting any kind of response. All that came was the rustling of the over-grown grass that towered over her little dog.

"Rudy…" she called out again, trying to sound firm despite feeling like her heart was lodged in her throat. After another agonizing moment of rustling, she let out a shaky breath and reluctantly glanced up at the dilapidated house in front of her. All five of its curtainless windows were pitch black voids, and the huge, thick walnut double door stood firmly shut.

She looked back down the street; five houses stood either side of her, and all ten stood darkened and asleep. The warm glow of the streetlights and the fat white moon hanging in the clear black sky were her only sources of light. Her own home, third on the left, was also in darkness, her parents tucked up in bed, which is exactly where Jilly wished she could be right now. Her clammy fists were tightly clenched as she looked at her parents' bedroom window, longing for her father to suddenly appear.

No, you're eighteen, you're a grown woman. It's just a garden.

Turning back to the house, Jilly took a couple deep breaths to steady her nerves, and gently raised the latch of the gate. Taking another couple breaths, she slowly pushed the gate open, cringing as the creaking grew louder with every inch it moved.

"Fuck, fuck," she muttered under her breath. Once the gate was open just barely enough, she turned her body sideways and slid her slim frame through the narrow space onto the weed-choked stoned path. Edging slowly up the path, her eyes constantly darted from the grass to the windows, to the door, and back again.

The rustling stopped.

"Rudy, get out here," she whispered sharply, casting an anxious glance at the house.

She jangled his leash, hoping the sound of it would bring him out of hiding. Another rustle sounded and Rudy popped out at the far end, wagging his tail with excitement at his adventure. Her eyes bulged in their sockets as the leash had the opposite effect, and the little dog bolted around the side of the house.

"No, please," she muttered to herself, as she instinctively broke into a jog after him.

The side of the house had the same cracked path with overgrown grass running down either side. Rudy sat at the far end, panting as he watched Jilly hurry toward him. *You little shit.* When she got within a couple feet of him, he turned and scampered out of sight, along the back of the house.

Jilly froze in place, as a pained look twisted on her face. With rising panic, she rushed around the corner and gasped when she saw Rudy's tail disappearing through the partially open back door.

"No, no, no, come on, why me?" Jilly whispered in anguish, stomping her foot on the ground. There was no going back now, though. Heart pounding in her chest and keeping as low as she could, Jilly lightly tiptoed toward the ajar door.

"Rudy," she whispered, pressing one hand against the weathered door as she gently pushed it open. Its chipped green paint splintered into the tips of her fingers.

She was met with only silence and no sign of Rudy. Swallowing a lump in her throat, Jilly gently pushed the door farther open.

As the door creaked, Jilly gasped and jolted upright at the nightmarish sight before her. The door opened into a dingy kitchen, covered with dust, cobwebs, and piles of dirty dishes and rotting food. Three of the chairs were occupied by three life-size clown dolls, their limp bodies slumped back as if engaged in some horrid tea party, with cups and a teapot in front of them.

Jilly stood paralyzed, skin crawling at the sight of their pristine white makeup and unblinking eyes. Blood red smiles were painted across each of their faces, a complete contrast with the grime and decay of the room.

Their eyes were outlined in thick blue circles, outlined in black. They wore puffy, red pinstriped costumes with curly red wigs on their heads. Jilly stared into their dead gazes, forgetting to even breathe, before the pitter-patter of little paws snapped her back to reality. *Rudy.*

Her eyes shot to the floor, which hadn't seen a mop or a broom in years. Muddy little paw prints broke up the filth, trailing through the doorway on the far side of the kitchen. After lightly knocking the door in a feeble attempt to announce her presence, she crossed the threshold and followed the muddy trail through the kitchen and out into the hallway. She didn't take a single glance up at the clowns.

The hall floor was bare, rough floorboards covered in a layer of grit and dust. One closed door was on the right, a staircase ascended into shadows on the left, and the front door, which had been boarded up, was at the far end. Rudy stood beside the front door, tail wagging happily as he ate some unidentifiable piece of meat that lay on the floor.

Jilly gasped the thought of what festering feast he'd found himself and tried to sneak up behind him. Before she could reach him, however, the middle door, now behind her, swung open.

Jilly spun around, blood running cold, as she came face to painted face with the mystery man of the house.

The clown's face was a polar opposite of the pristine dolls in the kitchen—his makeup cracked and peeling, with months of grime in each crevice. His waxen white face was stretched into an unnaturally wide red smile that extended to his ears. Black ringed sunken eyes stared out, from under the long, thin, straggly gray hair that hung limply around his face. His short, stocky frame was hidden by the black and red striped costume, complete with a tattered frilly white collar.

"I… I'm so sorry…" Jilly stammered, struggling to find the words to explain her presence. Before she could bring them to tongue, she was cut off by the clown releasing a bloodcurdling scream that echoed through the empty hall. Jilly nearly jumped out of her skin as the terrifying figure spun on his heels and fled back into the room from which he'd come.

"Please don't hurt me," the clown shrieked, his cries piercing Jilly to her core, as her heart almost beat out of her chest.

Her instinctive caring nature took over, overwhelming her fear, she hurried after the clown into the dingy living room. As with the kitchen, cobwebs and dust blanketed every surface. The old clown collapsed against the far wall, trembling as he continued to weep.

"I'm so sorry," Jilly offered gently, slowly crossing the grit covered floor toward him. "Your door was open, and my dog got in. I didn't think there was anyone home."

The clown flinched and cowered away from her as she got within arm's reach. "Don't hurt me," he cried out again between sobs.

"I won't, I promise," Jilly said, backing up with her palms raised. "I'll go, I'll get Rudy and leave you in peace. I'm so sorry for bothering you."

The clown bawled loudly, leaving Jilly with no idea whether to comfort him or leave him be. As unnerving as he was, and no matter how eccentric he might have been, she just couldn't bring herself to abandon the upset man.

"Are you sure you're okay?" Jilly asked, lowering herself to his eyeline.

The clown reached out and gently took hold of her hand. His long, yellow fingernails were caked in months of grime. His sobs slowly transformed into quiet laughter that steadily grew in volume. "You're not going to hurt me?" he asked. Jilly tried to free her hand from his grasp, but he kept hold. "You're not going to hurt me. You're not going to hurt me," he repeated between gasping laughs, as tears rolled down his cracked white cheeks.

Jilly pulled her arm back with all her might, but the clown's grip was vice-like. She frantically scanned the room for anything she could use to help break her free.

Eyes darting wildly, from the moth-eaten couch with its life-size clown doll occupant, to the ancient TV gathering dust in the corner. An iron poker leaned against the soot-stained wall beside the fireplace but was too far from reach.

"Let me go," she insisted. Her heart thundered violently, as the first of her tears ran down her cheeks.

"You're not going to hurt me," he laughed, his veiny hand keeping its grip.

As he began pulling himself to his feet, Jilly managed to twist her arm just enough to slip free of his grasp. She bolted for the door without looking back. Maternal instinct instantly turned her right, away from her escape route, but toward her oblivious dog.

Rudy was still happily devouring the unidentifiable food on the floor. "Rudy!" she snapped, but he didn't even glance up from his feast.

With no time to waste, Jilly sprinted for Rudy. The little guy, spotting her, assumed this was just a continuation of their game, and scampered up the staircase.

Jilly froze at the bottom of the stairs, gaze rapidly shifting between her runaway dog and the bone-chilling cackles of the old clown in the living room. It wasn't an option, there was no choice to be made, she would rather not leave at all than consciously leave without Rudy. Taking a deep breath, she bounded up the stairs two at a time, every step loudly creaking underfoot. As creepy as he was, the clown was still just an old man.

She reached the top just in time so see a wagging little tail turning into the left room at the far right of the landing.

"Rudy, we have to go!" she called. "Come here now and you'll get all the treats you want when we get home," she offered in pure desperation.

Only silence answered her pleas, as Rudy decided against taking up the offer. Jilly crept toward the open doorway, peering into the dark room. Moonlight filtered through the dirt-caked window illuminating years of dust and cobwebs coating every surface; the built-in wardrobe to her left, the bulky chest of drawers in front of her, and the iron-framed bed against the left wall. It was on the bed where she spotted Rudy, who was sniffing around another pristine clown doll.

Jilly gasped, her heart skipping a beat at the thought of Rudy messing with what was seemingly the only thing the old clown actually took pride in. She rushed to the bedside, finally managing to wrap her hands around Rudy's body. As she reattached his leash, she stole a glance down at the doll.

Her blood ran old.

It had human eyes. Deep blue eyes frozen open in an expression of sheer panic.

Jilly's gaze traveled lower, and she clasped a hand over her mouth to stifle a scream. This wasn't just a doll with human eyes. The doll was human.

Jilly's stomach twisted into knots, and she felt bile rise in her throat. *The dolls in the kitchen. The one in the living room. They're alive? What the fuck? What the fuck?*

The pleading eyes looked up at her, glistening in the

moonlight. "Are you okay? Can you get up?" Jilly whispered, voice quivering. She picked up the doll's hand, to find it completely limp. It flopped back down to the bed. "What the hell's he done to you? I'll get help, I'll come back with help, I promise," she said, backing away from the bed.

"You're not going to hurt me?" the old clown's voice suddenly echoed from the hallway.

"Fuck," Jilly muttered under her breath, glancing wildly around the room as she heard the slow drag of the iron poker on the wall. With no time to run, she darted into the wardrobe, pulling the door closed just as the shuffling footsteps entered the room.

Through the crack between the doors, Jilly watched the old clown slowly approach the bed, iron poker in hand, moonlight glinting off the rusted metal. Halfway there, he stopped, letting out a shocked gasp as he noticed the doll's hand had been moved.

"My angel, what has she done to you?" he said, voice trembling, as he hurried the rest of the way. "She won't hurt you; she won't hurt me, I won't let her hurt you again," he cooed, gently putting her hand exactly where it had been before, right by her side. From his sleeve, he pulled out a red tissue, which was connected to another tissue, this one blue. A yellow tissue was next out in the colorful chain, before he wiped his eyes with the final green tissue.

Jilly clamped her hand tight over her mouth, stifling screams as Rudy continued squirming in her other arm. The little dachshund was growing more restless by the second in the cramped wardrobe. She squeezed him against her chest, praying he wouldn't give them away with a stray bark.

Her mind raced. Should she make a run for it while his back was turned? There was no way of getting out unnoticed, so she had to give herself enough time to escape a potential iron poker attack.

"Where did she go, my angel?" the clown asked the doll in a whisper. "Is she… under the bed?"

Jilly's heart was almost in her mouth.

"Or is she… in the wardrobe?"

The instant that last word left his lips, Jilly jumped from the wardrobe, and sprinted for the door. The clown burst into a loud belly laugh, as he turned to watch her run toward the door.

"Don't run, I haven't properly introduced you both yet," he chuckled, as he casually walked after her.

Jilly went along the hall as fast as her feet could carry her, with Rudy clutched tight to her pounding chest. She rounded the corner and took the stairs two at a time, the old floorboards creaking loudly with every step. Behind her, she could hear the clown's shuffling footsteps leave the bedroom, following at a leisurely pace.

Reaching the bottom of the stairs, Jilly turned to sprint for the kitchen and the back door beyond, when she was stopped in her tracks. Not just stopped in her tracks but knocked back a step, in horror. All four of the human dolls from downstairs were now sitting in the hallway, their limp bodies arranged in two neat rows blocking her escape route.

Jilly's heart was thundering, her breathing was ragged, and she had eight pleading eyes staring right into her soul.

She looked back up the stairs to see the old clown now standing at the top, almost a silhouette in the darkness. In his hands, he held three white juggling pins, their ends sharpened to lethal points. A big yellow toothed grin stretched across his cracked makeup as he gazed down at Jilly.

"They're not going to hurt you," he said to Jilly, with a chuckle. "She's not going to hurt you," he said to his dolls, as he began juggling the sharpened pins, as if this were all just normal fun and games. The clubs continued twirling through the air as he slowly made his way down the creaking stairs.

Jilly looked to the dolls seated before her, face racked with anguish knowing she had no choice but to climb through their limp bodies to escape. Tears streamed down her cheeks as she carefully edged between the two rows, cringing as their limp, heavy arms brushed against her. All eight eyes followed her movements, silently pleading.

As Jilly tried to squeeze between the last dolls, a searing pain suddenly exploded in the back of her head. One of the clown's juggling pins struck her square in the skull, the force knocking her forward into the lap of the doll. Jilly screamed, the room was spinning around her. Clutching a whimpering Rudy in one arm, she struggled to regain her footing.

In a panicked attempt to stand, she stumbled backward, collapsing onto the lap of the doll behind her. "Please, let me go home, I'm sorry," she sobbed, finally managing to get upright between the macabre obstacles. A trickle of blood from her head wound ran down the back of her neck.

The clown was nearly at the bottom of the stairs, still juggling the other two pins. "But the fun is just starting, my angel," he said with a creepy smile.

Jilly forced her way through the human doll barricade and made the final sprint for the closed kitchen door. As she flung it open, she triggered a tripwire tied to the handle. A bucket of thick, viscous green slime poured down over her head, the shock briefly rooting her in place.

The old clown's raucous laughter jolted her back into motion. However, as she took her first step on the slimy floor, her feet slipped out from under her as if she were trying to walk on ice. Clutching Rudy to her chest meant she couldn't use her arms for balance, and she went down hard, landing flat on her back with a heavy thud that knocked the wind out of her.

"Did I hurt you?" The old clown giggled. "I wish you could see this, my angels, your sister just fell," he said, struggling to hold his laughter. "Flat on her back." The laughter took over him, his delight ringing through the hall.

Through the haze of pain, Jilly could hear him carefully moving the paralyzed dolls aside to clear his path to her own crippled body. She had to get up, had to move, but the thick slime stopped her from gaining any traction or footing. Between fighting against Rudy's relentless wriggling, slipping and sliding in the green ooze, and the throbbing gash on her skull, Jilly struggled to get back to her feet.

Using the edge of the table, she finally managed to slowly pull herself upright. The soles of her shoes were completely coated, leaving her with no option but to slow down as she made her way to the still-ajar back door.

The clown entered the kitchen, tossing an old blanket over the slick floor. The laughter was gone, his cracked and peeling face now completely straight.

Finally making it to the door, Jilly grabbed the handle with her slime-dripping hand and pulled it open.

She couldn't help but scream at the horrifying sight awaiting her.

A larger-than-life clown statue almost completely filled the doorway, its monstrous frame backlit by the moon. Jilly froze, expecting to see the same pleading eyes as the living dolls. Much to her relief, this clown's gaze was vacant and plastic. Its grotesque face was twisted into a snarling grin, and in its grip, was an eight-inch razor-sharp carving knife.

Jilly took the knife from the statue and was about to try and squeeze past it when she felt another explosive pain on the back of her head.

The old clown was behind her, using one of his sharpened pins as a club against her already bleeding head. Jilly staggered sideways with the force of the blow, crashing into the door frame to keep from crumbling to the floor.

Vision blurring, she gripped the knife handle with white-knuckled intensity, and with her last ounce of strength she lunged forward, driving the blade into his stomach.

The clown's eyes went wide in shock before his peeling painted mouth stretched into an eerie grin. A low chuckle rumbled up from his belly, quickly escalating into full-blown, manic laughter.

Jilly pulled the knife back and looked down in disbelief at the clean, unbloodied blade. She stabbed again, and again pulled back a clean blade.

The old clown looked down and laughed at the retractable knife. Then he locked his eyes onto hers. Pure terror meeting pure madness. "You can't hurt me," he grinned. Before Jilly could react, he plunged a syringe deep into the side of her neck, pressing a clear liquid straight into her bloodstream.

Jilly's world instantly went black, her legs crumpling beneath her.

When she woke, she found herself seated at the filthy dining table, surrounded by the three living dolls once again. Their sunken eyes stared painfully at Jilly as she realized she was now dressed and made up identically—her mouth painted into a horrific blood-red grin, eyes ringed in thick black and blue makeup. An oversized puffy costume and curly red wig adorned her paralyzed body.

She couldn't move a muscle.

A jack-in-the-box sat on the table in front of her. After a few agonizing moments of silence, the toy popped open to reveal a disembodied baby doll head with a painted clown face attached to the spring. Jilly's mind screamed in silent shock, but her drugged body could not react. The old clowns test to ensure that she couldn't so much as physically flinch.

At her feet, Rudy whined and cried, he just wanted to

go home.

Toys to Play With

Eric J. Juneau

Bradley asked Clive if they could play at his house today since Clive's grounding had ended. His parents weren't home— nine was too old for daycare— so they brought their *Mega Mercs* outside. Action figures with beefy arms lay in a pile in the grass while they took the two main guys on a mission.

"They're all around us," Clive said. "That bomb's gonna explode any second."

"Not with my Grim Blaster," Bradley said, wiggling Corporal Thunderbow's arm to brandish the plastic chip.

"There's bodies everywhere. Quick, retreat up the cliffs," Clive said.

Bradley broke character. "Where's the cliffs?"

"The trees."

"Why can't they be trees?"

"Cause they're cliffs."

Bradley followed Clive to the edge of his backyard, which bordered a deep and distant backwoods that served as a natural noise wall. He made Corporal Thunderbow ascend a hackberry, escaping from the Jab Jihadists. "Mac-Croft, throw me a rope!"

"Take this, you hajis. Blam, blam, blam." Clive made

Lieutenant MacCroft shoot the imaginary terrorists near the trunk. "Ugh, their brains and guts are exploded every-where…" He dropped his arm and looked into the forest. They had never breached its border before, never sure if they were allowed or not. "What's in there?"

"I don't know," Bradley said. "Trees."

"Let's go explore it."

This late in Fall, each tree was a bony claw reaching for the sky. Skeletal wobbly poles stuck in the dirt.

"What do you think's in there?" Bradley asked.

"I don't know. Maybe animal carcasses and bird's nests," Clive said.

"Maybe buried treasure?"

Clive scoffed. "There's no such thing as buried treasure."

"Yea-huh. Pirates used to bury treasure for real."

"There's no pirates in Ohio."

They kept walking, side by side but not together. The leaves looked like dead skin flakes.

"Did you hear that?" Clive perked his head up.

"What?"

"I… there it is again. It's a person." Clive took some cautious steps forward.

All Bradley heard was the crunch of his feet. Then a man shouted.

"I hear him," Bradley said.

"Hello? Help!" the voice said.

It sounded close, but they couldn't pinpoint it. The trees were too thin for an adult to hide behind.

"Hello?" Bradley called.

"Help! Please! I'm down here!"

Clive and Bradley paced in small steps with their eyes glued to the ground. Then Bradley noticed the hole. Over-grown grass camouflaged the pit with yellowed detritus.

Bradley toed for the edge and peeked down. He couldn't

see much inside, but the man inside wore a Day-Glo construction vest. They made eye contact.

"Is someone up there?" the man shouted. "I fell down this well. Can you get some help please?"

"Say something," Clive whispered to Bradley.

"Are you hurt?" Bradley called.

"I don't think so, but there's no room to move. Can you call the police?"

"Ask him what he was doing," Clive whispered.

"What were you doing?"

"Survey work. Please just go call the police."

"Like taking surveys?" Bradley asked, wondering why he needed a construction vest for that.

"No. Please, go call 911," Dave said.

"Okay." Bradley backed away from the hole. "Let's use your phone."

Both of them marched back to the house. On the way, Clive asked, "How long do you think he's been down there?"

"Probably not long. Or he'd be starving."

"Do you think anyone else would have found him?"

"I dunno," Bradley said. The only thing keeping people away from the hole was the vast uninteresting nature of the woodland.

Once through the basement sliding door, Clive rushed in and grabbed the phone from the wall in the kitchen.

"No, I want to call. I found him," Bradley said.

"It's my house, I get to call. Go get him some water. I bet he's thirsty."

"But I want to hear you talk to the police."

"He could be dying of thirst. There's bottles in the fridge."

Bradley plucked off a bottle from the plastic rings. Clive shooed him off, holding the phone to his ear.

Bradley rolled the bottle in his palms as he walked

across the backyard and through the forest. He couldn't find the hole until the man answered his shouts.

"I brought you some water," Bradley said, looking down into the hole.

"Oh… okay, thank you."

Bradley tossed it in. "My friend is calling the police."

The man gasped for breath after swigging. "Thank you. I thought I was going to be down here forever."

"Don't you have a cell phone?" Bradley asked.

"It's in the back of my truck."

"Oh." Bradley didn't know what else to ask. A stranger in a hole was still a stranger. "I got to get back to my friend now."

"Okay. You guys are going to be heroes. How about that?"

Bradley wasn't sure how to respond. "That sounds good."

He walked back to the house. Clive hung up the phone as he entered.

"I called them. They're on their way."

"Did you mention me? I found him, too."

"I said we both found him. But don't you have to go back home now?" He pointed to the digital clock on the oven. Bradley was supposed to be home fifteen minutes ago. All the excitement had made him lose track of time.

"I wanted to stay and see the cops. Did they say how long they would take?"

"I don't know. But you're already late. You better go home."

Bradley bit his lip and willed the clock to shift backward. But if Dad arrived home before he did, he'd be punished for sure.

"All right. Tell me everything in school tomorrow."

"Okay."

#

Bradley's house's storm door always slammed. Its springs were too old and cheap for delicacy.

His sister laid out on the couch, watching *Teen Mom* or *Pregnant Dad* or one of those shows. Each time she laughed, her nose chain that reached to her ear rattled.

"Amber, is Dad working late again?" Bradley asked.

"Yeah." She sipped a soda.

He headed into the kitchen, too hungry to tell her about the guy in the hole. He could tell her while eating.

On the table lay a plate with cold Chef Boyardee ravioli, corn chips, and a Pepsi.

"Is this my dinner?" Bradley shouted.

"Just eat it. It's all I could find," Amber shouted back.

"You're supposed to *make* something. Dad said so."

"Make your own dinner, then. He just said to make sure you have *something*," Amber said.

"I'm telling Dad when he gets home."

"Fine," she said. "Turd."

Bradley replaced the Pepsi with canned pears. While he ate, his mind roiled with scenarios where she was run over by a truck. This was the third time in a row she'd done this. He'd punish her by keeping his news to himself.

The garage door churned open. Bradley awaited his dad's entrance with the scolding on his lips. "Dad, Amber didn't make me dinner."

"You shut up! I did so make you dinner," Amber said.

"It was chips and Pepsi. You have to give me real food," Bradley yelled back.

"You were with your weird friend all day. I didn't know what time you were coming home."

For the next ten seconds, random shouting filled the room. Dad raised his hand. "All right, all right, ALL RIGHT!"

Bradley and Amber shut up.

"I am tired and I don't want to hear this. Amber, when I

say you got to make dinner, you got to make it. Bradley, stop complaining about what she gives you."

"But—"

Dad raised his hand higher. "Enough! I can't be here every night. Amber's got enough to do with laundry and vacuuming and all that. If she can't make the best dinner, then so be it. She has a life, too."

"I swear, I'm going to move out one of these days," Amber muttered.

"Don't start that crap again," Dad said.

Amber was always threatening to get emancipated or run away with her boyfriend of the month. She'd never do it, no matter how much Bradley hoped. Not while the house had free cable.

#

In class, Bradley ran up to Clive the moment he spotted him at his desk. "So what happened with the guy?" Bradley asked.

"It actually wasn't that exciting, but the police came and picked him up. He was nice. They lowered a rope, and he climbed out. He was really thankful. Gave me hugs."

"Did you tell them I found him, too?" Bradley asked.

"Yeah. It's not like there's a reward, though."

"Oh."

"Bradley!" Mr. Foster called. "Go sit down. I will not tell you again."

Bradley pulled away with a grunt.

He thought about the man all morning, but schoolwork and home stress over the next few weeks shouldered the incident away. When they played in the backyard, Bradley sometimes looked into the woods. But Clive never said anything. It became a faint moment, then history.

#

In the next two years, middle school separated Clive and Bradley. Adolescence and a new school deteriorated their relationship into a courteous nod in the hallway.

The interesting thing was that Clive's behavior improved. Back in fifth grade, his Friday detentions would cut into their playtime. Now teachers stopped giving him the evil eye when they handed back assignments. Becoming a hero had changed him.

One day, Bradley got home from school. Amber was watching TV while with alcohol-soaked pads on two new piercings--one labret and one on her reclosed cheek.

"Where's Dad?" Bradley asked.

"I dunno. Work."

A horn beeped outside. Amber leaped up, tossing her gauze aside.

"If Dad comes back, tell him I'm at Jordan's." The screen door clapped shut behind her.

Bradley was about to get a snack when the phone rang. The caller ID said it was Clive's house, which confused Bradley. He hadn't called for a long time.

"Hello?"

"Hey, Bradley. Whatcha doing?"

"Nothing."

"Wanna see something cool?"

#

No matter how much Bradley pestered, Clive would only say it was a surprise. On arrival, Clive grabbed a flashlight from the cupboard. They left out the back door and headed into the woods.

Clive stopped at a tiny clearing, then handed Bradley the flashlight. "Look down."

Bradley shined it in the hole. A white gangly monster looked up, shading its eyes.

No, not a monster. A person. Arms as thin as sticks, skin like moldy jelly. His long beard was dirty and gray.

Bradley fell back. The flashlight rolled away. Clive caught it, laughing. "What do you think?"

"Who is that?" Bradley asked.

"Who is *that*? The guy from before. Remember?"

A rattling voice drifted up. "Please help me."

"You… you said you called the police," Bradley said.

"I didn't. I just told you I did. I never actually called them."

Bradley grabbed the flashlight and pointed it into the well again. The man looked like a fish at the bottom of the ocean, one that never sees light. His eyes were white and red, like milk spots.

Bradley neurotically marched in circles while Clive giggled. "What, is he like a pet to you?"

"More like an experiment."

"Didn't anyone come search for him?" Bradley asked.

"I guess they never found him. It's hard to see that hole. And he couldn't climb out. Maybe it's too rocky down there to pull the dirt down. Anyway, he doesn't have the strength now."

"This is sick. I'm going to be sick. You kept him down there for two years?"

"He fell down the hole himself. I'm not keeping him there. He just can't get out. If I wasn't here to feed him, he'd already be dead."

"You're crazy. I'm going to call the cops."

Clive grinned. "And what are you going to say? You knew about this, too."

"But I thought they came and got him. I didn't know you *left* him there."

"Go ahead and call." Clive pointed to the well. "But he knows your voice. He knows what you look like. And he remembers that first day *very* well."

"They wouldn't arrest me…"

"They would."

Bradley sniffled. The mitten he used to wipe his tears scratched his eye. "Why did you even show me?"

Clive shrugged. "Not sure he's going to live much longer. I'm surprised he made it this far with what I've done to him."

"Like what?"

Clive's eyes lit up. "You want to see? I kept an album."

"No." Bradley backed away. "No, I can't. No."

He ran.

#

Bradley ran back into his house. When he saw his dad at the kitchen table, his wailing exploded. Thinking of Dad watching police take him to jail.

"Brad, what's wrong?"

"What happened this time? Stop being so sensitive," Amber said. "That's my brother," she said into her phone. "Can you hear him? I know, jeez…"

"Amber. Cut it," Dad said. "What's wrong, Bradley?"

Bradley was about to confess everything until he said *can you tell me?* Not with Clive's threats. He couldn't let his dad down like that. "No, nothing."

"I know. It's all the time. He's so screechy," Amber said.

"Shut up! Shut up!" Bradley smashed her with a throw pillow. She held up her arm and kicked her bare foot at him.

"Both of you, cut it out!" Dad held Bradley by his shoulders.

"But you heard her—" Bradley said.

"Son, you've got to grow up." He turned to Amber. "Don't you have to go meet Jordan or whoever he is?"

Amber huffed. She slipped on her sandals and exited the house.

"I'm making dinner tonight. Do you want ramen?" Dad asked.

"No, I'm sick of ramen."

Dad wiped his forehead. "Okay, well, help me look for something to eat."

Bradley didn't want to eat anything but comfort food:

McDonald's chicken nuggets, tater tots, macaroni and cheese. They searched the kitchen for fifteen minutes, but the closest they came was a single corn dog. Bradley shook his head.

His father slammed the freezer door shut. "Then I give up. You make your own dinner. I'm going to take a nap."

"But…   "

"Just eat something, I don't care what."

Bradley ate the corn dog. Then he drank water to feel full.

In bed, the ghost-man kept reappearing—sickly purple skin projecting, bulging frog eyes. He stared at the ceiling, knowing sleep would be impossible.

#

Clive walked up to him at lunch. They hadn't eaten together since middle school started. Bradley had his friends, and Clive ate with his. But now he was here, beaming." So what do you think? I know you're not going to try and stop me. Otherwise the police would have shown up last night."

"I'm going to tell someone. I just… haven't yet," Bradley said.

"You can't. Because if you do tell someone, they're going to come check it out first. So I'll know it was you." He leaned in. "And then you might have to go in with him."

"No."

"Do you think he'd eat you? Or just kill you," Clive asked.

"Shut up. Fine, I'm not telling anyone. I swear."

Clive plopped next to him. "I'm kidding. I wouldn't put you in." He unzipped his backpack. "You want to see my album?"

"No. I don't."

The album, bound in tan pleather, bulged with bulky scrapbook trinkets. "The first thing I tried was 'fishing'. I dangled some food on a hook but never let him get it. I'd see how long it'd take until he gave up."

He turned the page, past some newspaper articles about missing persons. From a glance,

"Oh, the smell log. I'd throw things down to see what he'd do, if he'd throw up or what. Eggs, garbage, rancid milk…"

Each page had charts, lists, or pictures of his transition from strapping man to cave monster. Bradley did his best to tune out Clive.

"I don't understand how you could do this."

"Cause he's not human anymore. He's off the grid." Clive closed the book. "How many chances like this do you get in life? To see what a person can take. How can you not be interested?"

"Didn't Hitler experiment with the Jews?"

Clive sat back. "Don't compare me to Hitler. *He* just wanted them dead. Science was an excuse to him."

Bradley kept still, waiting for all this to end.

Clive reopened the album and paged through for his own amusement. From the clippings, Bradley learned his name was Dave Acevedo. He had a family—wife and three kids. His job changed in each article--surveyor, construction worker, blue-collar. Insurance took care of his family, who had moved away.

The frequency of articles tapered off after a few days. He was forty years old. Not as newsworthy as someone younger who hadn't lived their life.

"What would *you* do to him?" Clive asked.

"Huh?"

"I'm looking for ideas. You've never thought about it?"

"I dunno. Put a board over the hole, no sunlight for a week."

"I did that already. For a month, in fact." Clive turned to the corresponding page. "Not much happened. What else? Come on…   "

"Throw some bees down there?"

"Bees? I've done other bugs, but not bees. I thought they'd fly away. But… if I covered the hole with a tarp." He flipped through until he came to a page titled "FINAL EXPERIMENT"

"What's 'final experiment'?" Bradley asked.

"Oh. That's—   "

The lunch bell rang. Clive slipped the album in his backpack. "Tell you later. Come to my house after school. It'll be just like old times."

Clive left before Bradley could answer.

#

Bradley arrived at Clive's house shortly after school. While they played video games for an hour, Bradley made furtive glances out the window at the backyard.

"You want to see him?"

Clive walked out with boundless energy. Bradley had trouble keeping up.

The ghoul hunched in fetal position, body rising with each breath. Stringy hair on his scalp fluttered.

"We're just going to look at him?"

Clive shrugged. "Sometimes that's all I do. Or throw down rocks. You want to feed him something?" Clive dug an unwrapped taffy out of his pocket. It was covered in lint and grime. "He'll love you forever if you feed him this."

Bradley tossed it down. It bounced off the man's shoulder blade. He twitched, as if disturbed from a nightmare.

"I started him off with regular food. But then I wondered what would happen if he got desperate. I've given him frogs, dead birds, roadkill."

"And he eats that?" Bradley asked.

"Sure. And branches, stones, cardboard. His teeth are all gone from breaking them."

"Wouldn't he get sick and die?"

"Oh, he got sick," Clive said. "But he didn't die."

Bradley gulped back his rising gorge.

"Don't act like you're better than this," Clive said. "I remember us burning ants with a magnifying glass. Pretended we were mad scientists with a death ray."

He remembered. They couldn't get the angle right.

"And we'd chase frogs and spear them with sticks. How about when we talked about putting all the homeless people in a meat grinder and feeding them to other homeless people? You used to love this crap."

Bradley shifted his feet. "So what was the 'final experiment'?"

"Oh, well…" Clive straightened like a lecturing professor. "I stole a dose of morphine from my grandfather. It's a lethal dose, I checked. I was going to throw it down and see if he uses it. You know, like the final test to see if he has any hope left."

"Why don't you pour some boiling oil on him?" Bradley sneered.

"That's not a bad idea. But I don't want to torture him. What I should have done was throw it in first thing. See how long until he uses it. If I find a second guy…   "

Cold sweat tingled on Bradley's forehead.

"I might have to do it soon. If I wait too much longer, he'll die on his own. He's about ready, don't you think?"

Bradley shrugged and edged away from the hole.

#

Amber wasn't in her usual spot on the couch, watching TV and doing her nails. He heard two voices in her room. One was a man's.

Bradley strafed away, moving to the kitchen for the phone. As he picked up the receiver, Amber's door opened. A man with a scruffy beard, a hemp necklace, no shirt, and jean shorts walked out.

"Hey, you got a cigarette?"

Bradley shook his head.

"How about a beer? Y'all got any beer?" He hunched in front of the fridge while Bradley held the phone. After finding a can, he went out the back door to the patio.

Alone again, Bradley dialed his dad. After two rings, the phone rustled. "Hello?"

"Dad? It's me."

"Bradley. What do you want?"

Bradley stammered. "I need some advice."

"Advice?"

"I have this friend—   "

"Is this an emergency?"

"N-no." The man in the well had been there two years already.

"I told you not to call unless it's an emergency. Every time I get pulled off the line, everything stops. You understand?"

"Yes."

"Okay. We can talk about this when I get home."

Bradley hung his head. They wouldn't talk about it when he got home. Dad would forget or Bradley's courage would fail or Amber would whine about something and distract them.

Amber came out of her room dressed in a tank top and cut-offs. "What are you doing here?"

"I live here."

"I thought you were with your friend."

"Came home."

Amber looked out the back door. "Don't you dare tell Dad about him."

"Fine." It wasn't his problem if she was having sex with skeevy guys who asked eleven-year-olds for cigarettes and beer.

Amber scoffed. "I can't wait to find my own place. Then I won't have to deal with your whiny bullshit anymore."

Bradley nodded to the back door. "Are you going to live

with *him*?"

Amber stooped into his face. "You know, you are so lucky I still live here. What do you think's going to happen if I leave? You're going to have to make all the food, do all the chores. The only reason I stay is to help Dad."

"You don't do anything to help Dad. You're supposed to empty the garbage and it's still full. Why don't you take out the trash instead of being it?"

Amber's head jerked back. "What did you say to me?" She leaned over him, arms hunching.

"Nothing."

Amber slapped him across the cheek. His face brightened red.

The man knocked on the sliding door. "Amber! You coming or what?"

Amber straightened. "Don't ever call me trash again." She turned and went outside. Behind the glass, her muffled voice said "I'm so done with this family."

Bradley went to the bathroom to wash his cheek. He wouldn't tell Dad. He wouldn't need to, since she was going to leave soon.

#

"Why don't we do it today?" Bradley asked.

"Do what?" Clive asked as he searched the bookshelf in his room.

"The final experiment. The morphine."

Clive's eyes lit up. "You think so? But you just learned about him. You didn't want to try anything yourself?"

"You said he's not going to last much longer. There's no point in waiting for me. And at least I'd get to see it."

Clive grinned. "All right." He reached under his bed and pulled out a small cardboard box. Inside was a single syringe and a small vial of clear liquid. Like a TV doctor, he held it upside-down and stuck the needle in the rubber tip.

As they approached the hole, Clive said, "I assume he'll

use all of it. I don't know why he wouldn't." Clive shined his flashlight down. "Can you hear me? Do you see this?"

The man stirred.

"This is an injection of morphine. You can end it all right now, if you want. All you—"

Bradley shoulder-checked Clive in the back.

Clive's sneakers tipped over the edge as he windmilled his arms. The syringe flew out of his hand, landing on the grass somewhere.

Bradley pushed. Clive tipped, twisted and clung to the edge of the pit.

"You stupid bitch! I knew you'd do something like this." Clive struggled up as Bradley stood frozen from the horror of what he had done. "I'm calling the cops. I'm telling them what you did. You—"

The man in the well jumped up and wrapped his bony arms around Clive's legs, making a screech. He clung like a monkey, yanking him down inch by inch.

Clive yanked clumps of grass for purchase. His eyes bulged. "Help, he's got me!"

Bradley followed the instinct that kept him still.

Clive's hands slid across the grass and disappeared. Grinding, gurgling, and hissing sounds emitted from the well. Bradley didn't look down, but he didn't leave. An hour passed in silence. Maybe they'd killed each other in the struggle. Maybe they'd both fallen into Hell.

#

"Where the hell were you?" Amber asked, walking out of the kitchen. "Dad said I had to make sure you were home before I could go out."

"Is Dad home?"

"No, of course not. Answer the question—where were you?"

"With Clive."

She sneered. "You're always with that kid."

"He had a man in a well. He had him trapped down there for two years, doing experiments on him."

"Huh?"

"A man fell into a well in the woods behind his house. Clive and I knew about it but didn't tell anyone. He was feeding him things like roadkill, dead birds."

"Are you serious?"

Bradley nodded.

"I'm calling Dad." She approached the phone. "If this is fake, he's going to be so pissed." She dialed, turning her back to him. "Either way, he's going to be mad. I bet this is a trick…"

Bradley snuck up behind her and stuck the needle in her neck. Clear liquid rushed out of the cylinder.

"What….?" She slapped herself as if bitten by a mosquito. Instead, her fingers fumbled around a syringe. Bradley took it out. He was done, anyway.

"What... what was that? Did you just inject me with something?" Her fingers came back dotted with blood. She stood suspended in confusion, allowing the morphine time to do its work.

The phone dropped. The battery casing broke apart on the linoleum. She fell on her knees and reached for Bradley.

He stepped back.

"Don't worry," Bradley said. "It wasn't the full dose. And you were always talking about running away, anyway."

White-faced, she curled up on the brown carpet. Bradley lifted her arm as a test. It offered no resistance. He slid open the patio door and tugged the wagon into the house. After heaving her in, he fit a bed sheet over her and started down the street.

No one in suburbia cared much about a boy pulling his wagon along the sidewalk. If they did, why would they say anything? Why would they remember when the news report floated by two weeks later? Probably just going to a friend's house, bringing some toys to play with.

Today's Special at the Forget-Me-Not Café: Muddy Bones and a Slice of Guilt

Terry Campbell

" So, this is how it all ends, huh?" Robbie Spencer says to the bloated, pasty-skinned corpse lolling in the gentle flow of the receding river, the inevitability of being swept far down river to points unknown delayed only by the tangled deadfall of branches and scraggly limbs, a corpse that until recently had been his best friend, a corpse that up until a few days ago would never have done anything to betray him.

Or so he thought, and what a prick he was for thinking that, folks. Besides, that was a few days ago. This is now. This is reality, and in reality, this corpse lies.

It also cheats. And it betrays him, oh yes, how it betrays him. This corpse is no longer his best friend, and Robbie Spencer is certainly no best friend to a decaying chunk of dead meat.

"Answer me, Wallace Davis," Robbie says sternly. He pauses a moment to roll up the legs of his jeans and carefully steps into the coffee-colored water of Rio de Diablo,

tenderly negotiating the twisted bramble of branches so as not to dislodge the body and send it merrily on its way toward the Gulf of Mexico like some macabre ferry manufactured from decaying tissue, giving passage only to the water bugs and turtles and snakes that might grab hold long enough to partake of the delicious edible vessel.

Robbie kneels, feeling the warm shallow water lapping at his thighs and spreads apart several smaller branches, revealing the swollen, mud-streaked face of one Wallace Davis. At this close proximity, Robbie can smell the process of decay that has begun to consume his former friend's mortal remains. It is not an altogether unpleasant odor, and it brings an ugly smile to Robbie's face.

"Hey," he says, tapping the corpse's cheek. The flesh gives slightly, and it's a weird feeling, because flesh isn't supposed to respond in that manner, creating a dimple which slowly smooths back over with rancid skin. Kind of like wringing out a wet sponge and watching it reclaim its shape. "Are you listening to me?" Robbie pauses a moment, as if waiting for an answer. He is patient, but not overly so.

When no answer comes, he leans even closer to the dead face staring back at him. The fish have chewed its lips away and completely devoured one eye. Robbie fleetingly wonders what happened to the contact lens, not that it matters. "Is this how you thought you would end up, Wally, Mr. Man of the World, Mr. Big Dick Lady's Man? Floating and rotting in this stinky shit hole? Is this what you pictured when you had to go and dip your stick in Trish, in my girlfriend, huh?"

Robbie stands and reflects on the moment, hands resting on his hips. He notices the corpse's other eye lying loose in the socket, bulging slightly, as if some water creature had tugged on it to claim it for its evening meal before being frightened away.

Robbie reaches down and takes the eye between his middle finger and thumb. The body does not create natural lubrication in a lifeless shell, and he is easily able to pluck the eye from its socket. Letting it roll in the palm of his hand like a fat shooter's marble, Robbie peers into the lifeless orb. It is a familiar eye, and yet, it is not. The sparkling blue—the girls always loved Wally's baby blues—has clouded over with decay, and that suits Robbie just fine.

What was the last thing this eye witnessed before it closed forever? Robbie knew it had seen the school bus, one of six carrying three hundred students and faculty members from Quinlan Christian School to a week-long retreat to Mount Lebanon, being swept off the bridge and into the rain-swollen, turbulent waters of Rio de Diablo.

Two other buses—like panicked bison stampeding over a cliff—followed the one carrying Wallace Davis.

This eye may have been privy to the terrible drowning of thirty-six fellow students and five teachers, and shared in the suffocating fear of their impending mortality.

Likely it wasn't thinking about anything but itself. Maybe it watched the raging waters rush by above it.   P erhaps it searched frantically for a low-hanging tree branch to grab. Certainly it paid rapt attention as the water climbed higher and higher, observed the head to which it was attached sink lower and lower into the violent waters, until it absorbed no more.

Then again, they say your life passes before your eyes at the moment of death, so maybe this eye recalled happier times. Its sixth birthday party, perhaps. Winning the city softball championship. Or maybe younger memories grabbed the final spotlight.

Going to the senior prom. Getting laid the same night. Perhaps—and, oh looky here, ladies and gentlemen, we've come full circle—just maybe, it recalled the time it gazed lustily into the glistening depths of Trish's pussy. Robbie's

Trish.

Robbie looks back at the dead eye, the trailing viscera drooping over his fingers and hanging lazily beneath. He tosses the eye behind him, not looking, and listens for the satisfying plop as it finds the surface of the calm river.

Until today, the remains of Wally Davis had not been found. His body was the only one of the forty-two unfortunate souls who perished in the tragic accident that was yet to be recovered. The murky waters of Rio de Diablo seemed willing enough to give up the others, but it had not been so keen to relinquish this prize. A massive search party had combed the riverbanks and surrounding forests for three days, and no trace of the body had been found.

Until Robbie stumbled across it. His lucky day. He would be a hero. The school would thank him. The local authorities would thank him. Wally's mother, grieving and eager to give her only son a proper burial, would thank him.

Trish might even thank him. Thank you for finding the body of the guy I fucked behind your back. I know we were taking this field trip together because the three of us are such good friends, Robbie, but you know, sometimes things happen, you don't mean for them to, you're not even sure you want them to, but you're working late at the store, and Wally comes over to look for you and he has some beer and he offers me one and we start drinking and then we're laughing and dancing and then we're holding each other and we're kissing and then the next thing you know we're fucking like we're the last two people on earth (sorry if we ruined your trip by telling you that) and neither one of us are thinking of you, Robbie, because if we were, we wouldn't be doing it in the first place but really, we're not thinking of you at all. But thank you for finding his body all the same, because now I can pay my proper respects. That's important. Don't you think? Paying your proper respects?

Respects? Robbie thinks. What the fuck do either of you know about respect?

No, this corpse Robbie now stares at lies, it cheats, and now it rots. And if this is where it will rot, then this is where it can stay. It can be buried with the fishes, the snapping turtles, the cottonmouths, the old, discarded tires and rusted bodies of automobiles, anything else that might rest at the bottom of Rio de Diablo. No fucking proper burial—Wally's mother could kiss his ass—no fucking proper respects, no fucking proper Trish anymore.

Robbie grabs the rope he has brought, a rope he had initially planned to use to possibly retrieve Wally's body if given the chance. Now he uses it to secure heavy stones to the boy's body, cumbersome rocks that will sink to the bottom, taking the lying, cheating corpse with it, where it will wait a long damn time for someone to pay it its proper respects.

Tell it to the seaweed.

What's that old saying? If the eye offends thee . . .

Robbie grabs the front of the corpse's jeans. They are heavy with the water they have absorbed, and a thin film of green algae has begun to grow on them, making them a bit slippery. Robbie pulls the corpse's jeans down to its knees so that the flaccid penis can float and bob freely in the river's slow, lazy current like some fisherman's rubber worm tempting a trophy bass. And if that little scenario were to actually play out, then so much the better.

This done, Robbie at last pulls the corpse free from the bramble in which it was trapped and pushes it toward the center of the river, where the current grabs it and takes it, listing and bobbing a moment before the weight of the stones coaxes it down.

The last thing Robbie sees in the foamy, swirl of dirty water is the corpse's hand protruding from the muddy water, as if waving good-bye or begging for mercy—hard to tell which—a final cry for help that goes unheeded.

* * *

Twenty years had passed since Robert Spencer stood on the muddy banks of Rio de Diablo in deep southwest Texas. *A long time.* He was merely a child then—a foolish, naive kid, standing at the edge of a new frontier naked of life experience with no concept of the consequences of his actions. A typical American teenager. He was thirty-eight years old now, a mature adult, a successful advertising executive. No longer that eighteen-year-old kid.

But goddamn, kids do some stupid things, you know? We've all done it. We're all guilty of that, he reasoned. Kids murdered these days and barely received any punishment for it.

So, was what he did that big of a deal?

Robert stared down at the water's edge, letting his gaze drift slowly from the bank, out across the surface of the gentle, flowing river (still muddy after all these years), across the great expanse of the body of water that could be so gentle and carefree one minute, so violent and angry the next.

I'm so sorry, Wally, Robert cried to himself. *I am so, so sorry.*

Robert tried to penetrate the surface of the water with his vision, tried to peer into its murky depths, but he could not break the brown film. *He's in there somewhere*, Robert thought, *and he shouldn't be. He should be resting eternally under a grand oak tree in a rural cemetery down some Texas back road with cattle lowing in the distance, not buried under hundreds of pounds of mud and silt.* But he's in there just the same. What's left of him, anyway. Scattered in the changing currents. Here and there. Some of him may have even made it to the ocean, sailing the seven seas for eternity.

How could he have been so stupid? How could he have

done what he did to a friend, even a friend who had betrayed his trust as Wally had? And for what? A piece of ass? Trish? Where the hell was she these days? When had he last thought of her? Oh, he'd thought of Wally plenty of times, hardly a day went by he didn't think about Wally, but when was the last time he thought of the catalyst for the senseless reason for which he had done this terrible thing?

Robert knelt at the edge of the water. The sun was sinking low. The warmth of the day would die quickly; it would be cooling off soon. He needed to head back to camp to rejoin the rest of his group. But still, it was hard to break away. Robert let his fingers caress the warm waters.

The vibration of his actions twenty years ago seemed to resonate on his fingertips; he could almost see them replay in the water's reflection, as if he was standing outside his body watching the event unfold through some other-worldly liquid reenactment.

"Please forgive me, Wally," he said to the trees, to the water, to anything that might be willing to listen.

Robert caught a whiff of roasting hot dogs and marshmallows drifting from the campsite, but it still could not overpower the oppressive odor of dank earth and dead fish emanating from the river.

In an attempt at remembering happier childhood days before girls and guilt and jealousy and anger had intervened and turned him into a man, Robert picked up a rock and skipped it across the water's surface.

One. Two. Three. Four skips. Not bad.

Robert picked up another rock. It felt lighter than the first rock. Rough. Coarse.

Almost like a piece of—

"Hey, you coming back tonight?"

Anthony from Copy-Editing.

"Yeah," Robert said. "I was just . . . thinking about old times."

Robert tossed the rock into the shallow water and turned to leave. If he had not turned away, he might've noticed the rock hit the surface, catch in a small rivulet and maneuver around a few larger stones, bob and weave, and finally float away on the lonely current.

* * *

Robert had not been camping since he was a young boy; he had forgotten how terribly dark it got in the dense woods on a moonless night. He curled up in a protective fetal position and attempted to bury himself deep within the confines of the down-filled sleeping bag. The night woods made noises; its creatures seemed to accuse him.

And possibly somewhere among these scraggly trees, the ghost of Wally Davis roamed.

Robert tried to listen to the sounds his friends made in their sleep—their breaths, their snores, tried to hum familiar songs in his mind, anything to drown out the sounds of the overwhelming night.

The hard ground. The chilly air. The magnified sounds. And the guilt he felt. All of these realities combined to make sleep very difficult. But sleep did come.

And it was not alone.

* * *

The stones he found protruding from the soft mud at the banks of the river would be perfect for the task at hand.

It was difficult for Robbie to hold the rocks against the bobbing corpse and still manage to tie the ropes at the same time. But it's amazing how focused one can be when there is but one single notion consuming the mind—the act of vengeance—and perseverance was definitely on his side.

He was glad he had excelled in the knot-tying sessions

in the Boy Scouts, although the thought of seeing his troop leaders' faces if they ever found out exactly what he had utilized this knowledge for brought a smile to his face.

He guided one end of the rope through the loop and pulled it tight until the rock pressed into the softening flesh of the corpse's chest. The added weight caused the corpse to dip a little deeper into the water despite being held in place by the drift of branches. Robbie shook the stone to test its stability. Finding it secure, he wrapped the slack end of the rope around the body's waist.

"Pretty pathetic, man," a voice behind Robbie said.

Startled, Robbie dropped the remaining stone into the water with a solid ka-thunk. He wheeled suddenly about to find the owner of the voice.

"What are you doing, Robbie?"

It was Wally, standing on the bank just downstream.

No, it can't be, Robbie thought. He looked back at the corpse. Wally's decaying body was still snagged in the brush. How can that be? He turned his attention back to the Wally standing near the water. The hard outline of his form drifted in and out of focus, and Robbie could see the trees behind him through his body.

"Is that the best you can do?" Robbie's friend said. "Shit, with friends like you . . ."

"How?" was all Robbie could mumble.

"Big man, getting your revenge like this. But hey, what do I care? I'm already dead. But do you have to be so . . . so dickless?"

Robbie blinked his eyes, squeezed them shut tightly. When he opened them, the transparent Wally was gone. Robbie turned his head from side to side, but there was no sign of the intruder.

Suddenly, Robbie felt something cold and wet grab his wrist.

"I'm already dead. The only person who's going to get

hurt over this is you."

The bloated, ugly Wally corpse squeezed its decaying fingers harder into Robbie's skin, and its rotted face, its eyes dripping a green liquid, its snaggled, brown teeth jutting from its purple lips, broke through the confining branches and came at Robbie.

* * *

The pleasant aroma of coffee boiling away and bacon frying helped to somewhat ease the nervous feeling with which Robert had awakened. The dream was just a dream; nothing could convince him there was anything more to it than that. He had lived with the cold reality of what he had done that spring for a long time. It was little wonder that returning to the figurative "scene of the crime" would wreak havoc upon his nerves and invade his subconscious.

But the dream had seemed so *real*. And he had heard Wally's voice; of that he was certain. He had not heard that voice from his past since its feeble attempt at apologies after Wally and Trish had confronted him about their sudden affair so many years ago. Still, he knew that voice.

"Just nerves," Robert whispered to himself.

The soothing sound of popping grease lifted his spirits a little more, and Robert could feel the dream slipping back into the dark recesses of his mind from whence it had come. But a dream like that would never completely disappear. It could drift in his mind, until it was almost gone, then snag in the river of his memory like a decaying body on a tangle of deadwood.

"Yo, Robert," Stephens called out. "I'm not guaranteeing there'll be anything left if you don't get your butt over here."

Don't let them see you're nervous.

"Save me a crumb at least," he shouted back, attempting

to sound jovial in an effort to hide his unease.

He slipped his right foot into one boot and stood to tie it when he felt the pain in his heel.

"Ow, shit!" he cried, dropping back down to remove the boot.

A rock had gotten caught inside the boot. Robert turned the boot over and shook it, catching the offending rock in the palm of his hand.

"There you are, you bastard," he whispered.

He let the rock roll in his palm as he inspected it. It was an odd shaped rock—

—an eye?—

—a creamy ivory in color, and a pair of tapered points jutted from one end. There was a splash of bright silver in the center of the rock—

—just like the one you held—

—and the top was flattened.

—after you yanked it out.

Robert's hand began to shake as he inspected the object nestled in his hand.

It wasn't a rock.

It was a tooth. A human molar. It even had a filling.

"What the hell?" Robert mumbled.

"We're starting without you!"

Robert turned the boot over and inspected the sole. Mud was deeply encrusted into the tread, and buried within, protruding from the dried earth like the fossilized remains of ancient creatures were three more teeth.

"What happened? You get a rock stuck in your boot?" It was Stephens.

Dumbfounded, at a loss for words, Robert merely held the tooth in the palm of his hand and extended it to his colleague. He couldn't stop his hand from shaking.

"Damn, that must've hurt. You have to be careful. It

pisses me off the way people don't clean up after themselves. Busted beer bottles everywhere."

"B-b-but," Robert stuttered. "Look." He held the tooth closer.

"Yeah, I see it. It's a piece of glass." He looked at Robert strangely. "Did it cut you?"

Robert shook his head, not comprehending the manner in which his colleague was reacting.

"Come on, I'm starving." Stephens slapped Robert on the shoulder, causing him to drop the tooth.

Robert tried to retrieve the tooth from the grass, but he couldn't locate it. He did find a piece of broken glass. There was another piece of glass and two small rocks embedded in the mud caked onto the bottom of his boot. Robert inspected his other boot. There was more mud, and a few tiny rocks, but no teeth.

Robert laughed nervously to himself. He picked the foreign pieces from the soles of his boots and tossed them aside. He removed his sock on his right foot, checking to see if the glass fragment had cut him. There was no blood. But there was a small indentation in the soft skin, and the area surrounding it was an angry red. Almost like a bite mark.

* * *

The summer sun was high in the sky, and the heat was beginning to swelter. The small aluminum fishing boat served as a magnifying glass in the hot rays of the sun as it floated slowly down the calm river. Robert absent-mindedly shelled the piece of bait shrimp destined to be impaled on his hook, but his mind was not really on fishing.

This morning's occurrences disturbed him still. The dream seemed more distant and less imposing. The incident with the teeth stuck in his boots—of the one tooth *inside* his boot—bothered him the most. He just couldn't fathom how he could've imagined a broken piece of amber-colored glass to be a tooth. It didn't make sense.

But he was trying to put it all behind him. He was here to have fun. He and his friends from Compton Advertising had planned this fishing trip to Rio de Diablo for months now in an effort to release some of the stress that had been building within the corporation, and he needed to relax.

But the fact of the matter was, he was feeling more stressed than ever. He should've known it would spell nothing but trouble for him when the guys had announced this particular river as the location of their vacation getaway. "The best blue cat fishing in the whole state," they had proclaimed. "You wouldn't believe some of the monsters they pull from the bottom of that river."

Monsters? Robert thought. Oh yes, I can believe that. Monsters. Ghouls. Skeletons.

Robert looked out across the brownish water as he guided the shrimp onto his hook. Any place on this river could be the spot where Wally's unfortunate body had become entangled in the twist of gnarly branches, any area could be where Robert had watched his hand disappear beneath the water forever.

Paying one's proper respects.

"Here, dip your bait in this," Desmond said. "This is guaranteed to attract the big cats."

Stephens jerked his head away. "Jesus, what is that shit?"

"Stinkbait, city boy. Haven't you ever been fishing?"

Robert crinkled his nose at the pungent odor of the cheesy concoction. The smell made him uneasy. It reeked of dead things. It brought long-buried, long-decayed memories floating to the surface.

Giving bones a decent burial.

"That's the most god awful stink I've ever smelled,"

Stephens said.

Desmond suddenly let out a whoop of excitement, and the others saw the tip of his rod was bending nearly double over the side of the boat. "See what I mean! Yes, yes, yes! Look at that bad boy fight!"

Robert watched the water churn as Desmond brought the sleek catfish to the surface, dodged the spray as the great fish flopped in a final futile effort to save itself. Bodies moved about the small boat as the others maneuvered to help land the blue.

"Grab the net, Robert! Help me land this monster!"

The excitement of the moment snapped Robert out of his funk, and he grabbed the large landing net. Moving over to the side of the boat, he could see the whiskered beast beating the water to a frothy foam.

He deftly slipped the net into the water, under the fish and lifted it up. The fish flopped within the confines of the net, its white belly exposed. One of its serrated fins was hung on the netting. Careful to avoid getting his fingers sliced open, Robert worked to free the fish. Eerie croaking sounds emanated from deep within its maw.

Why don't you just untangle it, Robbie? Let it float on down the river, sink to the bottom, rot in here with me?

Robert jerked his hand back and screamed.

He stepped backward, away from the net and stumbled over one of the bench seats, sending a tackle box flying and knocking over the jar of stinkbait.

Turning and twisting in the net, the bleached skull repositioned itself to face Robert. The black nylon hung over one empty eye socket, and for one comical, insane moment, Robert thought of a demented Jolly Roger. The jawbones clacked together, the sound deafening to Robert's ears, echoing down the long river.

Robert could swear the jaws curled upward into a sinister grin, and he could see there were several teeth missing.

My God, Robert realized. *The teeth stuck in my boot.*

Now that I've gotten inside your head, Robbie old buddy, you can get inside mine. Now it's time to find the rest of me.

Robert crawled backward frantically, his arms pin-wheeling, fighting for leverage away from the horrible visage. His hand landed on a hook, the sharp point digging into his palm past the barb. The pain did not register in Robert's brain.

The others laughed.

"Jesus, Spencer. Haven't you ever been fishing in your life?"

"Are you afraid you're going to get your hands all slimy?"

Robert halted his backward progress as Desmond lifted the sleek blue cat from the net, holding it up for all to see.

"Sweet," he boasted. "This baby'll go ten pounds, easy."

Robert clutched his chest, could feel his heart beating at an unsafe level. Sweat poured down his forehead and into his eyes. It was only when he moved to wipe the sweat away that he noticed the fishhook buried in his flesh.

"Christ, Robert. Scared of a little fish," Anthony chided. "Are you sure you're cut out for the outdoor life?"

Just a fish. Just a blue catfish.

Not a skull. Not a skull at all. Just like the glass wasn't a tooth.

Oh, he was scared, all right, but it wasn't because of a little fish. He was frightened of this river, more specifically, of what was in it. And he felt as if his sanity was being dragged down to join whatever lay beneath the dingy surface. Suddenly, Robert began to weep. He opened his hand and stared at the hook embedded in the palm of his hand, and hoped the others assumed he was crying tears of pain.

* * *

Robert had just nodded off to sleep, his bandaged hand throbbing with a dull ache, the events of the day still very much fresh on his mind. His memories were getting to him, that was all. There was a simple, rational explanation for everything that had occurred. The pieces of glass and small rocks stuck to the bottom of his boots.

It was easy enough to see how he could have mistaken them for teeth. The glint of the sun. The small streaks of mud on them. Sure, anyone could've done that. The catfish? Well, certainly, when the fish flopped in the net, exposing its bone white belly, and the dark spots on its side, looking similar to the recesses of eye sockets, anyone could've thought that was a human skull.

But would they have heard the skull speak to them, Robbie? Would they have heard it speak their name?

Yeah, sure, that could happen.

All of these strange occurrences. Easily explained.

But it was going to be much more difficult to explain away the shattered rib cage lying on the ground just a few feet from his sleeping bag. That was a tough one.

Yet, there it was, lying in the dark, glowing in the moon rays, looking like a tiny prison of bone from which there was no escape for Robert's sanity.

The rib cage lay flat against the black dirt of the campsite, broken into tiny pieces, parts of which were buried in the dried mud.

You broke so many hearts, Robbie. You're quite good at it. My ribs shattered trying to protect my heart when you stomped on it.

Robert sat up in the sleeping bag. The bones shimmered in the moonlight only an arm's length away, glowing horribly bright. He remembered for a fleeting moment sleeping on a cot at a cousin's house when he was eight.

From his position, he could see under his cousin's bed. There was something glowing under there, way at the back. When he woke his cousin, they had discovered that the mysterious, glowing entities were discarded glow-in-the-dark pieces from some of his cousin's Aurora monster models, still charged from the light of the day.

And even though he knew what they were, the young Robert still had trouble going to sleep, with the disembodied hands, feet and heads of the Wolfman, Godzilla, the Mummy and the Forgotten Prisoner staring back at him from the dark depths.

We're going to get you, Robbie. We're going to eat you and we're going to get inside your head and eat your brains and make you go crazy.

Only now it wasn't plastic pieces that threatened Robert. Now it was bones. Real bones. Bones that could not be rationalized.

Robert slowly reached out to touch the pieces of ribs. They were surprisingly cool to the touch.

"Go ahead," a voice said. "Pick them up. Bring them with you."

He knew that voice. Robert looked around the campsite to see if anyone else was awake. But his friends were sleeping. A comforting theory that this entire series of events had been an elaborate prank cooked up by his coworkers entered his head for a moment.

Robert collected the bones and stood. Ten feet away, underneath a tall tree, something radiated. Without hesitation, Robert walked to it and picked it up. A sliver of bone, possibly from the hand.

Robert peered beyond the perimeter of camp, into the deep woods. In the distance, he could hear the soft lapping of water at the sides of the banks. Stretching into the woods like a neon, morbid trail that might lead Hansel and Gretel directly into the witch's oven rather than safely back home, was a wake of phosphorescent bits of bone.

"Robbie," the voice said.

Robert followed the path, pausing to retrieve every piece he came across. Every few feet was another fragment, like pieces of some obscene jigsaw puzzle created by an insane craftsman. The last one rested in the shallow water at the edge of the river, near the place where he had skipped rocks his first day here. Robert knelt and put his hand into the cold water.

"I want them all," the voice said.

Robert turned, and there was Wally, as he had been before the bus trip, before Trish, before everything had fallen apart for them. He looked so young and innocent, but there was something in his blue eyes that told Robert he might be young forever, but that he would never be innocent again.

"Why are you doing this?"

"I want them all, Robbie. My bones. I deserve them."

"Wally, I . . . I am sorry. I am so sorry."

"I was so happy when you found my body. I was there, you know, standing right there on the bank, watching you. Oh yeah, watched your every move. My parents were going to be so relieved, as happy as they could be under the circumstances. They were going to be able to close the door on this terrible tragedy, were going to get to say goodbye to their little boy.

And wasn't it so fitting that my best friend be the one to find me? After all the cops and all the dogs and all the volunteers, it was just another kid who finds it. My parents really loved you, Robbie. You know that, don't you? They always credited you with keeping me out of trouble. And   , they were probably right. God knows I was always a screwup. But then, you started saying those things, those awful things."

"Please, Wally, can't you forgive me?"

"Forgive you? I don't know, Robbie. I don't think so.

You were such a coward. What I did wasn't right. God, I realize that, but what you did hurt me. I cried, Robbie. I cried when I watched what you did. I bawled and I screamed and I begged you to stop, but of course, you couldn't hear me. Maybe I had it coming, I don't know. It's a stretch, but maybe I did. But then you tied those rocks to me . . . and then . . ."

"I didn't kill you," Robert said.

The Wally ghost chuckled. "I never said you did. But I almost wish you had. It certainly would've been more dignified. For both of us."

"You were already dead, Wally."

"Fish ate my pecker, Robbie. My eyes. My fingers."

"You were dead. I didn't hurt you."

"But you did hurt me. You hurt me, and what's worse, you hurt a lot of others. Folks who were perfectly innocent. You went away to college a few months later. You never got to see what your little stunt did.

The stress drove my parents away from each other. When my mother finally died a few years ago, her and my dad were total strangers. They never got over my death, Robbie, because they were never able to put it to rest, never able to close the door on it.

They had to live with it as if it had happened yesterday, every day of their lives. I'm not saying their pain wouldn't have caused them to drift apart anyway, but at least they would've had some closure, some kind of goddamn ending.

"But now, what's left of me is buried in the mud, swept out into the ocean, covered in silt. You know, millions of years from now, some scientist will dig up my bones, and they'll probably put me in a museum in space somewhere. My mother couldn't say goodbye to me, Robbie, but some hundred-eyed alien will get to stare at me for the price of a freakin' ticket."

Robert began to sob. "I wish I could take it back."

"You can't take it back. It's already done. You can only do your part to make it right."

"How?"

"I already told you. By finding them. By finding my bones."

Robert looked at the collection in his hands.

Diggin' up bones. I'm diggin' up bones.

When Robert awoke the next morning, he wanted to believe the previous night's events had been a very bad dream, but there was fresh mud on the bottoms of his boots.

And no bones.

* * *

"Well, we did just good enough today to get to eat hot dogs, didn't we?"

The guys from Compton Advertising laughed, comfortable in the knowledge that the number of fish caught was not as important as the mere act of getting away for a while.

The fire blazed in the center of the campsite; wood chips popped and sent sparks into the twilight air. The woodsy smell of the fire rose with the smoke. Five sticks with wieners skewered onto them hovered above the orange and yellow licks of flame. The wieners blackened as the fire caressed them.

"Are you feeling any better?" Anthony asked Robert.

Robert slowly slipped the tubular slice of processed meat onto a stick he had whittled to a point with his pocketknife. He had not gone fishing with the rest of the guys earlier, content to stay at camp and listen to the voices in his head, to enjoy his gradual descent into insanity. Robert simply nodded and positioned the end of his stick over the fire.

I think you forgot something.

Robert did not look up; he had no interest in the walking corpse, only on his cooking hot dog.

You left something by the river. Seems to be a habit with

you.

Robert shut his eyes tightly. Maybe in denial, the voice would go away. Leave me alone, he said in his head. I didn't kill you.

You should've. I mean, if you had to have your little revenge, you should've acted like a man. That's what a real man would've done. But you had to take the coward's way out. You had to have your revenge, your sweet revenge.

I'm not going to listen to you anymore. You're not real. It's just because I'm here, where all this happened. That's the only reason. When I get back to Dallas, I'll be fine, and you'll still be dead.

Yeah, I'll still be dead. I'll always be dead. But I still want my bones.

Get them yourself.

Can't do that. Only you can. You're the one who let them get away. You're the one who has to round them up. Why don't you make a game out of it? Pretend you're an archeologist on a dig. You're looking for King Tut, digging through the desert sands, searching for the remains of the young king. It can be fun if you let it. Let it be fun, Robbie.

I'm not looking for your bones, Wallace. I didn't hurt you. I didn't kill you. That flood killed you; not me.

No, Robert Spencer, you did hurt me. I've not been at rest since my passing, and that's all directly related to what you did. So, you will find my bones—

I won't.

You will. I'll even help you look.

Robert looked up then, past his friends now busying themselves with the arranging of their hot dogs, at the transparent figure of his former friend. It held in its hands a skull, some rib bones, a few teeth. Robert could still see his coworkers through the apparition.

I told you to keep these last night. I'm helping you out here, Robbie. I think I'm being completely fair. Quite the gentleman, in fact.

I'm not finding your bones for you, Wally. I'm not responsible for what happened to you. You want them, you find them.

You will *find them, Robbie. You will.*

Robert returned his attention to his dinner and opened his mouth wide in a silent shriek. He was no longer holding a stick trimmed from a mesquite tree. Instead, he was holding an arm bone near the elbow, and the blackened wiener was gripped by a skeletal hand hovering above the fire.

Robert watched in horror as the bony fingers opened and closed, the action making a chilling *clackity-clack* sound that kept time with the crackling of the fire. Juice dripped from the plump, overcooked wiener and dripped down the length of the ulna, tinging it pink in the warm glow of the fire. Robert finally found his voice and dropped the arm, wiener and all, into the fire.

"Jesus, what is it?" Desmond cried.

Robert fell backward into the dirt, crawling away from the ghost of Wallace Davis. Even in the blaze, the skeletal hand continued its obscene action. *Clackity-clack. Clackity-clack.*

"Did you burn yourself?"

"Get away!" Robert screamed. "Get away from me!"

"Robert, what's wrong? What's the matter?" his friends asked.

This doesn't have to be difficult, Robbie. Just find my bones and I'll leave you alone. That's all I'm asking. Just find my bones. Give me my proper respects.

Robert stood and turned to face the apparition. Sweat soaked his shirt and his heart slammed in his chest. He clenched his fists and gritted his teeth. He had had enough.

"I'm not finding your bones, goddamn it! You're not real! You don't exist!"

Robert charged the specter of Wally and plowed into it,

sending them both sprawling down the sloping embankment toward the river. Robert's fist drove into the unsuspecting body, pounding out his fears and frustrations into his one-time friend. Their bodies slammed into trees and rocks and finally came to a splashing halt in the shallow water at the river's edge. Robert stood and kicked at Wally's ghost.

"Stop making me crazy!" he shouted. "Just go away and leave me alone! You're dead, and you can't bother me anymore!"

He continued to shove the ghost, sending it into the deeper part of the river.

Just shut up and find my fucking bones.

"Noooo! I'm not finding your fucking bones!"

Robert pounced on top of the drenched form beneath him, hands clenching its throat maliciously. He continued to scream at the ghastly spirit, the ghost struggling against Robert as he choked the life out of it. Finally, the resistance ceased, and the body slumped lifelessly into the brown water.

Are you quite done yet, Robbie? Have you gotten a grip yet? And most importantly, are you ready to find my bones now?

A ripple formed in the water and Robbie's eyes went to it. A familiar skull broke the water's surface and slowly rose, followed by several vertebrae, collarbones, ribs, until an entire skeleton stood dripping before him. Robert dropped to his knees and collapsed, sobbing fitfully.

Take a good look, Robbie. Here they are, all together. See them. Study them. Memorize them. Got that? Are you ready now? Good. Find them, Robbie. Find my bones.

Robert looked up as the skeleton fell in on itself. Small splashes of water splatted where the avalanche of falling bones entered the water. Robert watched in disbelieving terror as the bones were lifted onto the current and carried away, past the lifeless body that was being dragged down, into the powerful undercurrents of the unpredictable river, scattering once again.

* * *

Two months had passed since a small group of business associates from Compton Advertising watched one of their own snap and attack a coworker, choking him in the muddy waters of Rio de Diablo, and finally forcing him under the water to drown. The current had swept the body of Anthony Dennard away and evidently, intended to keep it; his remains were never recovered.

Robert Spencer was declared legally insane and incompetent to stand trial. He was locked away in the Terrell State Hospital for the Criminally Insane two weeks after the incident.

Robert enjoyed his room at the hospital. It was small, but cozy, and it kept most of the voices away. He had a small bookshelf where he kept whatever meager belongings the doctors allowed him to have, and a barred window looked out over the courtyard where he would watch visitors stroll by on sunny days. Overall, he was happy.

And content in the fact that he had work to do.

He was ready to find the bones.

I tried to help you, Robbie. Now it's going to be much more difficult.

"I know," Robert said to the voice inside his head.

He knelt at the concrete floor and closed his eyes.

Find my bones, Robbie. Remember what they looked like? Find them.

Behind his closed eyes, Robert could see the brown, babbling waters of Rio de Diablo, could smell the muddy earth, the stench of decay rising from their murky depths. He ran his fingers along the hard, rough concrete floor, could feel the smooth, cool sand of the riverbank.

Start digging, Robbie. Find my bones.

Robert scraped his fingertips across the unforgiving concrete, felt the tiny granules of sand part and give to his desires. He started to dig.

That's good, Robbie. That's real good.

Robert could feel the warm summer breeze on his back, could hear the wind whistling through the high tree branches, the birds singing in their hidden recesses. He continued to scrape his fingers across the floor, as the hole in the sand began to grow.

Blood started to flow from his ragged fingertips, splashing in hot drips on the hard floor. The hole in the riverbank grew wider but yielded no bones.

Keep going, Robbie. They're in there.

Robert scraped his fingers to the bone.

The bone? Robert giggled.

Find my bones, Robbie. Find all my bones.

Robert looked at his fingers. The skin and muscle was scraped away, revealing the first phalange of each finger. Ragged strips of meat clung to the ruined tendons and ligaments, hanging below what skin remained.

He held his hands up in the air. "Look, I found bones. Look, Wally. Bones."

That's good, Robbie. That's real good. Now, why not go for the mother lode?

Robert returned to his digging. The wide hole in the sand began to yield more tiny bones. The flesh on Robert's hands was eaten away up to his palms; brights flashes of metacarpal bones peeked through the mangled flesh.

"Lots more bones," Robert laughed hysterically.

He held one hand before his face, and with his other fingers, pulled at the phalange of his left middle finger. The remaining tendons linking it to the second phalange stretched like a gory rubber band and snapped, sending tiny splatters of blood flying through the air, freeing the small finger bone. He moved over to the ring finger, the index finger, and soon, Robert held ten small bones in his bloody palm.

He presented them for Wally to see. "Look, Wally. More bones."

That's good, Robbie. Very nice.

Robert looked up from the floor at the skull sitting atop his immaculately maintained bookshelf. Wally was nice enough to find his skull. The rest was up to Robert.

Robert continued to scrape his ruined hands across the rough concrete surface. Soon his hands would collapse into mushy piles of ragged flesh up to his wrists.

That's a good start, Robbie. But there are over two hundred bones in the human body. You have a long way to go, Robbie. But you're doing good.

The skull peered down from the bookshelf and smiled. Oddly enough, it had all its teeth.

Just keep digging, Robbie. I'll sit here and watch. Until you find them all. Every one of them. I'll watch and you'll dig, Robbie. Oh, how you'll dig.

Bon Appetit

Brett King

Ryan Leal could hear his husband fucking another man. He stood in the entryway and listened to the deep grunts and whining moans echoing from the bedroom they shared before dropping his keys and wallet on the hall table and heading into the kitchen. He popped in a pair of earbuds, cranked the volume up, and busied himself with cooking dinner. It was his duty to keep his husband happy, after all. A duty he felt he was failing at more often than not, but one he refused to give up on.

Before they married, Ryan and Travis lived in a shitty apartment downtown. They were broke, but it didn't matter; being together was enough back then. They didn't own a car, so Ryan would ride on the back of Travis's motorcycle with his arms wrapped around his waist.

Every day, Travis would drop Ryan off at work before going to his own job and every night the two of them would ride around town before heading back home. For three years, they saved every penny they had, surviving off the bare minimum. Three years of skimpy meals and holes in every pair of socks and underwear they owned, and they finally did it.

The wedding was small, with just a few of their closest friends. Neither of the men had spoken to their respective parents since they were teenagers. They didn't feel their absence at the wedding, though; their friends more than made up for it. They danced and laughed and drank way too much. At the end of the night, they mounted Travis's bike for the first time as husbands and they went home to that shitty apartment where they slept on a mattress with no frame, and they were happy.

Six months later they closed on the house and a week after that they moved in, oblivious that the happiness they once shared would fizzle and die there.

But life had been good there for a while. When they were still newlyweds and their house felt like a new adventure they were embarking on together. When they were making plans for renovations and vacations. In all the talks of future get-togethers and even the notions of maybe having kids. Back when Travis would lift him onto the very counter he was dicing an onion on now and they would make love with the sunlight filtering in through the kitchen window.

But then the cancer showed up.

It was a massive brain tumor that would take Travis's life within a year. It started with headaches and confusion and quickly became rage and random outbursts. It didn't take long for Ryan to put his foot down about the motorcycle. He couldn't fathom life without Travis.

He knew it was coming, but the bike was too risky. He begged him not to take it out anymore. Travis was irate. They argued all night and Travis put his fist through the bathroom door before locking himself in the garage. Ryan lay awake all night. Travis never came to bed.

The next morning, Ryan found him sitting on the living room couch. His hands and face were smudged with grease and his hair hung in sweaty tangles in front of his eyes. He apologized for the way he acted. After a much more civil talk than the previous night's, the two agreed Travis was in no state to be driving. Ryan went to work that day with his mind at ease. Looking back, it was the final happy moment he could remember them sharing.

The atmosphere at home changed after that. Travis, who once put all his attention on his husband, sunk into himself and their new home grew dark. The love they shared strained and resentment took its place. Travis spent large periods locked away in the garage working on his bike until the sickness became too great and he went to bed for what would be the remainder of his life. And yet Ryan persevered. What else could he do?

A cold chill ran down Ryan's neck and his shoulders tensed.

He looked up from the chopping board but didn't turn around. He knew what it was and as much as it made him want to run, he knew it was just watching. It lurked in the shadows at all times, observing and listening. Only once had it made itself known.

Ryan could feel it all around him most times. Whatever it was, he owed everything to it, but it was a parasite. It took everything in him just to get out of bed most days. His eyes and cheeks had sunken in leaving his face gaunt. His clothes hung off of his wasted body like a little kid in his older brother's hand-me-downs.

Ryan often wondered if his appearance was what made Travis start looking at other men. If he was being honest, he couldn't remember the last time they'd had sex. It had to have been after the diagnosis, but who could say?

Travis kept his distance from him. It had gotten to the point where they only interacted during dinner. It didn't take long for Ryan to notice the men. He had forgotten his wallet one day and came back home on his lunch break to get it. There was a car in the driveway he didn't recognize. He didn't stop. He simply turned around and went back to work. As he sat down at his desk, tears stinging his eyes, he decided it was a small price to pay for his husband's life. After all, his husband was a living miracle.

***

"It's starting." That's all Misty said to him. Pity, rather than empathy painted her wrinkled features.

Ryan couldn't speak. His tongue filled his throat and mouth. He nodded and the hospice nurse stepped out of his way. Travis's shriveled form lay in their bed at the back of the bedroom. The room stank like a hospital—a piss and vomit odor covered up by disinfectant that saturated everything it touched. Ryan often wondered if he would ever be able to sleep in this room again after Travis passed. The hiss of the oxygen tank hooked up to his husband pierced his ears. He stood frozen in the doorway. In the right corner of the room, near the bed, was a shadow of the deepest black. Ryan's hands began to tremble.

It had been there since the day Travis was diagnosed. It watched him night and day. No matter how bright the lights were, the room seemed shrouded in darkness. Was it Death? Ryan wasn't sure, but he could feel it feeding on them. There was no joy in its presence.

They never spoke of it, but he knew the nurse could feel it. She always approached Travis's bedside from the left—a habit Ryan adopted as well.

Misty spoke from somewhere off to the side, startling Ryan.

"He's stable right now, but I think it'll be soon. Maybe not today, but it'll happen before the week is over."

"Is he awake?" He pulled his gaze away from the corner.

"He seems to be, but he hasn't been lucid much since last night. I want to let you have some time alone with him before he progresses."

Ryan nodded and Misty nudged him inside, shutting the door behind him. With his eyes locked on his husband, he went to the dining room chair they'd placed next to the bed. Travis's eyes were closed and his throat crackled like hot grease with each breath. Ryan took his hand. It felt brittle and papery.

Veins bulged up through his loose skin. It was yellowed and hung from his bones like wet laundry. Travis opened his eyes just barely. He tried to turn his head to look at Ryan but gave up and looked at the ceiling. He coughed twice and closed his eyes again.

"Don't move, baby. I'm right here."

Travis took a ragged breath and coughed again. He cleared his throat with a grimace. "Scared."

"I'm right here."

Travis pulled his cracked lips back in a horrific smile but didn't say anything else. His labored breathing quieted, and he fell asleep. Ryan laid his head down on the bed next to Travis and he sobbed.

How could this be the same man he married? The same man who used to take him out on his motorcycle? The man with the most contagious laugh Ryan had ever heard? This creature in their bed no longer resembled his husband.

He had always promised to be there for him and now he was going to die. It seemed like a cruel joke. One minute they were moving into their first home together, and the next Travis was leaving forever. Ryan kept waiting for God to tell him, "Sike!" But it was no joke. It was real, and he was going to be alone for the rest of his life.

Not really alone, though. *It* was here, over in the corner, watching this last display of affection. He could feel how much it was enjoying this. And just like that he was exhausted. The fight was almost out of him. This was the end of the line and once it was over, he didn't know what to expect, but whatever it was, it started with him leaving this house forever.

He sat up and kissed Travis on his forehead. He was hot to the touch. Sweat stood out on his mostly bald head. Ryan could taste it on his lips. He sat that way with Travis for an hour when there was a knock at the door. Misty entered before he responded. At the sight of her, he began to stand.

"Oh, no. You just stay there. You don't need to get up for me. Jesus, it's dark in here. We should change those bulbs. How are you?"

He shrugged and looked at Travis.

She nodded and gave him that look of sympathy again. It made him feel like a child.

"I'm just going to take a look at him and then I'll give you some space."

Misty leaned over Travis and looked into his eyes. They were swollen and stood out harshly from the rest of his gaunt face. She leaned down and listened to his breathing. The death rattle was worse than it was earlier. It was a sound that haunted Ryan from the second it first began. It would echo in his head for the rest of his life, he thought. Misty picked up Travis's hand and raised her eyebrows.

"His hands are cold."

"What does that mean?"

"It's normal. His breathing has been uneven all day. Have you been talking with him?"

"No. I didn't think he could hear me anymore."

"You should try. It's reassuring. Sometimes they won't let go on their own."

"I don't want to let go, either." Ryan ran his finger over Travis's cheek.

"Maybe he knows that. Let him know you'll be okay without him. Let him have some peace of mind."

"You think that's why he's still here?"

Misty squeezed Ryan's shoulder. "There's a lot we

don't know about death, but in the years I've been doing this, I've learned that sometimes people are too scared to die. And sometimes, people are just too stubborn. Sometimes they need permission."

"I would do anything for him."

"Then do this. Let him know you're okay."

Ryan nodded and Misty left the room. He rubbed the back of Travis's hand. He didn't know if she was right or not—it didn't seem like Travis could hear anything that was happening—but if it meant giving him some kind of comfort, he would do it.

"Hey, baby." He paused and cleared his throat. "You've been so strong. Since the day I met you, you've been the strongest man I've ever known. You've carried so much weight—weight that was never yours to carry, but you don't have to anymore. Rest. I'll be okay. Just rest."

Snot threatened to run over his chapped lips. He didn't know if it was right to lie like this. How could he ever be all right without his husband? If Travis could hear him, though, he couldn't let him know he was lying. He needed to be strong for him.

And then Travis began to shake.

Ryan jolted backward and watched as his husband's body convulsed and rocked the bed. His head thrashed about on the pillow and his face twisted in pain. His hand slapped uselessly against the mattress, over and over. Ryan watched in shock, unable to move or think. And then he saw them—two yellow eyes in the dark of the far corner.

He screamed for help.

Seconds later, Misty burst into the room. She commanded him to stand back and shoved him away from Travis's bedside. All of the sound left the room and Ryan couldn't breathe. The eyes were gone now, but he could still feel them watching him.

The great blackness inched its way toward Travis's bed.

Whispers hissed from the shadows, too many and too faint to understand. He looked into the darkness, horror mounting in his heart, as he realized he could see the outline of something: a monstrous form made of shadow.

Misty grabbed him by both arms and spoke to him, but her words were muffled like he was underwater. She put her hands on either side of his face. Her words seemed jumbled up at first, but then they came to him.

"You need to be with him."

He nodded wordlessly and let her guide him to the bed. The convulsions had stopped. Somehow, Travis looked even more shriveled than he had earlier.

"Is it time?" he asked.

"He's still with us, but yes. I think so."

She sat Ryan down in the chair and told him she'd be right back. She left the room and came back with another chair from the dining room. She put it next to his and sat. She squeezed his knee. "I'm not going anywhere, okay?"

"Okay," he replied. "How long will it take?"

"I can't really answer that, but not long, I suspect."

Ryan held Travis's claw-like hand. He tried to channel everything he wanted Travis to know and feel into this simple gesture. He wanted Travis to feel safe and at ease, but how could he with that awful darkness watching over him? It crept its way across the room with every passing minute, stretching itself over the bed and blacking out the light. Its whispers grew louder until they were like screams inside Ryan's skull.

And then all at once, they became one voice.

"You can save him."

***

Ryan took a Ziploc bag of ground chuck from the fridge—red juice pooled at the bottom. The sight of it used to make him queasy, but he'd grown accustomed to it in the past few weeks. It took a few meals, but he realized early on the taste was fine. The real problem was the texture. He dumped it out into a skillet and soon, the kitchen was filled with the aroma of cooking meat. It was more pungent than most meats—almost akin to beef, but much richer.

With meat browned and drained and the aromatics cooked, he got the sauce simmering and water waiting to boil. He was about to taste the sauce when a small shirtless man—a boy really—came out of the hall and into the kitchen. The boy froze and then put on a fake smile. He couldn't have been older than twenty-one. He had shaggy blonde hair and his body was lean, yet defined. A tuft of blonde hair peeked out of the waistband of his shorts. He looked nothing like Ryan. It made his stomach hurt.

The boy's mouth moved, but he couldn't hear him over the music. He took out an earbud and said, "Come again?"

"Oh, uh," he stammered and then extended his hand. "I didn't realize he had a roommate. I'm Jake."

A sarcastic smile spread across Ryan's sallow face. "I'm not his roommate. Will you be staying for dinner?"

The boy's eyes widened and he dropped his hand. He tried to stutter out a response when Travis appeared behind him with his hand on his shoulder.

"It's all good," Travis whispered into Jake's ear. Ryan's chest ached at the sight of his husband touching this boy.

"There's more than enough. It's no bother, really." Ryan still wore the fake smile, but every cell in his body screamed for Jake to get the fuck out of his house.

Jake looked from Travis to Ryan and back again. "Uh, I think I should probably just go," he said, shrugging Travis off.

"I'll call you later?" Travis asked.

"How about I call you?" Jake said.

"Uh, yeah. That's fine."

"Don't forget your shirt," Ryan said.

Jake disappeared down the hall and the two men waited

until they heard the front door close before acknowledging one another.

"You're home early," Travis said.

"I had an easy day at work." He leaned forward for a kiss that Travis barely reciprocated. He could smell the boy on Travis's breath and lips. The stench of sex hung heavy on him and his skin felt sticky.

"How long until dinner is done?"

"Not long. Ten minutes maybe." Ryan sprinkled salt in the now boiling water. "Why didn't you go to the doctor?"

"Who says I didn't?"

"Unless that boy was your doctor, I assume you didn't go."

Travis crossed his arms. "No, I didn't go."

"You really should, you know. You could be the cure."

"I don't want to talk about this."

"I'm just saying."

"I don't really care what you're saying. Who knows how long I have before the cancer comes back? I'm not going to spend my final moments in some lab being studied like a fucking rat."

Ryan's lip quivered, but he smiled, anyway. "Dinner is about to be done. Go sit."

The dining room was dim when Ryan entered and he knew *it* must have been waiting there. He placed a plate of spaghetti in front of his husband. Travis looked at it and sighed.

"What?"

"Are you still using that cow?"

"Yeah, why?" Ryan seated himself opposite Travis. He felt eyes on the back of his head and realized *it* was hiding behind him.

"I don't love it." He twirled the noodles with his fork, lifted it to his mouth, and then put it back down. "So do you want to talk about this?"

"About what?"

"Don't do that."

Ryan took a sip of wine and cleared his throat. "Does he make you happy?"

"No."

"Is he the only one?"

"No."

Ryan thought about that for a moment. "You could have asked to open our marriage up."

Travis sighed. "And you would have agreed to that?"

"If it made you happy."

"Make me happy?" Travis scoffed. "What about you? What makes you happy, Ryan?"

"If you're happy, then I'm happy."

"Well, I'm not."

Ryan's guts twisted. "What are you saying?"

Travis sighed, pushed spaghetti around on his plate, and then dropped his fork with a clatter.

"I almost died, Ryan. I have no idea how or why I'm still here and it scares me. There's so much I never got to do. So many things I never accomplished. And I don't know when I'll get sick again. I want more from life than working a nine-to-five and paying a mortgage. I want excitement. I want adventure."

Ryan's hands shook on the table. This man didn't understand how much he loved him. He had no idea the things he'd done for him. The things that kept him awake long into the night. The things that made him throw up for weeks.

"I took care of you for months. I cleaned you and fed you and watched you while you slept. I put my entire life on hold to take care of you because you *are* my life. I did things you will never understand. What more could you need? What have I not given you?"

"You did take care of me. And I am grateful for that. But when I got better, you acted like nothing happened. We went right back to doctor's appointments and desk jobs. Right back to the same old boring routines we've been doing for years. And I guess I realized I want something you just can't give me.

"I was given a second chance that no one else has ever gotten before. My cancer disappeared completely on its own and all you want to do is pick fucking paint swatches together. I spent my first life trying to get this white picket fence life for you. I want to spend my second life living."

Ryan could feel the presence growing behind him. It loomed high over him like the shadow of a great mountain. The room darkened and the air around him began to fluctuate. It pulsed in his ears and chilled the back of his neck. Travis's words drowned in its oppressive atmosphere.

"I want to take the bike cross country," he continued. "I need to get away from this house. This place, it's not right. Too many bad memories. It's like it sucks the life out of you."

Ryan snapped back to reality. Travis could fuck all the men he wanted, but leaving was not an option.

"No."

"I'm not asking for your permission."

"No," he said again.

Travis took a bite of his spaghetti and chewed savagely. "Well, it's not really up for debate."

Angry tears blurred Ryan's vision. "You can't leave. If you leave, you'll die and I won't go through that again."

"I'm going to die whether I leave or not."

"You don't understand," Ryan said through gritted teeth. "You have to stay here or you *will* die."

Travis swallowed another bite of his dinner and put his fork down. "Ryan, are you threatening me?" His voice was calm.

Ryan laughed. He sounded like a lunatic. "It's not a threat. I don't know if there's anything I can say that'll help you understand."

The room was so dark now the overhead light might as well have been a tealight. Not even the sunlight outside could penetrate this darkness. Travis seemed to notice this for the first time. He surveyed the room, his eyebrows knitted together until his eyes stopped on Travis and his face went slack. He saw *it*. He stood from his seat and backed away from the table.

"Sit down. Finish your food. You have to eat it." Ryan took the first bite of his own spaghetti and shivered as it slid down his throat.

"No. I'm done eating this shit. I'm leaving. I'm already packcd."

Ryan slammed his fist on the table. "You're going to eat your fucking food!"

Travis looked down at his plate, back up to his husband, and then focused on the darkness that surrounded Ryan.

"Don't be scared. It won't hurt you. It saved you." Ryan forced down another bite of spaghetti. "Please, you have to eat."

"Why?"

"Just listen to me!" Ryan's voice shook and tears blurred his vision.

"Tell me why!" Travis demanded.

"I can't do that."

"What is it?"

"I don't know what it is."

"Not *it*. The food."

"It's spaghetti."

"Don't lie to me. What are you feeding me?"

"I told you; I went in on a cow with a couple guys from work."

The two stared at one another from across the table until Travis seemed to come to a decision. Without a word, he made to leave. He only made it two steps before a sinister laugh rasped from behind Ryan. The color drained from Travis's face. He snatched up his dinner knife and brandished it across the table. Hurried whispers and gurgled laughs erupted in the darkness. Travis shrieked and waved the knife around.

"Tell me the truth, Ryan!" he screamed. Ryan's features crumbled and he held his stomach, snot streaming from his nose.

"It's Misty!"

Travis stopped waving the knife and shook his head. He looked confused. "No, that thing can't be Misty."

Ryan swallowed back bile. "The meat, Travis. The meat is Misty."

Travis's face went blank and his eyes glassed over.

"It told me it could bring you back, but there would be a cost. I told it to do it. I swore I would take care of you. No matter how many times you hurt me, I'll always take care of you. Because I love you. You're the most important person in the world to me and I would do anything for you. Even things you're better off not knowing about. You had your secret and I had mine."

It started with his own blood. He used a steak knife to cut the tip of his finger and slid it into Travis's mouth. At first, nothing happened. And then Travis's eyes shot open. He seized Ryan around the wrist and latched onto him like a child at the nipple. It hurt immensely, but Ryan didn't mind. When he was done, Travis fell back asleep. He never brought it up after that, so Ryan could only assume he had no memory of it.

Keeping Travis fed became harder after that. He didn't think he could keep getting away with cutting himself into Travis's mouth without Misty catching him. He had to find a new method. Getting a practice kit for drawing blood was easy. Every night, he would draw some of his own blood and spoon it into Travis's mouth. In just three short weeks,

Travis was sitting up and having conversations. Ryan couldn't believe it.

The entity, whatever it was, told the truth.

Travis got stronger every day, but as Travis got stronger, Ryan grew weaker. He knew he couldn't keep this up. He would be the next one in hospice care if he didn't figure something out. And then he had an idea. It was time for Travis to have real food.

Travis's miraculous recovery disturbed Misty. She thought something must be wrong. It was impossible. How could someone come back from the brink of death like that? How could someone's cancer—brain cancer at that!—just disappear? It was she who urged Ryan to take him to be examined.

She had just finished her usual night shift. The two of them were in the garage sharing a cigarette. She had just given him the contact information for a specialist she'd been talking about all week.

Ryan had been apprehensive about going, but what could it hurt? It's not like they would ever believe how Travis recovered. After she stubbed the cigarette out, she started to head back into the house. It was then that Ryan made a choice. He grabbed a motorcycle chain from a shelf and wrapped it around her throat. They fell to the floor as she struggled against his grip. The chain dug into both of their skin while she kicked and squirmed. Their fingers tore to shreds. Ryan still had nightmares remembering the warm spray on his face as the chain ripped into her jugular. The rasping gasps and cries for help became gargled chokes and then silence.

Ryan was no hunter, so dressing the body was difficult. He wasted a lot more than he would have liked, but he used up as much of her body as he could.

Her death was probably the most meaningful thing that ever happened to her. Once he had cleaned the flesh from her bones, he used them to make broth that he would give to Travis until he was ready for solid foods. Until then, the rest of her sat in the deep freeze. When Travis asked about her, Ryan told him she didn't feel like she was needed anymore.

Travis looked between his plate of spaghetti, Ryan's solemn face, and the black figure that now towered over his husband. With one great heave, he threw up all over the floor and the front of his shirt. He steadied himself on the table and then threw up again and again until he was hacking and coughing up nothing, but spittle and stringy bile.

"I told you I would do anything for you."

Travis steadied himself on the table. "Fuck you," he said, making his way across the dining room with the table as his crutch.

"Where are you going?"

"I told you I'm leaving."

Ryan stood and took a step toward Travis. Travis's eyes widened and he held the knife out in front of him. "Stay the fuck away from me. I swear I won't tell anyone, just let me leave."

"You can't leave, baby."

"I can do whatever the fuck I want!"

Ryan took another step forward. "I won't let you."

"It's my life."

Another step. "Put the knife down."

"Stay the fuck back." He swung the knife in a wide arc. Ryan pounced.

He crashed into Travis and the pair slammed into the wall. He forced Travis's arm up and away from his body to wrestle the knife from his hand. Travis held on tight and tried to bring the knife down. Ryan cried and pleaded for him to stop.

His muscles strained at the effort to keep his husband's attacks at bay. He felt Travis's knee slam into his stomach.

The spaghetti and wine rushed up his esophagus and filled his mouth—another blow. The undigested food spurted from his lips and onto Travis's face. Travis retched and released his husband to wipe the vomit from his eyes, causing Ryan to lose his balance.

Ryan snatched Travis by the collar to steady himself but brought the both of them crashing through the dining room table.

Sharp pain radiated throughout Ryan's body. Splintered wood and shattered glass stabbed into his back and legs. He rolled over and got to his hands and knees. He coughed and spat the last remnants of vomit onto the floor.

He looked up.

Though he couldn't see its physical form, the presence was now standing over him. It filled him with dread, and he cringed away from it. He had to look away. His eyes landed on Travis. The dread of the presence could never match the dread he felt at the sight of his husband, the stem of a broken wine glass jutting out of the side of his neck. A puddle of blood had already formed around his head.

Every second or so a spurt would shoot out onto the floor. He made horrid choking sounds and blood bubbled out from between his lips. Ryan put pressure around the glass. His tears fell onto Travis's face and he chanted, "No, no, no."

"You can't die. I need you." The blood seeped out from between his fingers. Was he pressing too hard? What if the stem broke in half inside him? Travis's eyes were closed. How much blood had he lost? Could an ambulance get there in time? No. They wouldn't make it in time.

"Help me!" Ryan screamed at the presence. There was a deep chuckle, and they were plunged into total darkness.

"You ask me to save this man again? Even when he doesn't love you?" a thousand voices hissed at once.

"Yes!" Ryan sobbed into Travis's immobile body.

"What is it you are willing to give?"

Ryan wiped the tears, snot, blood, and vomit from his face. He leaned forward and kissed Travis on the forehead. "Anything. I'll give you anything."

The presence laughed. Ryan smiled as Travis opened his eyes—eyes that were filled with terror at the sight of him.

My Possession: An Introspective

James H Longmore

"*K*ill the cunt."
The voice in my head was as loud and crystal clear as if its obnoxious, otherworldly creator was standing right next to me and yelling at the top of his lungs into my damned ear.

Ignoring the shouting voice that had somehow managed to set my ears ringing, I smiled sweetly at the bedraggled stranger who sat looking up hopefully at me from the trash-strewn gutter by my feet, dropped a fistful of loose change into his tattered McDonald's soda cup, and wished him well.

"You're a scholar and a gentleman," the guy grinned up at me, proudly flashing the only three teeth that remained in his festering maw of a beard-covered mouth. "Thank you kindly, good sir, and have yourself a blessed day."

I nodded self-consciously, and cracked an inward smile at the vagrant's unintentional juxtaposition, although I was obviously the only one between the two of us who knew I'd only dropped him a few quarters and dimes out of guilt at the thoughts that were echoing inside of my head like bat squeaks in a dark, dank cave.

Had I really been contemplating killing this wretch of a man, human detritus that he was? Had I just actually found myself considering ending his presumably miserable life just because I'd heard some nefarious voice telling me to?

Demanding.

Oblivious to my internal dilemma, the hobo wrested his grubby placard—written on the back of a stolen real estate sign in handwriting so neat as to be almost feminine—from beneath his sleeping mongrel dog and drew hard on the glowing nub of his cigarette.

In another time, another place, my compassion would have registered a big fat zero on the Compassion-ometer and I would have commented quite loudly to anyone who cared to listen that perhaps this guy—and thousands like him—would be in less dire straits financially if he ditched the pooch and quit fucking smoking himself to death.

But things were different now.

I gave the poor, grinning vagrant my sweetest grin and went on my way.

"Pussy!"

I really wish Dave would quit yelling at me like that.

***

There's a well-worn and much overused saying that springs to mind: W   *e all have our own inner demons.* It's a rather clichéd and somewhat trite way of indicating one's internal struggles with anything from alcoholism to serial killing to obsessive masturbation, one which I feel people would be far less prone to using if they knew what those of us who actually do possess said demons, individuals for whom it is more a truism than a proverb.

He's been a part of me for almost as long as I can re-member. I call it a *he*, although there seems to be no gender

with these things as far as I can tell. I have no idea how—
or if—they reproduce, and consider it rude to enquire directly. But, from what little information I have managed to
gather from mine thus far, the things just *are*, and have always *been*.

Of course, this leads to all manner of difficulties in
naming them. Sure, you can have Abaddon, Melchon, Suc-
corbenoth, Incubus, and a whole legion—if you'll pardon
the pun—of handles by which to call them, but those are
simply names given to the denizens of hell by people, and
they tend to be more about what the demons *do*, rather than
who they actually *are*. And in all honesty, the demons don't
care much for the monikers we people stick them with all
that much.

So, I call mine Dave.

I've spent many, many a sleepless night trying desperately to pinpoint precisely how this all came about. Nights
rendered sleepless, I must point out, by the incessant chat-
tering that bounced around in my head, the constant questioning, analyzing and philosophizing that buzzed around
the inside of my skull - it was like being pestered by an
ever-present, insomniac five-year-old!

It is easy to hazard a guess that, were I not become quite
used to Dave's jabbering from a very early age, I could quite
easily have been driven insane by now.

There's a scene in one of the *Back To The Future* movies—the second one I think—where the crazy Professor guy
with the unmanageable hair explains to the forever youthful, pre-Parkinson's Michael J Fox how timelines can be
split at a particular point by a single incident. In the movie's
case, it was Marty McFly's nemesis getting his fat hands on
the Almanac of the future and thus altering the history of
the timeline from that point onward   .

I tend to think of such incidents as *Defining Moments*;

points in time which we all experience throughout our life-times that determine the course of our own history. Moments like *should I tell the wife I'm working late and then give the cute blonde in Accounts a call?* Or, *what if I quit my job and spent the rest of my days whittling mesquite sticks on the back porch?*

No, I'm not digressing. Here's my point:

There's one incident that sticks in my mind, nothing more than a silly childhood prank, but it was, perhaps, my very first—and in hindsight, most critical—*Defining Moment.*

The more I think about it, the more I am convinced it was that one, single moment that really was to define the remainder of my life.

We had a sad friend, as most thirteen-year-olds do, whose divorced parents vied for his affection with cash rather than love and affection. Subsequently, his behavior patterns had been duly programmed to buy our friendship.

Fair-weather friends that we were, we never complained, or refused the poor boy's grand gestures of fists-full of candy and all the latest trading cards, or his over-generous topping up of our relatively meager   allowances with his own. Yep, we were great friends to Bud, the very best he could have ever have paid for.

I think it was Joe who came up with the idea, but since Frank and I agreed with no hesitation, there's no blame to apportion other than three ways. It was a simple idea really, we were to perform an improvised séance to invoke some imaginary dark spirit or other—But was notoriously fascinated by ghosts, ghouls and all things nether worldly—and our main prop for attracting said entity would be that good old root of all evil - cold, hard cash.

Of course, the only one of us who could get our hands on the amount of money we figured would be required to summon the dark spirits was—yep, you guessed it—good ol' unsuspecting Bud.

I remember as clear as if it were yesterday's memory and not one over three decades old, cycling to Frank's house on my merry way to fleece our new friend and whistling *The Entertainer*; I'd not long since seen *The Sting* on TV and I guess I thought I was being funny, or ironic or something like that.

Frank had set up his parlor for our fake séance really quite well. He'd painted some regular candles up with black poster paint, created a Ouija board out of an old chunk of plywood he'd purloined from his tumble-down shed, and dug out his mom's old Gideon Bible which she had filched from a hotel room in Vegas a million years ago.

With the solemnity befitting our grim task, we lit the candles; the poster paints immediately gave off a God-awful stench which kind of helped set the mood a little—drew the drapes and took our pre-ordained places at the table.

Looking back, it was all pretty damned corny, we even had the whole '*is anybody there*' thing going on; Joe knocking on the bottom of the table and Frank pulling on the myriad strings he'd set up to pull things over.

Bud was living it.

He'd borrowed—and for borrowed read stolen—fifty bucks from his mom's purse. Of course, he fully expected to be putting it back long before she noticed its absence; I mean, how was he to know we would be stealing it from him?

After fifteen minutes or so of conversing with the dark spirits, it came time for the séance to go terribly wrong. Frank knocked the table over, Joe pretended to have been possessed by means of an undecipherable demonic message he'd pre-written in black Sharpie on his chest. I have to say, that Joe's ripping open of the shirt was way more dramatic than anything I'd seen in a movie before, or since.

Bud was wide-eyed with terror at all of this. Unbeknownst to us, he'd brought along his own prop—a tiny silver crucifix, also purloined from his mother's purse. He clung onto that piece of jewelry as if his very soul depended on it, which I guess he figured it did at that particular moment in time. We had him so damned scared he barely flinched when the newspaper scraps we'd surreptitiously substituted for his mom's grocery money went up in flames.

And that was pretty much that.

Joe bravely fought off his supposed demonic possession, Frank reassembled his parlor, and Bud went home fifty bucks lighter and looking way paler than he had when he'd come over.

Joe, Frank, and I spent the money on candy, soda, and nudie magazines, which we hid in Joe's dad's garden shed. The rest we just squandered.

We often reminisced with pride about our expert confidence trick, although we did feel a twinge of remorse when Bud's mom grounded him for a month over the missing fifty bucks. To his credit, the boy never once cracked and told her what had actually happened to it.

And I never told the guys what *I'd* felt that afternoon. *Different.*

Not just different, but somehow *different* than I had before the mock-séance, as if I'd been replaced by aliens and no one had told me about it, if that makes any sense.

I know now that one should never burn black candles at a séance because they invoke the darkest spirits—that is, if you believe in such things that

And I didn't.

I do now.

Something had been with us that afternoon in Frank's parlor. Something ephemeral, almost intangible, but there nonetheless. Even now, now that I have lived with the thing for all of these years, I struggle to find the precise words to describe what I felt following our mock-séance, and I'm supposed to be the fucking writer!

A presence, a ghost, a being from the Netherworld, call it what you will, but it was most definitely *there* with us that day.

And it chose me.

Dave and I have never actually discussed how he came to be, perhaps he takes it as read that I just know how—and *when*—he came into me. One day, I'll be sure to ask him.

In the days, weeks, months following our brilliant get-rich-quick scheme, and long after our ill-gotten gains had been spent, I became aware of the tinnitus ringing inside my head, it sounded to me like some high-pitched smoke alarm that was stuck perpetually onto *on*.

My Ear Nose and Throat specialist said it was most probably down to the aggressive ear infections I'd suffered as a small child, and I had it figured as space aliens attempting to make contact—I'd not long seen *Close Encounters of the Third Kind* and I think it may have left a lasting impression on me.

And that was all. A slightly weird feeling of not being quite the same as I was before that day, and an annoying ringing in my ears that the best specialists in the county said I'd just have to learn to live with. I've since read up on the condition, and learned suicide rates amongst tinnitus sufferers is far higher than in those who can enjoy silence. For me, perfect quiet is just a wishful concept.

What I know now, of course, is the sounds in my head were not due to some inner ear damage but Dave's early, developing voice; like a small child, he had to learn his language, practice, and grow with it. Like me, he simply had to mature and tune in.

As time marched by, I grew up as a pretty much regular

teenager.I was never one of the cool kids, but had my fair share of low self-esteem girls and was popular amongst my own peer group of misfits and introverts.

I did the expected college thing, got my degree in Biology and pursued a sales career that had no parallel whatsoever to my chosen education path, much to the chagrin of my parents.

I blossomed—under Dave's discrete tutelage, as I have since discovered—from a socially awkward boy who used humor as a defense   mechanism to the life-and-soul of every party. Class clown to fucking cliché in forty-eight years, that's me!

I married my high school sweetheart, created two beautiful children, and built up my lucrative career doing something I was exceptionally good at.

But all the while, there was this niggling feeling someplace deep in the darkest recesses of my mind that something was missing. A gaping chasm as black and empty as any sinkhole and along with it, the desperate craving for experience and knowledge.

And Dave was beginning to make his presence known.

Fast-forward to twenty-eight-year-old me. Successful sales executive for the globe's biggest vehicle manufacturer. Another dull Friday afternoon in a tedious sales meeting, fighting sleep and the thick headache of a hangover from the night before that was only just beginning to form. The night had been a wild one: too much booze, some barely remembered nightclub, and a stranger's face on the pillow next to mine the next morning in my expensive hotel room.

If she'd told me her name, I'd forgotten it, and I really didn't care all that much, anyway. Another ship passing in the night. Next month it would be a different face on a different pillow.

Dave's voice came through loud and clear, slicing through the sickly head pain like a lighthouse beam through thick, swirling fog.

What would it be like to...?

The impulse caught me unaware and before I knew it, I was standing up at the table, trousers down, dick in hand.

I wiggled it playfully at the Sales VP, oblivious to the sniggers of my fellow salespeople. I seem to remember slapping my manhood hard on the boardroom table a couple of times for effect before the VP's dumpy secretary with the improbably pendulous breasts ushered me from the room, doing her damnedest to get me to tuck my penis back into my pants without touching it.

My actions that day have since become the thing of legend in that particular institution. Some put it down to Good Ol' Jim horsing around, some to a nervous breakdown or stress or something similar. Others figured I was just still drunk from the night before and really didn't know what I was doing.

But I did.

I knew exactly what it was I was doing. I was finding out just what it felt like to do what every person in every boring meeting has mused about at some time or another; just what would it be like to wiggle my genitals at the VP?

And now I knew.

In my defense, for me it was more like watching myself from a place above the table as I did it; I was fully aware of my actions but knew there was not a goddamned thing I could have done to prevent it.

It was to become the beginning of the end, or to be more precise, an end of that particular part of my life. Dave had finally found his voice within me and he was exerting his newfound power over his more-than-willing host.

Okay, so let me try to explain this thing.

Demonic possession is a thing that regular—unpossessed folk—see only in the movies. They see the snarling, rotting body, the vile profanities, the preternatural movement and the head-spinning, bile-puking evil that looks great on the big screen.

In reality, and away from what the Catholic church wants you to think, it is more akin to catching a parasite than any other analogy I can come up with.

There is a parasite that lives in cat shit—*Toxocara gondii*—whose primary host is mice. Once infected, it grows inside its unwitting host where it sets up base camp in the poor, unsuspecting rodent's brain. From there, it alters the mouse's behavior, making it braver and more reckless than its naturally timid and uninfected brethren. Some studies have shown mice infected with *gondii* actually become sexually attracted to cats.

All the better to get eaten, my dear.

Naturally, a reckless mouse that has the hots for kittycats is far more likely to be gobbled up by Mr. Tiddles, which subsequently poops out yet more parasite eggs and thus perpetuates the cunning *gondii's* family line.

All by fundamentally altering its host's behavior.

I'm not saying for a minute that Dave made me inexplicably attracted to cats, but he did instill in me a certain recklessness, a confidence, and a thirst for new experiences. And he wasn't all in my head, either.

Yes, that's where I 'heard' his voice, most likely because that's where the brain's auditory center sits; but I felt his presence *everywhere*; in every fiber of my body. In that way, Dave was probably more comparable to a fungal infection, its mycelia snaking into every capillary, every nerve ending, and every muscle fiber that made up my physical existence.

Parasites? Fungal infections? Once the biologist, always the biologist, I guess.

But, you get the general idea now?

Dave was like a small child. As he continued to grow, he— *it*— was experiencing everything for the very first time. And, like said child, his demand for new things to discover was becoming insatiable.

What is? What if? What would? How does? The barrage was unstoppable, the floodgates opened with the board-room incident.

Dave—my inner demon—had found his voice all right, and I was damned well going to have to listen to it!

For anyone who still cares at this point in my story, I did return to work following a couple of week's forced rest. Just long enough for the hysteria and legend-building to have died down a little, and just long enough for my superiors to figure out the best way to persuade me that I really ought to be thinking about furthering my erstwhile lucrative career elsewhere.

And that suited me just fine. I was already making big changes in my life—under Dave's influence of course—and shedding the shackles of employment was just one on the laundry list that needed ticking off.

Dave wanted to write.

More to the point, Dave wanted *me* to write.

Although I'd hankered after a career in the literary arts since the beginning of Ever, I'd never done much more than tap out a few disjointed pages of pedestrian stories inspired by some movie or other. But now, now my head was filling with stories and images and dialogue and characters so fast I could barely keep up with them all.

And, it transpired that the only way to clear them from my cluttered brain was to write them down. Although, that seemed to have the effect of simply clearing room for fresh material; it was much like having a garage sale when you know damned well there's more crap to bring down from the attic.

And so I began to write.

And when my first story was out, laying there bloody, raw, bleeding, and glistening wet like a newborn, I felt for the first time since that fateful day of the fake séance that the bottomless, gaping hole in my psyche was a hair's breadth closer to being sated.

As a writer, people always—and I mean *always*—ask you that same old, conversation-killing question; *'Where do you get all your ideas from?'* They most likely think it makes them sound all intelligent and engaging.

It doesn't.

I always wanted to answer that dumbass question with *'and where do you get all your farts from?'* And, thanks to Dave, I actually have done just that now.

The reply is a short and simple one. A creative's ideas are generated inside our brains. Little more than a product of the complex bioelectrical and biochemical processes that any functioning brain performs simply to stay alive and maintain its god-like control of the human body.

Only some of us are different.

Some of us get *our* material from an otherworldly source, our very own, personal demon; in a sense, it's actually far more literal than the non-possessed will ever understand.

Lovecraft, Barker, Stoker, Poe, quite possibly King - all authors who have had the ability to dip into the seething currents of the unseen worlds that bubble and gurgle a hair's breadth beyond human comprehension. Worlds filled with torment and nightmares that would drive most people insane in a split second.

Why else do you think they—we—write about the vile, creeping things that inhabit our darkest, deepest nightmares?

Because we have been shown them. We *know* what's

out there, watching us with beady eyes, grinning at our frailty with snaggle-toothed maws and reaching out for us in the night with spindly, oozing, pustulant claws.

My marriage broke up. A necessary casualty according to Dave, although I put it down more to his '*I wonder what picking up hookers is like*' musings than anything else. Go figure.

As Dave grew stronger, I discovered a deepening feeling of being *pushed out*. You know how you felt as a kid when the group you were friends with one day suddenly and inexplicably decided not to include you in their games the next?

Much like that. More and more I found myself a passive observer in things I was doing. A little like an aware sleepwalker or someone having an alleged out of body experience. I say alleged because there really is a simple explanation for that—back to our friend the brain again. A release of chemicals to dull the pain and gut-twisting panic of impending death is what creates the illusion of tunnels and white lights and your favorite grandmother's long-deceased dog.

End of.

Well, believe it or not, there is an actual etiquette to picking up hookers off the street. Dave and I know that now—a lesson learned together.

The skill is to drive slowly around the designated red-light areas until you find the girl of your dreams—without getting pulled by the cops for curb crawling. A couple of drive-bys to catch her eye and then wait for *The Dip*.

Your chosen lady of the night will bend her knees to peek at you as you go by. A slowing down of your vehicle tells her you are interested in a business transaction and she will approach.

And before you can say *sexually transmitted disease*, you're in an abandoned parking lot somewhere dark having God-awful sex with a girl who reeks of cigarette smoke and nonoxyl-9 and has arms decorated with scabbed-over track marks.

And they say romance is dead.

So, Dave and I discovered what it did feel like to pick up hookers for soulless sex, and shortly thereafter, what it felt like to get caught out by your wife and thrown out of the home you'd spent ten years of your life paying for.

There's a well-worn saying: *The devil made me do it.*

In most cases it's just bullshit spouted by convicted felons trying to cop an insanity plea. But in a few cases— mine included—it really is the God's-honest truth. Not that it holds water with angry wives and pissed-off employers but as excuses go, it's a good one if it's genuine. Perfect too, for assuaging the conscience.

Dave's inquisitive nature began as innocent as a small child's. What do butterflies feel like? How do you eat spaghetti? What do farts look like?

And then, as my demon matured inside of me, I noted the less-than subtle change in his curiosity. What does a girl's tit feel like? What do you do with a rock-hard dick at two in the morning? What does a threesome feel like? What happens if you do drive too fast?

It was fun. Discovering all of these new things made me feel like a kid again, seeing the world as one of wonder and excitement instead of one of hard work and soul-destroying drudge.

And I was writing. And Jesus H.—was I writing? Pages and pages and pages of neatly crafted prose created from ideas and story lines that pretty much jumped fully formed into my head, all thanks to my nefarious lodger. And it was all original and unique material that, as it turned out, was highly saleable.

Dave had completely turned my life on its head; I had success and money doing the one thing I'd always wanted to do, and the glorious trappings that went along with it. An obscenely big loft apartment, a disgustingly expensive Aston Martin DBS (fully paid for) and a hot blonde girlfriend ten years my junior.

Well worth the pay-off of being another's puppet, I thought.

All was going swimmingly with Dave and me, until, one day a thought popped into my head: '*I wonder what fresh human innards taste like?*'

And sadly, as much as I tried to ignore Dave's constant, nagging voice chirruping around inside my head like some errant cricket about this, he was, unfortunately, all-too persistent.

Well, for the record—and I'm sure you're just itching to know—raw human innards taste pretty damned awful. And I'd swear to this day the hooker was still alive when Dave and I chowed down on her bloated, steaming transverse colon—I'm positive I saw her chest rising and falling. Ever so slightly, the faintest of movement, as was the flickering of her baby blue painted eyelids.

How best to explain Dave from that point on in our strange, symbiosis? Well, you know how you have that little voice inside your head that would really like to know what it would be like to mow down that sad-faced, little old lady tottering by on the crosswalk, or how it would feel to feed your hand into the garbage disposal and switch it on?

Now imagine that little voice actually having control over your actions.

And that's how come I had to deliberately torch a one-hundred-fifty grand car and tell the cops it was stolen *and* learn how to type one-handed. Hell, I have to do *everything* one handed nowadays. Although, I guess I should count my lucky stars that Dave had the good sense to try out his masochistic experiment with my left hand.

And so commenced what I guess I could call now—looking back with the 20/20 that hindsight offers—the beginning of Dave and mine's downward spiral. His desires, and along with them, his *demands*, became ever more sadistic in nature, initially involving just our body, but quickly expanding to pull in others.

Our body?

Yep, that's what I said.

I had come to view the corporeal vessel I had inhabited quite singularly—or so I'd thought—for the best part of thirty years or so as a shared thing by then. Dave was as much a part of *'my'* body as I was, and in some cases, more so—even if I insisted on pushing its physical limits to the extreme and then some.

Somewhere between us killing the doddery old woman, leaving her shattered body twitching and oozing blood and brains in the gutter, and butchering the hooker in order consume her slippery viscera, I happened upon a club for people who had developed a taste for life's more extravagant and experimental pleasures.

I say club, I was soon to discover it was more of a *society*; something more akin to the Freemasons or some such than a mere club. Highly secretive, one hundred percent underground and yet managing to pervade every level and aspect of the regular social order that regular folk take so much for granted.

And it had a large population of people just like me.

The possessed.

I guess that's how come I found out about The Society in the first place - through the bizarre network the demons have going on. I suppose it's only natural they communicate with one another in some form or another. God only knows how they do it, but it quickly became obvious to me that they do.

I'd been hanging out in some of the BDSM clubs with Rachel—the aforementioned blonde girlfriend *du jour*—first as a spectator and then as an active participant. It was good to be amongst like-minded people in an environment where Dave and I could indulge Dave's curiosity and very quickly we hooked up with people who were more than happy to be strapped to increasingly uncomfortable chunks of exquisitely carpentered equipment to be whipped and clamped and tortured in the most imaginative ways possible.

I remember one brunette girl who insisted I—we—bound her impressively sized breasts so tightly with harsh hemp rope that they turned a most unnatural shade of purple, and for her to have us thrash them soundly with leather riding crops until her nipples actually bled.

As Dave, Rachel and I progressed, I began to sense Rachel was becoming increasingly less enthusiastic and more detached as we advanced to the more extreme clubs. After a while, she preferred to remain a spectator—*tourists* the BDSM diehards call them—and on the few occasions I managed to persuade her to join in, whether as a perpetrator or a recipient, she made it obvious she was only taking part to please me and then would refuse to talk to me for days afterward   .

She looked damned hot in the black leather dresses I'd bought her, though.

It was on one such night, in a club new to us—rather unsubtly christened *The Tortured Vagina*—that I think I, well, *Dave and I*—pushed my beautiful blonde a little too far.

Stripped of her leather, bondage-buckled dress and deliciously naked, Rachel adorned the St. Andrew's Cross like she and it were a work of the finest art. Strapped to the upright wooden cross by her dainty wrists and ankles, her full, pert breasts signaled their invitations with hardened nipples and her freshly denuded pussy pouted and glistened in the flickering light of the countless candles that illuminated the dungeon room.

With the multi-colored ball-gag wedged firmly in her mouth, Rachel's pleasures began.

Thinking back with more clarity than possessed me at the time, the ball-gag was possibly where we went wrong. We had agreed our safe word—hammock—but of course the poor gal had no way of actually expressing it when she had reached her limit.

And I'd totally misread her eyes.

I don't know whether the last straw was the hot candle wax that was dripped down her breasts, or the cold, metallic intrusion of the huge, stainless-steel dildo that some fat guy in a translucent, latex bodysuit forced into her ass that did it. Or the bull dyke with the shocking pink Mohawk and ripped combats who fisted my poor Rachel until her eyes streamed and her pussy bled, or the nice young couple dressed as if for church who decided to practice their erotic asphyxiation techniques on my girlfriend until her baby blues bulged and her frantic wriggling against the biting leather restraints ceased.

Either way, once we had unstrapped Rachel and she'd revived enough to call me a *fucking sick asshole*, it was way beyond '*sorry*' and lame excuses. She'd stormed out of the club's *Torture Zone* with as much dignity as a naked chick with her ass crusty with cooled candle wax could muster.

And by the time I returned home, just a few hours later, Rachel—and all of her stuff—was gone.

But it was there at the *Tortured Vagina* that I learned of The Society. One minute I'd been standing there, dumb-

281

founded, watching as my girl's perfect peach of a bare bottom left the room, and the next I'm hearing a soft voice purring in my ear.

Whoever she was, I never saw her face.

She whispered that I was not to turn around, but that I had impressed her with my dark desires. She pressed a crisp, white business card into my hand, asked me to say hi to the friend inside my head for her, and then she vanished into the flickering ink of the shadows that danced amongst the dark, wooden torture equipment.

The card was damn near featureless, adorned with just a phone number. No name, no address, certainly no business title. Yet I—and Dave—knew precisely what it would lead us to; oh, what doors had just been opened for us!

The Society's gatherings were spectacular, opulent affairs. They were held in the grandest of mansions that belonged to the incredibly elite membership. Gone were our days of the squalid underground clubs hastily thrown together in the city's decrepit, abandoned places, which were invariably populated by the sick, the addicted, and the broken.

Although, deep down, I suspected Dave actually missed those sleazy, depraved times, we were both entirely captivated by the sheer luxury and whole new level of depravity that The Society had to offer. That and the fact that each and every one of the members was people like me.

The Possessed.

Every invited member of The Society was there as a player, and each one of those had their very own Dave. Of course, they gave different names to their demons, some even preferring not to be quite so familiar with the being that dwelled in the darkest depths of their soul as to give them a name. And those who weren't The Possessed? Well, they seemed to be there solely for our entertainment.

Dave was finally amongst his own kind.

And so was heralded the beginning of what I guess was the end for me.

The Society held their debauched soirees pretty much each and every weekend, and of course, a great deal of the pomp and ceremony revolved around perverse sexual practices—in most cases a simple, loosely disguised ruse to get the young, impressionable and decidedly unpossessed *Entertainment* naked and vulnerable as quickly as was humanly possible. I have to say   they did seem to be enjoying themselves for the most of it—the uninhibited hedonism of group sex, sado-sexual torture and on occasion, bestiality—as they cavorted with each other and The Society membership with joyful faces and orgasmic crics. It was almost as if they relished the closeness of we Possessed, perhaps even harboring the vain hope that by giving their bodies so freely to the demons that lusted after them would bring them one of their own.

Only it doesn't quite work like that.

And some of the *Entertainment* even giggled and squealed with sheer and absolute delight whilst we ate them.

Unlike the hooker Dave and I had tasted a million lifetimes ago, these young men and women gave themselves freely for consumption by the Membership. Again, perhaps they thought in doing so they would gain their own demons or fast track to the unearthly pleasures they assumed lie beyond death. And I must confess the added fear, pain, and adrenaline gave the flesh a soupcon of a tangy palette that fair caressed the taste buds.

And again, it doesn't work like that; the poor, deluded saps were in for one very big, if somewhat final, disappointment.

We would sit around the long, long tables in the cavernous dining rooms and pick out the choicest parts of our meal, some of us even preferring to carve those tender pieces of flesh for ourselves. The inner thighs were a much sought-after delicacy, as were the calf muscle, cheeks, and the breasts and vagina walls of the young women—the latter being a much sought-after delicacy, when prepared by the right chef. It was usually saved for the most senior Society members, or for those who had been asked to procure the next banquet.

The meats, once carved, were presented to the tableside chef who would then cook them to our preference and serve them back on a bed of rare and exotic leaf salad. To a casual observer, ignoring the living, breathing source of the meat, it looked for all the world like any other teppanyaki restaurant.

Although, there were those—Dave and I included—who preferred our meat raw, bleeding and still warm from the body from which it was sliced.

Through all of this obscene degeneracy, Dave was growing ever stronger within me, my will more and more playing second fiddle to his, and my demon eagerly allowed The Society to absorb us into its world almost to the exclusion of our own.

"And you, sir!" a ruddy-faced, rotund gentleman called to me from the opposite end of the ridiculously elongated table. All eyes—even those of our dinner—turned to inspect my reddening face.

"Me?" my voice squeaked out like a strangled fart.

"Yes! You!" he guffawed, taking great relish at my obvious discomfort. He shuffled in his seat and a young man, naked and shaved completely hairless, wriggled out from under the table between Fat Man's legs. "At our next gathering, it is your turn to procure something special for our table!"

This was news to me. No one had mentioned that Members had to procure anything at all. I was of the understanding these dinner guests—and the Entertainment—just magically appeared.

Perhaps they wanted me to find a rare bottle of wine, or a two-hundred-year-old scotch for after dinner drinks?

In my head, Dave laughed at my naiveté.

Then Fat Man clapped his hands in that theatrical way only the morbidly obese can carry off.

A squat guy with an odd, reddish tinge to his skin and an immaculate white suit appeared in an instant from one of the servant's doors at the side of the dining room. The door closed gently behind him, blending in perfectly with the heavy-pattern of the wallpaper and the white wainscoting. With him, the squat guy had a young girl.

She was no more than ten or eleven and was dressed demurely in a full-length cotton and lace gown; the girl looked like she'd just strayed from the *Little House On The Prairie*. She stared over at the living dinner tableau on the table before her as if she'd seen it all before.

"The other members and I have decided we would like to satiate our taste for something a little more—" Fat Guy paused, more for effect was my guess, "—delicate." He laughed again, loudly.

"Hey, come on—" I ventured, feeling all eyes burning into me.

Come on nothing, it would be so sweet. Dave chastised me.

"You *are* aware of the rules of The Society, sir?" Fat Guy raised his voice to me and it boomed across the now silent room to make my ears ring.

"I am, sir, but—" the words struggled to leave my mouth.

"But nothing!" Fat Guy countered. "If you are to remain in The Society, and enjoy all of the—" here, he swept an arm wide to indicate the all too willing flesh on and around the table, "—benefits, then you will adhere to the rules."

His voice had now adopted a hard, aggressive tone; any further protest from me was only going to fall on deaf ears.

And Dave wasn't helping either.

We like this place, these people. They're our kind. He chirruped inside me like some sick twist on Jiminy fucking Cricket. *So what if they want to eat children, the people you're eating right now were kids once, ya know.*

What scared me was that my demon's twisted logic was actually beginning to make sense.

"Just the one will do," Fat Guy boomed. "We don't want to spoil the treat for ourselves now, do we?" He clapped his hands again and smiled at Squat guy.

A flash of a blade and the little girl's throat was slit. To my dying day—and may that come very soon—I'll never be able to erase the image burned into my brain of her impassive doe-eyes and the scarlet cascade that soaked the front of her crisp white gown into a dark, wet scarlet.

And, of all the things I had experienced with Dave to that point, all the things we had seen and done together, it was that defining moment that divided us.

For the first time in our symbiosis, as we watched the girl slump lifelessly to the polished hardwood floor of the mansion's dining room, I came to see Dave for what he really was; a sick, soul-sucking parasite that I could never be rid of.

I avoided The Society the following week. And the week after that. A month or two crept slowly by, Dave's incessant chatter about complying with their demand and returning a deafening cacophony inside my head.

To placate him some, we frequented some of our old haunts but found the shabby pretenses of turpitude a bore and no longer able to meet our elevated desires. We procured a hooker or two—a sad cliché, picking on those in society whose job it was to get into cars with strangers, it was almost too easy—spiriting them away to the deserted parts of the industrial part of town where we would play with them for hours on end, reveling in their pain and terror, and ultimately their death. Yet all the while, that gaping chasm of *Not Enough* ate through our enjoyment like rust on an old car.

And all the while, Dave would whisper to my conscious; *one little girl, that's all they want, just the one. What harm could it do? Just one and we have all of that delicious debauchery back again.*

I truly want to believe Dave's heart—or whatever imagined lump of offal he had that passed for a heart—was not one hundred percent behind the constant goading. I know he missed his own kind, as did I in many, many ways, but I like to think that perhaps just a little of my humanity had rubbed off on my live-in demon over the years.

Just a little.

On the day I got word of my canceled book deal, I found out that Rachel had somehow managed to clean out my bank accounts, even the—as it turned out, not-so-secret—Cayman Islands offshore account. And then my bank foreclosed on my apartment without so much as a by your leave. There was something in the fine print of the mortgage contract—who the hell reads all of that?—said they could do that. Apparently.

The Aston Martin went next, a pair of the World's burliest repo' men in dark suits towered over me at five thirty, one humid Saturday morning and demanded the keys. Arguing was not even a consideration, let alone an option.

It would appear The Society's insidious influence stretches far and wide, like the infectious mycelia of some all-pervading fungal disease.

I had pissed them off and they were punishing me, it really was as simple as that. I tried making contact with them, to apologize and beg their forgiveness in order to save my sorry hide, but when you don't know exactly who you are supposed to be attempting to contact, it very quickly becomes an exercise in futility. I visited the mansions and panoramic-view penthouse apartments where they'd held their fabulous gatherings, only to be turned away by puzzled faces.

The Society, it would seem, had not just vanished from the face of our planet as far as I was concerned, it was as if they'd never fucking existed at all.

Only, I knew damned well they *did* exist; my rapidly ruined life stood testament to that.

Of course, Dave was all *I told you so* and *if you'd listened to me and procured what they wanted, you wouldn't be in this mess.* But at the time, I liked to think that, deep down, he was feeling sorry for me.

Are demons capable of compassion?

I sincerely doubt it now.

And here I am, everything lost, even my sobriety and sanity.

Dave stays pretty much quiet these days, I think the alcohol puts him to sleep, or at the very least it subdues him to the level of a faint mumbling in the darkest recesses of my tortured brain. Every now and then he will raise his metaphysical head to chastise me like a bored preschooler over what we have lost. But there's nothing I can do, not now.

There's a dark shadow blocking the one sliver of sunlight that ventures in through the gap in the freeway pillars. I look up, and see the guy standing over me. He's one of the kinds I have become, a homeless bum, and he's coveting the crap I lug around in two dirty, plastic *Circle K* bags.

He is also Possessed; I can see it in his eyes.

Kill the cunt.

The voice is so loud in the bum's head I can almost hear it, his very own Dave. I wonder what name he has given to *his* demon? Perhaps I should ask, strike up a conversation to distract the bum's attention from the folding knife he's clicked open and is absently fiddling with?

But I'm guessing he's not come over for a chat, or to ask for loose change.

We're going to die now. Dave stirred in my head. *It's been fun.*

Fun?

Not exactly the adjective I'd apply to the absolute wreck of my life - a life over before I'd even hit fifty.

One last experience to share. My demon informed me. *Embrace it, it's going to be interesting, to say the least.*

Probably for you, Dave, my internal voice raged at my demon. This was the definite end for me, I knew—don't ask me how, as I'd never asked him—Dave would go on. Either he'd return to where he came from and a lightless eternity of whatever it is they do there, or it would be onto some other poor schmuck who he can parasitize and destroy.

The chill steel of the blade slides easily between my malnourished, prominent ribs. It slices its cold, unrelenting way into my heart and I can smell the stink of the bum's breath in my nostrils and feel the coarse prickle of his un-kempt beard on my face.

You've done so much for me. Dave sounds quite sad. What was it Shakespeare said? Something about parting be-ing sweet, sweet sorrow? Bullshit it is. It's anger and disap-pointment and desperation, that's what it is. A parting of the ways with my demon, Dave, who had been a part of me for almost as long as I can remember meant death, and the dark finality that brought with it.

What can I do for you?

Well, Dave, you could get this piss-soaked hulk off of me for starters. Then you could get his knife blade out of my chest and stop me from bleeding to death in the gutter like some diseased animal.

That would be fucking nice for starters.

Then perhaps you could use your otherworldly powers to save my goddamned life - that's what you can do for me, sir!

But, of course, I know in my heart of hearts (a poor choice of phrase here, I know) that Dave can do none of those things. He is as rendered impotent by my physical limitations as I used to be by his overbearing presence in my mind.

You can show me Hell, Dave. My mind reaches out to my own very personal demon, inquisitive to the bitter end.

I slump sideways into the spreading, warm, viscous pool of my own blood, my consciousness fading in and out like a dimming light bulb and Dave's voice is hauntingly silent.

I know there is nothing more for Dave to say to me. He has no reason to show me Hell, no reason at all.

I've been living it all along.

My Friend Eddie

Sophia Cauduro

The last time I saw my special friend Eddie was when I was five years old. I don't really remember a lot about him now, just the important stuff. My therapist says it's difficult to retain memories of childhood as I get older, especially because my memories of him are confusing and disjointed.

My parents don't like to talk about Eddie, either, no matter how much I pry, but even through the brain fog of childhood and the consistent silence of my parents, I think I finally understand. All these years, all of my fond memories of my special friend Eddie have been subverted and now I dread the thought of him. Any odd creak in my house or movement in the shadows beyond the comfort of my bed, I see him waiting… watching.

I pray he will never come back to find me.

When I was four years old, I struggled to make friends in kindergarten. My teacher had always described me as "passive" which always made me an easy target amongst the other children.

My peers, who never got enough attention at home, would call me names and push me to the asphalt, knowing I would never do anything to retaliate. I was horrified to be labeled as a snitch if I tattled to the lunch supervisor but in being complaisant and allowing the name calling to continue, I inadvertently isolated myself more and more from my peers until I was a shadow on the wall with no friends at all.

After school, the majority of the kids in my class would go and hang out at the big playground in our neighborhood. We lived in a relatively small town surrounded by thick forest so there usually wasn't much to do. The playground was definitely the highlight of the town, complete with a huge jungle gym that had two different sets of monkey bars, a row of twisty plastic slides and a super-fast carousel that every kid got injured on at least once during their elementary school years.

My favorite was the swing set. The row of red, plastic seats always lay empty and out of the way of everything. A perfect view of the entirety of the park. I would spend my afternoons swinging away in the sun, watching my peers and their older siblings laugh as they chased each other around the park, playing games like grounders or manhunt.

I envied them as I swung like a ghost in the breeze.

I had always wanted an older sibling, an older brother specifically. Maybe it was because I was always jealous of my peers, watching them chase each other around at the park. Maybe it was because, like my bullies, I, too, was neglected at home. Both of my parents were always working and unconcerned about where I was during the day. As long as I was home before they came back from work, everything was fine.

Until it wasn't.

One overcast autumn day, I found myself on the lonely, red plastic swing set, watching two of my kindergarten peers and their older brothers practicing baseball tosses at the far end of the park. My dirty, gray Skechers brushed against the soft sand of the playground as thunder echoed in the distance.

That's the first time Eddie appeared.

"Mind if I join you?" a deep voice cut into my solitary daydream.

I turned my head to the left just as a figure came into my view. My memories of him are a bit jumbled but I'll always remember two distinct things: his long limbs and his crooked smile.

The lanky man jumped over the red plastic seat beside me and sat. I frowned at him.

"I'm not allowed to talk to strangers," I said matter-a-factly.

He smiled at me. That crooked smile. "We can't be strangers if we know each other's names now, can we? I'm Eddie."

"I'm Charlotte," I said hesitantly. My four-year-old self thinking it would be safe to say my name out loud. It wasn't like I was giving my home address away. "Where did you come from?"

Eddie didn't answer that question. Instead, he looked in the direction I was looking, focusing on the siblings happily playing catch together at the edge of the park. "Haven't you always wanted an older brother?"

My mouth hung open like a cod fish. "How did you know that?"

"Well," he responded. "I have always wanted a younger sister." He leaned over and tugged on one of my pigtails and I giggled at the display of affection. "Do you want to be friends?"

I smiled at him. A real, genuine smile.

My first friend, I thought. I finally had a friend. It was like he magically appeared right when I needed him the most.

Eddie and I spent all afternoon in the park together. I

told him about everything. He was a surprisingly good listener. I told him about my peers who bullied me, I told him about my parents, and I told him about my pet goldfish. I told him everything I could possibly think of, the words just rushing out of me like I had been holding them in since the day I was born. I hadn't even noticed it was well past curfew until I realized I could barely see the forest that lined the edge of the park.

"Uh oh!" I exclaimed. "I'm late! I don't want mommy and daddy to get mad at me. I have to go now, Eddie. This was a lot of fun!"

He smiled again, his crooked grin spreading across his face. "Do you want me to walk you home, Charlotte?"

I shook my head, jumping up out of the red, plastic chair. "I have to go now! But I'll be back tomorrow!" I started running away from the park and toward the direction of my house, a smile tugging on my face at the thought of seeing my new friend tomorrow.

I turned back briefly to give Eddie one final wave but when I looked back at the swings, he was already gone. It was like he vanished into thin air. The swing set was still and silent.

My parents were really upset when I got home. My mom had already called the local police and told them I hadn't come home after school. She was hysterical. I apologized a hundred times. She said I scared her, and she thought I was dead in a ditch somewhere. I shook my head over and over again, tears starting to form at the thought of my broken body lying on the side of the road.

"Mommy, I'm sorry. I'm sorry. I was with Eddie! I was with a friend!"

My mother and father looked at each other and then looked back at me.

"What do you mean you were with someone named Eddie? Is this a friend from kindergarten? I don't remember anyone in your class with that name."

"He's not in my class," I explained. "I met him at the park."

My mom's eyes bulged, my father's eyebrows raised.

"Charlotte, honey, what do you mean by that? Where did Eddie come from?"

I shrugged my shoulders. "He kind of just appeared. I was feeling kind of down today and then he was just beside me, like he heard my wish to have a friend."

I saw my mother's shoulders visibly relax. "And what did you and Eddie talk about honey?"

I crinkled my face up as I tried to remember our conversation. "Well, I did all the talking. He just sat and listened. Eddie's a really good listener. He's a really special friend."

My mom and dad shared another look but this time it was one of understanding. Maybe a little bit of pity.

My mom cleared her throat. "Charlotte, Eddie seems like a really special friend but it's important to talk to others as well and try to make friends with your classmates. Having an imaginary friend is normal at your age, but just remember Eddie is just that, imaginary. He's make believe. It's okay to play pretend when you get sad and lonely, just remember the other children might not understand."

"Imaginary friend," I repeated back to her. Eddie had felt so real. But then again, Sophie Bridgers had an imaginary friend that was a black Pegasus. She rode him every recess and told everyone he could shoot fireballs out of his nose and shape shift. His name was Jeffrey, and she probably also felt that he was real.

At first I was sad that I hadn't made a real life friend. But then I thought about having someone all to myself even if he wasn't real and that made me giddy with excitement.

Eddie appeared beside me at the swings the next day, too. The sky was overcast again, and light raindrops kissed the metal tops of the play structures. The park was mostly empty today because of the weather with only two kids from the upper grades using the wetness of the light rain to propel themselves down the slide at rocket speed.

"Did you have a good night?" Eddie asked me once he sat at the swing beside me.

I clapped my Skechers together in front of me. "My parents were mad that I was home late. I have to be extra, extra careful."

Eddie nodded. I could see him looking at me from the corner of my eyes as I watched sand spill from my sneakers.

"Eddie," I said adjusting my attention to him. "Promise you will never leave me. Promise you will be my friend forever. Promise that even if I outgrow you, you will stay. I will promise to never forget you, even when I make real friends."

Eddie gave me a funny look, but eventually the crooked smile returned to his face stretching wide across his cheeks. "I promise."

Eddie and I started hanging out together after school every day. I would wait for him at the swing set wishing for the appearance of my make-believe older brother and he would appear behind me.

I would tell him about my day at school, about my lack of friends, about the bullies, and about what my parents talked about at dinner. He would listen quietly, interjecting a handful of times to say things like "If only we could run away together" or "Parents suck, huh? I would never treat you like that."

I wished Eddie was my real dad sometimes. I never told him that. I figured he already knew since I had created him to be everything I wished for; I thought he could just read my mind.

At least the bullies didn't torment me after school anymore. The swing set had become a sort of safe haven for me. I knew the playground bullies were whispering about me and giving me weird glances. They stopped calling me names after school and it was all thanks to Eddie. Even though they couldn't see him, I knew he was there, and I believed he was protecting me with his presence.

I asked Eddie if he wanted to hang out at other places with me as well. The playground was fun and all, but I was getting bored sitting on the swings and talking every single day. Eddie seemed to fidget a little bit and then he said, "Well it's complicated. I'm trying to be a good imaginary friend, and it gets a little complicated if we hang out in super public places. I don't want to get you in trouble. You don't want to attract even more bullies."

I agreed with him and said it would be weird if a lot of people saw me talking to myself. He said he would always be there for me, and he would keep that promise, I just had to act like I didn't see him all the time.

His request was hard to adhere to at first but once I noticed him at different places throughout the week, my mood would drastically improve knowing I always had a friend nearby. At school during recess, I would gaze out toward the edge of the forest and smile, seeing Eddie's silhouette standing amidst the bushes and watching over the playground. At first, he was really hard to notice but I could feel his eyes watching me.

On Saturday mornings, I played U5 Mini Soccer. Eddie would sit on the bleachers several fields away and watch me. I started excelling in sports because I was eager to impress my make-believe brother. He cheered me on from a distance, giving a discreet thumbs up as I dribbled the ball to the net and scored a goal.

Some nights, when the weather was nice and my parents weren't home, I would stare out my bedroom window when I got lonely and wish for Eddie to appear. He would always come, stepping out of the shadows of the streetlights. He would appear out of thin air, on command, and stare up at me from the sidewalk.

I would smile and wave at him and he would watch me. His presence would remind me that even though my parents weren't home, there was always someone there for me. I would turn off the lights and sleep soundlessly.

As October crept to a close, Eddie and I bundled up in light winter jackets and found ourselves at the swing set once again. The now fallen leaves scattered in the wind as a cold chill encircled the playground.

"It's my birthday tomorrow," I told Eddie. "I know you can't come to my party because my mom and dad only want real friends to come but I got you something."

I reached into my jacket pocket and pulled out a pink bracelet. The letters E and C were etched into two of the neon pink beads. I rolled up my sleeve to show him the identical one I was wearing. "It's a friendship bracelet. I made them for us."

Eddie took the pink bracelet from me and inspected it closely before dropping it into his jacket pocket. "That's so nice of you, Charlotte. It's your birthday, though; I'm supposed to give you a present."

Eddie jumped up from his seat on the swing set and turned to face me, his dark eyes staring at me intently. His long limbs accentuated in the shadows of the dying sunlight. "I bought you something," he said.

I clapped my hands with glee and looked around him waiting for him to present me with a gift bag stuffed with pink tissue paper or a box wrapped in Disney Princess paper.

The sun was just peaking over the tips of the evergreen trees that lined the forest. My parents would be expecting me home soon for dinner.

Eddie unzipped his jacket and pulled out a clear plastic bottle from his breast pocket. Inside was a white, cloudy liquid that was almost filled all the way to the top. Murky white patterns swirled within the bottle as Eddie held it out to me.

I crinkled my nose. "What is that?"

"It's Gatorade. White Freezie flavoured."

I frowned at Eddie. "I'm not allowed to drink that."

Eddie stepped closer to me, trying to push the bottle into my hand. "It's a gift, Charlotte. It's your birthday. You can drink it just this once."

I shook my head at him, becoming agitated and impatient. "I thought you were my friend, Eddie. I thought you knew everything about me! I can't drink Gatorade! My parents told me I'm allergic to corn!"

I was upset at Eddie in that moment. Really upset. My imaginary friend was supposed to know everything about me. Gatorade contained a corn byproduct which could induce anaphylactic shock. Although my parents never bothered to invest in an EpiPen, they had drilled the dangers into my head. He had been perfect up to this point. How could he not know about my allergy? He was supposed to be my best friend.

Eddie frowned at me, his eyes narrowing. His hand tightened around the plastic bottle before he shoved it back into his breast pocket. "I have another gift for you," he said calmly. "But it's over there." He turned and pointed toward the edge of the forest.

I squinted at the edge of the tree line as the sun dipped below the first peaks of the evergreen trees casting eerie shadows throughout the park. I shivered despite my jacket.

"Where? I don't see anything."

"It's just over there," Eddie said pointing insistently to the same spot amongst the thick foliage. "Come on, follow me."

I didn't get up right away. A strange feeling had come over me. Something I had never felt before. Eddie sensed my hesitation. He became agitated.

"Charlotte, don't you want to see what I got you? Come on."

I didn't move from the swings.

"Charlotte! I said right now!"

Eddie had never raised his voice at me. He was shifting his weight from foot to foot and glancing around impatiently. I deduced that my current frustrations had started to impact the way he was acting now. I teared up at the thought of losing my best friend over my own hesitations.

"I need to go home now, Eddie. It's time to have dinner."

Eddie's jaw tightened as I propelled myself off the swing and started running for my house. The cold air rushed past me as adrenaline carried my Skecher-clad feet faster than they had ever gone before. That was the first and last time I didn't look back to wave goodbye to him. Whether I had understood it at that time or not, things had changed between us.

My feet dragged along the cool dirt as I waited for Eddie after school the next day on the swing set. He never showed up.

Even though our encounter the previous day had been far from pleasant, I was still excited to tell him about all the presents my parents had given me. I tried to think about him really hard and conjure his image next to me, just like I did all those nights before, but I was unsuccessful. I waited for him for a whole week and when he still didn't show up, I started losing hope I would ever see him again.

After almost a month of waiting alone at the swing sets, I realized Eddie wasn't coming back. He had made me a promise to be my friend forever and he had broken it. He had left me before I had outgrown him.

He had left me lonelier than I was before.

I never thought I would see my special friend Eddie

ever again; and then there was one night that changed everything.

I awoke in my small, dark room, startled by an unknown sound. I shivered beneath my blankets as the light snow fall whispered against my window. The clock on my bedside table was showing 2:34 AM. I rubbed my eyes groggily and yawned. I went to pull my pink and grey striped comforter over my head when a sound made me freeze.

The silence of my small bedroom stretched around me as I squinted my eyes against the darkness. I told myself I was just hearing things, but another sound cut through the silence, this time more distinct.

There was a creak near the bottom of the stairs. And then another one. And then one more. Soft footsteps ascended, closer and closer.

I lowered the comforter and hugged it to my chest as I sat up, trembling in the darkness. My bedroom door was always left ajar so my parents could check on me before they went to bed. From my position on the bed, I could see a portion of the stairs directly in front of me at the beginning of the hallway.

The creaking continued and I counted as I kept my eyes fixed to the staircase. "Eight, nine, ten, eleven," I whispered in the dark. My hands were white knuckled while gripping the sheets.

On the twelfth step, the hand emerged. Long fingers reached forward in the darkness, elongated by the shadows from the hallway window. The fingers reached down and rested on the thirteenth step, another hand reaching forward toward the next step, propelling a body forward on its hands and knees.

Something was crawling up the stairs. Long, gangly arms protruded from thin, bony shoulders. As the hands pressed down on the upper steps, the creaks became louder.

I sat wide eyed in my bed, afraid to make a sound as I

watched a head finally enter into my line of sight. The head turned toward me, and I could see eyes in the darkness that were fixated on me, watching me.

Eyes that had watched me previously for months. But they didn't look kind or understanding. In the moonlight that encompassed the staircase, they were wide, black holes, pits of uninvited darkness.

A smile spread across his face. An unhinged, lopsided grin that took up too much space. The teeth were too white against the pitch darkness of the hallway. There were too many of them as his gums curled back even further, leaving a gaping white hole where his mouth should have been.

I trembled as I watched his hands come to a rest at the top of the stairs. His spindly legs and arched back paused as well. We stared at each other in the darkness, his body bent like a hyena stalking its prey.

"Eddie," I whispered. My voice was trembling as it broke through the silence of the house. Damp tears streaked down my cheeks and onto my comforter. I was confused why he had finally decided to come back. After all this time. He had abandoned me, and he had come back, but it didn't feel right.

Something was very, very wrong.

Eddie looked different.

He reached through the baluster with one of his hands, stretching his fingers toward me in the darkness, his eyes widening as he beckoned me toward the staircase.

"Charlotte," he hissed. "I have something to show you downstairs."

My heart beat wildly in my chest as his index finger curled and uncurled, coaxing me to leave the safety of my bed and to follow him. I shook my head. I was too frightened to move.

"Eddie, where have you been?" I whispered back to him in the dark, ignoring his plea to follow him.

"Come here, Charlotte and I will show you."

I didn't move. I stared at his eyes that were too big, his smile that was too wide, his long limbs that stretched out like tentacles. Tears came faster now as he watched me. I took a deep breath, conjuring up all the confidence I could muster.

"I don't want to be friends with you anymore, Eddie."

His smile dropped. His eyes narrowed into two slits of black. He rose from his hands and knees, his frame rising as he towered over the banister and began to walk down the hallway toward my bedroom.

Panic began to set in. "You're not real," I whispered to Eddie, willing him to go away. "You're not real. You're not real. You're not real. You're my imaginary friend and I don't want to see you anymore."

Eddie didn't vanish, though. He crept closer and closer to my bedroom door. A quiet determination set on his face. Shadows clung to him as he radiated darkness. His steady breathing was ominously louder than the beating of my heart.

I threw the covers over my head, shaking violently as I listened to his footsteps cross the threshold of my bedroom. And then I did what any five-year-old would have done at the time.

I sucked in my breath and I screamed.

Chaos erupted around the house. Doors were opening and slamming. There was yelling, jumbled footsteps and glass shattering. I sat still with the cover over my head afraid to look back out into the darkness, praying Eddie would go away.

Tears slid violently down my cheeks as exhaustion washed over me. Sleep had found me as my comforter soaked through with my tears. I cried because I lost the only friend I cared about. I cried because I never wanted to see him again.

Sleep came but it was unwelcome until the sun broke through the crevices of my frost covered window.

I shuffled downstairs to have cereal, eyes puffy from crying all night and from lack of sleep. I wondered if it was all just a nightmare, a cruel illusion of my five-year-old mind creating monsters in the dark. When I turned the corner, I discovered the police were in the kitchen with my father, inspecting the broken glass of our sliding glass door that was completely shattered. A cold chill swept through the room.

One of the officers reached down and picked up something pink from the floor. He walked over to me and crouched down to get to my level.

"Does this belong to you, sweetie?" the officer asked, holding out a pink bracelet with the initials E.C on it.

I shook my head no and rolled up my right pajama sleeve to show the officer my matching one.

"It belongs to my friend, Eddie," I said to the officer. I frowned at my wording. I should have said we weren't technically friends anymore.

"Who's Eddie?" the officer asked me, concern creeping into his features.

My dad froze from beside the smashed glass door and slowly turned toward us, his face turning pale as an understanding slowly began to form. The officer turned around to look at him, taking in his ghostly white complexion.

"Her imaginary friend," my dad said.

The officer and my father looked at each other, fear etched into their expressions as the horrors of what just happened finally clicked into place.

A scenario I couldn't even fathom until I was much much older.

My special friend, Eddie sure was special, but he was never imaginary.

Photographs

Christina Meeks

I've never been a pretty girl.

I've worn the thickest glasses that turned my eyes into tiny marbles since I was seven. My hair was frizzy, like I had a permanent hand on one of those lightning balls. Once puberty hit, I got an awkward contralto voice and skin riddled with acne.

Joo-Mi was the complete opposite.

She was the new girl at school, which already made the slightly-more-male student body flock to her. On top of that, she was from Korea, making her an exotic luxury to behold. She introduced herself with two names: "My name is Joo-Mi An, but I go by Junie." She'd later tell me only her boyfriends were allowed to call her Joo-Mi.

To make matters worse, she was *gorgeous*. She had silky black hair that hung tantalizingly over her breasts. Her unblemished skin was porcelain, and her almond eyes were a deep pool of brown that grabbed anyone's attention. Her smile was small and coy; her small, plump lips would be upturned, but her eyes didn't follow. It made anyone to know what *exactly* she was smiling about.

She seemed to pick me out of the crowd at that first lunch. She locked eyes with me, shifting her whole body so our shoulders were parallel, and walked toward me.

"May I sit?" she asked. Her high-pitched voice rang through the crowd of people in the courtyard.

I raised an eyebrow. I was sitting on the concrete, against a brick wall—hardly comfortable—and I didn't think I was good company. "Sure."

Joo-Mi sat next to me, our knees only inches apart. She silently unpacked a tin box from her backpack, revealing the contents of kimchi fried rice with an egg on top. My ham and Swiss sandwich looked utterly pathetic.

"You're from Korea, right?" I asked, taking another bite. I had one leg bent and one sticking out while Joo-Mi sat on her feet, straight posture and hands on her lap.

She nodded.

"How come you don't have an accent?"

"What, should I have one?" she answered with that smile. I blushed, feeling stupid for even asking. "My family goes back and forth. My father works for *Nissan*; he's like a liaison."

I hummed in thought. "Do you like Korea or California more?"

Joo-Mi gave a small, cute chuckle. "Pros and cons. My brother is going to stay here for college to escape military service."

"Yeah, that does suck."

"Where are you thinking of going to college?"

"Not sure. I'm kind of boring. I don't have any dreams, you know?"

Suddenly, Joo-Mi reached out to my chin, holding it in her palm, as she wiped mayonnaise off my cheek with her thumb. "I think you'd make a fascinating subject."

#

Joo-Mi and I spent our lunches together. She assured

me she liked me, but I knew it was because I was a natural boy-repellent. All the Palm Springs white boys chased after her like starving dogs in front of a steak, wanting her to be their anime waifu or something.

I wanted to grab them by the shoulders, violently shake them, and say *"She's from Korea, not Japan, you idiots!"*

No one understood her like I did. Joo-Mi was polite but not particularly nice; she spoke her mind but in such a nice way that you couldn't be mad at her. She loved photography, too. She took the photography class and baffled her teacher with her technical skill and love of unconventional subjects. I once saw her pull out her camera and take a picture of the dumpster before we headed back to class after lunch.

"Hey, I wanna do a portrait of you," Joo-Mi suddenly said between scoops of Korean potato salad.

"Me?" I nearly choked on a hot Cheeto.

"Yeah. Just for fun."

"Why me?" I looked down at my T-shirt and jeans, praying she wouldn't make me wear one of the floral dresses she wore every day to school.

"I told you," she replied, pointing at me with her chopsticks. "You'd make a good subject."

I groaned. "You're not gonna put this anywhere where anyone can see, right?"

"It's just for me. And you, too."

"Fine, I'll indulge you."

She told me to meet her on the football field after school. She said the wide, white wall on that side of the school was perfect for photography. When I got there, she had a whole set up: a tripod, a whiteboard, one of those lights that flashes, and, of course, her camera that used film. (She insisted they were better than the modern stuff.)

I immediately regretted everything when I saw the equipment, but I pulled through when I saw her genuinely smile for the first time. She was a kid on Christmas, bouncing around and excitedly directing me.

She took a picture from each angle, and I couldn't help but feel like she was taking mugshots. Like there was a crime she knew I committed, but I didn't know. I felt naked, especially when I saw nothing but her smile when she looked through the viewfinder.

And then it was over. Joo-Mi thanked me, and we departed for the weekend.

#

Joo-Mi convinced me to let her sleepover at my house Monday evening. Even when I had friends, I didn't like sleepovers. Something about inviting someone to your private space for them to see everything you own and make judgements about it made me feel exposed and ashamed. But Joo-Mi won me over. Again.

When she walked into my purple-and-gray bedroom, she looked around with her small mouth parted into a silent gasp, soaking up the surroundings with her dark brown eyes. "Huh. My bedroom is bigger than yours."

It was probably true, so I couldn't get mad at her. My bed was only two feet away from the closet on the other side of the room. That and my desk were pushed up against the wall opposite of the door.

Joo-Mi walked over to my desk and picked up at picture frame. Her delicate finger pressed against the glass. "Who's this?"

I walked over to her. "Oh, that's my baby brother, Thomas."

The picture was the Disneyland trip we took during spring break earlier that year. Thomas was in my dad's arms, wearing one of those dorky Mickey Mouse ears with his name on it.

"I didn't see him when we walked in."

"He, uh, passed away."

"Oh…" Joo-Mi put the photo down, her eyes still fixed on Thomas.

I then noticed how close together we were standing and shuffled back. "Did those photos of me ever process?"

She whipped around. "Oh, yes! Let me show you."

She sat on my rug with her usual poise and dug through her backpack. I sat across from her, anxious to see what they looked like. I usually didn't like how I looked in pictures, but Joo-Mi's photography was always good. She handed me the first photo, face down.

I looked at her with a frown. Did it turn out bad? I turned it over.

I was greeted by a grotesque figure. Its face was concave and wrinkly as if it was bashed in and the skin grew around the wound. One arm was small and tiny, and the other was large and muscular. It hunched over, the same pose you do when someone punches you in the stomach.

But it was me.

It had my hair and my glasses and my acne and my clothes.

I grabbed the wastebin from my desk and vomited. Out of the corner of my eye, Joo-Mi had a large grin, spanning from ear-to-ear, and her small, dark eyes were wide and wild.

"Is this a joke?" I yelled at her.

Still grinning, Joo-Mi slowly shook her head. "That's *you.*"

"That's not me! That looks nothing like me!"

"My camera…" She tapped her fingernail against the lens. "It bares into the soul. It shows me *secrets.*"

I covered my mouth, wanting to throw up, as she laid out the other shots we took. She *knew.* I just met her, and she *knew.*

"This was all the confirmation I needed," she murmured. "You killed your brother, didn't you? I was keeping up with the news the summer before we moved. Cars just don't flip down cliffs randomly like that."

I was crying. "I wanted to go with him. My dad… he makes me feel small. I wanted to go and take Thomas before he felt small, too."

Joo-Mi hunched over and crawled to me slowly like a panther. "I don't think you're small."

"You don't think I'm a monster?" I gestured to the photos. "Even though…"

She was so close to my face I could feel her hot breath on my chin. "No. I think you're beautiful."

Her eyes were looking directly into mine, filled with adoration. Maybe lust. Maybe love. Maybe just *hunger*. I believed it when she said it at that moment.

"Why?" I whispered.

"Because you're just like me."

She brushed her lips against mine.

She was the most beautiful girl in school. Every boy wanted her. Every girl wanted to be her. But she was in my room. She was mine. Deep down, I wanted her to kiss me when I saw her. In that moment, though, with the photos on the floor, I didn't want her lips anywhere near mine.

#

Joo-Mi kept the photos. I would've said yes if she had asked, but she didn't ask. She just tucked them back into her backpack.

At school, we went back to normal. It took me a few weeks, but I eventually saw her the same way. In private, though, it was different. She'd pull me into closets and hastily make out with me as if she were about to die in an hour. We once touched ourselves in front of each other, and I was struck with a sense of intimacy that made me blush during class. We had a secret together. A lot of secrets together, actually.

Sometimes, I enjoyed trysts. Even if I didn't, I'd glance

at her backpack and remember the photos. Joo-Mi never said it, but I knew what she was thinking. Besides, the euphoric high brought about by orgasms washed it all over with a rose tint.

We were at her house once, and she was right about her bedroom being bigger. Hell, *everything* was bigger. It was the biggest goddamn house I had seen in a suburb. Everything in her room was dainty and pink.

I was laying my back against her pink rococo-style sheets with a full-length mirror propped up against the edge of the bed. I had just finished touching myself in front of it, as Joo-Mi wanted to show me just how beautiful I looked when I came. She was also touching herself behind the mirror. We came together.

When we were both finished, Joo-Mi crawled onto the bed next to me, propping her head up with her hand, stroking my hair with the other.

"Told you you looked beautiful," she said in a hum.

I grunted in agreement. I didn't feel beautiful, though. I just felt sick and perverted and depraved. Joo-Mi told me that was just society telling me that. I figured she was right.

I turned my head toward her. "Hey, I should take a photo of you sometime."

Her face melted into a scowl. "Why?"

I was choking on my words, instantly regretting them. "I-I want to know what it's like to be behind the camera. I wanna know what it's like to be you."

Joo-Mi smiled like she was trying to remain composed with a rail spike in her foot. "Fine. Just once, though."

While she was getting her camera from her nightstand, I sat up and pulled my pants back up. She handed it to me, and I held it to my face. To my disappointment, Joo-Mi looked the same through the viewfinder. Hell, she looked *angelic,* even, with the light pouring from the window behind her and that usual small smile on her face.

Click!
"Happy?" she said.
"Happy." And I sealed it with a kiss.
#
My feelings toward Joo-Mi changed in an instant.

I was grabbing my books from my locker when I overheard Joo-Mi talking to some guy. I kept my eyes focused on my locker. I didn't want anyone to know she was anything more than my friend who I ate lunch with. He was asking her out on a date. My heart throbbed in my ears as if my body was protecting me against Joo-Mi's answer. Like a knife, her voice cut through all the noise: "Yes."

I couldn't look now. If I looked, *then it would become real.* But I still felt a knife twisting in my chest. It all became apparent what I was to her: a plaything. Something to take all her confusing feelings out on, and there was nothing I could do because she had those photos.

I had to get those photos back.

As I heard her heels click past me, I turned around.

"Hey, Junie!" I blurted out louder than I wanted.

She turned around, her hair moving around her in such a serene way. Fuck, why couldn't I be mad at someone uglier?

"Sleepover at my place tonight?"

That small smile and a nod.
#
We passed out on my bed after another make out session. Joo-Mi was slow and methodical this time, not in a rush. It was tender, and it was exactly what I wanted when we made out; not the usual clashing against teeth. It felt nice, but it was unusual. Something was wrong, I knew it.

We were spooning in my bed. I insisted on being the bigger spoon, telling Joo-Mi I was scared of my dad coming in. She conceded after that; she hated my dad for all the shit he put me through. Her perfectly shaped ass was pressed against me, and she smelled like roses and vanilla; she was making it *very* difficult to get out of bed.

I moved an inch. I held my breath as she stirred. I managed to slide out without her waking up.

I crawled over to her cursed yellow backpack and opened it. I dug through as quietly as possible until I felt a glossy page. I pulled it out, but in the dim lighting, I could tell it wasn't me. It was *her*.

It was the photo I took of her, but her silhouette was entirely different. Her black hair looked unkempt, and her eyes were freakishly huge and milky. Her tongue hung out between sharp teeth, extending all the way to her chest. Her tits poured out of her dress, cascading out of frame.

I suddenly felt nails dig into my wrist, as I was pulled toward my bed.

"The fuck do you think you're doing?" Joo-Mi hissed. There was a fury on her face—an expression I had never seen before. I wouldn't have recognized her if I hadn't seen her moments before.

I held up the photo to her in response. Her expression changed into silent horror.

"So now you see me," she whispered, tears running down her cheeks. "For the *freak* I am. Everyone sees me as this beautiful, perfect girl… but not you. You see me for the depraved lesbian *monster* I am."

She let go of me, and I shuffled toward her, placing my hands on her knees.

"This is it, huh? You're gonna show everyone that photo and tell them what I did to you."

I shook my head.

"Why? Why still be with me, then?"

I placed the photo on her lap. "I think you're beautiful."
#

I took Joo-Mi out for a drive one Saturday. At first, she was hesitant to go anywhere remotely public with me, but she agreed when I told her I wanted to show her where I crashed the car. I drove her out of Palm Springs, toward Oceanside.

She held my hand on the center console, as 80s rock ballads played over the radio. We drove on the cliffs along the coast when I pulled over and stopped at a promenade by the time the sun was setting.

They had carved it out, poured concrete on it, and placed a park bench. There was a knee-high cross there with teddy bears and flowers all around it. To those people, the person who killed my brother was a drunk driver. An unfortunate accident.

We got out of the car, and Joo-Mi immediately walked past the cross to the edge of the cliff, staring down. She had left her backpack in the car, so I took out the photos, tucking them into my jacket. She was getting careless around me. I walked over to her, rubbing my arms as if the glass shards were still in it.

"The remains aren't there," I said. "They cleared it out almost immediately."

Joo-Mi straightened her back but kept her eyes down. "Oh." She turned to me. "How do you feel being here?"

I shrugged. "Weird, I guess."

"Why did you bring me here? Why now?"

"I wanted you to see me." I took out the photos and a lighter from my pocket. "We only get to see ourselves. Our true selves."

Her eyebrows scrunched together, and her eyes were wide. "What are you doing?"

I flicked the lighter, and she pounced on me. It was too late, though. In the scuffle, the photos were lit, and the heat made me throw them toward the cross. It, the flowers, the teddy bear. All on fire.

Joo-Mi had me pinned down. Her face was contorted with anger, but tears were running down her face. "You bitch! Why would you do that?"

I was crying now. "No one gets to see me. No one gets to see you. Only us."

"You idiot!" She began pounding her fists into my chest. "I hate you!"

I let her do it until she stopped. She needed it, I could tell. She eventually collapsed on top of me, wailing into my shirt.

"You're beautiful," I whispered. She slowly lifted her head, and for the first time since I met her, she looked confused. Before she could ask, I grabbed her waist and threw her off me.

I walked into the flames. Maybe my clothes and my flesh and my hair was on fire. I couldn't tell. I felt nothing when I saw Joo-Mi's face through the fire. For a moment, the dancing of the flames made her look like the monster in the photograph. Her true self. It made everything easier.

I leaned back and fell down the cliffs.

Side Effects May Include:

Kody Greene

The exam room table was cold, and the paper crinkled as Jackie shifted her weight. Her feet dangled off the edge of the examination table, her coat discarded on the ground beside her. She wanted to leave. The clinic was sandwiched between a payday loan store and a pawnshop, tucked away in a rundown strip mall in the East end of Edmonton.

The door opened abruptly, the noise too loud in the small exam room. Doctor Coffer came in clutching a thick folder. He flipped through it, oblivious that he had almost caused Jackie to piss her pants.

He looked to be in his early forties, with dark espresso colored skin. He had a long narrow face and dark circles under his eyes. He wore a dark burgundy dress shirt with sweat stains in the armpits and smelled like onions and chemicals.

She wished Doctor Johnson hadn't referred her to this man. Every cell in her body was telling her to run.

He flipped through the file folder, his back to her.

Jackie cleared her throat, wondering if maybe he forgot she was here. Which would be difficult in this broom closet.

He held up one impatient finger, shuffling the paper methodically.

Jackie rolled her eyes, glancing at her phone. *12:10*. She had to get started on her kinesiology assignment before work at the bar. There was a playoff game tonight, so it was sure to be busy.

"You're here for the trial?" The doctor asked without looking at her. He flipped the page again, revealing a splash of red.

"Uh, yeah… I think so," Jackie said.

He closed the folder then looked at Jackie finally, pivoting in the office chair. He rolled the chair forward until his head was level with her crotch.

Jackie turned to the side, crossing her arms. It was freezing in here.

"You are aware *Insoculum* is an experimental drug and there may be some adverse side effects," he said, his voice almost a whisper. But he didn't look at her when he spoke. He stared straight past her.

"What kind of side effects?"

Doctor Coffer shrugged slowly.

"Some patients have reported hallucinations, nausea, and headaches. But this was only reported in fifteen percent of patients."

"And it works? Doctor Johnson said two pills a day and I won't need to sleep anymore."

Doctor Coffer stared through her for a moment, his head tilted to the left.

"That is correct. *Insoculum* allows the brain to recover neural pathways during wakeful hours. Though many patients elect to nap for an hour or so a day, to rest their muscles."

"What's the catch?" Jackie asked. A full twenty-four-hour day to get things done. It sounded too good to be true.

"There is no catch, and the medication is fully covered by the research team. I just need you to come back in one week to follow up."

"That's it?"

Doctor Coffer nodded slowly, a small smile entering his face.

"Yes."

He withdrew a small bottle of pills from his pocket. It didn't have a label on it, but she could see two dozen large pills through the plastic container.

She licked her lips, her palms sweating and heart racing.

Two years sober, and still the sight of pills gave her a near sexual attraction. She had been lusting for a fix.

Doctor Coffer seemed to notice her distress and put a sympathetic hand on her knee as he passed her the small bottle. His hand touched hers and it was as cold as ice.

"Doctor Johnson mentioned your history of substance abuse. Rest assured, these pills have no evidence of creating a dependency. You can stop taking them whenever you want."

Jackie brushed his hand off her knee and stood. "That makes me feel better," she said, her stomach in knots.

"Come by next Thursday for a follow up, and we'll take it from there." He then turned back to the folder on the small desk.

Jackie grabbed her coat and made her way to the door. "Thank you," she said mechanically and left the exam room with the small pill bottle.

She put her coat on as she passed the overweight receptionist and went out the front door. She made it outside and inhaled the sharp February air. Her breath fogged in front of her as she withdrew the pill bottle and opened it.

The pills were a mustard yellow color and smelled of Sulphur. She took one and gagged. It had a metallic taste, like blood. She dry swallowed it and got in her car. She tossed her purse on a pile of empty coffee cups on the passenger side. When she looked up again, she saw Dr. Coffer watching her from the doorway of the clinic.

It was too hard to tell from that distance, but it looked like he was smiling at her.

She gave him a sarcastic wave that he didn't return.

"Creep," she muttered. She put the car in drive and pulled out of the snow strewn parking lot.

*

She didn't notice the pills take effect as she went through her day. She spent a few hours catching up on an overdue assignment, then worked at the gym as a personal trainer. She led a bike spin class and did some one-on-one appointments. Overall, it was the same as most of her days over the last year. Frantically busy.

Thanks to that dumbass in Ottawa, rent in any major city was triple the average household income. So, she had to work two full-time jobs, live paycheck to paycheck, and rack up debt. She had a hard time living with other people. All the people she trusted weren't on speaking terms with her. She burned a lot of bridges that last year she was on pills. And she had never been able to mend those wounds.

So, she worked a billion hours each week and filled every spare second with school. It wasn't all bad. This self-induced state of hyper productivity left her little time to think about using.

She showered at the gym and changed into a blouse and leggings. She took the time to do her hair and apply makeup. She wasn't a big fan of cosmetics, but she did like tips.

The bar was already full of the regulars when she got there, tables crowded with pitchers of beer and towering stacks of nachos.

"Hey Jackie," Seema said as she poured a pint.

Jackie waved back, dropping her coat and purse in her locker. She washed her hands and joined Seema behind the bar. Off to her right was an older gentleman who wasted away his free time sitting in front of a cold glass of beer, chatting idly with whoever would listen. His name was Dean.

"Jackie, when you gonna let me take you out on that date?"

Jackie looked at him and smiled. Dean was old, fifties or sixties and looked every day of it. His gray hair was unkempt, but he had a wide easy smile that almost made up for it. His hands were folded across his belly, a half-finished pint in front of him.

"When you stop drinking, I'll think about it," she said with a grin. It was their running joke. With other guys it would have been creepy. But Dean was a sweetheart. Some asshole had grabbed her butt one night and Dean had put him on the ground before security could get over to her.

Dean laughed, taking a long sip of his beer. "But then I wouldn't get to see your lovely face anymore!" He laughed loudly. A couple of the other regulars laughed as well.

Jackie smiled. "Refill?"

He drained the dregs of his beer, and she went to the tap with a new glass, pouring the beer. To her left sat the Old Man. He had been coming in every day since before Jackie had started working there.

He sat at one of the bar stools from open until close, every single day. He wouldn't talk to anyone except to quietly ask for a drink in a thick Eastern European accent. Vodka double, neat. He would nurse one of those for an hour or more. Over the course of a shift, he would drink a handful of them. And then pay with a single hundred-dollar bill and leave the remainder as a tip. He shut down any attempts at communication, staff and other customers alike.

During her slower shifts, Jackie wondered what haunted him. Who was he? Was he wasting his life away in this decrepit bar to punish himself for perceived sins? Or mourning the loss of a loved one?

Maybe he fought in one of the wars and was plagued by the horrors of some battlefield. Jackie would pass the time, puzzling over this man's mysterious life. Sometimes for her whole shift. She would watch him stare at his glass, lost in his own world. Occasionally, he would look up at the other patrons as if he didn't know where he was.

But tonight, Old Man was laying with his head on the bar, resting on his arms. An empty glass in front of him.

Dean's beer began overflowing, the liquid spilling down the glass and over her fingers. She cursed and wiped the glass before handing it to Dean.

She couldn't take her eyes off Old Man, though. She had never seen him do that. *Is he okay?*

She walked over. "Hey, would you like a refill?" She picked up his empty glass.

Nothing.

He didn't even stir.

Crap, is he dead?

"Hey," she said, putting a hand on his arm.

He lifted his head, and his face was gone. Where his eyes, nose, and mouth should have been was a barren stretch of flesh.

Jackie gasped, taking a step back. She dropped his glass, and it shattered on the ground as loud as a gunshot.

Old Man's hands went up to where his face should have been and tore at the flesh. It pulled the skin apart, blood streamed down his neck. The flesh tore away and revealed a single massive eyeball. The iris flicked back and forth, blood gushing forth. It saw her and the pupil contracted as

Jackie let out a shrill ear-piercing scream.

The bar went silent, heads turned to look at her. The only sound came from the two talking heads discussing the impending hockey game on the TV's.

Jackie looked back at Seema, stepping away from the Old Man.

But Seema looked only at Jackie. The Old Man looked at her with a perplexed expression. His face was normal. Two brown eyes, a small nose with a mole on it, and a mouth.

What the hell?

Seema stepped forward, smiling at the Old Man. "I think you startled Jackie, sir, let me get you a refill. On the house." Seema gave Jackie a look. *What's wrong with you?*

Jackie ran her fingers through her hair, taking a deep breath. She ignored a smart comment Dean made. She left the taps and went to the small employee locker room. She took a minute to collect herself, wiping the tears.

Seema came in, eyes narrowed. "Jackie, I need you out there," she said and stormed back out.

Jackie checked herself over quickly in the small broken mirror, and then went back to the bar. She froze. The bar was at max capacity, rowdy patrons watching the TV's intently while filling their faces with food, spilling beer on their orange and blue jerseys.

The game was already in the second period, Oilers beating the Flames 2-1. Which was impossible… She had only been in the locker room for a minute.

She stepped behind the bar and saw Old Man was gone, and his seat was taken by a middle-aged woman with comically large breasts, talking animatedly about her recent divorce.

"Jackie," Seema hissed impatiently as she filled up a pair of beers.

She turned, smiling to the two younger guys standing in

front of her. "Hey, what'll it be?" She asked.

And so went the rest of her shift. Aside from the cold shoulder from Seema, everything else went routinely. But Jackie had a sense of discontinuity. There was a gap in time she couldn't explain and the nightmarish thing she had seen had sunk its teeth into her. It felt like that horrifying eyeball was still watching her.

Seema barely spoke to her as they gathered glasses and cleared the bar to close for the night. And Jackie didn't know what to say.

It wasn't until she got home that she realized the drugs were working. She didn't feel tired at all. Her legs were sore from standing, but that was it. Normally, she would be dosing off on the short cold drive back to her apartment.

It was *2:35* when she got in her door. Instead of sleeping, she did the assignment she had requested an extension on. Then she got to work on the next reading assignment. She went to the gym early to get a morning workout in, a gruelling cardio session that left her breathless and her legs burning. She showered afterward, and even had time to grab a coffee before her first client.

Jackie spent the rest of the day teaching people how to work out. She led Zumba with a local Seniors Day program, modifying it so it could be done standing or sitting. She took her third pill afterward, gagging again on the metallic taste.

Her last client of the day was a guy named Cole. He was an introverted nineteen-year-old who was woefully addicted to video games. His parents made him get a gym membership as a way for him to get exercise and much needed socialization. He had thick, moppy hair, and despite being six foot, he probably didn't break one hundred pounds. When they first met, he had clearly been shy with girls.

He was probably one of the guys who bragged about

their online scores or kill/death ratios between browsing the latest selection on Pornhub. But speaking to a real live girl? He hadn't unlocked that skill yet.

Jackie had brought him out of his shell with their shared affection for 80's horror classics. She had only done a handful of sessions with him, but already there had been a definite improvement. Not to his muscles, though that would come, but to his self-confidence. The way he carried himself and spoke.

This was why she loved being a personal trainer. The empowerment of physical fitness. It had saved Jackie from herself during a battle with addiction.

Presently, she watched Cole's form as he descended on a squat, barbell resting on his back. His torso leaned forward too much as he reached the bottom and pressed up, exhaling sharply.

"Brace your core," she reminded him. His next rep was better. She guided him through his set, pretending not to notice him checking her out every time she looked away.

"My legs feel like Jell-O," he complained at the end of his three sets of squats.

Jackie smiled. "I'd still like for you do another leg exercise today. Lunges or single leg press. Or we can move onto some upper body movements."

He pretended to consider for a moment. "Upper body."

Of course. Guys usually only cared about working out chest and arms. She led him toward the pully station, already compiling a list of accessory movements.

She froze. The gym wasn't busy yet but was beginning to fill with after-work gym goers. But that wasn't what caught her eye. In the reflection of the mirror, she saw something at the back of the gym, near the locker room.

She stared at it for a moment, her mind grappling to make sense of what she was seeing. Then she realized it was another mirror at the far end of the gym. A reflection of a reflection. She looked back and didn't see anything un-usual. When she looked at the mirror again, she saw a mas-sive bloodshot eye across the room watching her.

With her heart racing, she turned around again. Nothing was there. Just two older ladies leaving the locker room.

"Jackie?" Cole asked.

She looked in the mirror again, unable to respond. The massive eyeball blinked once with torn, bloody eyelids. A long, bone thin appendage reached up and touched the glass of the mirror, twenty feet away. Cold dread froze her in place, and she felt warm pee trickle down her pant leg and collect in her shoe.

The creature pushed an impossibly long limb through the mirror, scuttling forward like an insect—massive, jointed limbs that were oddly human pushed forward. Creeping toward her on six tall, jointed limbs. Its torso was covered in thin purple tendrils.

Slowly, she managed to turn her head.

"Jackie?" Cole called her name again, more concerned now. He stepped back from the puddle of urine on the floor.

Jackie looked back and the eyeball monstrosity was gal-loping toward her like a horse, climbing over gym equip-ment and patrons to reach her. Jackie screamed, running through the gym.

She looked back to see it grasping for her with its im-possibly long limbs, that horrible bloodshot eye lusting for her. She screamed again, tearing her way out the front door of the gym. She didn't even look back until she was a block away. By then her exposed arms were cold in the February air. It was already dark despite it being dinner time. She had left her car, purse, and coat at the gym. And there was no way she was going back.

*

She was shivering against the cold Alberta winter, the wind biting at her exposed flesh. She had crossed her arms, clutching her cellphone. She didn't know what to do, who to call.

So, she had gone to the only place she could think of. Doctor Coffer's office. She passed a group of men smoking outside the nearby convenience store. Cigarette butts scattered the snow. They looked at her as she passed, their conversation dropping.

She went down the alley and stopped in her tracks. It was dark, but she could still see the unit where the clinic had been, next to the payday loan store.

But the unit was empty.

No, not just empty.

Abandoned.

Like it had been unoccupied for ten years. Gone was the desk with the overweight receptionist and plain infographics about the importance of safe sex. The unit was empty, only a broken wooden chair remained. Cobwebs covered the arms. An overhead light dangled precariously by wiring, and the window to her right was shattered and covered with plywood.

Jackie's eyes teared up. She turned around and went up the alleyway to the men smoking outside the convenience store. There was only two of them now. She walked up to them, her arms red from the cold, tears streaming down her face.

"Ex-excuse me," she said to them.

The men turned to look at her.

"Do you know where the doctor's office moved to?"

The man closest to her was bundled up in a dirty oil stained Carhartt and toque. He laughed, ashing his cigarette with a flick.

"Doctor's office? Here?"

"It was just—" She pointed down the alley, letting out

a whimper.

He shook his head. "There was a barber shop down there years ago."

"Just the loan sharks and pawnshop now," his partner agreed, itching at a bandage covering his left eye.

Jackie's legs trembled. Her pants were frozen where she had peed herself.

"Okay, thank you," she said walking away.

"Lady, you should go inside and warm up," the bigger guy called after her, but she ignored him.

Jackie swiped through her phone with stiff, frozen fingers. Already her tears were freezing on her face. She found the contact in her phone. *Big brother.* She pressed call, hoping the battery would hold.

"Please, pick up," she sobbed as it rang.

"Hello?" came a rough voice.

"Steven, it's me," she said her voice wavering. "I need help; something is going on. I think something's after me."

A heavy sigh. "Jackie, are you using again?"

"What? No, I swear! Look, I know how this sounds,"

"Enough, Jackie. I'm sorry, but I can't do this with you."

"Steven, wait!"

The call ended, and she was alone.

Jackie collapsed to the icy concrete, her phone dropping beside her. She sobbed as the wind howled through the alleyway. Sirens rang out in the distance, as her world cascaded around her.

The door to the vacant unit stood open, swaying softly in the wind. And in the darkness, she could see the pale glow, of a single tire-sized eye.

"No," Jackie muttered.

One long jointed limb stepped through the doorway, followed by another.

"Please… No!" she sobbed.

The eyeball came into view, illuminated by distant streetlights. The tentacular appendages on its torso wriggled, shrinking against the cold air.

Jackie's breath fogged in front of her, and she didn't even have time to scream when it pounced. She could feel its thin fingers penetrate her mouth. The eyeball blazed in front of her as its arms slid down her throat, choking out her screams as she beat frantically at the brick wall. She heard the monster chirp happily as its appendages slipped into her body and Jackie's world faded to black.

*

Seema unlocked the bar. She dragged her feet to the locker room and ditched her purse and coat. She went through the monotonous task of prepping for another day of slinging beers. She had been working extra shifts all week, by herself for most of them.

Aaron, their manager was pissed that Jackie had no-showed her last four shifts. She should be here today, too, though Seema wasn't holding her breath. She had called Mike, the dude who ran the desk at the gym Jackie worked at. He said Jackie had some sort of mental breakdown. Just up and left in the middle of a session. Ran off, left her car and belongings. No one had seen her since.

Seema thought of the last night she had seen her. Her screaming, the fear in her eyes. And then disappearing. That was so unlike her.

Seema did a quick inventory on the booze and glassware.

The door opened, as she was ducked behind the bar, checking for another bottle of crown.

"We're not open yet," she called out. She stood up and saw Jackie standing there. She had a wide smile on her face, but her skin looked ghostly pale. Almost like a layer of frost covered her. Her clothes were dirty, and her hair was messy and full of twigs.

"Jackie, you scared the shit out of me. Are you okay?"

She tilted her head to the side in one sharp motion.

Seema took an involuntary step back. She could smell her now, too.

God, she smells awful.

"Jackie…"

Slowly, Jackie's hands reached up to her head. One hand grabbed her lower teeth and jaw, the other hand gripped her upper teeth. She began pulling.

Seema put a hand over her mouth.

Jackie pulled hard, a soft moan escaping her mouth as the flesh at her cheeks ripped. Bright red blood poured down her neck and hands.

"Jackie, stop!" Seema screamed, reaching for her phone.

Her lower jaw dislodged and hung limply to the side, bloody flesh barely holding it together.

Seema began dialing *911*, then she saw something thin and pale slither out of Jackie's esophagus.

A jointed limb slithered out. The hands opening and closing with far too many fingers. Jackie's chest was pulsing, as if she was laughing, or dry heaving. Then, her neck bulged like an over inflated balloon, turning a horrible purple shade as blood vessels popped. Extruding from her mouth was a large, horrible eyeball, looking left and right from within the bloody remains of Jackie's mouth.

OTHER HELLBOUND BOOKS
www.hellboundbooks.com

ROAD KILL: TEXAS HORROR BY TEXAS
WRITERS - VOL 9

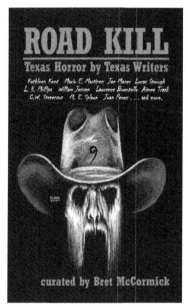

Road Kill: Texas Horror by Texas Writers, Vol. 9 is packed with harrowing depredations, grim manifestations and terrifying implications.

Suggesting this historic anthology is just a regional horror collection is like calling Frankenstein's monster a simple misstep in medical technology.

Road Kill is no longer just an annual anthology of horror stories. It's a serial collection of some of the most serious voices in Lone Star literature. It's a chronicle of Texas terror, and Vol. 9 is eerie, edgy and feral. It will haunt you long after its first reading.

It's as fine a selection of horror fiction as you'll find today.

With stories of exceptional horror from:

Mario E. Martinez, L.H. Phillips, Lucas Strough, Aimee Trask, Armando Sangre, W.R. Theiss, C.W. Stevenson, Jae Mazer, M.E. Splawn,Kathleen Kent, Andrew Kozma, Julie Aaron, Robert Stahl, William Jensen, Todd Elliott, Lewis B. Smith, Derek Austin Johnson, Juan Perez, Bev Vincent, Lawrence Buentello, & Bret McCormick

To Hell and Back

To Hell and Back serves as a mosaic of contemporary fears and timeless terrors, curated and edited by the Bram Stoker Award-winning Joe Mynhardt. This collection of horror stories brings together a diverse array of tales from both beloved and emerging voices in the horror genre, each story a unique exploration of the dark corners of the human psyche.

Published in collaboration with Crystal Lake Entertainment, with an introduction by Lee Murray, this horror anthology includes disturbing tales by Jeff Strand, Gage Greenwood, Gregg Stewart, Jasper Bark, Kenneth W. Cain, James Aquilone, Taylor Grant, Colin J. Northwood, Chad Lutzke, Felix Blackwell, J.P. Behrens, Bridget Nelson, Jay Bechtol, Nick Roberts, Kyle Toucher, Diana Olney, Devin Cabrera, Naching T. Kassa, John Durgin, Francesca Maria, James H. Longmore, and Rowan Hill.

To Hell and Back invites readers on a journey through cityscapes and small towns, into office blocks and family homes, along lonely roads, and wooded trails. It confronts external threats like predators and cults as well as internal battles with ambition, mental illness, and moral weakness. Themes of road rage, childhood trauma, the horrors of war, and the supernatural intertwine, offering a chilling snapshot of contemporary societal fears. With stories that range from political and cultural tensions to tales of creeping unease, this anthology not only aims to terrify but also to offer a means of confronting and reflecting on our fears from a safe distance.

Uncover the shadows lurking within and beyond with To Hell and Back—dare to turn the page and confront your darkest fears.

The Horror Zine's Book of Monsters Stories

With an introduction by Shirley Jackson Award-winner Gemma Files, this outstanding anthology of all things monstrous includes spine-chilling stories from Bentley Little, Simon Clark, Elizabeth Massie, Tim Waggoner, Sumiko Saulson, plus some of the best emerging horror writers working today.

"This anthology gives us a chilling glimpse at the dark and dangerous things prowling in the minds of some of today's best horror writers." – JG Faherty, author of *Ragman* and *Songs in the Key of Death*

"Throughout the pages are creepy tales by up-and-comers who you may have read, plus writers brand new to a horror reader's discerning eye. Embark on a journey to the realm where monsters—familiar or unique—dwell. Highly recommended to horror aficionados obsessed with eldritch fiction—this one's for you!" – Nancy Kilpatrick, author of *Thrones of Blood Series* and *the Darker Passions series*

Flanagan

"Straw Dogs meets Fifty Shades - heart pounding, gut-wrenching, sexy as all hell and with a twist you'll never see coming!"

Meet the Sewells, your typical, all-American couple; happily married for ten years, respected high school teachers, still crazy about one another and with a secret, shared dark side.

During their annual Spring Break vacation to recharge their batteries and reconnect as a couple, they are waylaid by a perverse gang of misfits in the one horse, North Texas town of Flanagan.

Taken hostage as the focus of the gang's twisted games, the Sewells are brutalized into performing increasingly vicious physical, sexual and emotional acts upon one another, until events take an unexpected turn - triggered by an unintentional death.

As their circumstance descends into the worse nightmare imaginable, the Sewells find themselves involved in an altogether different situation...

The Gentleman's Choice

"A clever twist on the age-old adage, Art imitates reality, drives this terrifying possibility into the deepest places of your imagination." Andrew Neiderman, author of *The Devil's Advocate* and the V.C. Andrews novels.

A sleazy internet dating show blamed for a viewer's death, a host with a dark, secret past, and a killer with a sadistic grudge…

Someone is kidnapping and murdering previous contestants from the popular streaming show *The Gentleman's Choice* – a strictly adult hybrid of *The Bachelor and Love Island.* Private Investigator, Vanessa Young, is hired by a victim's family to infiltrate the show as a contestant to expose and capture the killer. Vanessa and Cole Gianni, the show's charismatic star, begin to fall romantically for each other, until Vanessa's plan goes terribly awry when they're drugged and taken to a remote location to take part in their captor's own brutal, ultimately fatal, version of *The Gentleman's Choice.* With the clock ticking toward their fateful final night, Vanessa and Cole are forced into a battle of wills to survive their tormentor and escape with their lives before it's too late…

A HellBound Books Publishing LLC
Publication

www.hellboundbookspublishing.com